River Road

AND OTHER MYSTERY STORIES

River Road

AND OTHER MYSTERY STORIES

JOHN M. FLOYD

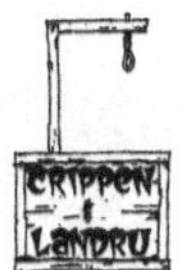

Crippen & Landru Publishers
Cincinnati, Ohio
2025

Previously published stories contained within this volume copyright 2017, 2018, 2020, 2021, 2022, 2023, 2024 by John M. Floyd.

This collection copyright © 2025 by John M. Floyd.

"A Trivial Pursuit," "Overlooked," "The Three Dolphins" copyright © 2025 by John M. Floyd.

Introduction is copyright © 2025 by John M. Floyd.

For information contact:

Crippen & Landru, Publishers
P. O. Box 532057
Cincinnati, OH 45253 USA

Web: www.crippenlandru.com
E-mail: Info@crippenlandru.com

ISBN (softcover): 978-1-936363-99-5
ISBN (clothbound): 978-1-936363-98-8

First Edition: November 2025

10 9 8 7 6 5 4 3 2 1

Table of Contents

AUTHOR'S NOTE   7

PART 1 – SHERIFF RAY DOUGLAS MYSTERIES
TRAIL'S END   13
SCAVENGER HUNT   27
FRIENDS AND NEIGHBORS   41
THE DOLLHOUSE   51
GOING THE DISTANCE   65
THE POD SQUAD   73

PART 2 – PI TOM LANGFORD MYSTERIES
MUSTANG SALLY   91
SENTRY   97
A TRIVIAL PURSUIT   113
OVERLOOKED   125
THE THREE DOLPHINS   141
R.I.P., VAN WINKLER   155

PART 3 – OTHER STORIES
GUN WORK   173
MOONSHINE AND ROSES   189
WELCOME TO ARMADILLO   203
RHONDA AND CLYDE   217
RIVER ROAD   239

SOURCES   255
PREVIOUS CRIPPEN & LANDRU PUBLICATIONS   259

For Carolyn

Author's Note

An old classmate once asked me, at a booksigning, how it could be possible that I graduated from college in Electrical Engineering and wound up writing mystery fiction for magazines. I remember replying that I thought it made perfect sense, because you have to be crazy to do either one. Especially the mystery-fiction thing.

Yes, I've had two so-called careers. The first was with IBM Corporation, where I worked as a systems engineer for thirty years; the second is this one, where I work at dreaming up stories. I was probably lucky in the order. If I had discovered my love of writing when I was a young man, I wouldn't have ever wanted to do anything else, and my family might've starved.

By *stories*, I mean short stories, most of them in the mystery/suspense genre, which only means a crime of some kind is central to the plot. I suspect their short length is because I grew up watching those half-hour anthology series like *Twilight Zone* and *Alfred Hitchcock Presents*, and the crime element is because a lot of prime-time TV back then was about cops and private eyes (and of course, cowboys). My heroes were Joe Friday, Richard Diamond, and Matt Dillon.

When I was a kid and *not* watching cops and Westerns on TV, I was usually reading. Not just novels but shorts as well. I discovered *Alfred Hitchcock's Mystery Magazine* and *Ellery Queen's Mystery Magazine* as a teenager, and still remember some of those little tales. Never did I dream that I would eventually write stories for those publications. I didn't even like English much, in high school and college. I liked math and science. Go figure.

For whatever reason, I didn't start writing until my mid-forties. I was traveling a lot with IBM at the time, usually alone, and during those trips I began writing stories in my head. This was in the mid-'90s, shortly before personal computers were commonplace, so anytime I was home I banged my stories out on an ancient Underwood typewriter that probably weighed fifty pounds. I soon had manuscripts stacked everywhere, in desk drawers and dresser drawers and on tabletops. Finally my wife suggested I send some of those stories to magazines—in other words, get them out of the house—and see if somebody might want to publish them.

I wasn't fond of that idea. I loved my stories, and wasn't eager to mail them off to someone who might *not* love them. Besides, I had no clue about how to submit something to a magazine editor.

My wife didn't see that as a problem. She just pointed and said, "You know where the library is. You can learn how."

So I did. I found a book called *Novel & Short Story Writer's Market,* which listed hundreds of publications receptive to unsolicited fiction, and another book about how to format and submit manuscripts. Thus armed, I chose and prepared five of my short stories and snailmailed them to five different magazines. To my complete surprise, four of those first five stories were accepted and published, and I thought, *Whoa, this is easy.* I was, of course, wrong. The next dozen manuscripts I submitted were rejected. Twelve in a row. But I wasn't discouraged; I had seen, with my own eyes, that it could be done. So I kept sending them out.

Now, many years later, I still get rejections. But my acceptance-to-rejection ratio has improved a bit, thankfully, and I've been fortunate in terms of sales and awards. My stories have been published on five continents, taught in high schools and colleges, optioned for film, distributed in Braille, adapted for animation, translated into Russian, and selected for inclusion in five best-mysteries-of-the-year anthologies. (I should note, after all that horn-tooting, that I've also probably collected more rejection slips than any other author—but I've thrown most of those away, so no one can prove it.)

In summary, I've had more luck than I deserve, not only with stories in magazines and anthologies but with a collection of my published poems—*Lighten Up a Little* (2020)—and seven collections of my short stories: *Rainbow's End* (2006), *Midnight* (2008), *Clockwork* (2010), *Deception* (2013), *Fifty Mysteries* (2015), *Dreamland* (2016), and *The Barrens* (2018).

Which brings me to the book you now hold in your hand. For a long time now, one of my bucket-list goals has been to have a collection of my stories published by Crippen & Landru. I couldn't be more proud and pleased that it's finally happened, and I'm also pleased by the *kinds* of stories they said they wanted for this book. Most of my short fiction has been crime/suspense stories in general, not traditional mysteries. They're more howcatchems or howtheygotawaywithits than whodunits. For this collection, though, C&L editor Jeffrey Marks told me he wanted detective/ puzzle-type stories, fair-play mysteries with logical solutions.

Partially because of that, I've divided *River Road and Other Mystery Stories* into three sections. The first part of the book is six stories originally published in *Alfred Hitchcock's Mystery Magazine,* all of them starring rural Mississippi sheriff Ray Douglas and his sometimes-girlfriend Jennifer Parker. Three of those stories feature two separate mystery cases within the same story, and two more of the six stories feature three cases each—so there are a total of thirteen "solvable by the reader" mysteries contained in those six stories. I hope that kind of thing'll make it fun for the reader. It was certainly fun for the writer.

The second part of the book is made up of half a dozen stories about a Southern private detective named Tom Langford and his fiancee Debra Jo (D.J.) Wells. The first of these stories, "Mustang Sally" (which won a Shamus Award in 2021), was published in *Black Cat Mystery Magazine*, the second ("Sentry") appeared in *Strand Magazine*, and the sixth ("R.I.P., Van Winkler") was in *Black Cat Weekly*. The other three of these stories are new, and have not been previously published. Once again, I had a great time writing them. I've always been fascinated by private-eye stories.

The final third of the collection are just stories I *like*. Each of these five include a mystery and three of them feature private investigators, but—unlike the first dozen stories in the book—only one of these last five has a Southern setting. The others range from the Old West of the 1880s ("Gun Work," from *Coast to Coast: Private Eyes from Sea to Shining Sea* and reprinted in *Best American Mystery Stories 2018*) to the mountains of Kentucky ("Moonshine and Roses," *Alfred Hitchcock's Mystery Magazine*) to the Arizona desert ("Welcome to Armadillo," *Strand Magazine*) to present-day Wyoming ("Rhonda and Clyde," *Black Cat Mystery Magazine*, reprinted in *Best American Mystery Stories 2020*). The last tale, "River Road," from *Prohibition Peepers: Private Eyes During the Noble Experiment*, is set in depression-era Mississippi and features one of the most unusual and interesting historic spots I've ever visited. I won't reveal that here, but I hope you'll enjoy the story.

In fact, I hope you'll like the whole book. And that you have as much fun reading these stories as I had writing them.

—John M. Floyd, August 2025

Part 1 – Sheriff Ray Douglas Mysteries

TRAIL'S END

My name is Raymond Kirk Douglas. Everyone calls me Ray, and yes, I've heard all the *Spartacus* jokes, so spare me. I'm a thirty-six-year-old bachelor, a lapsed Methodist, a relapsed fisherman (I tried to stop and realized I have no other hobbies), and the sheriff of Pine County, Mississippi, where I was born and raised. The only other thing I should mention here is that this story would never have happened if my friend Jennifer Parker had taken my advice and visited the ladies' room one more time before she and I started our drive home from New Orleans last Friday night. But she didn't, so it did.

We'd been gone two hours, cruising along in the middle of nowhere. Jenny was in the passenger seat of my patrol car, her luggage in the trunk and a Yankees ball cap on her head, humming a little tune and watching the dark woods drift past her window. Neither of us had spoken for a while. Then, from the corner of my eye, I saw her turn and look at me.

"Thanks again, for the ride," she said.

"My pleasure." The fact was, I'd been trying to decide whether to give her a call anyway, after we got back. Jenny Parker and I had been dating, off and on, for several years. We had even come close to getting married once, before both of us came to our senses. Currently our relationship switch was in the "off" position, at least the romantic side of it. Though I wouldn't have minded changing that.

"I bet your training conference was more fun than my week with Margaret," she said. Which was probably true. Jenny's cousin Margaret had been our classmate at Pinewood High, and after college the always-complaining Margaret had decided to move from the backwoods to the big city to chase fame and fortune. I suspected she was still in pursuit of both, since she was neither famous nor wealthy, but at least she now lived someplace that got cable TV.

"Mine was just a day-trip," I replied, agreeing without rubbing it in. I let a few minutes and a few miles go past, then took a deep breath and asked, "How about a movie or something, tomorrow night?"

She gave me a long look. "I thought we were in a cooling-off period, Ray."

"I could use some warming up." Mr. Smooth Talker—that's me.

"Oh, you could?" She seemed to find that amusing. "Try

Maryanne Sims, why don't you? I've heard she has her eye on you anyway."

I'd heard that if Maryanne Sims were a bird she'd probably fly north for the winter. "I have enough problems as it is," I said. "Besides, she's dating that real-estate guy—what's his name? Doofus?"

"Dolphus. James Dolphus. And no, she's not."

"How do you know?"

"Because I've been dating him."

That, I hadn't wanted to hear.

"Just a couple times," she said. "He seems okay."

"He did two years for mail fraud, Jenny."

"And paid his debt to society."

"Well, I didn't see him volunteering to drive you home from your trip to Margaret's."

"He probably doesn't know my car's in the shop."

He probably doesn't know enough to get in out of the rain. I didn't say that, though. What I said was, "Well, I'm glad I could save you a bus ride."

"Even if I have to ask for a pit stop?"

"What?"

She pointed to a cluster of lights, just ahead. "That place looks like it's still open."

I squinted at it. "You sure you can't wait? We'll be home in twenty minutes." We'd just passed the county line, so we were officially back in my jurisdiction. Not that it mattered—this was still the back side of beyond.

"Sorry," she said. "When you gotta go, you gotta go."

I dutifully slowed down and steered the car toward the gravel lot just as someone else's headlights pulled out. I parked near the front door, leaving plenty of room at the grimy Exxon pump for anyone crazy enough to refuel at a dump like this. Seriously, it reminded me of that gas station in *Deliverance.* And this is a redneck, speaking.

Inside, we found a lunch counter, a dozen racks of chips and candy bars, and an old guy with an apron and a broom, talking on the phone. After a moment he hung up, turned to face us, and introduced himself as Isaiah Cole, owner and manager. With a shaky finger he directed Jenny to a restroom, and—when I asked—poured me some coffee and managed to get most of it in the cup. He had noticed my badge, but before he could say something like

It's on the house, I paid him anyway. This place looked like it could use every penny, and so did he. It was only when I plopped down on a stool at the counter that I realized how tired I was. I took a swallow of the coffee, which tasted like river mud, and said, "You alone here?"

"I was till you came in," Cole said. Even his voice was trembly. "Had three customers a while ago, boys who'd been working the carnival over near Milltown. Oh, and Bucky Branson—he's out there in the side lot, loadin' his Jeep."

"Excuse me?"

"Maurice Branson, everybody calls him Bucky. He and his wife own a motel down on the lake, about a mile south."

"If you don't mind me asking, what would he be loading up this time of night?"

"Restaurant supplies. I can buy 'em cheaper'n he can, so I always sell Bucky some."

"Well, he must've finished already," Jenny said, returning from the bathroom. I was pleased to see she had survived the experience. "Somebody was leaving just as we drove in, and no other cars were parked outside."

I could tell from his raised eyebrows that Isaiah Cole was wondering how in the world Jenny could've heard what he'd just said to me from so far away. That was one reason I liked her company. Jenny heard and saw everything, important or not. That way, I didn't have to.

She climbed onto a stool, I introduced her to Mr. Cole, and they shook hands like this was a business meeting. Cole had perked up a bit, I noticed—Jenny has that effect on people—and the two of them fell into a long discussion about whether some of his kinfolks might know some of hers. They didn't seem to care about mine. This had gone on for ten minutes or more when the telephone rang. Cole excused himself, answered it, listened a moment, and gasped.

"You won't have to call it in," he replied, into the phone. "I'll tell the sheriff now—he's sittin' right here." He hung up and looked at me, his eyes as wide as half dollars.

"Tell me what?" I asked him.

"That was Bucky Branson, the guy I just mentioned." He turned to Jenny. "You was right, ma'am, he's finished and long gone now— he's back down at his motel."

"And?" I said.

"He says somebody just murdered his wife."

For a moment the three of us stared at each other. Then I drained my cup, set it down on the counter, asked Cole for directions, and said to Jenny, "Stay here."

She didn't, of course—she never did anything I told her to—and on our way out to my cruiser I noticed that Cole was locking up and coming with us. I secretly thanked him. Getting lost in the woods on my way to the crime scene didn't sound too appealing.

All three of us piled into the car; the old man pointed ahead and to the right, and I took off in that direction. After three or four bumpy minutes on a pitch-dark side road we arrived at a long wooden building beside a moonlit lake. Cypress trees as big around as my kitchen table poked out of the shallows, and gray veils of Spanish moss hung from the oaks lining the bank. A neon sign—TRAIL'S END, which seemed appropriate—lit up a parking lot containing nothing but (1) an old stick-shift Jeep Wrangler, (2) a weeping man in a Western shirt and boots, and (3) a woman lying face-down on the ground.

I checked the body, verified that the victim was deceased, and used my cell phone to contact my office, which would in turn notify my deputy and the county coroner. Jenny stood nearby, watching silently, taking everything in.

Something I haven't yet mentioned about Jennifer Parker: she's smart. I mean like *really* smart. She'd gone off to law school on a full scholarship, set all kinds of records, and spent two years at one of those fancy New York firms before returning to Pinewood to write mystery novels, of all things. She was still as brilliant as ever; the downside was, she sometimes didn't have much common sense. She was one of those folks who could probably assemble a parachute within thirty seconds and give you all the specs on air density and rate of descent, and then forget to put it on before she jumped out of the plane. Even so, it was comforting to have her and her deductive abilities here tonight.

The distraught man, Bucky Branson, agreed to answer a few questions while we waited for the medical and law enforcement reinforcements. He seemed to realize that although time was no longer important to his wife, it was indeed important when it came to trying to find her killer. All of us moved a respectful distance from the body, and I took out my notepad and pen.

I also shot a worried glance at Isaiah Cole. Even in the fruity lighting, he appeared a little green around the gills. The last thing we needed was another corpse lying in the gravel tonight, and it was my fault—sort of—that the old fellow was here in the first place. I should've insisted he stay put. But he seemed as interested as we were in hearing what Branson had to say, so for the moment all attention was focused in that direction.

Branson, who looked a little like Willie Nelson after a long road tour, wiped his leaky nose, took a hitching breath, and began his story. He had indeed been at Cole's station earlier, he said, loading boxes of repurchased goods into his Jeep like he does every Friday night, and had come outside carrying two cases of bottled water just in time to see the Jeep disappearing in the direction it had been pointing, down the dirt road toward the motel. He threw down his burden and followed on foot, and had finally arrived at the Trail's End to find that someone had emptied the cash register, shot his wife, Alice, on the way out, and apparently escaped across the lake in the speedboat Bucky kept at his pier fifty yards away.

Both Branson and Cole agreed, before I could even ask them, that whoever stole the Jeep—and was therefore the killer—must've been one of the three carnival workers they'd seen at Cole's place just before Jenny and I arrived. No one else had been in the area.

I said to Cole, "You have any security cameras?"

He blinked as if I'd shaken him awake. "Cameras? You kiddin' me? I'm lucky to have locks on the doors."

"You both got a good look at these guys, though, right? How about descriptions?"

"Well, it was an odd group," Branson said. "They was performers, not just workers. One was a dwarf, no bigger'n a toddler; one was a giant at least seven foot tall; and one was an acrobat—least he said he was—on crutches, with a cast on his left foot. Speakin' of foot, they was *on* foot, didn't have no car. I heard 'em saying good-byes when they left, like they was fixin' to go in different directions—to hitchhike further on, prob'ly, or head for the bus station down the road apiece—but I didn't see which way nobody went."

"Me neither," Cole said, when I looked at him.

"And you're sure they were the only people around?"

"Positive," Branson said. "It had to be one of them three, that stole my Jeep."

"Why only one of them?" I asked.

"'Cause there's only room for a driver." He pointed to the vehicle, and I could see he was right. The back and passenger seats were packed full of boxes and crates.

Jenny, her eyes narrowed, spoke for the first time: "But if somebody else—one of them—drove your Jeep . . . how'd *you* get here?"

Branson stared at her as if she'd asked him if he was a space traveler. "I just told you. I ran after it."

"A mile?" she asked.

"I can run pretty fast when I'm mad."

"In the dark? In *cowboy boots?*"

Branson's world-weary face hardened. "What exactly are you sayin' to me, missy? You think *I'm* the one drove down here? And shot my own wife?"

"I think," she said, turning to speak to me but keeping her eyes on him, "we should bring divers in to search for a sunken speedboat, near the pier there. Or maybe tied off to the shore, someplace nearby."

Branson's jaw dropped. Isaiah Cole was staring, dumbstruck, at Jenny.

"Wait a minute," Branson managed to say. "You're accusing me of murder—and of blaming it on somebody else—based on my *footwear?*"

"No, Mr. Branson. I'm accusing you based on logic." She pointed north, toward the highway. "The sheriff and I saw the lights of a vehicle leaving Mr. Cole's place of business as we arrived there, and even though it was too dark to tell what kind of vehicle it was, I do know we didn't see anybody running after it. Which reminds me, I think we ought to have those divers also search for a gun, on the lake bottom near your pier. If I were you, that's where I would've thrown the murder weapon." She paused and added, "And I'd be willing to bet that with Mrs. Branson out of the picture, you stand to inherit that motel of yours. Am I right?"

Bucky Branson's neon-lit face had gone even redder. He looked at me, a vein pulsing in his forehead, and said, "Sheriff? You gonna say anything about this?"

"I say we listen to her," I told him. "She's making sense." Even if she was a lawyer.

"But—"

"To make sure we're clear," Jenny said, "yes, I think you drove down here yourself, shot your wife, covered the whole thing up, and phoned Mr. Cole there, to report it."

"You're crazy," Branson blurted. "Both of you. How could I—"

"That's the only way it could've happened. None of the three strangers you say you both saw at Mr. Cole's could've done this."

"How do you figure that?"

"Because none of them could've driven your Jeep."

It was suddenly quiet in the parking lot. Even the crickets and night creatures seemed to have fallen silent. All of us—Branson, Cole, and I—stood there staring at Jenny Parker.

"Think about it," she said. She held up a forefinger. "One was too short. . . ." Another finger. "One was too tall. . . ."

"And the third," I added, as I caught onto her reasoning, "had a cast on his left foot. He couldn't have operated a manual-transmission clutch."

Jenny nodded. Bucky Branson was breathing hard now, looking at each of us in turn, his mouth opening and closing like a fish.

"Go ahead," I said to him. "Tell us we're wrong."

He swallowed and looked at Cole, who avoided his gaze. How did the old saying go? When you eliminate the impossible, what's left, however improbable, is the truth. None of the three suspects he'd described could've come down here and committed this murder. The process of elimination pointed straight back to Bucky Branson.

Very slowly, the deep lines in his face smoothed out. The color drained from his cheeks, his eyes drooped, his shoulders sagged.

"Mr. Branson?" I said.

With what seemed a great effort, he focused on me.

"She wanted to sell," he murmured.

"What?"

"Alice. She wanted to sell the property and move to Jackson, where our nephew lives. She hated this place, hated it almost as much as she hated me. Said it had never made any money." His eyes took on a dull, empty look. "Don't you see?—She forced me to do it. I didn't have a choice."

"You had a choice," I said, unclipping the handcuffs from my belt. As for the motel, his wife had probably been right—it was located at the end of a dirt road, for God's sake, and not really close to anyplace. I doubted it had *ever* had many customers, Friday night or not.

As I was cuffing him my deputy, Cheryl Grubbs, arrived in a spray of gravel, followed by the coroner and an ambulance. I handed a dejected and shell-shocked Branson off to Cheryl, who read him his rights and ushered him into the backseat of her cruiser before joining the rest of us, gathered now in a group around the county coroner and the body. Sure enough, when the victim was lifted from the ground, the coroner's flashlight revealed a small-caliber gunshot wound to the chest. Moments later, after some discussion and a dozen photos, the late Alice Branson was loaded into the ambulance and headed back to town.

The rest of us stood there in the lot watching them leave, except Maurice "Bucky" Branson, who was watching from the rear seat of the patrol car. Or at least he was looking in that direction. I suspected he had other things on his mind.

Actually, I had other things on my mind, too. I turned to Deputy Grubbs and said, "After you lock him up, you mind giving Jenny a ride to her house? I need to stay behind for a minute." I expected an argument, but both ladies amazed me by agreeing. The truth was, Jenny was by now looking as exhausted as I felt. She and I made plans to get together later to transfer her luggage, and—although we held eye contact a fraction longer than necessary—said nothing more to each other. She climbed into the passenger seat, and I added, to Cheryl Grubbs, "I'll take Mr. Cole back to his place."

Just before Cheryl's cruiser pulled out of the lot with Jenny and the prisoner aboard I tapped on the driver's-side window. When Cheryl lowered it I said to her, in a hushed voice, "You know a realtor named James Dolphus?"

"Yeah. Why?"

I knew Jenny couldn't hear me above the idling engine. "If you see him," I said to Cheryl, "pull him over."

"What for?"

"Just tell him we're watching him."

She nodded, looking puzzled, then buzzed the window up and drove off. Sometimes it's good to be the sheriff.

I shifted my attention to Isaiah Cole, who was still looking like an ad for acid reflux pills. I hooked my thumbs into my belt and waited to see if he would speak first. When he did, what he came out with surprised me.

"That lady," he said, glancing past me at the road. "Miss Parker. Is she a cop?"

"She's a writer."

"Are you two . . . together?"

"Just friends."

He nodded, as if deep in thought. Finally he took a breath and said, "What's going on, Sheriff? Why are we still here, you and me?"

I scratched my chin, which really didn't need scratching, and fixed him with a stare.

"A couple things are bothering me, Mr. Cole."

"What do you mean?"

"Well, for one thing, the timing. According to Branson, these three suspects that both of you saw, they supposedly drove away in a stolen vehicle, then Branson ran off chasing them, then Ms. Parker and I showed up, then ten minutes later you got a call that a murder had been committed."

Cole hesitated, and did a palms-up. "What do you want me to tell you?"

"I want you to tell me how that could happen. I don't like coincidences."

"What's the second thing?"

"The three men. They're a little too perfect. Too *planned*. It's like the beginning of a joke: a midget, a giant, and an acrobat walk into a bar. . . ." I shook my head. "A group of weird-looking carnies, who just happened to be passing through?" I took a step closer, watching his face. "And on *foot*? With one of them injured and using crutches?"

Cole shrugged, though his heart didn't seem to be in it. "Who knows? I figure somebody dropped 'em off. Besides, your lady friend didn't seem to find it strange. She used their descriptions to catch old Bucky in a lie."

"That she did. Ms. Parker is bright, a lot brighter'n I am. She's especially good at puzzles, and using information she's seen or heard in order to prove or disprove things she hasn't seen or heard. But what if some of the information was false?" I paused, looked him straight in the eye, and said, "What if Branson dreamed up three guys who would immediately seem suspicious—nobody trusts circus people—when what he should've done is dream up suspects who are *believable*."

I couldn't hear him swallow, but I saw his Adam's apple bob up and down.

"If that's true," I said, "then Branson wasn't the only one lying."

Another pause. Drops of perspiration dotted his forehead; one of them trickled past his eyebrow and down his cheek.

"You looked scared just now, when we were questioning him," I said. "If anything, more scared than he was." I watched him a second more, then pushed my hat back and rubbed my eyes. I said, very quietly, "What does Bucky Branson have on you, Mr. Cole?"

This time he didn't ask what I meant. His face actually seemed to relax a bit. He raised his head and gazed up at the black sky as if trying to count the stars. As if somehow relieved that the waiting was over.

Even his voice, when he finally answered me, sounded calmer.

"He said he'd burn my business down."

"He what?"

"He said he'd burn it to the ground. My house, too."

I took a moment to process that. "Unless . . ."

"Unless I helped him," he said. "I wouldn't have to lie outright, he told me—all I had to do was feed you some facts and agree with what he told you." He paused, then added, "I didn't do nothing illegal."

"You're wrong, Mr. Cole. You helped a man murder his wife."

"Without knowing it," he said. He heaved a sigh, the sound strangely loud in the emptiness of the night. "Some of what he told you was the truth. He was out there loading up what I'd bought for him, like I said, and I heard him leave not long before you and your friend come into my place."

A thought popped into my head. "It was Branson you were on the phone with, when we first walked in. Wasn't it."

"Yes. He was already down the street by the time you'd parked in my lot, but he'd caught a glimpse of the lights on top of your car, or the SHERIFF sign on the door, or some damn thing. Anyhow, he knew you was the police. So he musta took a couple minutes to think it through, and saw it as a chance to do this—to kill his wife—and get away with it. That's all I can figure. He'd have somebody to blame it on, he'd have a cop right there to see his grief, the whole works. So yeah, he called me on his cell phone, just before you opened my door and come in. He threatened me, said he'd call me again in ten or fifteen minutes, after he drove home. I didn't know then what I know now. I figured he might be about to do something crazy, maybe accuse his wife of stealing from him, or fire-bomb his motel, or drive his Jeep into the lake for the insurance, I don't know—but I never dreamed he'd kill Alice. I didn't know that until he said he done it, in that second call a while later, the one you heard my end of. He told me in that call what I should relay to you, and said that since you'd probably come right away I should come along with you, to back up his story." Suddenly Cole frowned. "It was then, right at that moment, that I shoulda told you everything. I realize that now. I shoulda said,

'This guy's nutty as a pecan orchard, Sheriff, and he's told me he'll get me back if I don't help him.' But I didn't do that. You say this Parker lady is a quick thinker? Well, Bucky Branson might look dumb but he's pretty quick, too. I'm not. I wasn't thinking fast enough to ask you for help."

Cole stopped then, as if talked out. He stopped and just stood there, watching me.

"I didn't know, Sheriff," he said again. It was almost a moan. "I swear I didn't."

I studied his face for a long moment, then felt myself nod.

"I believe you." I did. I'd been a cop long enough to know if somebody was lying.

He made no reply. I think he was holding his breath.

"Get in," I said, pointing to the car.

With me in the driver's seat and the old man riding shotgun, we bumped and lurched back up the winding road to the highway, where I pulled up to the front of his Depression-era café and gas station, stopped, and cut the engine. It was quiet in the car, and dark except for the glow of a single street lamp. The one that must've shown Bucky Branson my lightbar, earlier, or the lettering on my car door.

As we sat there I reminded myself to find those divers to search the lakebed near the pier. I agreed with Jenny that the murder weapon was probably there. I doubted the speedboat was—I suspected, as she'd also mentioned, that we'd find it hidden and tied off to a cypress somewhere along the bank, to have been retrieved and secretly sold once all this had died down. Maybe we could requisition it, for use by the department.

"What you fixin' to do now?" Cole asked, bringing me back from my thoughts.

"I'm fixin' to come in and use your restroom. That okay?"

"When you gotta go, you gotta go."

We climbed out together, and a moment later he unlocked the front door, stomped in ahead of me, switched the lights on, and sagged down onto one of the barstools to wait. When I returned from the bathroom, I walked over and stood facing him.

"More questions?" he said. I could hear the fatigue in his voice. And the concern. I hadn't arrested him yet, but I hadn't left yet either.

"You think Branson will give you up?" I asked. "Tell us you were helping him?"

Isaiah Cole drew a long, shaky breath. "I'm not sure. It would just make him look worse. And he's not the kinda guy who wants other folks to know he *needs* help. You know?"

"But he might," I said. "Implicate you, I mean. If he does . . . well, I'll do what I can."

"Thanks, Sheriff."

I turned to leave, got as far as the door, and remembered something. "In your men's room a minute ago," I said, "there was a little step-stool sitting there, beside the toilet."

"Musta got moved. I use it to stand on when I clean the top pane of the window. It's usually in the corner."

"I don't think it was there by accident. It was pulled right up to the commode. Any small kids ever use that restroom?"

"No. Unless . . ."

Then he blinked, and I could see that the answer occurred to him the same time it occurred to me.

"The dwarf," I said.

He nodded. "I remember now—he made a trip to the john just before they left."

"So he was real."

"I told you he was real. I saw him. The tall guy, too, and the one with his foot in a cast. Bucky told the truth, at least about that. I told you about it, too, when you two first walked in. But you was right about the timing. Them three left at least an hour before you got here."

I gave that some thought. Maybe I *hadn't* been a cop long enough.

"So it wasn't that he made up unbelievable suspects when he should've kept it simple," I said. "He told us about real people . . . who weren't really suspects. If he hadn't he might've gotten away with it."

"In a way, that's even sadder," Cole said. "Ain't it."

"I think it's called 'ironic.'"

Several seconds passed, as both of us thought all this over. Finally I nodded to him and opened the door to leave.

"Sheriff?"

I paused once more, looked back at him.

"That Parker lady. You said you two ain't together?"

"That's right. Why?"

"You should be," he said.

I felt myself smile. "Good night, Mr. Cole."

Outside, in the car, I kept replaying the things he'd said to me. All the way home I thought about truth and lies, good and evil, things that were clear and things that weren't. Most of all I thought about the way we sometimes keep doing the things we don't want to do just because it's easier than changing, and that we don't do the things we want to do because we're afraid to.

I took out my phone as I drove, paged to Jenny Parker's name, and pressed the button.

Why not?

SCAVENGER HUNT

I had risen from my desk and had picked up my hat with one hand and sunglasses with the other when Jennifer Parker appeared in the office doorway. Staring at her, I dropped my sunshades into what I thought was the pocket of my uniform shirt, missed, and was vaguely aware of them clattering onto my desktop. The hat got no further than my chest—I held it there as if about to pledge allegiance to the flag.

"Going somewhere, Sheriff?"

I cleared my throat. Jenny Parker always made me feel like I was eight years old. Come to think of it, I'd probably loved her since I was eight years old. "Down the street a ways," I said.

"I won't keep you. I just dropped by to say hello."

"I enjoyed the movie the other night," I said, as she turned to leave. "Maybe we could do it again. Maybe Friday."

She smiled. "We need to go slow, Ray. Remember our past, you and me."

I remembered. A few years ago our on-again-off-again relationship progressed all the way to the point of blood tests for a marriage license, and shopping for a house. We even had wedding invitations printed up. The coming-to-our-senses moment happened at roughly the same time—I still remembered us sitting there in rocking chairs on the porch of her childhood home, sitting there stopped in mid-rock and staring at each other with *What the hell are we doing?* looks on our faces. At least we didn't mail out the invitations (saved fifty bucks on postage, right there). I wished I hadn't already bought her a ring. It was still in its little box, in my sock drawer.

"You're right. Go slow," I said. "Let's wait till Saturday."

Her smile widened. A good sign.

"Walk with me," I said, raising my hat to where it belonged. "It's a nice morning."

"Where?"

"I don't know—it's probably a nice morning everywhere."

"I mean, where are we going?"

I shrugged into my coat, steered her through the outer office, waved to Lizzie the Dispatcher, and held the front door open. "To see a lady named Barb Sandifer. You know her?"

"Sounds familiar. I knew a Joe Willie Sandifer, before he died."

"That was her daddy. Apparently she left here years ago and moved back." *Like you did*, I thought. "When she called she said she's living in the old family house, on Third and Franklin."

"Why'd she call?" Jenny asked. We passed the post office next door and turned south, on Third Street. It was cold but clear, our breaths smoking as we talked.

"She told me she'd been robbed, last night."

"Robbed how? Burglarized? Mugged?"

"We're about to find out," I said, pointing to the small frame house on the next corner.

"We?" she said.

I stopped, and we stood squinting at each other on the sidewalk. I wished I hadn't left my sunglasses in the office.

"Come talk to her with me," I said. "You like this kind of thing, I know you do."

"I'm not a lawyer anymore, Ray. Remember? I'm a writer."

"A *mystery* writer. I also remember it was you who put Bucky Branson in jail."

"I was lucky. I smelled a rat, for all the wrong reasons," she said.

"Doesn't matter. He was guilty and you figured it out."

She was looking at the house and frowning. "You sure it's okay?"

"If Ms. Sandifer complains, I'll tell her you're my deputy."

"In jeans, sneakers, and a fuzzy coat? Your real deputy would love that."

Actually my real deputy, Cheryl Grubbs, wouldn't have minded a bit. To Cheryl, Jenny Parker was the small-town girl who'd made it big—law degree, fancy job in New York—and who'd then left it all to return to the small town. If Jenny told Cheryl pond mud was ice cream, Cheryl would gulp a double scoop.

"Cheryl's off this week," I said, and without waiting for a reply I marched across the brown lawn to the house and rapped on the door. By the time I heard someone opening it, Jenny was standing beside me.

Barb Sandifer looked to be around fifty, which in Pine County meant she was probably around forty. "You the sheriff?" she said, by way of greeting.

"Raymond Douglas," I said, hat in hand. "This is my assistant, Jennifer Parker."

Assistant? Jenny gave me an annoyed look but let it go. We followed Barb inside and sat down on a leather couch. She sat in a matching wing chair. Between Barb and us was an expensive-looking glass-topped coffee table. I looked down through the glass and saw my booted feet underneath, and Jenny's Reeboks, and Barb's house shoes. Jenny was looking around like a field hand in a cathedral, taking everything in. Nothing about this room was what we'd expected.

"I do remember you," Jenny said suddenly. "You won the Riverway Giveaway."

Barb smiled for the first time. I remembered, too, now: Riverway Furniture in nearby Brookhaven had held a widely publicized contest two weeks ago, and the winner had received a completely furnished living room: leather sofa and chairs, brass lamps, paintings, lush chocolate-colored carpeting, the works—along with a cash prize. Quite a deal.

Then the smile faded, to match her eyes. Barb Sandifer looked tired. "I'm not sure all my luck was good," she said. "A guy I used to know—Calvin Gunn—showed up last night and asked me for a loan. Lotta folks been hitting me up for loans lately." She let out a sigh. "Anyhow, I told him to leave, but, well, he knows me, Calvin does, knows I like to gamble. The casinos in Natchez and Vicksburg, down on the Coast, that kind of thing. And I occasionally have a drink, and, well, I'd been doing some of that, too, last night, before he got here."

I stayed quiet, watching her and listening.

"So when I turned him down on the loan—it wouldn't have been a 'loan' anyway, if you get my meaning—he asked me to take a bet. To bet with him, on a card trick. If I won, he said, he'd leave and I'd never see him again. If he won I'd loan him two thousand dollars, cash."

"Doesn't sound too fair, to me," I said.

"I told you, I'd had a few drinks," Barb said. Actually I wondered if she'd had a few this morning as well. "Anyhow, he told me the terms: he'd let me pick any card out of a deck, then I'd hold the card out so he could see the back of it, that's all, then I'd put it back into the deck. He'd never touch it, he said."

"And?"

"And he'd tell me what card it was."

"Without ever looking at it," I said.

"Right. Except for the back."

"He must've planned to use a marked deck."

"Nope. We used one of mine. I got it out of the junk drawer there in the kitchen."

"Then he must've been going to mark it himself, somehow."

"He never touched the cards, Sheriff. Not once."

I waited for a beat, but she didn't continue. "So what happened?" I asked.

She pressed her palms together as if in prayer. "I fetched my deck from the drawer, shuffled it right here on the coffee table, took out a card, and looked at it: the eight of diamonds. Then I held the card out facedown between us, just like this." She pulled her chair up, facing the two of us, and extended an arm. "Then, when Calvin nodded, I put the card back into the deck, squared it up, and set it down. And he looked up at me and said, 'The eight of diamonds.'"

Jenny and I sat there silently, gawking at her.

"That's impossible," I said.

"Not impossible," Jenny murmured. "Unlikely, though. Odds are one in fifty-two."

"So what happened then?" I asked Barb.

"Then I accused him of cheating me. And he said, 'How about we do it again?'"

"Did you do it again?"

"We did it three times. He named the right card every time."

All of us had fallen silent. I thought I could hear a TV going, somewhere in the back of the house. A talk show—Kelly Ripa, maybe.

"And you gave him the money?" I asked.

"I had to," she said. "He won the bet. He did exactly what he said he'd do."

"But you told me you were robbed."

"I was. He cheated me. I just"—she swallowed, her face reddening—"I just don't know *how*."

Jenny and I exchanged a glance. Finally I looked at Barb and said, "I don't know either, Ms. Sandifer. I sympathize, but I don't have any way to help you, here."

Her face stayed brick-red, but the anger leaked out of it. "I know," she said. "But I just had to tell somebody."

"How about this?" I said. "We'll watch him. We'll see if Calvin does anything else, tries this anywhere else. If he does we'll try to catch him at it, and prosecute him. Okay?"

She nodded, staring off into space. Suddenly, with that crystal clarity that seems to occasionally dawn on the faces of those who partake in Demon Rum, she said, "Calvin's not that smart, you know. Not intelligent. He's just sneaky."

I didn't know how to respond to that. We sat there a moment longer, then I glanced at Jenny and we rose together to our feet and bid our farewells. When we let ourselves out the door, Barb Sandifer was still sitting there in her new chair, staring at nothing.

"Well," Jenny said, as we retraced our steps to the office. "That was strange."

"It was. And you know what?—I believe her."

"You believe it happened that way? And that he cheated her?"

"Yes, to both. He knew she had windfall money, knew about her gambling, and knew he could win it." I studied Jenny's face. "You're the brains, on this team. How'd he do it?"

"The trick?" She shook her head. "Don't know. We're missing something obvious."

"Which reminds me," I said.

"Of what?"

"Of something Calvin's father did, once."

"His father?"

"I've run into Calvin Gunn before," I said. "Nothing criminal, but he's always been trouble. She said Calvin was sneaky? Well, the rotten apple didn't fall far from the tree."

We'd made it back to the Pinewood post office, and I nodded toward a bench in an alcove by the sidewalk. We detoured and took a seat. It was early December, plenty chilly but not yet bitterly cold, and the sun helped a little. I could smell breakfast cooking in the café across the street. Strings of Christmas lights draped every tree in sight.

"You have time for this?" I asked her.

"I'm sitting here, aren't I?"

I drew a long breath and let it out in a white cloud. "Several years ago," I began, "when I was a deputy here, I heard about Calvin's daddy. Lester." I paused, remembering. "Lester Gunn was a slick operator. Our sheriff at the time, Robbie Neal—"

"Him I remember," Jenny said.

"Well, he knew Lester was into all kinds of illegal ventures, but never could catch him."

"Gunn control can be a problem," she agreed.

I took off my hat and scratched my head. "Do you want to hear this or not?"

"Sorry," she said.

"Years ago," I continued, "Lester Gunn worked as an assistant manager at Burton's Emporium, on East Main." I pointed with my hat. "Store's gone now, burned to the ground."

"I remember that, too."

"Well, Lester was cocky. Arrogant. He was always bragging to his friends at the store that he could steal the place blind if he wanted to, and he once made a bet with somebody—a really expensive bet—that he could sneak five hundred dollars' worth of merchandise out of the store over several weeks' time. Undetected."

"More bets," Jenny said. "And?"

"One of Lester's co-workers was the sheriff's cousin," I said. "The cousin heard about the bet, told Sheriff Neal, and a few days later Robbie Neal stopped Lester on his way home and searched him—you could do things like that back then. But Robbie didn't find anything. He did another search two days later, and two days after that, and still came up empty. Robbie even let me come along and watch, now and then."

"What did Lester do, about all this?"

"Nothing," I said. "The sheriff's source told him Lester actually thought it was funny, the way he was fooling everyone—even the Law. Instead of getting scared and calling off the bet, Lester kept at it. It got to be a game between them: Robbie Neal watched Lester march in to work every morning with his pipe and briefcase and lunch bag and watched him come out every afternoon with his briefcase and sunglasses and a milkshake, grinning and carefree. And every few days Robbie would stop him and frisk him on the way out, to no avail."

"How about the briefcase?"

"It was searched too. Always contained regular stuff, including the empty lunch sack."

"Any hidden compartments?"

"Nope." I squinted up at the sun and put my hat back on. "And there was never anything suspicious in Lester's pockets, either. Sometimes he was ordered to turn out the contents."

"How about jewelry?"

"Another dead end. He wore the same Timex wristwatch every day, and never wore rings, bracelets, neck chains, et cetera."

Jenny frowned, mulling that over. "Did Neal ever do, like, a full-body search the way they do now at airports?"

"No. There were limits, even back then—but he always patted Lester down, and did it well. Never once did he find a hidden pocket in his clothes or things sewn into linings or strapped to the inside of his leg, anything like that."

"But the sheriff didn't search him every day?"

"Not every day," I said. "But there was never more than a day or two between searches, and they were always unexpected. It would've been almost impossible to beat those odds—and Lester wasn't crazy."

Jenny stayed quiet a moment more, thinking. During the silence my cell phone buzzed in my pocket. I fished it out and heard Lizzie's voice: "Get back here, Ray. Something's up."

I disconnected and rose from the bench. To Jenny I said, "Gotta go."

"Wait a minute. What finally happened?"

"With Lester? He got caught. We figured out what it was that he was stealing."

"What *was* he stealing?"

"Sunglasses," I said.

I was twenty feet down the sidewalk toward the office when I heard her hurrying after me. "Seriously?" she said, as she pulled alongside.

"Yep. Sunglasses. Different pair every day. Same style, mostly—black frames and so on. Obvious but not too obvious."

"Like the card trick."

"Exactly," I said. "Except this time we can't solve it."

We reached my office building and were climbing the steps when Jenny stopped me, her gloved hand on my arm. "You were the one who figured it out, weren't you. You caught him."

I shrugged. "It wasn't that hard. I started watching Lester closer, talked to the clerks. It finally dawned on me. He didn't wear—or need—sunglasses going *to* work. Just when he left."

"You solved it without me."

"You were in New York," I said.

Her face softened. "Good old Kirk. My hero."

"Don't call me that."

"It's your middle name, isn't it? I bet Kirk Douglas even played a sheriff or two, in his prime."

I grinned a little in spite of myself. "Is there anything about me you *don't* know?"

My brightened mood changed as soon as we pushed through the door. Lizzie hopped up and handed me the message, and I saw the *it's bad news* look on her face. Jenny and I read the note together. Then I entered my office, picked up my desk phone, and punched in the number.

"Mr. Simpson?" I said. "Raymond Douglas, sir. I just received your message. I'm sorry to hear about your wife." I hit the speakerphone button so we could listen together as Jacob Simpson repeated the info from the note he'd left: twenty minutes ago he'd found his elderly wife, Minnie, lying dead on the steep, icy steps behind their hillside home. But it was no accident, he said. Someone had killed her. When he wouldn't go into more detail, I told him I was on my way and hung up.

I looked at Jenny's face, an act that usually diluted my attention considerably. This time it didn't. Murder tends to focus the mind. "Are you beginning to wish you hadn't stopped by today, to say hello?"

She stood there hugging her elbows as if still cold. "I've heard about two mysteries this morning, and only one of them was solved. I don't want to get left out of the third."

"The more the merrier." I dug around in my lap drawer, found a spare deputy's badge, and tossed it to her. "It matches your earrings." As we exited the office I shouted over my shoulder to Lizzie, "You haven't told anybody about this, right?"

"Just you and the coroner," she called.

"Well, don't," I said.

It didn't take much longer to drive to Jacob Simpson's place than it had taken to walk to Barb Sandifer's. The home had indeed been built on the side of a hill. I pulled over to the edge of the narrow access road to allow the county coroner's van to pass in the opposite direction, then we drove on to the house, parked out front, and trudged down a steep slope and around to the back. Jacob, who must've seen us coming, met us there. After exchanging introductions and more condolences, the three of us gravely studied the steps that ran downhill from the two-story home's back porch to a little wooden cabin with floor-to-ceiling windows.

"Her studio," Jacob said. "She took up art a few years ago. I think she was happiest out there in that house, painting the hills and reading her books." Even from outside, and at a distance, I could see a wall of neat bookshelves inside the cabin. "She hadn't been able to do much of either, since her stroke several months ago. But she was recovering." His eyes misted over. "And now this."

I stayed respectfully silent for several seconds, then took out my notepad and pen and started doing my job. "You said she didn't come out here often?"

"Not since her health problems started. I suspect she wouldn't have come out today either, if not for this." He swiped at his damp eyes with a coat sleeve and dug a folded envelope from his coat pocket. "I found this on the kitchen table this morning. I must've brought it in from the mailbox with everything else late yesterday afternoon, and never noticed it. We ate in the den last night, watching TV, so I assume she found and opened the letter this morning, before I got up. She was always the early riser. I'm the night owl."

Holding the envelope by its corner, I studied the front. It was addressed to Mrs. Jacob Simpson, no return address, no postmark. It must've been hand-delivered to their mailbox, yesterday. I opened the flap and carefully removed the single sheet of paper inside. On it were the typed words: AN URGENT MESSAGE FOR MINNIE SIMPSON HAS BEEN PLACED BETWEEN PAGES 85 AND 86 OF THE MALTESE FALCON.

Jenny, peering over my shoulder, whispered, "That's a novel."

"I know that." I turned to Jacob. "Your wife owned a copy, I assume."

"Yes."

"And—you think this message is related to her death?"

"I do," Jacob said. He pointed to the note. "What does that sound like, to you?"

"Something in a scavenger hunt," Jenny said.

"Exactly. I think whoever sent that note knew my wife loved mysteries and puzzles of any kind, and that she had a copy of that novel in her studio bookcase." He paused, and let a hard edge creep into his voice. "I think he also knew how frail she was, and that it was dangerous for her to go down these tall steps alone. Especially with the weather we've been having."

"You're saying this message was to lure her outside, in the hope that she would fall?"

Jacob shook his head. "More than that. I think the sender waited, crept up behind her, and pushed her." He nodded toward the stone staircase. "Those steps are wide as well as tall, and she fell down the left side, away from the handrail. Minnie *always* held onto the handrail."

"What if she'd found this last night?" I said. "What if she'd taken you with her, to look?"

"I don't think she would've. That studio was her territory, and hers alone."

After a silence Jenny said, "Assuming all that's true—who might've wanted her dead?"

Jacob took a long, ragged breath. "Only two people," he said. "Both of whom had visited her studio in the past. One's Walter Harmon. Y'all know him, right? The fights he and Minnie had over censorship of new books got him fired as county librarian. He hated her."

"Enough to murder her, with a careful plan like this one?"

"I wouldn't have thought so—but who knows?"

"Who's the second possibility?" I asked.

"Our nephew, Calvin Gunn."

Jenny and I exchanged a look. *Calvin?*

Jacob made a face. "He was the no-account son of Minnie's no-account brother, Lester."

"But why might you suspect him?"

"Because of something that happened last week. Minnie was with me in Brookhaven, at Riverway Furniture, having a good day and doing pretty well with her walker, and told Calvin she was fed up with his drinking and carousing and was going to cut him out of her will."

"Wait," Jenny said. "What was Calvin doing with you two at Riverway Furniture?"

"He works there," Jacob said.

"What?"

"A stock boy, or some such. Nothing that would require much brainpower, I would hope."

Jenny was staring off into the distance, her face a blank.

"My God," she murmured.

"What?" I said.

She turned to me, eyes wide. "I know what he did," she said. "I know how Calvin tricked Barb Sandifer."

I glanced at Jacob, said, "Excuse us a minute," and steered Jenny aside. "What are you talking about?" I asked her.

"He worked at the furniture store, Ray."

"So?"

"If he worked there, he knew what the prize was. The Riverway Giveaway. He knew ahead of time what furnishings she won."

I was getting frustrated. Jenny could do that to me sometimes. As calmly as possible, I asked, "What does that matter?"

"Remember what Barb told us? During the trick she was

instructed to hold the card she'd picked facedown in front of her, between them. Right?"

"Right. So?"

"Calvin knew she had a dark-colored carpet, Ray. And a glass-topped coffee table. That's why he went there. The dark background of the carpeting made the glass act like a mirror, so—"

Suddenly I understood. "—So he could see the underside of the card reflected in the glass tabletop," I said.

"Correct." Her cheeks were flushed now, and not just from the chill. "She was dead right: Calvin's not smart. He's just sneaky. He cheated her." She leaned closer to me, eyes glittering. "He needed money, she had it, and he knew how to get it out of her," she said. "Just like here."

"What do you mean, like here?"

Jenny turned and spoke to Jacob.

"The will you mentioned," she said. "Your wife was going to cut Calvin out?"

"Yes," Jacob said.

"But she hadn't done it yet?"

"No. And Calvin knew that."

"How much of an inheritance are we talking about?" she asked.

"A lot. Her father left her well off."

"How well off?"

"Calvin's share would be a hundred grand or more."

Jenny looked again at me, and I could see the cold certainty in her face. I felt it myself.

"Okay," I said. "We've established motive. Sounds like we need to question both Walter Harmon and Calvin Gunn. Mr. Simpson, have you been down to your wife's studio yet, to look between the pages of that book of hers?"

"No. I figured I should wait for you, to do that."

"Well, let's go do it."

"Let me run fetch the key," he said. "It's in the house." He hurried back up the hill.

When he'd disappeared inside, Jenny said to me, "You won't have to look at the book."

I felt myself frown. "Why?"

"Because there won't be anything there."

"You sound pretty certain."

"I am."

"So do you also know who killed her?"

"I do if there are only two suspects," she said. "Because this particular scavenger is not Walter Harmon."

"Why not?"

"Because Mr. Harmon was a librarian for thirty years, Ray. He knows books, backward and forward. Everything about books. And . . ."

"And what?"

"No one who knows books would have written that note."

"Why do you say that?"

Jacob arrived with the key. Jenny stepped back, held out an inviting hand, and said to me, "See for yourself."

I followed Jacob Simpson down the steps, and when he'd unlocked the door to the studio I headed straight to the bookshelves. A minute later I took down a beautiful hardcover copy of *The Maltese Falcon*, flipped to page 85—and froze.

"See what I mean?" Jenny said, from the doorway.

Jacob leaned over to look, and his jaw dropped as far as mine had.

Jenny was right: there was nothing between pages 85 and 86. There couldn't have been.

Pages 85 and 86 were—as they are in any book—the front and back of the same page.

She was also correct that a librarian would've known that.

"If there are only two suspects," she repeated, "the guilty party is Calvin Gunn."

I nodded. "I believe you. But—"

"But what?"

"We need proof."

She thought a moment, looked at her watch, and raised her eyes to meet mine. A slow smile spread across her face. "I have a plan," she said.

"What kind of plan?"

"Mr. Simpson?" she said. "You've talked to nobody about this, right? Nobody at all."

"Right. Only you two and the dispatch lady."

"Lizzie's kept it quiet," I said. "So has the coroner."

Jenny kept her gaze fixed on Jacob. "It's past eleven o'clock now," she said. "What time did you discover your wife's body, sir? Ten or so?"

"About that time. I called the sheriff's office right away."

"But the murder was committed much earlier, right?"

"Yes, it had to have been. I woke up around eight and ate my breakfast alone; I thought Minnie was in the downstairs bedroom, where she's been staying since the stroke—but of course she wasn't—so I didn't start looking for her until much later. Whatever happened must've happened before eight o'clock."

"More than three hours ago, at least," Jenny said. "My guess is, the killer figures you found the body shortly after it happened. He'll figure everybody in Pinewood knows about it by now." She looked at me. "But Calvin isn't in Pinewood. He works in Brookhaven. You see what I'm thinking?"

"I believe I do," I said.

Ten minutes later I placed a call from my cell phone to Riverway Furniture and asked for Calvin Gunn. When he came on the line I looked at the script we'd prepared and said, "Mr. Gunn? Sheriff Douglas, Pine County. What can you tell me about your aunt Minnie Simpson?"

I waited several seconds, holding my breath.

"I . . . still can't quite believe it, Sheriff. We were very close, Aunt Min and me."

"I understand, Mr. Gunn. But I must tell you, we have reason to suspect foul play. If you happen to think of anything that might help, anything at all . . . please contact me. All right?"

"Absolutely, Sheriff. And if, well, if it wasn't an accident—I hope you find whoever did it, and fast."

"I think I will, Mr. Gunn. Many thanks."

I disconnected, switched off the RECORD feature on my phone, and gave Jacob Simpson a solemn thumbs-up. We now had proof that Calvin Gunn knew that Minnie was dead when there's no way he could've known that, unless he was the one who'd killed her. To Jenny I smiled and said, "You know what you are? You're smart and sneaky."

"Even so," she said, "I think you better go on over to Riverway right now, and bring him in. Don't give him too much time to think."

"You don't want to come along?"

"No. Just bring me back some info about their next Giveaway."

"I think I'll keep it for myself. I could use a new living room."

"Yes, you could," she agreed.

I remembered she'd left her car outside my office. "I'll take you back. It's on my way."

"Okay. But drop me off at Barb Sandifer's. I want to give her the good news."

"And play some cards?"

"And have a drink," she said.

On the drive to town I watched from the corner of my eye as Jenny, in the passenger seat, took the gold deputy's badge from the pocket of her coat. She looked at it, tilted her head, turned it over and over in her hands.

"You were right," she said quietly. "I do love this kind of thing."

"Keep it. You can wear it to the movies."

She turned to me and grinned. "Saturday, right?"

"Friday," I said.

FRIENDS AND NEIGHBORS

Jennifer Parker was digging with a shovel in one of the flower-beds in her front yard when I pulled my cruiser into her driveway. I climbed out, took my time putting on my hat and adjusting my gunbelt, which always makes me feel sheriffy, and strolled over to where she was working.

She didn't seem to be accomplishing anything except turning over dirt, and since she didn't seem inclined to stop doing it, I pointed and said, "What are those?"

Finally she leaned on her shovel and squinted up at me. "Which ones?"

"The purple ones."

"Pansies. And they're blue."

"Look purple to me."

"Take off your sunglasses."

I did, and sure enough, the damn things were blue. When I looked at her again, she was grinning, and I thought—not for the first time—that she was the prettiest lawyer I'd ever seen.

I guess I should tell you: I'm Raymond Douglas, Ray to my friends, and I'm the sheriff of Pine County, Mississippi. And, technically at least, Jenny Parker wasn't a lawyer. She was a novelist who'd once been a lawyer, and that's a big difference. I'm not overly fond of writers either, the few of them I've known—but I *really* don't like lawyers. Unless maybe they're district attorneys.

Except for Jenny. Jenny could be an assassin for the Dixie Mafia and I'd still follow her around like a lapdog. The truth is, I love her. I've even told her so, though I'm not sure she believes it. I've told her she loves me, too, and she's even said it herself a time or two, but I'm not sure she believes that either. Still, we hang around together. With Jenny and me, there seems to be a fine line between boyfriend/girlfriend and just friends. It's an odd relationship.

Her voice snapped me out of my thoughts: "You look pleased with yourself," she said.

I smiled back at her. "You can say that again."

"You look pleased with yourself." Still breathing hard, she sleeved sweat from her forehead and added, "What's the occasion?"

I put my shoulders back a little and sucked in my stomach. "I solved a case."

"You what?"

"Well, I didn't *solve* it. But I caught an error, and wound up ID'ing a burglar."

"How? Tell me about it."

Another note: Jenny wasn't just being kind, when she asked me about police work. She loved it, and had been helpful to me in solving some pretty crazy cases the past couple years. I don't think she misses lawyering, but she seems to like the challenge of dealing with crimes and criminals. Of figuring things out.

"First, tell me why you called me," I said, relaxing a bit. It was hard holding my stomach in. "A legal issue, you said?"

Her smile dimmed a little. She wiped her face again, stabbed the shovel into the dirt like she was setting a boundary marker, and sat down in a patch of grass. Suddenly she looked tired, and from more than just digging in a flowerbed.

"No," she said. "You go first."

I didn't argue further. I put my sunglasses in my shirt pocket, pushed my hat back, and sat down beside her. Choosing my words.

"My old buddy Alan Collums at the Jackson PD called me this morning about Ellie Limpkin," I said. "Remember her, from high school?"

"She was a year behind us, right? Always studying."

"Apparently still is. She's the head of the biology department at one of the colleges up there now, and Alan said somebody broke into her office last night. Stole some fancy exhibits, or some such. Bug collections."

"Bug collections?"

"Insects. Butterflies, beetles, ants. Valuable exhibits, Alan said, but they were probably just a diversion. Also stolen was the department's safe. Several thousand dollars. No signs of forced entry to the room, and—get this—Ellie was the only person who had a door key."

Jenny took off her work gloves and studied my face. "Is she a suspect?"

"Not really. She's a workaholic, been there ten years. Says her key was missing this morning from her purse. Alan's call to me was mostly to ask about any of her family that might still be here in Pinewood, to try to find some kind of a lead he could chase. As it turned out, all I could do was confirm part of what he already knew: Ellie's married with no kids, her parents live in Texas now, her father's an only child, and her mother had one sibling—a sister who recently passed away."

"How about Ellie's husband? Do you know him?"

"No, but he's the prime suspect. Auto parts salesman, police record, out of town at the moment."

Jenny thought that over. "And Ellie swears he's innocent, I suppose."

"Yep. She says he's been gone a week, but her uncle from Memphis visited her yesterday, and that *he* must've taken her key, maybe from her purse when she was making them Sunday lunch."

"What does this uncle do?"

"He's a koley . . . koley op . . ."

"Coleopterist?" she said.

"Yeah. Doctor something, I forget his name. Ellie says he'd done some work with her college in the past, and was familiar with her department."

"And?"

"He left again last night, and now nobody can locate him."

"Hmm. And there are no other clues?"

"Nope."

She waited, and when I didn't continue she said, "Is all this leading someplace?"

"It's leading to the fact that I solved the case. And I did it the way *you* always do: I spotted something obvious, something in plain sight, that the cops up there had overlooked."

"What?"

I paused a moment, then said, "She invented the uncle."

"She what?"

"She must have. Nobody saw him during his visit, except her, and his name doesn't seem to be listed with any hospitals or clinics in Tennessee. Ellie made him up." I plucked a blade of dry grass and twirled it in my fingers. "Her dad has no siblings, remember, and her mother had only the one sister, who's gone now."

"So . . ."

"So Ellie couldn't have *had* an uncle," I said.

Jenny gave me a long stare. Birds chirped in the trees that shaded her yard. Somewhere down the street, a dog barked.

Her doubtful expression wasn't the reaction I'd been hoping for, but I was still proud of myself and my deductive powers. In all fairness, she had her own problems, and I hadn't even heard them yet.

"Anyhow, that's my story," I said. "Ellie must've either stolen the cash herself, and the bugs to throw us off the track, or—more likely—she's lying to protect her already-familiar-with-the-cops husband." I flicked away the sprig of grass. "Your turn. Why'd you call me?"

She seemed to refocus, and took a long breath. "Because I need your help. You know more about this kind of thing than I do."

"What kind of thing?"

As she began telling me her story, it turned out that her situation was as much a surprise to me as it must've been to her, when it happened. And hers, unlike mine, was personal. Jenny's cousin and neighbor, a professional photographer named Julia Parker, had stolen and altered a property deed that their Aunt Millicent had signed over to Jenny shortly before the aunt's death last month. It was a deed for a small parcel of land, outside town. The document had gone missing two nights ago from a file box Jenny kept in the trunk of her car. Her mobile office, she called it.

"I know that box," I said. "I thought you only kept writing stuff in there."

"I keep anything there that's important to me. Contracts and backups of my manuscripts are important, yeah, and whatever research I'm doing at the moment. But so was this." She heaved another sigh. "I had intended to put it in my safe deposit box at the bank and just hadn't gotten around to doing it."

"And now it's not there," I said.

"Right." She ran a hand through her sweaty hair. "I was looking for a file yesterday, and saw the box wasn't shut all the way. When I checked further, I found the deed was gone."

"Why do you suspect Julia took it?" I asked. As I spoke, I turned and looked across the street, at the tall house one door down and to my right. Julia Parker lived there, alone like Jenny—but I knew the two of them seldom saw each other, and hadn't spoken in years. Talk about odd relationships . . .

"I suspect her because she showed me the deed," she said.

I blinked. "The one that was stolen?"

"Yeah. She told me yesterday she'd found it among Aunt Millie's things, last time she was out at the old home place."

"You mean . . . she came right out and showed it you? Even though you knew it had been taken from your car?"

"Yep. And she knew it, too. It was all I could do not to slap her face."

"How could she have known about the file box?" I said.

"How could she not? She's not blind. She lives across the street, I always park in my driveway, and I take papers in and out of my trunk all the time."

"Could there have been two copies?"

"Of the deed? No. Aunt Millie told me that."

"You said it had been altered. Altered how?"

"It now had Julia's signature on it, as the new property owner, instead of mine. The typed name was still J. Parker—I'm Jennifer Lynn and she's Julia Anne—but I'd signed it J. L. Parker, which is my legal signature. And Julia had changed it. The J. L. had become Julia—easy to do, if you're careful, and with the right color ink."

"Do you have anything else that might confirm that the property was transferred to you?"

"No. Apparently Millie didn't leave a will, and nothing about her estate was filed at the courthouse. Just the fact that I loved that piece of land, and she'd always told me she wanted me to have it. Both Julia and I knew that."

I took several seconds to think this over. "But wouldn't an examination of the signature show the last name to be in your handwriting, rather than hers?"

"Probably not. Aunt Millie gave me the new deed to sign the night of her ninetieth birthday celebration, and I was dead tired. The signature doesn't look like Julia's, but it also doesn't look much like mine."

For a long moment neither of us said a word. A bee buzzed past, hovered for a while over the pansies, and took off again. Probably looking for one that was purple.

"If there's really no other record," I said, "the document Julia has, forged or not, might not even be legally binding. You know that, right?"

"That'll depend on the judge. But it's going to complicate everything, to say the least." Another silence passed, both of us lost in thought. After a minute or so I rose to my feet and crossed the yard to Jenny's car, a twenty-year-old Grand Marquis parked beside my cruiser in her driveway. There was a long story behind the big Mercury. The house had been her parents' and the car had been her mother's, after her dad died. It was old but roomy and well-made and ultra-comfortable on the road, and Jenny loved it.

I didn't have to ask her why it wasn't in the garage. The garage was still full of stuff she hadn't unpacked since she moved back here from New York, a few years ago. And it didn't take me long to see that there was no visible damage to the trunk. Whoever had stolen the deed must've somehow gotten into the car elsewhere, and opened the trunk from inside. But there was no damage to the door or any of the windows either.

I asked her about that. She told me she kept the Mercury locked, and never loaned the car or the car key to anyone. At first I wondered if the thief—Julia—might've written down the vehicle identification number off the dashboard and somehow used it to get a replacement key from the dealership, but that reasoning didn't hold water. For one thing, it wouldn't be easy to do. For another, Jenny's car's VIN was obscured by a map that had slipped down between the windshield and the dash, making the number unreadable from outside, and she assured me the map had been lying right there for months. In fact the only odd thing Jenny had noticed was that on two separate mornings her outside driver's mirror had been askew, and had to be adjusted after she'd gotten behind the wheel. She figured she must've bumped the mirror without realizing it, maybe when washing the car or walking past while unloading groceries.

"For what it's worth," she added, "I lost my remote key-fob awhile back, and haven't replaced it."

"So how do you unlock the car door? Manually, with the ignition key?" Our police cruisers used to all be Crown Vics, which are essentially the same car as the Grand Marquis, so I knew the startup key could also be used to open the doors.

"No. I just enter a four-digit unlock code into the security keypad on the driver's door, beside the handle. Easy as pie."

I nodded, then said, "Think somebody could've seen you entering the code?"

"No again. I always stand close to the door when I key in the number, so no one from the street would be able to see past me."

"Hmm." I walked out to the curb, looked up and down the road, looked across it at the front of Julia's house, came back again, studied the car from stem to stern. When I was done, I turned to Jenny and said, "I think I know what happened."

"You what?"

"Mind if I walk over and talk to your cousin? I have some questions I'd like to ask her."

"Go ahead," Jenny said. "I hope you scare her silly."

Julia Parker's residence was, as I've mentioned, a white two-story on the lot just across from and one house down from Jenny's. Cousin Julia worked out of her home, Jenny had told me, and had an upscale photography studio on the second floor. Which was where Julia told me she'd been working this morning, after she answered my knock on her front door. She was an attractive lady, a bit taller than Jenny, with darker hair and darker eyes. I said I needed to talk with her and she invited me inside, a little reluctantly.

Half an hour later I came back across the road. Again Jenny put aside her shovel and gloves, and this time I looked her in the eye and handed her the deed. The Julia part of the Parker signature had been scratched out and changed back to J. L.

"You shouldn't have any more trouble out of your across-the-street neighbor," I said to her. "Julia confessed that the deed and the property are yours after all. She even signed a separate statement to that effect." I handed Jenny that piece of paper as well.

Jenny was stunned. "But—how . . . ?"

"I accused her of stealing the document from your car trunk, and described the way she'd done it. I also said we have hard evidence of the theft, but that if the altered deed was corrected and returned, no charges will be filed. Your cousin would make a lousy poker player, by the way."

"Evidence? What evidence did you say we have?"

"The works," I said. "Photos, video, fingerprints, you name it."

"In other words, you lied."

"I exaggerated."

Jenny just stood there, looking back and forth between me and the deed. Finally she said, "What do you mean, you 'described the way she'd done it'?"

"It's pretty simple, really. Since you always unlock your car using the manual keypad on the driver's door, it was always possible for somebody to watch you and see the code. It'd be hard, of course, even with binoculars, because you said you always shield the keypad with your body to block the line of sight, right? But you also said your side mirror had twice needed adjustments before you left in the morning, which suggests someone might've turned it during the night. And the view from the second-floor windows of Julia's house, since it's across from and just offset from yours on the correct side, would've allowed a camera with a telephoto lens to see past your body and watch the car's keypad through the driver's-side mirror, if the mirror was properly positioned. It must've taken two nights to get it done, but once Julia knew the right key-code, she could then unlock your car door while you slept, pop the trunk-lid using the release button inside, and steal the deed from the files in the open trunk."

Jenny stayed quiet a moment, watching me. Slowly, she nodded. "And that was it."

"That was it," I said.

She looked at me with something like wonder. "You solved it, Ray. You not only figured out what happened"—she held up the deed like a trophy—"you made everything right." She put a warm palm on my cheek, and I saw the satisfaction in her eyes. "My hero," she said.

But . . .

"But something's wrong," I said. I knew her face pretty well, by now. "What's wrong?"

She shook her head. "Nothing, with all this. You did great. But the other case . . ."

"What other case? The burglary, at the college?"

"Yeah."

"What's wrong with that?"

"Well . . . remember, you said Ellie couldn't have had an uncle?"

"What about it?"

"Actually, she *could*'ve had an uncle."

I felt my forehead scrunch together in a frown. "How?" I said. "It's impossible."

"No. It's not. What if her deceased aunt was married, Ray? The aunt's husband would be Ellie's uncle."

I gave that some thought, and gulped.

"Whoa," I murmured. "I didn't think of that."

"You can say that again."

"I didn't think of that."

"Well, luckily, you can recover," she said, setting the papers aside and pulling her gloves on. "Tell your cop friend—Collums?— that Ellie was right. The uncle's the thief. But the 'diversion' was probably the cashbox. What he wanted were the bug collections."

"What? How do you know that?"

"Because I read books. And magazines."

I frowned again. "I read magazines, too."

"Yeah, but I read magazines that have something besides race cars on the cover, or deer hunters, or football players, or girls in swimsuits."

She had a point, there. "Okay," I said, "let's say Ellie *is* right, about having the uncle. Why do you suspect he's the burglar?"

"Because he would have a special interest in insect collections."

"So you mentioned. And why's that?"

"A coleopterist," she said, "is an expert on beetles."

I stared at her. "Are you serious?"

"Yep. Look at it this way—the uncle exists, the uncle's guilty, and the case is solved."

"But I didn't solve it."

"You must have," she said. "One of us did, and I'm not in the law business anymore. I'm just a writer."

By now both of us were smiling. "And a landowner," I said.

"And a gardener." She pointed. "Hand me that shovel."

THE DOLLHOUSE

When my office phone rang, I was leaned back in my chair with my boots propped on my desktop, reading a confidential memo forwarded to the sheriff by the mayor. Attached to the memo was a letter from a local resident requesting the installation of speedbumps on the city street behind his chicken house. His argument was that cars using that street as a short cut were occasionally squashing hens that had made good their escape from the coop. The mayor's argument against this request was that reducing the amount of high-speed traffic would also reduce the amount of money collected via speeding tickets. Welcome to small-town government.

I should mention here that we don't have a police chief in Pinewood, Mississippi. The Pine County sheriff does both jobs. This arrangement has the full approval of the city *and* the county since the sheriff's increased responsibility is balanced out by a decreased salary. The sheriff, as you might've guessed, is me. My name is Raymond Kirk Douglas (yes, I'm serious) and, in the words of the late Joe Friday, I carry a badge.

Since it was ten minutes to noon, I barely heard the ringing of my desk phone above the rumbling of my stomach. And since our dispatcher/receptionist was out of town, it eventually dawned on me that I should answer it myself.

"Ray?" the voice on the phone said. "Donald Benton."

"Donny. What's up?" Benton and I had graduated together from Pinewood High in the previous century and had somehow managed to stay in Pine County while most of the rest of our class had fled (like uncooped chickens?) to greener and faraway pastures. I remember hearing him say, when we were kids, that he wanted to one day be principal of our alma mater. So far he'd just been a history teacher, but since the retirement of old Mr. Finkley last month, little Donny Benton had at last realized his dream. I wondered if he now felt like the car-chasing dog that finally caught one and then didn't know what to do with it.

"I need your advice," he said. Confirming my suspicions.

For the next several minutes he filled me in: A woman named Arlene Poole had called him to say an expensive bracelet had been stolen from her eleventh-grade daughter Laura's locker this morning, and that Laura had received a note naming her class-mate Courtney Cook as the thief.

"Slow down," I said. "Are you saying this student's mother wants to press charges?"

"Not exactly," Benton said. "She just wants the Cook girl expelled, and wants her daughter to be declared winner of the election."

"Election?"

"Courtney Cook was chosen yesterday as junior class president. Laura ran against her."

"Don't those elections usually happen at the end of the school year?"

"There was a vacancy. The family of the current prez moved to Gulfport."

I took my feet off the desk and rubbed my eyes. "All due respect, Donny, this doesn't sound like a law-enforcement matter."

"What you mean is," Benton said miserably, "it's my headache and not yours."

That was exactly what I meant. "Let's just say, school problems are usually resolved by school officials."

I heard a groan. "Help me out here, Ray. I'm new to the job, and I'm under a microscope right now. I want to do the right thing."

I let out a long breath and checked my watch. Donald Benton was a good friend, but the former Love of My Life would be here any minute to meet me for lunch, and . . .

A little background, here. Breaking up with girlfriend-and-almost-fiancée Jennifer Parker many years ago was the biggest mistake of my life, and despite a long separation—Jenny fled with all the other escapees after graduating college—she was now back home, having given up a promising law career with a famous New York firm to live here in Pinewood and write mystery novels, of all things, and lately I'd made what I hoped was some headway toward a long-overdue reconciliation. My progress involved lunches with her on Tuesdays and Thursdays for the past couple weeks, and even though that would be a small step for mankind, it was a giant leap for Ray Douglas. I had no idea what to do next, but that was nothing unusual.

I forced my mind back to Benton's problem. "You said the girl with the missing bracelet—Laura?—received a note?"

"This morning, after second period. Taped to the door of her locker. She was so upset, her mother took her home."

"Came to school and picked her up, you mean?"

"No, Ms. Poole's company helped sponsor the the local science fair, so she was already here to help with that."

"Her company?"

"Her employer. She sells real estate."

"Hmm." After a moment I said, "Was the note signed?"

"I asked that. The question seemed to take Ms. Poole by surprise."

"And?"

"She finally said yes, the note was signed by"—a short pause, a riffling of paper—"Barbara Millicent Roberts."

"Is that a student?" I said. Somehow the name sounded familiar.

"Not here, she isn't. Wait a minute—I guess she could've been here to compete in the science fair. I'd have no way of knowing, about that."

"Have you seen this note?"

"No. Ms. Poole said she threw it away."

"How convenient."

Perking up at that, Benton said, "You think she could be lying? A frame job?"

"I think you've been watching too many cop shows," I said. "But something about that signature bothers me. And I don't like coincidences. Why would the winner of a student election steal something from her opponent a day later?"

"I have no idea."

I thought a moment. "Who exactly is Arlene Poole? I thought I knew most of the folks in my fiefdom."

"You probably do. She and her family just moved here. Said her husband works offshore, some kind of rig supervisor."

"So they just moved here, and the daughter still ran for class president?"

"She ran. Didn't win."

"So you mentioned." Another pause. "You said Ms. Poole's a realtor?"

"Part-time," Benton said. "In her other career, she said she's had considerable experience dealing with young girls."

"What career is that?"

"She designs dolls."

"What?"

"Yep. For a toy company. That's all she said. Seemed proud of it, though."

I stayed quiet a minute, mulling that over. Finally I said, "You say this woman was there at the school this morning. Have you actually talked to her, in person?"

"No, just by phone. That's why I'm calling you. She told me she wants to come to my office this afternoon at five, to discuss this."

"After quitting time?"

"Cops aren't the only ones who work late," he said.

"And let me guess—you want me to be there."

"Could you? I'd owe you."

"You already owe me," I said, just as Jennifer Parker marched into my office. "Gotta go, Donny. Duty calls."

"Wait a minute. Will you come?"

"I'll be there at five."

I hung up the phone, rose to my feet, and tipped over my coffee cup. Thank God it was empty. I fumbled it upright and looked up at the only woman—except my mother—I'd ever loved, and the only person in the world who could make me act like this. And I didn't even mind.

Jenny grinned, enough to make me dizzy, and glanced at the phone. "Be where at five?"

"Long story." I shrugged into my coat, socked my hat on my head, and picked up my sunglasses. I always felt cooler with my sunglasses on. "You ready?"

"We can't go yet," she said. "Nobody's at the front desk."

"I know—Lizzie's off today. Cheryl'll be here in a second." And just as I said those words, I looked through the window and saw Deputy Cheryl Grubbs—bless her sweet soul—pull her cruiser into the lot. Normally she would grumble at having to come in and man (woman?) the phones, but when I'd reminded her who I was having lunch with, she happily agreed. Cheryl is half law officer and half mother hen, and she thinks Jenny Parker is God's first cousin.

"Donny who?" Jenny said, looking again at my telephone. "Benton?"

"I'll fill you in at lunch."

"Okay—and it's my turn to pay."

I just grinned. "Whatever you say."

#

We never made it to the restaurant. It was a five-minute drive to the Hootin' Holler Café, just outside town, and we were halfway there when the radio in my cruiser spat a glob of static. I picked up, and a metallic female voice said, "Ray?"

"Lizzie would not approve," I said into the mike. "If she was there, she'd tell you to say 'Calling Unit One.'" My car was Unit One and Cheryl's was Unit Two. That was our entire fleet. Jenny was rolling her eyes.

"Yeah, well, Lizzie's not here, and you better be glad I am," Cheryl said. "We just got a call from Martin Dahl at the Dollhouse. You need to get over there."

"What does he want? I'm starving, and so's Jenny." Which was half-right. Jenny ate like a bird.

"Go right now, Ray. They're waiting for you."

"Can you tell me why?"

"Because somebody's murdered Randall Wells."

I almost ran off the road. "Good reason," I said. "Let me drop Jen at the Holler, then I'm on my way."

Jenny gaped at me. "Are you crazy?"

"What I meant, Cheryl, was *we're* on our way."

"Ten-four, Unit One," she said. "Over and out."

I heard her disconnect, the mike still in my hand. I felt numb. I'd known Randall Wells half my life. When I took my eyes off the windshield long enough to glance at Jenny, she looked as shocked as I was.

"Lizzie would approve," I said, into an unhearing radio.

#

Crime scenes are usually grim, and this one fit the bill. The law office of Dahl, Hauss, Stanley, Wells, and Yates—Dahl Hauss for short, and the Dollhouse to everybody in the county—was attractive from the front, but the parking lot behind the building was typically drab. A strip of unlined blacktop bordered on one side by a board fence, on another by a field with grass as tall as I am, and on the back by a patch of woods with drooping oaks stripped almost bare from the early arrival of winter. A cold wind tugged at the clothing of the half-dozen people gathered in the lot, and heavy gray clouds darkened an already somber scene. Parked in the middle of all this was an ambulance with flashing lights, and a body lay facedown on the leaf-littered pavement.

It took half an hour for the county coroner and me to do our work, and by the time the deceased was carted away, we had a pretty clear picture of what had happened, and when.

Fifty-year-old Randall Wells had been murdered when approaching the driver's-side door of his late-model Lexus at the rear of the parking lot, sometime this morning. A young paralegal named Julie Atwood had found the victim's body around eleven-thirty, when she got back from an errand to the courthouse and almost ran over it in the next parking space. According to the coroner, the cause of death was a single blow to the left temple—blunt instrument—between maybe ten and eleven. Colleagues confirmed that Wells had been in the office this morning and had planned to meet a client for lunch in nearby Hattiesburg.

Jenny Parker sighed as she and I stood and watched the ambulance drive away. Cheryl Grubbs was there too, now, cheeks rosy and hands stuffed into the pockets of her uniform jacket. She'd talked one of our retired deputies, Buster Dalworth, into spelling her at Dispatch long enough for her to join us. She looked as if she was sorry she had come. All of us had known Randall Wells, at least in passing, and murder wasn't something we saw much of, in this town.

"Guess the firm'll have to change its name," I said, more to break the silence than anything else.

"And hire another lawyer," Cheryl said. "Just what the world needs." Her face suddenly turned even redder. "No offense, Jen."

Jenny, who was no longer a lawyer anyway, gave her a sad smile. "None taken. Truth is, Randall was a good guy." In a lower voice, she added, "A lot nicer than his partners."

The crowd had dispersed except for the employees of the firm. They stood in a quiet group on the other side of the lot, dry leaves whirling and skittering around their ankles. Watching them, Cheryl said, "What do you think, Ray? Are they suspects?"

"The partners?" I drew a deep breath and let it out in a cloud of white fog. "Yeah, they are—for several reasons. One, they were all here, at the time of death. Two, Wells's wallet was intact, which rules out robbery. Three, this isn't a bad area of town. And four, I figure Wells might've known the killer, since he allowed whoever did it to approach close enough in broad daylight for the blow to the head." I paused again. "Besides that, Jen's right—they're all jerks, especially Yates. And Dahl's a Yankee. Though you didn't hear me say that."

"Sorry," Cheryl said. "I didn't hear you."

"So that's all we have, for now. We'll know more when we've talked to everybody."

After a moment of thinking our own thoughts, Cheryl said, "Well. I better get back to the desk before Buster decides to put the mayor in jail." She looked at Jenny. "Need a ride home?"

Jenny looked at me.

"Stay," I said. "I need all the help I can get."

When Cheryl was gone, I took out my notepad, made sure I had a pen that worked, and walked with Jenny toward the remaining partners and staff. I checked my watch, and wrote the time on the first clean page of my pad. It was 12:43.

#

At two o'clock Jenny and I drove back to the office. Cheryl, who'd missed lunch also, ordered three cheeseburgers and fries from the café across the street and joined us at my desk at two-thirty. By then Jenny had typed up our notes and printed them out and I'd listened to a brief audiotape I'd found in Randall Wells's desk drawer, Outside the windows of my office, the sun seemed to be trying to burn through the overcast. Our moods remained gloomy.

"Fill me in," Cheryl said, unwrapping her burger.

I looked over the printed notes. "There's not much, from the interviews. Most of it we already knew. Wells is —was—married, comfortably wealthy, not too ambitious. Also a teetotaler and sort of a straight-arrow, which rules out several possibilities. But we did find something interesting in the parking lot, and something *really* interesting in his office. I'll save that until last." I motioned to Jenny, who handed me her cell phone, and I showed Cheryl the pictures we'd taken of the pavement where the body was found. The photos showed a cluster of rough white markings on the blacktop beside where Wells's right hand had been. Five printed letters, the first and last of which were uppercase and larger than the middle three. It said: "SandY."

"Sandy?" Cheryl said.

"We almost missed it," Jenny told her. "Fallen leaves had hidden the letters, afterward. But these letters were obviously written by Wells. We're told he often used an office blackboard, and carried a piece of chalk in his pocket. Sure enough, we found it in a clump of leaves. We're wondering if what he wrote was a message, sort of a dying clue to the killer's identity."

Cheryl made a face. "What? Are you kidding me?"

"I know—TV and movie stuff, right? But I guess it could happen."

"So if it *is* a clue, what does it mean?" Cheryl said, looking at both of us.

"Don't know, yet," I said, and took a bite of my cheeseburger. "Meanwhile, look at this." I handed her one of the sheets Jenny had typed, a list of detailed information about Wells's four partners. Detailed, but nothing suspicious.

Martin Dahl was seventy-five, married, three children, Vermont native, former Navy officer who walked with a cane but still came to the office every day. Second on the power ladder was Wayne Hauss, sixty-eight, born and raised locally, divorced, two sons, Vietnam veteran, Purple Heart, Silver Star. Gerald Stanley was fifty-six, married, no kids, former state senator, Baptist deacon, avid sportsman. Fourth and last was Maurice Yates, fifty-seven, twice divorced, one daughter, model-airplane enthusiast, health nut. All the surviving partners, also known at this point as prime suspects, had excellent academic and professional credentials.

"Nothing that jumps out at us," Cheryl said. "Right?"

"Except for Hauss's military record," I replied, taking anther bite. "A combat veteran, unlike most people, might prefer a quiet, quick, close-quarters attack like this one."

"The cause of death *is* odd," Jenny said. "Murder weapon's usually a gun of some kind."

I shrugged. "Guns use bullets, and bullets can be evidence. Who knows?"

All of us looked again at the photo of the chalked message on the pavement. SandY.

"This means something," I said, "and we have to figure it out. The sooner the better."

"Before you ask," Jenny said to Cheryl, "we've already tried." She picked up another notepad and read what she'd written there. "First, Maurice Yates has sandy hair; second, Sandy's the nickname of Dahl's wife, Sandra; third, Sandy sounds a lot like Stanley." She added, "Pretty lame connections, but that's all we've been able to come up with."

Cheryl seemed to ponder that. Finally she said, pointing, "Don't you want those fries?"

"Help yourself," Jenny said. She'd already given me half her burger.

"What was it you found in his office?" Cheryl asked me, coating her new fries with ketchup.

"A tape. A mini-cassette recording Wells made a week ago. I took it, along with his pocket recorder, with me when I left. I already listened to it, once."

"I'm surprised Dahl's people let you take it," Jenny said.

"Officially, they told me I could have whatever I needed. Unofficially, I assure you they didn't know what's on the tape."

"What *is* on it?"

"A conversation in Randall's office at the Dollhouse between him and two other men, who I strongly suspect weren't aware they were being taped."

"And?"

"They proposed a dirty business deal. Wells flatly disagreed with them."

"That's motive," Jenny said.

"It *could* be motive. But even if we identify the others by their voices, it's not enough by itself to incriminate anybody, or imply anything like murder."

"Let's hear it," Cheryl said.

I produced the mini-recorder, pressed PLAY, and we listened to the short tape. When it was done, all of us looked at each other. I said, since no names had been mentioned, "I recognize Wells's voice, but not the other two."

"Me either," Jenny said. But she'd been strangely quiet, these last few minutes. She was staring again at the photo on her cell phone.

"I know the voices," Cheryl said. "They're two of the other partners. The first one to speak was—"

"Don't say their names yet," said Jenny.

"Why?" I asked.

She raised her head and looked at us. "Because I've been thinking about that message we found scratched on the pavement. And I want to see if we're on the same track."

I frowned. "What does that mean?"

"It means I want to confirm a suspicion." She paused, her gaze going from me to Cheryl and back again. "I think I know who murdered Randall Wells."

I felt my eyes widen. "What?"

"And I don't think it was just one person." Jenny tapped the photo on the screen of her phone. "SandY," she said. "Remember, the three middle letters aren't capitalized."

"So?"

"Give me a drumroll, here." She turned to Cheryl. "Whose voices were they, on the tape? Who were the two partners trying to talk Wells into that shady deal?"

"The first to speak—the deep voice—was Gerald Stanley," Cheryl said. "The other was Maurice Yates."

Jenny nodded. Her eyes were shining.

"What?" Cheryl and I both said.

"It really *was* a dying clue." Jenny pointed to the chalked message. "SandY."

Understanding dawned. "Stanley and Yates," I said.

When I looked up at her, she was grinning.

#

The final step was as quickly accomplished as it was anticlimactic. Jenny stayed at the office while Cheryl and I drove back to Dahl Hauss and confronted both Gerald Stanley and Maurice Yates, interviewing them separately, telling them about the tape and the message on the pavement and accusing each, outright, of Wells's murder. Perry Mason would've been proud: In a surprisingly short time each of them broke down and pointed the finger at the other, and an hour later we had in our hands not only the signed and witnessed confessions but the murder weapon itself, a bloodstained brick that had been tossed afterward into the grassy field beside the parking lot. We also had, handcuffed and downcast in the back of my cruiser, two of the remaining four partners of Dahl, Hauss, Stanley, Wells, and Yates.

It was the fastest—and luckiest—resolution of a case that I could remember. I still had plenty of forms to complete and lawyers to deal with and papers to sign and calls to make, but by 4:45 Jenny and I were sitting together at my desk with satisfied looks on our faces and two prisoners locked in the seldom-used cells of the adjoining jail.

"The Dollhouse," Jenny said, as if she still couldn't quite believe what we'd been able to do. "Still standing, but missing three of its big shots. I wonder if it'll recover."

"I hope so," I said. "I like the name. A lot better'n Merrill Lynch."

"Those were brokers, not lawyers."

I shrugged. "It's still a catchy name."

And just like that, a bell went off in my head. I sat up straight in my chair.

"Ray?" Jenny said. "You okay?"

"Dollhouse," I whispered, thinking hard. "That's the answer."

"The answer to what?"

But I wasn't listening. I was looking at the clock.

"Come on," I said, grabbing my coat and hat.

"Where are we going?"

"To a meeting. Let's take your car."

I even left behind my sunglasses.

#

We arrived at two minutes past five. Through the window in his office door I could see Donald Benton, sitting at his desk talking to a plump, scowling woman in her forties.

I was about to knock on the door when a thought struck me. Jenny was not only smarter than most people, she could be a little intimidating. Benton would be distracted and the complaining mother would be irritated.

"Can you wait for me, out here?"

She opened her mouth to protest—probably Why'd you bring me if I can't sit in?—then stopped. Patiently she took a seat in the outer office, close enough to the door that she could listen. When I knocked, Benton saw me through the glass and hopped up to let me in. Introductions were made, and I sat in the second of two chairs facing his desk.

"I told Ms. Poole you might join us," Benton said. Arlene Poole gave me a hard look but made no reply. She obviously wasn't happy I was here. Neither was I, but after seeing her sour expression, and since the answer to all this had come to me in Technicolor brilliance back at my office, I found myself almost looking forward to the next few minutes. Especially after the shock and the stomach-churning stress of the Randall Wells murder, only hours ago.

"Start at the beginning," I said to Ms. Poole. "Tell me what happened."

She did. It agreed, pretty much, with what Benton had already told me—her daughter Laura had discovered, this morning, a folded note taped to the outside of her locker, saying Courtney Cook had stolen something valuable from her. Sure enough, when Laura looked inside, a bracelet given to her by an aunt had disappeared from where she'd put it when she went to P.E. earlier this morning. She'd called her mother's cell phone, in tears, and Arlene, who was already here because of her employer's science-fair sponsorship, took Laura straight home. Where they had both remained, the daughter distraught and the mother growing more and more angry.

After Ms. Poole finished making her case, all three of us sat there a while in silence. Benton was frowning with a combination of sympathy and worry and Ms. Poole looked disgusted. I couldn't see my own face, but I imagined myself looking appropriately thoughtful.

"Ms. Poole," I said, "you called the principal before noon. Why wait until now to meet?"

She stared at me as if I'd lost my mind. "I had to show a house," she said.

I nodded. "I'm not at all surprised."

She probably suspected she'd been insulted but wasn't sure, and while she tried to figure it out I turned and said, "Mr. Benton, are the student lockers secure?"

He seemed glad to be asked a question he knew the answer to. "They have combination locks. But not many students use them."

"They shouldn't have to," Poole snapped. "I'm sure most of the students are honest."

Ignoring her, I said, "Can one of these locks be engaged without using the combination?"

"Yes. Each has a hasp that goes through the slot in the locker's door latch. You need the lock's combination to open it, but anyone can close it. Just snap it shut."

"I bet Courtney Cook's locker's locked," Ms. Poole said. "I bet my Laura's bracelet's in there."

"You sound pretty certain of that," I said.

She stood up. "Let's look. Right now." She glared at the principal. "And when we find the bracelet in her locker, I want that girl expelled, and I want my Laura installed as president of her junior class. With apologies from everyone involved." Including you two, her gaze said.

I kept my seat and said to Benton, "Another question. Do the cleaning crews wipe down the students' lockers at night?"

"The door handles and locks, yes. Ever since that flu outbreak a while back—"

"Then I suggest we dust Courtney's locker for any fingerprints left there this morning."

Poole blinked. "What?"

"My deputy carries a print kit in her car," I said. "I'll call and have her come check."

"But—you'd just find Courtney's prints."

I shook my head. "Courtney's home sick today. I know because I phoned her mother on my way over here."

Arlene Poole looked stunned. A silence passed.

Finally I gave her a long stare and said, "You don't want us to check for fingerprints, do you, Ms. Poole? Because you know whose we would find."

She swallowed. Even through a heavy layer of makeup, her face had gone pale.

"Your daughter doesn't even know what you did, does she?"

Poole stood there, teetering a bit, looking dazed. "Let's just forget this," she murmured.

But I wasn't finished. "We'll retrieve and return the bracelet you planted in Courtney's locker this morning," I said, "and Principal Benton will decide whether to prosecute you. If it were my decision, I'd hang you upside down from the flagpole."

Arlene Poole deflated like a punctured tire. Silently Benton and I watched her slink from the office. When she was gone and I looked at him, his eyes were wide as goose eggs.

"What just happened?" he whispered.

"I'm not sure justice was served," I said, "but an injustice was avoided. You won't have any more trouble from Ms. Poole."

"But—why did she do it? Why would anyone do such a thing?"

"You heard her. She wanted her daughter to be class president."

Benton blew out a sigh. "How on earth did you know?"

"That she was lying? Because of the name she gave you, earlier. The signer of the note."

"Barbara Millicent Roberts?"

I nodded. "Ms. Poole made a mistake, saying it was signed. When you then asked her who signed it, you said she hesitated before answering, right? And since she had to come up with something quick, she came up with someone she knew wouldn't be a real student."

"So the name—it isn't real?"

"Oh, it's a real name. It's just not a real person."

"What?"

"Ms. Poole said she was a doll designer. Correct?"

"Yes . . ."

I couldn't help grinning. "According to a series of novels written in the sixties, Barbara Millicent Roberts is the real name of . . ."

"Who?"

"Barbie," I said.

He blinked. "You're kidding."

"Nope. Barbie Roberts, from Willow, Wisconsin. I googled it

in the car just now to make sure, but it occurred to me earlier, when Jenny Parker and I were talking about dollhouses."

"Dollhouses? Why were—" He shook his head. "Never mind." He stood up, looking almost as drained as Poole had been when she left. He held out his right hand. "I do owe you."

"Your tax dollars at work," I said, shaking his hand.

When I'd left the office, I found Jenny sitting there staring at me. "You heard?" I asked.

"Every word. But I have a question."

"What?" We headed out the door toward her car. Despite the earlier brightening of the sky, the sun seemed to have given up the battle. It was not only dark and dreary; a light rain was falling. Just as well I'd forgotten my sunshades.

"I assume you didn't play with dolls," she said, "as a kid."

"You assume correctly."

"And you once told me you weren't a reader, growing up."

"I wasn't."

"Then how—"

"My mother was. She'd read that whole series of Barbie books, in high school, and after I came along I think she told me about every single one."

Jenny nodded. I could see she liked that. We climbed into the car, my mind turning again to the upcoming work to square away the Wells case. We were pulling out of the school lot onto the rain-wet highway when I realized Jenny had said something else to me.

"What," I asked.

"I was saying there's one other thing I heard, while I was waiting for you back there."

"What's that?"

"I heard you tell them you'd called the Cook girl's mother, in the car, and found that Courtney was out sick."

"So?"

"I was with you on the way here, Ray. You fiddled around with my phone while I drove, but you didn't make any calls."

I smiled. "You're a fiction writer, Jenny. Are you implying I shouldn't stretch the truth now and then?"

She didn't bother replying to that, but I could see her face, even though she was watching the road ahead. And she was smiling, too.

It had turned into a bright day after all.

GOING THE DISTANCE

I arrived at Pinewood General Hospital around five p.m., just before the ambulance did. I'd already seen the flashing lights in my cruiser's rearview mirror, and when I stepped out into the falling snow I heard the siren. My old friend Jennifer Parker was already there, waiting inside the lobby of the ER. I wasn't surprised to see her. As Jenny's part-time boyfriend and Pine County's full-time sheriff, I had long ago decided that Jenny Parker had some kind of built-in radar that sensed trouble. What she actually had, of course, was a police scanner, and time on her hands.

"Merry Christmas, Jenny," I said, shivering and stomping my boots in the doorway.

"Hi, Ray."

That's me. I'm Sheriff Raymond Kirk Douglas. And yes, that's my real name. What can I say?—My dad was a movie addict.

"What do you think?" I asked her.

"I think the weather outside is frightful."

"Dean Martin," I said. "Right?" She just gave me a blank look. I get that a lot.

Deputy Cheryl Grubbs showed up seconds later, her face solemn, and filled us in while an unconscious James Thomas Wallace—Jato to everyone who knew him—was wheeled out of the ambulance and into the warm hospital. Jato, Cheryl said, had been stranded on a back road miles from town in the freak snowstorm and had called his daughter Heather, who lived in Nashville, on his cell phone. Heather Wallace, who'd kept Pinewood's emergency numbers handy ever since her father's heart attack last year, had immediately mobilized the sheriff's department and the hospital, and both Cheryl and the ambulance had arrived at the scene to find Jato half-frozen in his pickup.

We stood there and watched as the assistants pushed their new patient down an echoing hallway and through a set of double doors. I found myself feeling a little guilty about having taken the day off and leaving all this to my only deputy—but it was December 20th, and I'd needed to do some shopping. Not that I had many people to buy gifts for.

"What was he doing way out there, anyhow?" I asked Cheryl. "And why had he stopped his truck?"

"Don't know. He was passed out behind the wheel," she said. Deputy Grubbs was easygoing and lighthearted by nature, but today she looked as serious as an undertaker—I knew she and Jato were good friends. "His truck was pulled off onto the shoulder, not in a ditch. Tires looked fine, what I could see of them in the snow, and his headlights were on. If I hadn't checked the trip odometer I would think he ran out of gas."

"Odometer?" Jenny asked. "Why would that tell you anything about his gas tank?"

A word of clarification, here. Jenny Parker, who was as smart as anyone I've ever known, was a relatively young lady—mid-thirties, about my age—but when even younger she'd been a member of a hotshot team of attorneys at a New York firm. Eventually she lost either her love for the business or her love for the stress that went along with it and switched from lawyer to mystery author, and then, for reasons that weren't entirely clear to me, decided to leave the Big Apple for good and come back home to the slightly smaller apple of Pinewood, Mississippi. I often entertained the hope that one of those reasons might've been me, but on that score Jenny was as mysterious as the characters in her novels. I had made several attempts to rekindle the sizzling romance she and I once had, as teenagers and in college, but those attempts had been only partially successful. We were both still single, she was still smart, and I was still confused. I've been confused most of my life.

Anyhow, in answer to her question, Cheryl said, "Yeah, odometer. I know it sounds funny, but I've heard Jato say that since his truck's fuel gauge broke last year he's been relying on his trip odometer to keep up with how much gas he's used. He always resets it to zero when he fills up, so when the odometer reaches something close to three hundred miles he knows he's almost empty."

"You're kidding."

Cheryl shook her head. "He says that works fine, for his purposes, and fixing the fuel gauge would be too expensive. For that old truck, he's probably right."

"And what did the trip odometer say, when you looked at it?" I asked.

"It had just been reset. It said '0006.' Meaning the tank must've been almost full."

"Six miles? There's no gas station six miles from where he was found."

"Right," Cheryl said. "But I saw a card on his dashboard from Woody's Garage—which has a gas pump, and *is* about six miles away. So I called there on my way here, to see if they might've filled his tank."

"And?"

"Harry Logan was working late at the garage, and sure enough, he said Jato brought the truck in for an oil change a few hours earlier. But . . ."

"But?"

"But they didn't gas him up, or reset anything."

Everybody seemed to take a while to think that over. The three of us had gravitated to the waiting room off the lobby, and I glanced at the window. The snow was coming down harder now. It was beginning to look a lot like Christmas. Perry Como?

"Who's Harry Logan?" I asked, getting my thoughts back on track.

"New in town," Jenny said, before Cheryl could answer. "He bought Woody out, three months ago."

"Nobody tells me anything around here," I grumbled. Woody's Garage was off the beaten track, and I never went there, but still. I'd lived in Pinewood all my life; Jenny had been back only a year or two. And she seemed to know everything about everybody. Maybe it was a girl thing. As the thought occurred to me, I added, "This Logan, is he a good mechanic?"

"Don't know. I doubt he'll be here long, anyway. Says this is too far south for him."

"What does he miss?" I pointed at the winter wonderland outside. "Cold weather?"

"He just doesn't like it down here," Jenny said. "When Rosie Crump suggested he visit the parks and the war memorials here in town, he just smirked. Said he used to be able to see the nation's tallest monument from his own backyard."

"Where was that? D.C.?"

"I guess." Jenny stayed quiet a moment, probably picturing— as I was—the white spire of the Washington Monument against a blue sky. Or maybe she was just thinking about what was shaping up to be a good mystery. Writers, I had come to realize, were a strange bunch. So were lawyers—and Jenny was a little of both.

"There is one other possibility," I said.

"What's that?"

"Attempted suicide."

"What?"

"Think about it." I'd already been thinking about it, and the more I did, the more sense it made. "It was crazy for Jato to be out there in this kind of weather, with the heart trouble he's had. He must've known the risks. And I'd heard he's been depressed. He had casino debts, everybody knew that."

"*Except,*" Cheryl said, "that he was about to come into some money."

Both Jenny and I turned to stare at her.

Cheryl shrugged. "Word around town is, someone owed him a lot of cash, from years ago."

"I really *am* out of the gossip loop," I said.

"Me too, this time," Jenny murmured.

"Any idea who owed him?" I asked Cheryl.

She shook her head. "Somebody from Missouri, I heard."

"We'll check," Jenny and I said, together. Then I had another thought: "If Jato had a cell phone, why'd he call his daughter in Tennessee—what's her name? Heather? Why didn't he just call for help, locally?"

"Because his phone was dead," Cheryl said. "I checked. Battery must've quit just after he phoned his daughter."

"Great." Wearily I pulled my gloves and overcoat on and turned to Cheryl. "You got time for another errand?"

"Let me guess. You want me to take another look at the truck."

"Yeah—see if there's anything we're missing. I'm headed to the office."

"Don't run out of gas," Jenny said.

#

I was sitting at my desk half an hour later, trying to put together the beginnings of a report, when the phone rang. Outside the two windows of my corner office, the white stuff was still floating down. I hadn't seen snow like this since I was a kid. This was Mississippi, for cryin' out loud—the land of cotton and kudzu and sweaty, dusty days. Down here the only thing we shovel . . . well, you know what we shovel down here.

But that wasn't what was on my mind, and neither was the report. What was on my mind was my earlier suggestion of attempted suicide. Who would stop to get his oil changed just before trying to kill himself?

I picked up the ringing phone.

"Ray, it's me," Jenny's voice said.

"You found something?"

"Maybe. I contacted Jato's daughter Heather a minute ago, and caught her still at home—she has to wait till the storms ease up before she drives down here. She said she'd forgotten to mention that her dad had also called her just after he left that garage—Woody's—to tell her he was going to go get a Christmas tree."

"A Christmas tree?"

"She said the garage owner—Harry Logan—had told Jato he'd gotten one last year from Earl Haskell's farm, way up north of town."

"How'd you know Jato's daughter's number?" I asked.

"I asked Deputy Grubbs for it, before we all left the hospital—the number was in her phone, from the earlier calls. Have you heard back from her yet?"

"Cheryl? Yeah, she just called in. Sure enough, she confirmed that Jato's truck's out of gas. Bone dry. And there's no sign of a leak."

"Makes sense," Jenny said.

"What do you mean?"

Jenny hesitated a moment, as if gathering her thoughts. "I think Harry Logan knew how Jato used that trip odometer, Ray. I think Logan, while servicing the truck, saw that it was very low on fuel, maybe even drained some of it just to be sure, then told Jato it had been filled up even though it hadn't, and reset the counter to zero anyway. Then I think Logan pointed him toward Haskell's farm hoping he'd run out of gas in the middle of nowhere in the snowstorm and die from exposure. Like you said, he already had health problems."

I paused, mulling that over. "Wouldn't Logan have known Jato had a cell phone?"

"I don't think so. He carried it in his pocket, and his daughter told me it was new."

Another silence passed. "That's not enough, Jen. I couldn't prosecute based on that. I'd need a confession, or more proof—"

"I'm not finished," she said.

"Let's hear it."

"Three things," she said. "For one, I don't think Jato was trying to kill himself. I mean, stopping first to change his oil—"

"I agree. What's the second thing?"

"The fact that Harry Logan lied."

"Lied about what?"

"If Logan moved here this fall," Jenny said, "he couldn't have bought a Christmas tree from Earl Haskell last year."

I blinked. I should've caught that. "True enough," I said. "But answer this: the most important question of all. Why would Logan try to kill Jato Wallace?"

"To keep from having to pay him."

"*What?* You're saying Harry Logan was the one who owed him money?"

"I think so."

"Why?"

"That's the third thing," Jenny said. "Something I found on Google."

"What?"

"I've been checking my geography. Remember your deputy saying Jato Wallace's debtor was from Missouri?"

"Yes . . ."

"Well, I was wrong. The tallest monument in the nation, the one Harry Logan had said was visible from his backyard before he moved south? It isn't in Washington at all."

"Where is it?"

"It's the Gateway Arch," Jenny said. "In St. Louis."

I sat up straight, then stared at the wall for a moment, taking this in. Finally I nodded. "I think I better go have a talk with Mr. Logan."

"What you better do is take your deputy with you," she said.

"I don't think so. Cheryl and Jato are pals, from way back. If Logan really did what we think he did, she might shoot him."

"Yeah, well, he might shoot *you*."

"I doubt it," I said. "Remember what Tom Selleck said, in that *Quigley* movie? 'This ain't Dodge City.'"

"No, and you ain't Wyatt Earp."

I didn't point out that I was Kirk Douglas. But I saw what she was saying. "Maybe I *will* take Cheryl along."

"Good," she said. "Call me when you get back."

"Why? You think Logan might need a lawyer?"

"No, I want you to take me out to dinner."

"Excuse me?"

"I'm in sort of a fix. The oil light's on in my car, I'm hungry, I have an electric stove, and my power's off."

I couldn't help grinning. "I knew this weather was good for something," I said.

I hung up and sat there a minute, looking at the phone—probably longer than I should've, since I had to go question a suspect. Then I snapped out of my dreams, called Cheryl, arranged for her to meet me at Logan's garage, put on my winter gear, and trudged outside.

I steered my cruiser out of the parking lot, still smiling a little, and switched on the radio: ancient Christmas songs were playing, as expected. One was just finishing up, and sure enough, it was old Dino. As he crooned the final verse, I found myself agreeing with him.

"Let it snow," I said.

THE POD SQUAD

Nothing else on Earth smells like a school gymnasium. That was only one of the pleasant memories jangling in my head as I entered my old high school gym several weeks ago, following the arrows on signs that said TRI-COUNTY SCIENCE FAIR. I once played basketball in this building for the Pinewood Pirates, and while no one would say I was a great athlete, most would agree that I did lot better on the court than in the classroom. Both are far behind me now.

I guess I should tell you, my name's Raymond Douglas, and I'm the sheriff of Pine County, Mississippi, a place that's said to have more alligators per capita than any area outside Florida. That's not true—I've spent some time in south Louisiana—but what *is* true is that folks here are more familiar with welfare than wealth, and with George Jones than the Dow Jones. Part of that's because we tend to lose our best scholars. Those who aren't overly smart or overly adventurous, like me, usually come back home after college, and the rest head for higher-paying jobs either out of town or out of state, and remain there. Except for a few, like Jennifer Parker.

All this, and especially Jenny, was on my mind as I stepped onto the hardwood floor that morning among roughly two hundred clueless students and a dozen bored teachers. The noise around me was deafening. Many were here from surrounding schools, and I noticed only one local I couldn't name: a sad-faced boy who was familiar only because he looked just like his mother, one of my old classmates. After awhile my grown-up height advantage allowed me to pick Jenny out, standing at a small table covered with plaques and trophies underneath the north backboard. She saw me and smiled. God, I loved that smile.

Jenny Parker had made good her post-graduation escape, suc-ceeded up North as a big-firm attorney, and then gave it all up a few years ago to come back here and write mystery/suspense novels. The reason for that decision remains unclear, but I know part of it was me. The two of us were madly in love when we were younger, but then she left and I stayed, and now that she's returned, our on-and-off, hot-and-cold relationship is complicated. All she wants, it seems, is for us to be friends and go on the occasional date. All I want is for us to finally get married. I figure she secretly does, too, and just hasn't told me yet. And if you believe that, maybe I should be the one writing fiction.

She pointed to a corner of the gym, and when we'd both weaved our way through the crowd to that relatively quiet spot she said, "What're you doing here? You stalking me again?"

"Not again. I never stopped."

"Good," she said, and gave me a peck on the cheek. I immediately felt better. "How'd you know I was here today?"

"I had to come ask Donny some questions," I said. Donald Benton is the high-school principal, which is one of the great mysteries of the universe, since he'd also been the biggest doofus in our class. "He told me about the fair, and that you'd volunteered to be a judge, so . . ."

"What kind of questions?" she asked, as I had known she would. Probably because of her crime-writer imagination and her legal knowledge, Jenny is always fascinated with police work, a fact that I have often used to my advantage. So I spent the next few minutes filling her in.

There wasn't a lot to tell. Sixty-eight-year-old Maria Cardenas, the widow of a local businessman, had been robbed and assaulted sometime yesterday, presumably by one of a team of workers who were doing yard chores at her home south of town. Specifically, she'd been struck on the head with a blunt object and was discovered by a concerned neighbor this morning, lying on her bedroom floor. A jewelry box was open and empty on her dresser, and drawers had been ransacked. Paula Murphy, the neighbor, told me Ms. Cardenas had murmured only one word to her—*Gordo*—before being loaded into the ambulance.

"Gordo?" Jenny repeated. "That's all she said?"

"That's it. Which might've been just as well—apparently she doesn't know a lot of English, and the neighbor doesn't speak Spanish."

"Will she be okay?"

"The doc thinks so. But she lay there on the floor all night, probably in and out of consciousness, with a head injury and a broken hip from the fall, so she's not in great shape. No telling when we'll be able to question her."

Both of us were quiet awhile, letting that sink in. The noise level in the rest of the gym was maddening. Everybody seemed to be talking at the same time.

"So . . . you think she was describing her attacker?" Jenny asked.

"That'd be my guess."

Thoughtfully she said, "In Spanish, 'gordo' means 'fat.'"

"I know. I googled it."

She stayed quiet a moment, then said, "How'd you know about the yard workers?"

"The neighbor told me. She'd seen three of them, mowing and edging the Cardenas property late yesterday afternoon. Their van had GREEN LAWN SERVICE on the side."

"Did she get a good look at the work crew?"

"After I saw the googled translation, I called her back and asked her that. She said she did, and all three were thin. Skinny, even."

"Maybe the robber wasn't one of them."

"Maybe. But Ms. Murphy hadn't seen anybody else around, yesterday or last night. And she said she keeps a close watch." I paused. "There's one more thing."

Jenny waited, watching me.

"Before I left my office an hour ago, I called the lawn service, and asked owner Lamar Green about the crew. He said there were two part-timers—a Ron Webb and a Lindsey Hinton—and one regular employee, who's worked at Ms. Cardenas's before. And he confirmed that none of them were overweight. But—get this—the regular's name is Gordon Bailey."

Jenny raised both eyebrows. "Gordo."

"Yep. Green agreed that Bailey has used that nickname."

"So you're picking him up?"

"We will when we find him. Green says Bailey lives alone and he's off every Saturday, goes fishing somewhere in the hills in Smith County. But nobody knows exactly where, and there's no cell service out there. We'll probably wind up waiting for him at his house."

Jenny fell silent again, thinking. A female teacher at a podium with a microphone on the raised stage behind us announced to the exhibitors that judging would begin at ten o'clock.

"That gives me an hour," Jenny said. Then: "Keep going."

"That's all I have," I said. "I asked Green to email employee photos of all three workers to Cheryl at the office." Cheryl Grubbs is my only deputy, and probably the most efficient person in law enforcement I've ever known. I decided long ago that if she ever decides to quit or retire, I will, too. Jenny treats her like an older sister, and Cheryl treats Jenny like a rock star.

Jenny seemed about to reply when she looked past me, smiled, and said, "Hey, Billy."

I turned to follow her gaze, and saw the long-faced boy I'd noticed earlier. He was standing there staring cautiously at both of us.

Jenny said to me, "Sheriff Douglas, you remember Billy Osmond, don't you? Billy lives on my street. We rode together today."

I shook his hand and said, "I know your mom. So you have a project here?"

"No sir, I'm a sophomore—I can't compete till next year. My teacher told me to come."

"Good for her," Jenny said. "It's a nice way for you to spend a Saturday. Right?"

The even sadder look Billy gave her reminded me of one you might see if you handed a kid a broccoli stalk instead of an ice-cream cone. When I was in school, science fairs were held on school days, not weekends. I felt for him, but he appeared smart enough not to argue.

He broke the heavy silence by pointing to a boy standing beside him and saying, "This is Michael Zubrick, from Hallman Academy. We just met, and he needs to ask you a question."

Jenny focused on young Michael, who seemed to be wishing Billy had kept his mouth shut. Especially disturbing, I figured, was the unexpected sight of my badge.

Michael took a breath and said to Jenny: "There's a kid from my school, Kevin Moss, who has a project here today, but he's not at any of the tables. You know how I could find him?"

"I sure do," she said. "The exhibits are laid out alphabetically, by the students' last names." She pointed. "They start over there, at that end of the gym, and end up over . . . there. Since your friend's name starts with an M, he should be someplace right there, in the middle. He's probably just gone to the bathroom or to get a snack." She gave him another look. "Got it?"

"Yes ma'am. Thanks a lot." Michael Zubrick flashed a smile of his own and, with a final nod to Billy, headed off through the milling crowd, presumably in search of Kevin Moss.

Afterward, Jenny said to Billy, "Why's Michael here, if he doesn't have an exhibit?"

"He said it's because his sister does, and she didn't want to drive here alone," Billy said. "He's pretty glum about it, said she not only has a driver's license, she has a cell phone. I asked him if it's because she's older, but he said no, they're twins. Said he doesn't have a cell 'cause his grades aren't good enough."

I knew Billy had a phone, too—I'd seen him looking at it, earlier. But I also knew grades weren't always the deciding factor. Most students his age had cell phones regardless.

"He told me his sister's ringtone's the Darth Vader theme," Billy said to us, brightening a little. "How cool is that?"

I didn't mention that my ringtone is the intro to *Blazing Saddles.* I was afraid that might prolong the conversation, and I was guiltily hoping Billy Osmond would hurry up and leave so I could resume chatting with my True Love. But he didn't. He stayed put, watching me with an odd expression. Finally he said, his cheeks flushed a bit, "There's something you don't know, Sheriff, about Gordon Bailey."

Jenny and I exchanged a look. I said, "So you just heard everything I've been saying to Ms. Parker here?"

Now his face turned beet-red. "I guess I did, yes sir." He swallowed and added, "I didn't really mean to. I was just waiting here with Michael so he could ask her about his friend—"

"It's okay, no harm done. What's this about Mr. Bailey?"

"Well . . . I know him. Or I used to."

I shouldn't have been surprised. This isn't a big town, or even a big county. Still, the small-world connections in the rural South are sometimes amazing. "Tell me about him," I said.

"He took my dad and me fishing a few times, when I was little."

"Fishing where?" Billy's father was deceased now; I knew that much.

"A place on Abe Garner's farm. But it's been sold since then, and the pond was filled in." Billy paused. "What I want you to know is, Gordon Bailey was good to me. He was good to everybody. I can't see him doing anything like what you said happened to the Cardenas lady."

Which doesn't mean he didn't, I thought.

Billy seemed to be thinking that, too. After a moment he cleared his throat, the downcast look returned, and he said, "Well. I'm supposed to go look at some of the projects. See you later, Ms. Parker. You, too, Sheriff."

As he walked away, Jenny said, "What do you think?"

"I think that doesn't really change anything. Gordon Bailey's the only lead we got."

"I agree." An uneasy silence passed. The place was still buzzing. Most of the crowd was now gathered around the exhibits.

"New subject," she said. "You told me you left your office an hour ago. How long did you visit with our fine principal?"

"Not long. I'd remembered that the school uses a lawn service for the baseball field, but turns out it's not Green's, so questioning Donny did no good. Why?"

"That leaves at least half an hour. What were you doing for all that time?"

I gave her a look. "Do I need to call my lawyer?"

"I was just wondering, Ray."

I sighed and said, "I stopped off at Watson's Pharmacy on the way here, to get some perfume for Lizzie, at Dispatch. Next Thursday's her birthday."

"You bought perfume at a drugstore?"

"What's wrong with that?"

"Nothing. You're a sweet and considerate boss."

"And a brave sheriff," I added.

"I was about to say that. How's Mattie doing?"

"I didn't see her—her helper sold me the gift. Said Mattie was home sick today." Which was disturbing news in itself. Mattie Watson is probably in her late seventies.

Jenny frowned. "Helper? Has Mattie hired someone?"

"Must have. This woman was the only person in the store."

"Would I know her? What'd she look like?"

I felt myself squint, remembering. "Brunette, very short, thirtyish, brown eyes. Single, I guess. No wedding ring."

"Hmm. You noticed that, huh?"

"I'm a detective," I said. "Besides, her finger would've been hard to miss—she had her hands in my mouth."

"Excuse me?"

"She told me she was once a nurse, so I asked her to look at a tooth." I opened wide and pointed. "Second from the back, bottom right. It's giving me fits."

"News flash, Ray. Nursing and dentistry aren't the same thing."

"Well, she checked it anyhow. Said it looked okay to her." I added, "Her name's Linda Quentin. Told me her great-granddaddy invented Q-Tips."

"What?"

"Interesting, right? Apparently they started out as Quentin-Tips."

Jenny frowned again and seemed about to say something when I heard a bloodcurdling scream. The place was loud already, but this drowned everything else out. We turned to see a student sitting at the last table in the line of exhibits jump to her feet and flap her hands as if signaling a rescue boat. Her huge nametag, readable even at a distance, said MICHELLE.

"Help! Somebody stole my backpack!" she wailed. "Just now—with my phone and money inside!"

While everyone stood frozen, I spotted Billy Osmond and motioned him toward me. Within seconds the two of us maneuvered through the crowd to each other, and amid the noise I shouted instructions into his ear. God bless him, he understood fast, and took off for the robbery victim's table. By the time I reached the podium on stage, I could see Billy handing her his cell phone and telling her what to do. As Michelle punched the numbers with trembling fingers I pulled the microphone to me and said, over the PA system, *"Everybody be quiet!"*

The entire gym fell silent, every stunned and wide-eyed face watching mine. After a long pause I heard what I'd hoped for—the deep bass notes of "The Imperial March" from *Star Wars*—and everyone else heard it too. It came from the bulky coat of a thin-faced teenager. All heads turned toward him.

"Grab that kid," I said into the mike. *"He's a thief."*

Two male teachers did just that, pinning the boy's arms behind him. I joined them as fast as conditions would allow, and a quick look underneath his overcoat revealed a pink backpack with Michelle's ID and cell phone inside. The phone, which was pink also, had finished its majestic ring and was issuing a recorded message that Michelle was busy and would call back.

It took less than five minutes to turn our hapless and sulking thief over to Principal Donny Benton. On my walk back to Jenny, interrupted by numerous kind words and pats on the back, I saw a beaming Michelle plant a movie-worthy kiss on the lips of a red-faced but obviously pleased Billy Osmond. A few minutes later Billy, Jenny, and I stood together in roughly the same place we'd been before the incident. Jenny, beaming also, asked us, "How'd you know?"

"I didn't," Billy said. "It was the sheriff."

"You picked up on it quick," I said to him.

Jenny poked my chest with a finger. "Answer my question."

"Two things," I said. "First, Michael had told us his twin sister was here. So when I saw MICHELLE on the screamer's nametag—"

"Michael and Michelle," she said. "Boy-girl twins."

"Right. I figured she must be the sister."

"But that's crazy, Ray. They don't look anything alike. And there are a lot of Michelles, even these days."

"That's the second thing. Since their last name's Zubrick," I said, pointing, "that would place the sister—alphabetically—at the table where the robbery happened. The one on the very end. And since Michael had already told us his sister's ringtone . . ."

Jenny thought that over, then tilted her head and studied me a moment, smiling. "Sheriff Douglas, I am impressed," she said. Billy was grinning like a possum eating persimmons.

I was impressed, too, actually. In fact I thought I deserved a reward at least as good as my young partner had received. But before I could suggest that, Jenny's eyes turned serious again.

"What?" I said.

"How would you like to help another damsel in distress?" she asked.

"Can't, right now," I said. "Donny and a security guard are detaining our thief until we can make sure this wasn't a prank and see if the victim wants to press criminal charges."

"Can't they do that themselves? Or can you delay it for a few minutes?"

"Why?"

She held up her own cell phone. "I've been puzzling over what you told me, about Mattie Watson and the drugstore. And what her 'helper' said to you."

"And . . . ?"

"I called her a few minutes ago, after all the excitement," she said.

"You called Mattie?"

"Yep. I phoned her at home. That's where you were told she was, right? Home sick."

"So, what did she say?"

"She didn't answer," Jenny said. "She wasn't there."

"Maybe she felt better, went in after all."

"Nope. I called the store, too. No answer."

"Not even from this . . . what did I tell you her name was? Linda Quentin?"

"Not from anybody. No helper, no Mattie. No one answered the drugstore phone."

For a moment neither of us spoke. Billy, still there, looked from Jenny to me and back. I realized he hadn't heard the whole story, so I gave him the thirty-second mini-version. I finished by turning to Jenny and saying, "So . . . you think something's wrong."

"No, I'm pretty *sure* something's wrong. And there's more."

"Like what?"

"I'll tell you in the car," she said. "We need to go there." She turned and marched toward the table where I'd first seen her. I followed her, and Billy followed me. When I started to object he pleaded, "You gotta take me along, Sheriff. I earned it. Besides, Ms. Parker's my ride."

Which was true. I nodded and phoned Donny to say I'd been called away, and when Jenny had fetched her purse the three of us hiked out to the parking lot and piled into my cruiser.

I didn't use the siren or lights, but I also didn't waste any time. Speeding toward downtown, I said, "Okay, talk to me."

Jenny said, from the passenger seat, "It worries me that no one answers the phone at the store or at home—"

"I know that already."

"—but other things don't make sense either. This Linda person, who told you she'd been a nurse and sold you the perfume? I don't think she works for Mattie at all."

"Why not?"

"Well, Q-Tips, for one thing."

Billy said, from the back seat, "Q-Tips?"

"This woman told Sheriff Douglas the Q is for Quentin," Jenny said. "Actually, the Q is for Quality."

"Quality-Tips?" I asked.

"Yep. And I'll give you another quality tip: You said you saw her ring finger was bare. Well, no nurse, current or former, would've stuck her hand in your mouth without gloves on."

That stopped me, for a beat. "Maybe she didn't have any around."

"Then she wouldn't have checked your tooth. Not that she would've anyway."

"Maybe you're right," I said, also worried now. "I hope you're not."

"I hope I'm not, too."

I saw a red light ahead, and almost ran it but decided at the last second to stop. As we sat there waiting for it to change, my cell phone played its tune. It was Cheryl, at the office. She said she'd received the photos and other info about the three workers from Lamar Green, and was headed to Gordon Bailey's address to check things there. I asked her to text me the photos and descriptions, and to be careful at Bailey's. When I disconnected Billy said, "*Blazing Saddles*."

I grinned. Nobody else had ever recognized my ringtone. "You know Mel Brooks wrote that song?" I asked.

"Yep. And Frankie Laine sang it."

"My God," Jenny said, her eyes on the stoplight. "That's all I need, another movie nut."

"Cinema aficionado," I corrected. To Billy I said, "What's yours?"

"My ringtone? *The Great Escape* march."

"Excellent choice."

Jenny let out a sigh. As I accelerated again, she turned in her seat, pointed to me, and said to Billy, "Did you know his middle name's Kirk?"

"Kirk Douglas?" Billy said. "No way."

I nodded tiredly. "It's true. You actually know who he was?"

"Are you kidding?" He straightened his back and raised his chin. " 'I am Spartacus.' "

I sat up straight, too. " 'No, *I* am Spartacus.' "

Both of us looked at Jenny, waiting, but she just rolled her eyes. "Deliver me," she said.

At that instant Watson's Pharmacy appeared ahead, and as I parked at the curb in front of the building I felt my momentary good mood evaporate. I dreaded what we were about to find, and mumbled a quick prayer that Mattie Watson was someplace safe and sound.

"Both of you stay in the car," I ordered, and climbed out. They of course climbed out, too, and followed me like puppies to the front door.

The store was deserted—door open, lights on. Not a good sign. I drew my pistol, something I've not often felt the need to do, and told them to by God, stay your asses outside this door. This time they did.

After a quick search I discovered Mattie bound and gagged in a back room. I called out to Jenny and untied the relieved storeowner while Jenny phoned for an ambulance, but Mattie was thankfully unhurt and, despite her ordeal, more angry than scared. As expected, "Linda Quentin" had—after pulling a gun, tying Mattie up with a computer cord, and stowing her out of sight—stolen a fair amount of cash and prescription drugs. The hardest part, Mattie said, had been listening to me have a casual conversation with the thief while she sat strapped to a chair in the dark, forty feet away. I wished fervently that I had sensed something amiss, but I hadn't, dammit, and that was now water under the bridge. I apologized anyway, and got a fierce hug in return. "Forget that, you silly boy," Mattie said. "You rescued me."

"Jenny was the one who figured it out. I'm thinking I should deputize her."

"You should marry her instead," Mattie said, making both Jenny and me blush. Billy stood there grinning like a fool. I found myself getting attached to the kid.

Mattie cancelled the ambulance call but agreed to go to her doc and get checked out. Jenny and I helped her make a quick tally of the items stolen, and I talked her into closing the store for a while. I also promised her, there on the sidewalk before we left, that I would somehow catch the woman who did this. But I had my doubts. We both knew what the robber—and fake nurse—had looked like but there was little else to go on, unless she'd left some fingerprints on my back molars. I was glad I hadn't asked her for a flu shot.

It was past eleven o'clock by the time Pinewood's new crime-fighting team climbed back into my cruiser. Before I could start the engine Jenny said, "Change of subject, again. Let's look at the stuff Cheryl sent you."

The descriptions and photos on my phone were unhelpful. Ronald James Webb, 45, six-foot-four, had dark eyes and hair and a full beard and looked like an axe-murderer; Lindsey Ann Hinton, 31, four-foot-eleven, was blond and blue-eyed, with rosy cheeks and glasses and looked as innocent as a sleepy kitten; and Gordon Arthur Bailey, 52, six-foot-one, green eyes, looked like a kind and friendly farmer but remained the target of our one and only piece of evidence.

"The woman seems pretty small for yard work," Jenny said.

"Green told me she does the weed-eating and leaf-blowing."

All of us studied the information for a minute more, with Billy leaning over between us from the back seat.

I was about to quit and put my phone away when Billy spoke up: "What if Ms. Cardenas didn't say 'Gordo'?"

Both Jenny and I turned to look at him. I said, "What?"

He pointed to the photo of Lindsey Hinton. "Look at the eyebrows. They're not blond like her hair, or even dark brown. They're black."

He was right. They were.

"What does that matter?" Jenny asked. "She probably colors her hair."

Still looking at the picture, Billy said, "Do you recognize her, Sheriff?"

I re-studied the photo, and heard a tiny alarm bell in my mind. Just a ding, but still . . .

I stared through the windshield at the front of the now-closed pharmacy, remembering, then looked again at the photo. With a lot of makeup, and dark hair, and brown contacts, and no glasses—

"You're right," I said. "With a few changes she could be the woman who helped me, in the store. I'll ask Mattie about it, too. But that doesn't match what we were told the Cardenas lady said." I shook my head. "To try to connect these two crimes—that's a big stretch."

"I don't think so," Billy said. "One's Lindsey Hinton, one's Linda Quentin. Both were robberies. And did you hear what I asked you? What if Ms. Cardenas didn't say 'Gordo'? Maybe she said 'Corto.' "

"Which means . . . ?" I asked.

"Short."

It was suddenly very quiet in the car. I glanced at Jenny, who nodded dazedly.

"I had to take Spanish, this year," he explained.

I stared at the descriptions. Six-foot-four, six-one . . . and *four-eleven?*

It made sense. My gloveless dental inspector had been tiny. Less than five feet tall. Lindsey Hinton and Linda Quentin.

The same woman had robbed two old ladies in less than a day's time.

Stunned, I called Cheryl and gave her this new information. We would still have to talk to Gordon Bailey, and find and interview Ron Webb—no stone unturned—but above all we needed to get Lindsey/Linda's photo and description, along with suggested variations, out to all the usual places, and stake out her home address shown in Lamar Green's records. We'd also need to find and check any camera footage outside both the lawn service and the drugstore, to see if we could get her vehicle's description or, ideally, a plate number. What a break this was.

Got you, Lindsey, I thought. When I saw Billy watching me in the rearview mirror I said, "Kid, if you ever tie somebody up and rob 'em, don't tell the cops your kinfolks invented a cotton swab."

"Or that the robbee went home sick," he said, grinning.

Jenny didn't seem amused by either of us, but I didn't get the scolding I'd expected for my mentorly advice, and our ride back to the high school found all three of us in a better mood. Especially after Donny Benton called and said Michelle Zubrick had decided not to press charges. The backpack thief would be disciplined by the school—he was theirs now, not mine.

"You're still gonna be late for the judging," I said to Jenny, after I disconnected. I'd been careful not to tell Donny that Jenny was with me.

She shrugged. "They'll manage."

"Think they could manage till after I buy us lunch?"

"Don't see why not."

I looked at Billy again in my mirror, and it occurred to me that his face had changed a lot from its sad and hangdog look, earlier this morning. "What'll you tell your teacher tomorrow, Sherlock? About your day at the science fair?"

He smiled. "I'll tell her I had more fun that I ever had before."

"You know, kiddo, you wound up in some projects after all," Jenny said. "Criminology's a science, too."

"I never thought of that."

After a mile or two, each of us off someplace in our own thoughts, Jenny said, "Remember *The Mod Squad?*"

"That was TV," I said. "Not movies."

"It was both. But my point is, we could be the POD Squad, the three of us. Parker, Osmond, Douglas. What do you guys think?"

"I like DOP better," I said. "Douglas, Osmond, Parker."

At that moment, Jenny's cell started playing "Unchained Melody." She looked at the display and said, "It's Donny. The principal." She switched it off. "I'll call him after we eat."

Silence. No one said a word.

"What?" she said, frowning at both of us. "You think I should call him back now?"

Billy and I exchanged a look and said, together, "We think you need a new ringtone."

And grinned all the way to lunch.

Part 2 – PI Tom Langford Mysteries

MUSTANG SALLY

My client, a red-haired young woman in jeans and a yellow T-shirt, sat silently in the chair on the other side of my desk and inspected my office. I hadn't even heard her come in, over the sound of the ceiling fan; my door's always open, and when I looked up from my morning paper there she was. She of course wasn't yet a client, since she had yet to speak to me, but I hoped she would be. I needed the work.

Her gaze had settled on my window, and she seemed to study the trees in the park across the street a moment before turning to face me. She had green eyes.

"Thomas Langford?" she said.

"That's me."

"Your ad said you're a private detective."

"Investigator." I folded my paper and took my feet down off the desktop. "And your name is . . ."

"Sally Marshall."

Her cheeks, I noticed, were almost as red as her hair. I figured she was either embarrassed or overheated. Maybe both. This was, after all, summertime, and even though fish were jumping and the cotton was high, the living wasn't necessarily easy. It was hot as the hinges of hell, even at ten in the morning, and the A/C in my building wasn't the best. That's why I kept the fan on and the door open.

"Want a cup of coffee?"

"It's too hot for coffee," she said.

"You're right." I leaned back and put on what I hoped was a professional face. "How can I help you, Ms. Marshall?"

A word of explanation. At the time that I met Sally Marshall, I'd already been in this job a few years. I wasn't as smart as Holmes or as brave as Spenser or as handsome as Magnum, but I was a former cop and a pretty good investigator. And I thought I'd heard it all: *My supposedly disabled employee is teaching an aerobics class; I think my Russian brother-in-law has bugged my apartment; My neighbor's cat keeps peeing in my flowerbeds; My husband ran off with my best friend and I miss her.*

But I'd never heard anything like this.

"My ex-boyfriend's father's dog," she said, "ate my diamond ring."

I stared at her a minute. "It's also too hot to be April Fool's Day."

"I'm not fooling," she said.

But she admitted her story was strange. Ms. Marshall, it turned out, was a freelance writer, and had taken a taxi earlier this morning to the home of a Mr. George Neely, to pick up a car she had loaned a week earlier to his son Wilson—the aforementioned boyfriend. "Will parked it in the barn," Neely told her. "Stay here, I'll back it out." They said nothing more; she and the old man had never liked each other. It was while she waited in the driveway, she said, that a skinny black-and-white-spotted dog with one ear missing popped up out of nowhere and approached her, growling and baring its teeth. She backed away, suddenly aware that there was no place to run. Then she remembered her heavy, hard-soled sandals. Slowly she bent her left leg and reached down with her right hand to slip off a shoe while at the same time holding her left palm out in a stop-right-there gesture to the dog. In a terrified but soothing voice she said, "Take it easy, doggie. Good doggie—"

And it lunged forward and bit her.

"On the hand?" I asked. My eyes immediately went to her left hand, expecting to see the ragged stub of a ring finger. But her hand looked fine—not even a bandage.

"I was lucky," she said. "Technically he bit me—his jaws snapped shut on my fingers—but the ring must've got in the way. It was brand new and loose anyway, and when I snatched my hand out of his mouth, his teeth dragged it right off my finger." She held up her hand, and I could see a long pink mark above the nail of her ring finger. "Probably one chance in a million, but that's what happened."

"So, this ring—you're sure the dog swallowed it?"

"Positive. Gulped it right down. I think it scared him—might've scratched his throat—because he jumped back for a second, and when he did I whacked him in the nose with my shoe and he yipped and took off running, around the side of the house."

"What happened then?"

"Mr. Neely backed my car out and pulled up beside me. He looked at me a little funny when he got out—I mean, I was standing there shaking and sweating and holding one shoe in my hand—but he didn't say anything. I'm pretty sure he hadn't seen what happened, with the dog."

"And you didn't tell him?"

"No. I was pretty flustered, and old George wouldn't have done anything about it if I had. I just hopped into the car and drove off. He probably thought, *Good riddance.*"

"And you came straight here?"

"Not at first. I drove around awhile, thinking. I'd seen your ad someplace, a week or two ago, and for some reason I remembered it."

Probably my stunning photo. But right now I was wishing she hadn't seen it at all.

"You sure this dog belongs to George Neely?"

"I'm assuming he does. It was there at his house."

"But you never saw him before, right? The dog, I mean."

"No. This was only the second time I've been to George's house. It's pretty close to my apartment. Wilson lives on the other side of town."

I paused a moment, thinking. None of my thoughts were good. I studied her face, which seemed a little less flushed now. Her red curls stirred in the breeze from the ceiling fan.

"You said this was a diamond ring?"

"Two carats," she said.

"A wedding ring? I thought you said—"

"Engagement. Wilson and I were supposed to get married."

"Supposed to?"

"We broke up," she said. "Two nights ago."

Which explained the *ex*-boyfriend. "But you kept the ring."

"Damn right I did."

"Even though you're no longer engaged."

Her eyes hardened. "He gave it to me. It's mine now."

"Did Wilson agree with that?"

"Doesn't matter if he did or not. He has plenty more where that came from." She paused then, and focused on me. "So, are you gonna take the case, or what?"

"Get your ring back, you mean?"

"That's what I mean. That's why I'm here."

"And how do you propose I do that?"

She shrugged. "That's up to you. You're the investigator. My suggestion would be to get the dog and keep him until he . . . well . . ."

"Produces the goods."

"Right."

I drew in a long breath and let it out. "Ms. Marshall, have you considered talking to the police about this? Or maybe Animal Control? I mean, the dog did attack you, and they could—"

"No police," Sally said. "No dogcatchers, no veterinarians, none of that."

"Why not?"

"I have my reasons." Her face had reddened again. "Are you gonna help me, or not?"

We stared at each other awhile, and I heaved another sigh. I guess nobody ever said this job was easy.

I took a minute to give her the standard spiel about daily rates and expenses, but both of us knew they wouldn't apply. What had to be done here would probably have to be done today, over the next few hours. Instead we agreed on a one-time fee of two thousand dollars, payable if and when I deliver the ring. I felt like one of those bloodsucking, ambulance-chasing lawyers—you pay us only if we win the case.

Sally Marshall and I shook hands across the desk. Then she stood up, we exchanged a final frown—smiles had not been part of our meeting today—and she left. I watched, from my window, as she crossed the street and climbed into a bright red Mustang. It looked a little like my Camaro in the parking lot behind the building, though mine was older and plainer and had trouble getting started. Like me.

I tucked George Neely's address into my pocket, sat again at my desk, and googled several sources describing the average dog's digestive tract and how long it might take an ingested foreign object to pass from point A to point B. I saw nothing encouraging and many things disgusting, but I was now at least armed with some basic information. I figured I had from six to twenty hours to locate and secure the treasure. Anything longer than that, my quest would be over and my modest reward lost.

My last thoughts, as I locked the office and headed down the stairs, were about business opportunities and life decisions and taking pride in one's chosen career. I had studied accounting in college, for cryin' out loud. I could be doing someone's taxes right now.

My car started on the third try.

#

My first stop was Walmart, where I bought a packet of latex gloves, a sturdy leash, a small Igloo cooler, a bag of ice, and a fat sirloin steak. If I couldn't find the dog, I would at least have a good meal. I dumped the ice and the steak into the cooler, piled it and the rest of my purchases onto the passenger seat, and took off. En route, I phoned my longtime and infinitely patient girlfriend, Debra Jo Wells, and left her a message that I might be late for our date tonight. I didn't tell her why. We rarely shared details about our work with each other anyway—she was a paralegal at a law firm five blocks from my office—and I sure didn't plan to start now.

George Neely's home was a tired-looking ranch house at the edge of a patch of woods just south of town. I parked in the gravel driveway and waded through weeds to the front door with a cautious eye on the shrubbery. For all I knew, it might be hiding a mean, one-eared dog.

The man who answered the door looked like John Huston, the late actor/director. Big guy, bags under his eyes, long face, maybe seventy. I introduced myself and shook his hand. Unlike what I'd expected, he seemed friendly. "What can I do for you?" he said.

And I gave him the only story I could think of, the first part of which was true.

"I'm working for a young lady who says she came to see you this morning," I said. "Sally Marshall. Says she knows your son."

"Yep. Sally and Will was a big thing for a while there. Thought they was gonna get hitched. Don't know the whys and wherefores, but things didn't work out. Can't say I'm sorry—that gal's a little odd. Anyhow, she came today to pick up the car she'd loaned him."

"You don't mind me asking, why'd she loan it to him?" Something, I only just realized, that I should've asked her myself.

He shook his head. "Beats me. Maybe his was in the shop."

"And why would he leave the car here for her, instead of taking it back to her place?"

"'Cause they broke up, I guess. All I know is, Will left it here yesterday, said since Sally lives close by, she could pick it up whenever she wanted."

"Sounds like the two of them didn't split up on good terms."

"I can't say, there. My chillun don't tell me much."

"What does he do, your son? For a living."

"You know, I ain't really sure, no more. Don't see him nor talk to him often. These kids, they got their own lives now, too busy for the old folks. He does well, though, moneywise."

"I believe you," I said. Two-carat diamonds don't come cheap. Actually I was beginning to give some serious thought to Wilson Neely. I was fairly sure I'd seen or heard the name before. "Anyway—what I really came here for was to ask if I could borrow your dog for a day or so. I got a leash in the car. I'd be happy to pay you for the favor."

I don't think I could've surprised him more if I'd told him I'd just beamed in from Mars.

"You want to borrow my dog?"

"More like rent him. Just for a while. The thing is, Sally says she saw him here yesterday, the spotted one with a missing ear, and she's being paid to write a piece for the paper about a new dog park here in town, and she wants to go spend some time there but she needs a dog to take with her, and well, you see where I'm going, here. . . ."

He huffed out a laugh. "You're going back empty-handed, is where you're going. I seen that one-eared dog, too, earlier today, but he ain't mine. Don't know whose he is or where he belongs. In fact, last I saw of him he was headed out to them woods over there, about the time Sally left."

Whoa. "So you don't have any idea where I might find him."

"Not a clue. It'd be a needle in a haystack, I expect." He shrugged. "Sorry."

Oh well. So much for my "Frodo Finds the Ring" adventure. There was just one more thing.

"That car of hers," I said. "It's a red Mustang, right?"

"Yep. A twenty-ten , I think."

#

Sally Marshall's apartment house was less than a mile west, but I headed north instead, to my office. Several things were nagging at my mind, and though I could've probably found the answers via my phone, the computer on my desktop would be easier.

One thing that bothered me was the name Wilson Neely. It was definitely familiar, and the faint bell it rang in my mind was more an alarm than a jingle. The other thing was, if Sally's former boyfriend was so well off, financially, why borrow her car for a week, and why drop it off at his father's place when he was done? Even more to the point, why hide it in the barn?

And why had Sally been so dead set against involving the police?

Finding what I needed didn't take long. The online editions of recent newspapers gave me the story I wanted. One of the biggest jewelry stores in the city had been robbed by a masked gunman five days ago—I vaguely remembered hearing about it—and the local TV stations' websites said the suspect was still at large and unidentified. And a call to my old buddy Ronnie Robertson at police headquarters gave me two facts that the news stories hadn't included: (1) Wilson J. Neely was a convicted felon, having served time in the state pen for fraud, assault, and assorted other crimes, and (2) a red fifth-generation Ford Mustang had been spotted leaving the jewelry store the night of the crime, and had also been seen parked in the area twice in the two days prior to the robbery. Sally had been right when she mentioned something about her ex-boyfriend not needing her ring because he had "plenty more where that came from." He probably had a bagful.

Wilson Neely's father might not know what shenanigans his son was up to—I somehow believed him, there—but I had a feeling Sally did know.

Even so, she was my client and I felt I owed her a report. First things first.

I drove across town for the second time that day, the leash and other dog-catching supplies still lying unused on the passenger seat, and found Sally sitting on the little patio in front of her apartment building. I pulled up a chair and told her the bad news. The dog that bit her was a stray, he didn't belong to George Neely, and he was gone with the wind. So was her ring. Although by this time I knew, and so did she, that it wasn't hers at all, and hadn't been Wilson's either. I shook her hand one last time, put the chair back where I'd found it, and left.

I turned right on Magnolia, not far from her apartment and about halfway between her place and George Neely's, and had aimed my Camaro north toward home and was thinking about lunch when I saw the dog. Skinny, black-and-white spotted, one ear missing. He was sitting in a clearing beside the road, calmly watching the passing traffic as if taking a count.

I pulled over and parked. He was still there. Holding my breath, I took the cut of steak from the cooler, picked up the leash, got out, and walked toward him.

#

That night Debra Jo and I met for a late dinner, downtown. As we climbed out of our cars my cell phone buzzed, so I stayed outside the restaurant to take the call while she went in and found a table and looked over the menu. I joined her five minutes later, and we had no other interruptions. After dessert and coffee we strolled the two blocks to the park across the street from my office building and sat together on one of the wooden benches. It was still humid—we were used to that—but the nighttime temperature was down to something at least reasonable. A warm breeze riffled the leaves of the oaks that lined the sidewalks.

"Who was it on the phone, earlier?" she asked me.

I turned to study her profile in the dim light of the street lamps.

"Ron Robertson. He was working late."

"Your old partner?"

I nodded. "He called to say they'd caught the guy who robbed that jewelry store the other day. Recovered most of what was stolen. Came from an anonymous tip, phoned in to Ronnie this afternoon. Says he's a hero now." What I didn't add was that Ronnie also assured me that Sally Marshall would be kept out of the story. I had told him that she'd almost certainly known about what happened, but only after the fact. And keeping her out of it would keep me out as well. I doubted George Neely would remember my name, if he even remembered my visit.

"I'm happy for Ronnie," Debra Jo said. "But I'm also happy you're not there anymore. On the force, I mean."

"Me too," I said.

She snuggled into my shoulder. It was quiet in the park. Overhead, visible through the leafy branches, a quarter moon floated in and out of the clouds.

"Thanks again for the ring," she whispered. "It's beautiful."

"I should've done it a long time ago."

She raised her left hand, turned it a little to catch the light. "Where'd you get it?" she asked.

I smiled into the darkness, enjoying the smell of her hair, and the trees, and the city around us. I'd had my share of bad smells this afternoon.

"You wouldn't believe me," I said, "if I told you."

SENTRY

Friday afternoon, 4:50. Quitting time, for most people. Not me. I was still on the phone in my office. Well, I wasn't *talking* on the phone—I was leaning back in my desk chair and playing chess with Boris, my electronic opponent. He'd mated me in five minutes, as usual.

I was about to lower the skill-level setting—take *that*, you sneaky Russian—when Tony Soprano walked into my office.

I knew, of course, that the actor who played T.S. died several years ago. But this guy sure looked like him. Barrel chest, sleepy eyes, receding hairline, solemn face, mid-forties. I found myself wondering if he worked for my building's landlord, and wishing I'd paid the rent on time.

"Thomas Langford?" he said. He even sounded like Gandolfini, in maybe the first season.

I put my phone down. "That's me."

"Private investigator. Right?"

"Right."

"Marty Rooks," he said. I didn't know the face, but I knew the name. I took my feet off the desktop and sat up straight.

He didn't offer a hand to shake, and I didn't offer him a chair, but he sat anyway.

"How can I help you, Mr. Rooks?"

He took a long look around the office, like most of my visitors. My digs aren't exactly upscale. Then he focused on me and said, "You can help me protect my wife."

Yet another surprise. "Protect her from what?"

"It's a long story."

#

As things turned out, the story wasn't long. But it was scary.

First, a little backstory. I'm a former cop, currently single but engaged, and my only real vices are that I drink a little too much and I watch too many movies, often at the same time. Workwise, I try to stay on the correct side of the blurry line between right and wrong, and I am neither well known nor powerful. Martin Rooks was both, and although he'd spent a number of years on the other side of that line, he seemed to be pursuing legitimacy, or so I'd been told.

I'd also been told he hadn't reached it yet. Ours is not a big city and we don't have big crime, at least not like Atlanta or Miami, but we have our share, and most of that, at the time of my meeting with Marty Rooks, was controlled by two families: the Rooks and the Knights. Yes, those were really their names. It was as if several mid-level chess pieces decided to take over the game. On the north side of town was Fenimore Knight, whose trucking business was a front for prostitution, migrant smuggling, and gunrunning, and on the south was my unexpected visitor today, whose recycling organization specialized in gambling, money-laundering, and loansharking. The problem was that both camps had now moved heavily into drug trafficking, a gold mine that had caused several bloody disagreements and would certainly cause more.

One of the recent clashes, a retaliatory attack for the torching of one of Martin Rooks's warehouses, had made national news. It was unusual and especially tragic in that it happened in the front driveway of Fenimore Knight's mansion and resulted in the death of his wife.

Which is where Rooks began his story.

"It was an accident," he said to me. "Stray bullet. She wasn't even supposed to be there." He shook his head sadly. "Our people weren't supposed to be there either. These were new guys, sent by one of my late father's lieutenants to, ah, let's say . . . take care of Fenny. I didn't know about it. In any case, it happened and they failed, and I made sure it won't happen again."

I didn't ask how. What I did ask was, "How does all this involve me?"

Rooks, who'd been off in his own thoughts, came back to earth and said, "We ain't the Mafia, me and my group, and neither is Fenny Knight and his band of idiots. No code of silence, no 'made men,' none of that. But we do have rules, Mr. Langford, and one of 'em is simple. Stay away from the enemy's wives and kids. My men violated that rule when Susan Knight died, accident or not, and now Fenny's sent me a message that he plans to get even."

He paused and looked at me.

"He told you he means to kill you?" I asked.

"I said 'get even.' He told me he means to kill my wife."

Both of us let that statement hang there in the air awhile. I had sense enough not to suggest getting the police involved. Finally I said, "I'm not a bodyguard, Mr. Rooks."

"I don't need a bodyguard. Annie never goes anywhere. What I need is a sentry."

I let out a sigh. I wanted no part of this, and I could see he knew that, but I could also see he was dead serious. "What do you mean, 'sentry'?" I said.

"Someone to stand guard in my house every night, outside her room, between, say, six and ten. For the next month or so. By then, this'll be resolved."

Again, I didn't ask how. In fact I shelved most of the questions that came to mind and said, "I would think you'd already have dozens of men who could do that."

He gave me an odd look then, a combination of amusement, sorrow, and anger. "The thing is, how many of them can I trust? My father's passed, my brother's left the business, and two others are, for now, covering for me in all my meetings, traveling, et cetera, so I can watch Annie. The only other man I trusted ordered the unauthorized . . . mission . . . I told you about." He leaned forward. "For this job I need somebody besides one of my workers, Mr. Langford. I've checked you out: job record, military record, everything. You're the man I want."

I studied him a moment, trying to get into his head. I couldn't. I knew, and so did he, that these workers of his were really *soldiers*—he was right when he'd used the word lieutenants—and that probably made the suspected lack of loyalty even worse. And more dangerous.

I still couldn't quite believe I was getting this behind-the-scenes, *Goodfellas* look at a Southern version of the mob. Leave the gun, take the gumbo.

He added, interrupting my thoughts, "Two hundred thousand, for four weeks' work."

I blinked, but otherwise tried to keep the shock off my face. *What?*

"And you might never have to get up out of your chair. How about it?"

I cleared my throat and tried to remember the questions flitting through my head a minute ago. "Why six to ten?" I asked.

"Because I'll be with her the rest of the time."

"Can I ask where you'll be during those four hours?"

"I'll be in my office, about thirty feet from her room. But I'll be occupied. And since you're about to ask why . . . I'll tell you that when you've agreed to take the assignment. What you need to know now is that it's nothing illegal, or even questionable."

"Then why not tell me now?"

He hesitated, and his face reddened a bit. "Because you'll think I've lost my mind."

Slowly I shook my head. "No. You've told me you want to hire me to do something you could obviously do yourself. I need to know why."

We sat and stared at each other. I waited him out.

"I've started writing," he said. "Fiction. I'm writing a novel. I haven't told anybody. And I need that isolation, that undisturbed time every night, away from Annie and everyone else." He sighed. "I know how that sounds, but it's the truth."

I wouldn't have been more surprised if he'd told me he was sewing a ballerina outfit. "You want to pay me two hundred grand," I said, "to fill in while you indulge in . . . a hobby?"

"While I indulge in something that allows me to keep my sanity. If there's any of it left."

I let half a minute go by, then nodded. To each his own. *Just don't put me in your book.*

"So you agree? You'll do it?"

In other words, would I forget my pride and climb into bed with a known leader in organized crime? For nothing but money?

"Yes," I said. I hoped my mom and dad down in Florida never found out, or the pastor of the offbeat church I'd been talked into attending with my fiancée. But the truth is, this would be an incredible paycheck for a one-man private-eye firm. Besides, I'd already decided I wouldn't break any laws or get involved in any of my employer's activities. It was like he'd said: I would stand guard and make sure no harm came to the person in my charge. At worst I would shoot anyone who needed shooting and at best I would be a bored baby-sitter. Either way, it was a sound business decision.

He nodded. "Good."

#

The tension of sitting across my desk from a crime boss was nothing compared to what I felt that night at dinner, sitting across the table from Debra Jo Wells. I'd almost decided not to tell her about my deal with the devil, but honest boyfriend that I am, I spilled the beans while eating my beans. The strange thing was, she didn't seem overly upset by my rubbing shoulders with underworld figure Martin Rooks, a name she'd never heard before. What irked her was that I might be swapping hot lead with Fenimore Knight, a name everyone had heard before.

"Knight's a killer, Tom. A psychopath, some say."

"I know that, D.J. I was a cop here, remember? The truth is, though, Fenny Knight's old now, and almost always stays home. And to most people he's a war hero."

"You're right, there. He's scheduled next month to dedicate a statue of some kind, to Vietnam vets. But like you said, you know the truth." She fixed me with a stare. "And now you want to make yourself a willing target for a man like that?"

That irked *me* a little. "I can take care of myself, Deej. If I couldn't I wouldn't do this. Hell, if I couldn't, Rooks wouldn't have sought me out in the first place."

"Okay, okay. Who is this Martin Rooks, anyway?"

I gave her a brief summary, and showed her an Internet photo of him on my phone.

"I remember now. I've heard about him." She handed my phone back and said, "Looks a little like the guy on *The Sopranos*. By the way—how *did* he know to seek you out?"

That was a question I had asked him myself before he left my office that afternoon. I said, "He got my name from Charlotte's husband. Trenton Carlisle."

Her eyes widened. "Well. That's interesting."

"That Rooks and Trenton know each other? Interesting maybe, but not surprising." After all, both had acquired their considerable fortunes by less than honorable means, and there are all kinds of snakes in the jungle. FYI, I don't much like Trenton Carlisle. I've heard that a lot of divorced guys don't like their ex-wives' husbands.

Trenton's misdeeds didn't seem to bother D.J. Her mind, I knew, was still on my new endeavor. "I don't know," she said, shaking her head. "Even if that part does turn out okay—"

"What part?"

"Sentry duty. Even if that works out, and you keep her safe . . . it still sounds wrong."

I felt another twinge of irritation. D.J.'s a paralegal, and spends most of her time around people who think everyone's a crook and everything's a conspiracy. I once did, too, but I quit that job. "What specifically?"

"I don't know. The whole deal sounds fishy to me."

"You mean, like, the novel writing?"

"Yeah, that, for one thing. And this story about him not trusting any of his men."

"Okay, let's say he's lying about that, or other things, or everything. If there's really no threat to his wife, I'll be paid a boatload of money for taking no risks. Right?"

She didn't reply, but clearly wasn't happy. She did, though, make sure she got the last word: "I think there's something about this you're not being told."

As it turned out—and as usual—she was right.

#

The following afternoon, before my first evening on what D.J. was calling the don's payroll, Marty Rooks asked me to arrive an hour early so I could meet his wife and her assistant (assistant?) and take a look at the house and grounds. As requested, I showed up at his front gate at five p.m., armed with my shoulder-holstered revolver under my coat and my best behavior.

Annie Rooks was almost what I expected: an attractive middle-aged woman with a pleasant but disinterested smile. What I hadn't expected was the fact that she was barely aware of her surroundings. Early-onset Alzheimer's, Rooks told me later, which explained the presence of her assistant, Olivia Logan, who was not only a constant companion but a caregiver as well. The suite of two bedrooms where the women spent most of their time—and every night between dinner and breakfast—was lined with books and photos and prescription medicine bottles. Rooks explained to me afterward that during my "guard sessions" I was never to contact Annie, who when she was lucid was fiercely insistent on her privacy, but that I would have Olivia's cell number and could check with her on anything at any time. I had a brief image of me texting her to take cover while I shot it out with invading gangsters in black ninja suits.

"Have you ever lost someone dear to you?" Rooks asked me, when we'd made our exit.

"Not a family member," I said. "But I had a partner on the force, Benny Ramirez, who was like a brother to me. Murdered, for no reason. Seems like yesterday."

He nodded and said, "Then you understand. I know Annie's not actually gone, but . . . this is almost as bad."

I didn't know how to respond to that, so I didn't, and our tour continued. It was mostly limited to the north wing of the house, which contained (1) Annie's rooms and a bathroom; (2) Rooks's bedroom, home office, and a bathroom; and, situated between the two suites, (3) the large room where I would be posted during my time here each evening. (Which did not have a bathroom.

I guessed I'd just have to hold it.) As for my duty station, it looked like what it was: a security operations center, with two computers and ten HD monitors showing surveillance-camera views of the first two floors of the giant three-story home. Not monitored were the third floor, which was inaccessible from outside, and the basement, which Rooks assured me had four always-locked doors and no windows and a secure three-car garage. "Even I don't know everything about this house," he said, looking embarrassed. "It's got hidden fireplaces, two-way mirrors, secret passageways, you name it." And encircling everything was an eight-foot-high stone wall with two barred gates, in front and on the east side. An escorted walk around the perimeter showed me all this firsthand. It was more a castle than a residence.

When we finished and returned to my station it was almost six o'clock and the sun was dipping behind the west wall. Rooks asked me if I'd had dinner already, I said yes even though I hadn't, and he walked through the door to his suite of rooms, shut it behind him, and left me to it.

I spent most of those first four hours getting used to the computers and the surveillance system. (Rooks had been right: if anyone entered or left this house, the cameras would show it, and if anyone entered or left Rooks's rooms or Annie's they'd have to walk past me.) One of the computers was similar to my own, so I pulled my chair over to that part of the long desk and made it my home base. When ten o'clock rolled around, I'd seen neither hide nor hair of Rooks or his wife, which he'd said would be the norm. I tidied up my workspace, sent a good-bye text to Olivia, whose number he'd given me, and left, locking the office door behind me.

It occurred to me, on the way to the car I'd left parked at the curb near the front gate, that if this gig indeed lasted four or five weeks—and if my math was right—I'd made around seven thousand dollars tonight.

I decided I could live with that.

#

Since I was now working the biggest part of every evening, D.J. and I started meeting for lunch every day at a little café halfway between our offices, which put it within walking distance for both of us. It was also halfway between in terms of luxury, which meant less fancy than her office and fancier than mine.

She was still nervous about the whole arrangement but agreed that even though I was yet to be paid, I was making money on a grandiose scale, and she was always eager to hear my latest news from what we had begun calling the Rookery. And there was, thank God, never much to report. I checked in at my duty post, kept my butt glued to the chair and my eyes glued to the monitors, did my time, and left. On three separate occasions I caught glimpses of Olivia, passing through my office to run some errand or another to/from the rest of the house, but never during my four-hour stretches did I lay eyes on either Rooks or his wife and—as impossible as it might seem—never did I speak a word to anyone except to Olivia on her cell phone. Tough duty.

I found myself wondering, not for the first time, what Ben Ramirez would've thought of all this. Benny and I had agreed on most things, both here in the local PD and overseas in what he referred to as Allscrewedupistan. After the Army we entered the police academy together, a skinny kid from the Mississippi Delta and a pudgy kid from Corpus Christi. Anytime I bragged about the South, he reminded me that he was from farther south. I still missed him every day.

I found it fairly easy to follow the rules, at the Rookery. The only time I overstepped the established bounds was one night about a week into my employment. I had arrived ten minutes early, and noticed that the garage door was open and two cars were sitting in the driveway—a late-model Mercedes and a big, sensible Buick. A burly young man had just finished washing the Benz and was working on the Buick with an almost-empty soap bucket when I walked past. I was struck by a rare bright idea and asked him, "Which one is Mrs. Rooks's car?" He pointed to the Buick. "But she don't drive it much no more," he said. I walked back out to my car and returned to the driveway a few minutes later to see that the kid had gone around the corner as expected to refill his bucket. Knowing there were no cameras out here and feeling a lot like Sean Connery, I took a tiny magnetic GPS tracker from my pocket and hid it underneath and behind the Buick's rear bumper. The device was one I had used a month earlier to track the movements of a client's wandering husband, and had later returned it to my glove compartment. And even though it seemed the chances were small that Annie Rooks would be going on any unannounced outings, I would now know it if she did.

I'm not sure why I didn't tell Rooks about this. I guess I figured he might not approve. But it was a resource that I thought might help, and (1) I doubted if anyone else would ever know and

(2) if caught I could always say I was trying to better do my job, which was true.

As luck would have it, I got a hit on the device the following night—my iPhone had the tracking app—and I immediately called Olivia just to "check in" as I sometimes did. Olivia said all was well, and I could even hear Annie's voice in the background, humming a tune. So—no big deal—someone else must've taken the car out. Rooks hadn't emerged from his office (he never did) and there was no other way out without my seeing him, so it must've been one of the help. Maybe the car-washing dude, running a late errand for the boss. I watched the moving dot on my phone as it approached a spot north of town, stopped around eight o'clock and stayed there awhile, and returned. Not anything to get excited about. I went back to monitoring my monitors, and nothing else of note happened that night.

I was living the American dream: earning money for doing nothing.

#

And then something did happen.

On my seventeenth evening of sentry duty, around nine p.m., I heard a shot ring out—a rifle, from its sound, somewhere nearby— and then the breaking of glass. I vaulted from my chair and, in violation of all my orders, charged through the closed door to Annie Rooks's suite of rooms. She and Olivia, both already in pajamas, gaped at me for a second, then went back to what they'd probably been looking at before I burst in: a spider-webbed pane of glass with a bullet hole in its center, in the last west-facing window at the far end of the bedroom.

My gaze went straight to the opposite wall, and I spotted the bullet's final resting place, near the ceiling and away from anything else in the room. Using both points of impact to draw an imaginary line, I saw that the shooter had to have been on the grounds just inside the west wall. I rushed to the smashed window and spent a quick moment scanning the scene below.

"Lock the door," I said to Olivia, and sprinted back through it and into my office. No movement on any of the screens—but, as I mentioned, all the cameras faced the house. Revolver in hand, I dashed outside to the second-floor landing and down the stone stairway and across the west lawn, focusing on the branches of the oaks that overhung the wall there. It was no use. Whoever fired the shot must've climbed back into the trees and over the wall and was long gone.

I went back upstairs to find Marty Rooks's door open and him standing in my office, talking to Olivia. She was assuring him that Annie was fine, although Annie herself was nowhere to be seen. I got the impression, not for the first time, that Rooks and his wife had an odd relationship, with or without Annie's illness. Even though Marty was obviously concerned for Annie's wellbeing—to the tune of two hundred thousand dollars—neither of them felt the slightest need for the other's company. And I thought *my* family was dysfunctional.

When things settled down, Rooks and I had our first sit-down conversation since I'd taken the job. We reran the footage of what had happened and saw the window break, and when I described to him the relatively harmless placement of the shot, we agreed that this had only been a warning, to convey the message that the threat was real and, probably, that next time someone could shoot from the trees instead of from the ground, for a more deadly result.

Maybe I would finally earn my pay.

#

Four nights later—on my three-week anniversary here—I again got a ping on my phone and saw the red dot from my tracking device heading north through town. I glanced at my watch. 7:42. At around eight it stopped for several minutes, as it had last time, and then headed back home. More than curious now, I checked the online maps and found the spot where on both trips the Buick had stopped, and Google Street View gave me a good look at the area. It was a stretch of deserted road through wooded hills, and the exact site was a small patch of cleared ground overlooking a park below. It didn't make sense, but to investigate further would mean asking questions I shouldn't ask and would reveal my hidden tracking device, and besides, I was again certain that neither Annie nor Marty Rooks had been the driver during that night's trip. Marty was sealed away as usual and both Annie and Olivia were playing some kind of board game—I'd heard their voices for the past hour. Bottom line was, it was an interesting puzzle but didn't concern me. I cautioned myself not to look for storms in a cloudless sky.

Debra Jo, when I told her about it at lunch the next day, wasn't so sure. "Something's funny, with that," she said, "and at the house, too. I'll be glad when you're done with all this."

"I will too," I said, taking a bite of my chili dog. "I've needed a new car for a while now. And a vacation to Fiji."

Ignoring me, she said, "Haven't you wondered why he hasn't given you an end date?"

"Rooks? Because he doesn't know yet."

"But don't you figure he has something planned, to eventually wind this up?"

I sighed. "I suppose. And yes, of course I've wondered about it. To tell you the truth, I've always figured Rooks was hoping for an external solution to the problem."

"What kind of solution?"

"The kind that involves something happening to Fenimore Knight before Knight can make something happen to Annie Rooks. Marty, you see, is not Fenny Knight's only enemy. If one of those other enemies should decide to eliminate the head boss-man of the Knight empire—and with these people that's always a possibility—Rooks's problem is solved."

But D.J. was probably thinking the same thing I was: that kind of solution was leaving a lot to chance.

She fiddled a moment with her salad and said, "I also wonder—and I can't believe I'm saying this—I wonder why he doesn't just dispatch somebody to whack Fenny once and for all."

"I suspect he's considered it," I said. "But these people have strange ways and ideas. Remember the old movie *Once Upon a Time in the West?*"

"No."

"Well, at one point late in the film, the hero—Charles Bronson—shoots a few gunmen who were about to ambush his arch-enemy, Henry Fonda. Afterward, the woman who also wants Fonda dead accuses Bronson of saving his life. Bronson replies that he didn't let *them* kill him and that wasn't the same thing." I nodded to myself, remembering that scene. "I think Rooks feels that way, too. If he wants Knight to get whacked, he's honor-bound to do it himself."

"He seems more interested in writing his novel," D.J. said.

"It does seem so."

"You figure Knight feels that way, too? That he'll have to be the one to kill Annie? And, eventually, Marty?"

"I don't know. I can't seem to think the way they do. They're both warriors, these two. Rooks did two tours in Afghanistan, as—of all things—a sniper, and Knight won a string of medals in Vietnam. But I also know that whoever fired the warning shot at the house the other night wasn't Fenny. He'd be too old to move that fast, or to climb into a tree to clear a fence. I'm told he almost never leaves his house."

"So you said."

I heaved another sigh. "We got all kinds of unknowns going here."

"Focus on the car with the tracker," she said. "I bet that's the key to the mystery."

If there even *was* a mystery. Maybe things were really as they appeared, and we were grabbing at straws, or jumping at shadows, or whatever cliché fit the bill.

But my true love didn't think so, and that worried me. She was the brains of this partnership, and we both knew it.

#

After lunch I picked up a newspaper at a stand outside my office building, but wound up never looking at it. I had to finish up a background check for one of my other clients, and by the time I was done with that and played two quick (and painful) chess games on my phone with Boris and grabbed a burger across the street at five, it was time to report in for Night #22 at the Rookery. I took the newspaper along, folded under my arm like a spy.

All seemed to be well on the surveillance front, and after watching some back footage and checking in with Olivia to remind her about pulling the shades to all the windows—the broken one still hadn't been repaired—I shook out the paper and scanned the headlines. I hadn't watched or read any news for a week. The world appeared to be as gorked up as usual, and by the time I got to the sports page I was wondering why I'd bothered to buy the paper at all.

And then I saw it. An article on the last page of the main section titled VIETNAM VETERANS TO DEDICATE MONUMENT AT BRISCOE PARK. I flashed back to what D.J. had mentioned, and sure enough, one of the three participants would be James Fenimore Knight. The public was cordially invited, etc., etc.

I raised my eyes from the paper and stared blankly at the wall.

I'd lived and worked here for years, but on the east side of town, and had never heard of Briscoe Park. It was probably new. But in that moment I knew exactly where it had to be.

With flying fingers I again pulled up Google Maps. There it was, neatly labeled: Alton Briscoe Park. It was about two hundred yards from, and below, the spot where the car bearing my tracker had stopped, on those two nights. What was its driver doing there?

But I knew that also, as surely as I knew my name. He was surveying the killing ground. Checking the wind, the light, the cover. And, more than that, he was probably fine-tuning (sighting in, it was called) a rifle scope. At eight o'clock on both those nights, the park would've almost surely been deserted, a perfect setting for some long-range practice shots.

I looked back at the article. The ceremony would begin promptly at eight p.m.

Tonight.

I picked up my phone, opened the tracker app, and saw what I'd expected to see. The big Buick, blinking and on the move. Heading north.

Staring at the red dot, still wide-eyed, half a dozen thoughts zinged through my head. First, the dedication ceremony must've been planned and announced some time back, since D.J. had mentioned it more than three weeks ago. Which meant Rooks would've known about it, too. Second, Martin Rooks had been a sniper in the military. Third, and maybe most important, I had a feeling Rooks was at this moment not where he was supposed to be. Just as he'd not been there on those two other nights. Martin Rooks was the driver of the Buick.

To make sure of that, I rose from my chair, marched to his door, and tried the knob. Locked. I kicked it open and looked around the book-lined office. Empty. So was his bedroom.

I should've suspected this long ago. He'd told me there were secret passages throughout the house. One of them undoubtedly led from one of those "locked" basement doors, or the garage, up here to his suite of rooms and back again. If I had the time, I was sure I could locate the entrance/exit from this room—probably a swiveling section of wall or bookcase. That's how he was able to fire into Annie's room the other night from outside and then hustle unseen back upstairs to his room, stow his rifle, and go through to my office by the time I got back from running around the grounds. Again, I should've known. A warning shot? For what reason? The reason, I knew now, was to reassure me that there was really a threat. Even though there wasn't.

All these revelations ricocheted through my head in a matter of seconds. D.J. had been right all along. The whole deal—my employment, Rooks's need to isolate and write, Knight's note threatening

Annie's life—was a lie. I even knew, in a flash of sudden insight, *why he'd hired me*: Rooks knew he would need an alibi. A witness—me—from outside his organization who could swear that Martin Rooks had been right here in his rooms between the hours of six and ten every night for the past few weeks, including the evening of Fenimore Knight's murder.

I blinked and thought about that. Knight's murder.

I looked again at my phone. It was 7:35.

#

The following afternoon, I sat in my office across the desk from my fiancée. Between us on the desktop was a bottle of wine she'd brought, along with two paper cups. We hadn't opened the bottle yet. Both of us knew, without saying so, that the wine was to celebrate my return from the Dark Side. I couldn't help remembering the day almost a month earlier, when Marty Rooks sat there where D.J. was sitting.

I'd spent most of the morning answering questions at the police station, during which time D.J. was apparently a nervous wreck. She said her bosses finally told her at noon to take the afternoon off, so she had bought the wine and had come here and used her key to unlock my office and wait for me. I asked her if she'd gotten me any new clients in my absence.

"Are you gonna tell me what happened," she said, "or not?"

"I told you last night what happened."

"I mean with the police." She paused. "Are you okay?"

"Why wouldn't I be okay?"

She studied me for a long moment, then scooted her chair closer to the desk and leaned toward me. This, I had found, was the only problem with finally meeting the love of your life. They eventually come to know you better than you know yourself. "Tell me again," she said.

I exhaled a breath, rubbed my forehead awhile, and said, "When I saw the write-up in the paper and realized that this event, this rare public appearance by Fenny Knight, had been scheduled for a long time, I connected the park with the location I'd seen earlier on my tracking device, and I put the pieces together. Rooks planned the killing, hired me so he would have an ironclad alibi—which would be worth every penny of the two hundred grand—and did it well ahead of the fact so it wouldn't raise any suspicions afterward. It was all deception: Knight's threat, Rooks's seclusion in his room, the fake attack a few days ago. Everything except Annie and her illness and her caregiver; that was real and they're real. But Rooks cared nothing about her, and she'll be better off without him."

"So he's going to jail? For sure?"

"Oh yeah. And for a long time. He was on that road above the park, exactly where I told the cops he would be. Easiest confession they ever got."

"But in another way, they were too late," she said.

"Yeah, they were." Rooks had already shot Fenny Knight dead as a gatepost on the celebration stage, and was in the act of stowing the rifle in his trunk when the cavalry arrived. Subtract not one crime boss, but two.

D.J. leaned back again in her chair, but her eyes remained locked with mine. I knew something was coming.

"How long did you wait to report it?" she asked. "How long after you figured it out?"

I thought a moment before answering. I had lied about this to the cops, but there was no use lying to her, and besides, I didn't want to. "About twenty-five minutes," I said. "Maybe thirty. I stood there in Rooks's room and watched the red dot on my phone move north. When it stopped I went back to the security office, turned on the radio, found the broadcast for the event, and waited until they said the three veterans were taking the stage. Only then did I call it in." I paused, remembering. "I wasn't certain I'd guessed right on the timing, but I figured I was close. And sure enough, I'd given Rooks just enough time to make the shot but not enough to get away. Even if he'd left before the cops got there, they would've caught him on the way home. Since he thought he was safe, I doubt he'd have tried to ditch the murder weapon."

"So you made the conscious decision to give him enough time to kill Fenimore Knight."

I nodded again. "I did. Does that bother you?"

"Not a bit," she said. "The only thing I'm wondering is, how long have you known?"

"Known what?"

She gave me a hard look. "That Fenny Knight was the one who murdered your partner."

I turned and stared out my window awhile. It was cloudy today, no sun shining on the trees. That was okay. The view was good anyway.

Finally I faced her again and said, "I've known for a long time. Knight's M.O. was always one shot to the heart and one to the head, with the same kind of ammo they dug out of Benny's chest.

Besides, Knight bragged about it to one of our informants. Said Benny had become a threat. But Knight had the power and the lawyers and the witnesses, liars though they were, who swore he was someplace else at the time." I paused. "When did *you* find out?"

"This morning. One of the partners remembered the killing, and mentioned Ramirez's name. I've heard you talk about him a thousand times. Apparently it was common knowledge that Knight pulled the trigger, personally."

"Murder's always personal," I said.

"You know what I mean."

"I know. All I can tell you is, twenty hours ago Fenimore Knight got what he deserved."

We both fell silent then. At last she looked at the bottle and said, "Want to open it?"

"You're better at it than I am." I handed her a corkscrew from a desk drawer—my office is primitive but not ancient—and said, "We need dance music—did you bring a radio? Where I'm from, D.J. means disk jockey."

Ignoring me as she often does, she twisted the cork and said, "I guess the novel was a lie too. Correct?"

"Yep. Either that, or he had the world's worst case of writer's block. I took a look at his desk while I was in his office last night. No manuscripts, pages, outlines, notes, nothing. He was apparently *reading* a novel, though. Get this: *The Godfather.*"

"Too bad." She'd opened the bottle and was pouring. "The movie's better than the book."

"You're missing the point," I said. "Movies give you images you can't erase. With the book, Marty could probably picture himself in a lead role. Maybe his father was the don, and he was Michael. Or Sonny without the bullet holes."

"Maybe so." She sipped her wine, and I gulped mine. It wasn't bad. I savored the taste and tried to picture myself at a poolside bar underneath the swaying palms of Fiji, but it was hard to do in my uncomfortable chair with the A/C growling and farting.

On that subject, D.J. said, "I suppose this means you won't get paid."

"Afraid not. Since I was hired to provide an alibi and did pretty much the opposite, I think I'm on my own." I gave her a hangdog look. "Will you still marry me?"

"I guess. Tell me something romantic."

"Pass the wine," I said.

A TRIVIAL PURSUIT

The best thing about my office is its view of the park across the street. On nice days pretty young ladies often stroll past, and on days that are too hot or too cold for my iffy A/C and heating, I can look out my window and watch people who are even hotter or colder than I am.

Another plus is that there's free parking down there around the free park, and I can sometimes spot people from a distance who I suspect are on their way to visit me. If they happen to be creditors or salesmen or old enemies—I've made a few—that gives me time to lock up and hotfoot it down the stairs and out the back door.

Then again, I'm not always looking at the right moment.

"Hello, Tommy," a familiar voice said, from my open doorway.

In the way of background, my name's Tom Langford—Tommy to friends and family and Thomas to those reading the printed letters on my office door. The second line says PRIVATE INVES-TIGATOR. Some folks outside the business seem to think that's a romantic and mysterious line of work. Others, like my ex-wife, Charlotte, think it's a job you take when you've failed at more worthwhile endeavors. Before getting my license, I was a cop for several years, and while I don't consider my previous career a fail-ure, I do like this one better. At least I'm now my own boss, which Charlotte figures might also be a problem.

I once told her, while working my first case as a PI, that the slow time of the week at a bank is said to be from ten to eleven a.m. on Tuesdays. She replied that the slow time of the week for a small private-eye company must be from nine a.m. Monday to five p.m. Friday, since she hadn't noticed any busy times. That of course wasn't the only thing we disagreed on.

"Did I catch you at a busy time?" my visitor added.

"Hello, Charlotte," I said. I put down my iPhone and removed my feet from my desktop. "It's been awhile."

"But not long enough, right?" She smiled, took a look around, and made her way to one of the chairs on the other side of my desk. My office, I should mention, is small but primitive. Desk, three chairs, filing cabinet, ceiling fan. She studied the chair a moment, seemed to consider wiping the seat off, and sat anyway. She looked uncomfortable, but Charlotte always looks uncomfortable. It occurred to me that I should install one of those drop-through-the-floor-when-you-push-a-button chairs like one of the James Bond villains had in his conference room. Pointing to my phone, she said, "I see you've finally embraced technology."

"I play chess on it," I said.

"Against other players?"

"Against the computer. His name's Boris."

"Let me guess," she said. "Grand Master level."

"Dummy level. But today I've got him worried." Both of us smiled. Even awkward meetings should begin with a few pleasantries.

"So, how's Darla Jo?" she asked.

"Debra Jo. She's fine." Unlike Charlotte, I hadn't yet remarried, but Debra Jo Wells and I were well on our way. The two of them hadn't met yet, which was fine with me. I made it a point not to ask about Charlotte's new and wealthy husband. Why, I wonder, do they call them pleasantries? I took a breath and said, "To what do I owe this honor?"

She cleared her throat and shifted a bit in her chair. "I need your help."

That grabbed my attention. Charlotte had never asked me for anything—before, during, or after our marriage. She liked to be in complete control at all times. She also never apologized and never admitted a mistake. I remember discovering, after she left me, that she'd also left some personal items—jewelry, clothes, etc.—behind. When I called to inform her of that, she informed me that anything she hadn't taken with her she didn't want and didn't need. Like me.

"Did you hear me?" she asked.

"I heard you. How exactly do you need my help?"

"I'd like to engage your services." She took out a checkbook and held it up as if flashing a badge. "Professionally."

By now my mixed feelings were narrowing down to suspicion. "To do what?"

"To find a name," she said. "One of my husband's employees is selling trade secrets, about our business. Well, Trenton's business."

"Oh yes. Good old Trenton. He makes glue, right?"

She closed her eyes a moment, probably praying for patience. "Adhesive products," she said. "Tape, sealers, coatings, et cetera. You know that."

I pictured, just for a moment, smug and obnoxious Trenton

Carlisle with his wrists taped together and his mouth sealed shut and his ass glued to a tiny raft surrounded by crocodiles.

"What are you smiling about?" she asked.

"Nothing." I frowned and said, "What kind of secrets are we referring to?"

"I told you. Trade secrets. Confidential information about the company's products."

I let several seconds pass. Outside my window, rust-colored leaves fell gently from the oaks in the park. A horn honked in the street below.

Finally I said, honestly, "I think you're in the wrong pew, Charlotte. Industrial espionage—corporate espionage—is a crime. You should be talking to the police."

"Trenton doesn't want the police. He says there's nothing they can do." She took a breath, looked down at the hands folded on her checkbook, and raised her head again. "It's complicated, Tommy. Corporate espionage is usually tied to things like hacking or break-ins or wiretaps. In this case, someone's just passing along information to a competitor, and even if the cops caught him—or her—doing that, it'd be hard to prove and prosecute. It could be argued that it's more unethical than illegal." She leaned forward, pinning me with her gaze. "All Trenton wants is to stop it from happening. And he can do that if he knows who's behind it."

I did a palms-up. "I doubt I could find that out. I could keep an eye on some of the employees, see where they go and who they meet with—following folks is part of what I do. But I probably can't find out what was said, or revealed."

"You might not have to," she said.

"What do you mean?"

"Trenton thinks we have an ally in our ranks."

"What kind of ally?"

She leaned back, frowning as if choosing the right words. "He found a note on his desk the other day, when he got to work. It's sort of"—she paused—"a puzzle."

"A what?"

"Let me back up a little," she said. "Trenton thinks—and I think—somebody in his company is trying to help us and remain anonymous. We think this somebody knows who the spy is, and is trying to tell us in a roundabout way."

"Why roundabout? Why doesn't he just give you a name?"

"We don't know. Maybe whoever wrote the note is scared. Maybe he doesn't want to reveal anything outright. Maybe he wants to feel Trenton is clever enough to deserve the help."

I heaved a weary sigh. What did I do, I thought, to deserve *this*? "Let's say you do discover the spy's identity. What happens then?"

"Several choices. Confrontation, termination, maybe prosecution. Or maybe just keeping quiet and feeding them false information." She grinned a little. "I saw Captain Kirk do that once to the Klingons, when they were listening in on his plans. Remember showing me that episode?"

I was surprised *she* remembered. But I had to agree, the options sounded reasonable. I rewound to what she'd said earlier and asked, "What kind of puzzle are we talking about, here?"

"Well—puzzle might not be the right word. It's more of a riddle. In the form of a poem."

"Are you serious? You mean, like . . . a rhymed poem?"

"Yes."

"So you think the author is saying, 'Solve it and earn the prize, fail to solve it and lose?' Sorry, Charlotte, this sounds like something you really *would* see on TV—"

"Look," she said, again with the closed eyes, "I know how silly it sounds. But it's the only lead I have, okay? And I think you're one of the only people who can help us."

A long silence passed. My ceiling fan was beginning to squeak a little. I needed to oil it.

I found myself tempted to backpedal out of this, right now. But how? I couldn't very well say I was too busy. She'd been right, long ago, about my busy times. Clients weren't exactly lined up outside my door. There wouldn't be room out there for them anyway.

"One more question," I said. "And then I'll look at the poem." Dammit.

"Okay."

"Why are you so sure I'll be able to solve the riddle?"

"Because of the movies."

"The what?"

"In all my life," Charlotte said, "I've never known *any*one who knows as much as you do about movies and TV. Do you deny that?"

What could I say? I'd spent half my life in front of both the big and small screens, I owned thousands of DVDs, and if asked I could describe the kind of guns preferred by both the men from U.N.C.L.E., tell you how many bandits stormed the village in *The Magnificent Seven*, and name the nomad riding the third camel in the caravan in *The Mummy Returns.* Did I remember the episode Charlotte mentioned, of *Star Trek?* Hell, I remember *all* the episodes.

"Even so," I said, "what does my cinematic trivia knowledge have to do with anything?"

"It usually doesn't. I always thought it was stupid, wasting all that time gawking at make-believe when you could've been—" She stopped in midsentence and did a re-deal. "What I'm saying is, I think in this case you're especially suited to help me."

"Because of what's written in this note of yours."

"Yes."

"All right," I said. By now I was getting curious. "First, a little more about this spying. How many possible suspects are we talking about, here? Who has access to these vital secrets?"

"Only five people." Charlotte took a hand-printed list of names from her purse and handed it to me. "One of these employees has to be the information thief."

I put on my reading glasses and scanned the list:

HANNAH MEEKS – MANAGER, RESEARCH & DEVELOPMENT

GEORGE McVALE – SENIOR CHEMIST, RESEARCH & DEVELOPMENT

PHILIP HAYES – SUPERVISOR, QUALITY CONTROL

SARA HARPER – CHEMICAL ENGINEER, PRODUCT DEVELOPMENT

RANDALL MASTERSON – TEAM LEADER, PRODUCT TESTING

I looked up at her. "Any priorities here? Would any of these people have more access than the others, or be more likely or motivated to do something like this?"

"As for access, it's probably about the same for all of them. Plus Trenton, of course. As for most likely or most motivated, who knows? A couple of them are a little hard to get along with, but we thought they were all loyal. Apparently one isn't." After a moment she added: "I know for a fact that Phil Hayes and Randy Masterson have had some heated arguments with Trenton, and George McVale has been with the company only a few months."

I nodded, mulling that over and thinking, *As if Charlotte and*

Trenton aren't hard to get along with. "How do you know you can trust what this . . . anonymous ally says?"

"I don't know that. But, as I told you, it's all we have to go on."

I took a minute more to study the list of names and responsibilities.

"Okay," I said. "Let's see the note."

She took out another slip of paper and handed it over. It contained only four lines, typed.

The thief was a new man in movies, I've heard—
It starts with an H and is only one word.
In addition, the name of our disloyal friend
Sounds a bit like a place that was gone with the wind.

Weirder and weirder. But I felt myself thinking, to use a cliché I had come to hate, *It is what it is.* If this was all the info we had to work with, so be it. I had solved cases with less.

"This'll take some thought, Charlotte." I knew that was a little abrupt, but Charlotte would stay here all day if I let her, and I had a lunch date in half an hour. "I'll be in touch."

She sat there a moment more, looking at me. "So, you do think you can figure it out?"

"I'll figure it out."

She gave me a smile. "I'll say this for you, Tommy. You were never short on confidence."

Even when I was wrong, I thought—but I didn't mention that.

I also didn't watch her leave. I sat there listening to the hum of my ceiling fan and staring at the stupid poem and the list of suspects, and wondering what I'd gotten myself into.

#

Debra Jo Wells, who despite her trendy name was the most stabilizing thing in my life these days, was waiting for me outside our usual lunch spot, halfway between her place of business and mine. Inside, I steered her to a table apart from the most of the others, which told her right away that I wanted to discuss a case. As things turned out, she did too; D.J. was a paralegal at one of the downtown law firms, and loved it. Half our time seemed to be spent discussing crime and criminals. The difference was, I had to *solve* my cases, while she got paid no matter who won the legal battles. Also, she had to work with six criminals every day, in her office. Sorry, that's a little harsh.

After we'd ordered our usuals—a garden salad for D.J. and a lumberjack-sized burger for me—she gave me the details of the latest fiasco facing her distinguished employers. It was unusual, to say the least: the lawyers for the grandson of an elderly socialite named Hocksmidt had filed suit against the descendants of the producers of a 1902 Chicago stage play of *The Wizard of Oz*. According to the lawsuit, the dog that played Toto in the stage adaptation was badly mistreated by everyone in the production, and had later died in its owner's—Ms. Hocksmidt's mother's—arms. One of the long-ago actors was quoted as saying, "Who cares, it's just a damn dog."

I found myself wishing the waitress would hurry up with our food. "Keep going," I said.

"Well, the thing is, the sued dude is one of our firm's most valued and most demanding clients. The case sounds like a total waste of time, I know—but it's time my bosses will have to spend regardless."

I shrugged and said, "So what? Don't they charge by the hour?"

"Yes, but they have at least some scruples. This needs to be exposed as frivolous litigation, and dropped like a hot potato."

"Besides which, they don't want to become a laughingstock to their fellow attorneys." Like some of the personal-injury lawyers you see on TV, I thought.

"True," she said. "I can see it now: Local law firm becomes crusader for animal rights violations 120 years ago."

I groaned. "I think I remember now why I'm self-employed. At least the bad decisions and bad assignments are my own."

"There was a lot of Maalox being passed around in the office when I left." She shook her head. "Anyhow, that's my news. What's yours?"

By this time our waitress had brought us tall glasses of tea, and after I took a long swallow I said, "Mine's more of a riddle than a situation." For the next ten minutes I told her about the problem my new client had spelled out to me this morning, although I—wisely, I thought—neglected to mention Charlotte's name. In the visual-aids part of my briefing, I showed her the printed list of possible spies and the dazzling work of poetry the client's husband had found in the desk drawer in his office.

I loaned D.J. my reading glasses—the light was dim at our table—and watched her as she read the poem several times, and then the name list. She looked cute in my glasses. "This is wild," she said when she'd finished. "Industrial espionage?"

"Yep. That's a first, for me. So is getting a clue-filled puzzle from a hidden helper." I looked around at our fellow diners, who didn't seem to be listening, and said, "Any ideas?"

"A few." Her eyes were going back and forth now between the poem and the list of names. "The thief was 'a new man in movies'? 'New man' might point to one of the three males on the list. Right? Or specifically to McVale, who you said hasn't been with the company long."

"Could be." I wanted to give her time to brainstorm a bit.

"And this second line: 'It starts with an H and is only one word.' I'm guessing 'it' refers to a movie title. A one-word title beginning with H."

That much, I figured, was correct. "Go on."

She took out her phone, tapped a few commands, and said, "Google shows dozens of those. The best-known are—let's see—*Halloween, Hondo, Hidalgo, Holes, Hannibal, Hook, Highlander, Houdini, Hairspray, Hoosiers, Harvey, Hud*—"

"*Hud*," I said. "I saw that when I was a kid. Sort of a Western without gunfights."

"So?"

"It starred Paul Newman."

"*So?*" she said again.

"Maybe *that's* what 'new man' means."

D.J. blinked and nodded. "That's possible."

I stared into my tea glass, deep in thought. I could feel her eyes on me.

"Also," I said, "Newman was in *Hombre*. A Western *with* gunfights."

She was nodding in earnest now, like one of those dunking-bird toys. "Paul Newman," she said, warming to the idea, "and two movies with one-word titles that start with H. That makes sense."

Our food arrived. She ignored hers, but I dug in. Chewing, I said, "How would either *Hud* or *Hombre* tie in with one of the five suspects' names?"

D.J. studied the list for a few minutes, lips moving as she silently read each one. "I don't know. '*Hombre*' is Spanish for 'man,' right? Maybe it really is one of the three males."

"Maybe. That still wouldn't narrow it down enough." I pointed to the poem. "How about this other part? 'Sounds like a place that was gone with the wind'? Any thoughts on that?"

"Well . . . the name 'George' sounds like 'Georgia,'" she said. "And 'Hannah' rhymes with 'Atlanta.' Those were places in *Gone with the Wind.*"

I took another bite of my Paul Bunyan Burger. "Those seem pretty farfetched."

"I agree. But I think it's close."

"I do, too." A long silence passed, and nothing useful came to mind, for either of us. Finally she gave in and picked at her salad awhile. I was already done with my hamburger and was mopping up ketchup with the last of my fries.

"Sorry I'm not more help," she said. "Guess my mind's still on that Wizard of Oz thing." She looked at her watch and waved to the waitress for a doggy-bag . "I better get back."

"Me, too." I refolded the list and poem, stuck them into my pocket, and said, "By the way—you can tell your lawyer bosses they won't need to pursue that case."

"What do you mean?"

"I mean the guy doing the suing—I love these rhymes—is full of Toto poop."

She blinked. "What?"

"In the 1902 stage version, Dorothy didn't have a dog. She had a pet cow named Imogene."

She sat up straight in her seat. "Are you kidding? This sounds like kidding."

"Dead serious. Your guys would find it eventually anyhow, but this'll save time. In fact it should keep them from having to get involved at all." I wiped my hands and put some bills on the table. "The play opened at, I think, Chicago's Grand Opera House sometime in 1902 and moved to Broadway in '03. It's the only adaptation I know of that didn't use a dog."

Her eyes widened as that sank in. "My God."

"You can call me Tom," I said.

#

All the way back to the office—it's not a long walk—I thought about the list and the mysterious verses of the poem. The answer to all this really was close; I could feel it. I kept replaying those one-word movie titles in my head. And that question about a place in *GWTW*. Maybe "George" or "Hannah" was correct . . . but I didn't think so.

I stomped up the flight of stairs to my office, switched on the fan, and stood by the window. Some of my best ideas came from the always-soothing view outside my window.

My mind kept drifting back to the line about single-word titles. If there was a key, that was it. The sound-alike clue would be secondary. More of a confirmation.

For a long time I stood there motionless, adrift in my thoughts. The sun was bright on the autumn-tinted trees, but it had moved well into the afternoon side of the sky now, which didn't help the temperature in my office. Even so, there was a steady breeze through the open window, and my ceiling fan was trying its best. Below me, a noisy truck rattled past. Somewhere in the park across the road, a child laughed. A dog woofed. He sounded way bigger than Toto.

And then it happened. The answer came to me with no warning, out of the blue. I was surprised I hadn't seen it sooner. *Newman had done three movies—not two—whose titles begin with H.* After that, it took me only seconds to connect that to *Gone with the Wind.*

I knew who the information thief was.

Smiling, I took out my cell phone to call D.J., but before I could hit her speed-dial the phone buzzed in my hand. It was Charlotte.

"Where are you, right now?" I asked her.

"What? Just down the street from you. Jeaneane's Boutique."

I'd never heard of it, which wasn't surprising. "Come up to the office," I said.

She wasted no time getting here, and probably knew as soon as she saw me that I had good news. I let her sit down first, then said, "I think I know who your spy is. Or at least who the informant—the author of the riddle—thinks your spy is."

Charlotte looked down at the poem and the name-list that I'd put on the desktop between us, then up again at me. "Well? Who is it?"

"Sara Harper."

For a moment she didn't reply. Then: "Sara? The chem E.?"

"Her name fits. And it's the only one that does. " I pointed to the poem. "It finally occurred to me: Paul Newman—'new man'—starred in three movies that had one-word 'H' titles. *Hud* in 1963, *Hombre* in '67. . . and *Harper* in '66. Believe it or not, Harper was a down-on-his-luck private investigator."

Charlotte stared bug-eyed at me, transfixed.

"And the clincher," I said, pointing now to the name list, "is the second part. The word Sara rhymes with Tara, which is—"

Her eyes got even bigger. "Scarlett O'Hara's plantation."

"Yep. Which covers all the bases."

Very slowly, she nodded. "Sara Harper."

"Only if your Good Samaritan poet is right," I said. "But I have a feeling he is."

"I do, too." She looked dazed. "This is just what we needed. Trenton can control this now, stop it in its tracks. It can save the company." She blinked and focused on me. "Sara Harper. You did it, Tommy."

I spread my hands. "What can I say? I knew this kind of expertise would one day be good for something."

"And worth something, too," she said. She flipped her checkbook open and took a ballpoint pen from her purse. "How much do I—"

I raised a hand. "It's on the house." I picked up both pieces of paper and gave them to her. "This was more fun than chess with Boris anyway."

"But—well, no offense, but . . ." Charlotte waved a hand at the simple surroundings. "You could use the money."

I shook my head. "I'm doing fine. Lately there seem to be more bad marriages"—*like hers and mine*, I thought—"and that means more following the hubby or missus around with a camera." I held up my iPhone. "This thing has a lot of uses."

Before she could reply I heard footsteps on the stairs, and wondered who else might've slipped past my surveillance. Probably the IRS. I really needed to move my desk closer to the window.

The visitor this time turned out to be D.J. She breezed into the office without knocking, said, "You forgot your reading glasses—" and then stopped dead. As the two women looked each other up and down, I made awkward introductions and they shook hands and smiled in a way that I couldn't begin to decipher, which was probably for the best.

I did see, however, that Charlotte had noticed the engagement ring I'd given D.J. some time ago, a ring that I couldn't afford but had acquired via a strange case involving a dimwitted jewel thief, a red Mustang, and a one-eared dog with intestinal problems, but that's another story. Charlotte made no comment, and moments later she thanked me again, pocketed her checkbook, hitched her purse over her shoulder, and shook hands once more with D.J.

Well, I said to myself. That was fairly pleasant. I had expected either a hair-pulling, a necklace strangling, or a nail-file stabbing. Maybe I wasn't as big a prize as I'd thought.

"Nice to see you again, Charlotte," I said.

She was still looking at my fiancée, and both were smiling. "It's a great pleasure to meet you, Donna Jo."

"Debra Jo."

Then Charlotte paused.

"Are those my earrings?" she asked.

OVERLOOKED

It had the makings of a good day. It was sunny and warm, my rent was paid, I was caught up on paperwork, and the humidity was so low I had my office window open, something you don't see much anymore. I'd even beaten my computerized opponent, Boris, in a game of chess on my iPhone. I admit I'd asked him to let me replay several moves, and the skill level was set to "Idiot"—that's just below "Fool"—but a win is a win. All seemed to be well in my world.

Then Al Ratzen walked in.

Ratzen was a character from my past, specifically from my days as Homicide Detective Thomas Langford, and our relationship had never been pleasant. Neither was the look on his face. I assumed he was still on the force, and that the guy who walked in with him was, too. Cops, at least to criminals and fellow policemen, look like cops. One thing was interesting, though. I'm a film nut, and in movies and TV, anytime you're confronted with two members of law enforcement, one's short and one's tall. Both these dudes were giants, at least six-five. "Let me guess," I said. "You're recruiting for the basketball team."

"I don't remember you being a team player, at anything," Ratzen said, dropping into one of the chairs facing my desk. "Is that why you became a PI?"

He was more right than he realized. I've always liked the word *private* in *private investigator.* "I don't think I've met your twin," I said.

"Andrews," the second guy growled, folding himself into the other chair. Maybe this was the "bad cop/bad cop" routine.

"Please," I said to them, "have a seat." Neither seemed to think that was funny. "What can I do for you?"

Ratzen looked the office over and focused on me. "Ever had a client named George Willard?"

"Come on, Al. You know I can't reveal the names of clients."

"You can this time. He's dead."

That got my attention. I hadn't known Willard well, only as an employer for several weeks last spring, but it was long enough for me to feel both regret and surprise at this news. The surprise was mostly that his death would interest the police. George Willard was an accountant, one of the most boring and safe and low-profile occupations on earth, unless you kept the books for the mob. Which George hadn't. It took me several seconds to gather my thoughts and ask the logical follow-up question.

"How'd he die?"

"Suicide, looks like. Or an accident. Fell off a cliff west of town, called the Overlook. He and his wife were out camping, last night. We found your business card in his wallet." Ratzen studied me a moment. "Answer my question, Langford. Was he a client of yours?"

"He was. A few months ago."

"We've talked to his wife—Alice. She didn't recognize your name."

"I'm sure he never mentioned it to her."

"Why's that?"

"He hired me to find out if she was cheating on him."

That seemed to take the Rat by surprise. After a pause he said, "How'd that turn out?"

"She wasn't. She's a real estate agent, so I agreed she couldn't be trusted, but she was Little Miss Sunshine for the seven weeks that he engaged my services." I shrugged. "He was pleased, I got paid, end of story."

My two visitors seemed to think that over. At last Ratzen said, "Anything else you can tell us, about either of them?"

"Don't know anything else. I met Willard only once, at his home, and I updated him by phone once a week afterward until the job was done. His wife wasn't home at the time. I never met her."

"You just followed her for seven weeks."

"That's right. You boys protect and serve, I inspect and observe."

A silence passed, during which I wondered what they weren't telling me, about all this. After a little more staring at each other I decided I'd had enough.

"If it was suicide, or an accident," I said, "why are you here? What's to investigate?"

Neither of them liked that. I could tell because they both suddenly looked as if they were trying to pass kidney stones. "We'll ask the questions," Andrews said.

Apparently, though, they had run out of questions, and were as tired of me as I was of them. "Call us if you think of anything," the Rat said. Without another word he stood and marched to the door. Andrews followed him. They both turned, gave me a parting glare, and left.

Just another happy meeting between cops and private eyes. But this morning's visit had been especially strange.

I smelled a rodent, and it wasn't just Ratzen.

#

Fortunately, the next two people I talked with—Robbie Robertson and Debra Jo Wells—*did* like private investigators, or at least this one. Robbie was an old pal on the police force and D.J. was my current love interest, who I guess was my permanent love interest since we were engaged to be married. My phone call to Robbie was to ask if he knew anything about the death of a George Willard (he didn't) and to ask him to find out about it and tell me (he said he would). My call to D.J. was to ask if we were still on for lunch. Both conversations did a lot toward overcoming my bad mood, and by the time noon rolled around I was practically cheery.

"I had a good morning," I said to her, "except for Starsky and Hutch."

Debra Jo looked up from her salad. "You should probably be glad they stopped by. Otherwise you wouldn't even know about this Mr. Willard."

"I wish I still didn't." But since I did, I wanted the straight story, about his death. He'd seemed like a good guy, to me.

At that moment, as if summoned, my cell phone vibrated in my pocket. I took it out, checked the display, said to D.J., "It's Robbie," and listened for the next several minutes. I even took out a pad and pen and made some notes. When I disconnected, she was watching me and obviously waiting for a briefing. On the one hand, I was always amazed at Debra Jo Wells's love for investigative matters of any kind, but on the other, I figured it was appropriate: she was a paralegal for a firm of criminal lawyers. Which I'd once told her was a redundant term.

Anyhow, I gave her my summary, between bites of cheeseburger. According to Robbie, the call had come in early this morning: Mrs. Alice Willard said she and her husband were camping in Overlook Park when she woke up to find her husband George missing from their tent. She went outside looking for him, still talking to the policeman on the phone, and when she peeked over the edge of a nearby cliff, she saw her husband's body lying on the rocks at the bottom. Later, after several cops and the meatwagon crew arrived at the scene and hiked down into the gully to recover the body, and after Mrs. Willard had time to recover her own body from shock and grief, she tearfully told Ratzen and Andrews about what had happened beforehand.

At this point things got detailed, and I consulted my scrawled and mayo-stained notes. Mrs. Willard, I read to D.J., said her husband suffered from agoraphobia—a fear of large, open spaces—but had made steady progress for months, to the point that he could now approach and stand at the edge of a drop-off like the one near their campsite—which he did, late yesterday afternoon—and not be bothered by it. On an impulse, she said, he had decided to declare himself cured of that disorder and throw away the pills he took every night to treat it, and he even went back to their tent to fetch the pill bottle and dump its contents dramatically over the cliff. Then the two of them had returned to their tent and ate the sandwiches they'd brought along for supper. She said they played cards afterward, George took his other medicine as usual before going to bed, and they turned in fairly early. Around seven this morning she woke up to discover he was missing. That's when she called the police.

I pocketed my notepad, took another chomp of my burger, and said, chewing, "You see anything odd about that report?"

D.J. stared back at me. "What part of it? The whole thing sounds strange, to me."

"Okay. Why would she bother to tell the police all that, about his medical condition and the pills he took for it, and his thrill at overcoming it? What does that have to do with anything?"

"I don't know," she said. "Unless she was just reporting every-thing, no matter how trivial. Don't *you* tell interview subjects to do that? But there's another possibility: Maybe she wanted to convince them it was an accident and not suicide. I mean, if her husband was so pleased with having beaten this crippling disorder of his, why would he then take his own life?"

"Good thought. Also, whatever life insurance he had probably wouldn't be payable after a suicide."

"What a suspicious mind you have. I was thinking the same thing." D.J. seemed to consider all that, then said, "What did she mean by 'took his *other* medicine'?"

"Beats me." I felt, even more than before, that the whole story had a fishy aroma. "By the way," I said, having saved the best till last, "Robbie said there was an eyewitness."

This brought D.J.'s eyebrows up. "To Willard's death?"

"Not exactly. To those events I just told you about, in the hours before he died." I hesitated, getting my thoughts straight, and said, "This witness—an older lady—called in this morning to report a 'suspicious incident' she'd seen just before dark last night, and the sergeant who took the call was the same one who, less than an hour earlier, had taken Mrs. Willard's call. This second woman was later visited and questioned by Ratzen and Andrews, after they'd been to the Willard home and—apparently—just before they came to my office. Anyhow, they clammed up after that, and Robbie doesn't know what they might've learned from the witness." I paused again. "He was able, though, to give me the other woman's name, and said she was a retired and widowed employee of the state Department of Motor Vehicles—but he didn't have her contact information." I took another bite of my neglected burger and added, "I bet you ten bucks that what this witness saw would explain some things."

D.J. sat there nibbling on her lettuce like a rabbit. "But I guess you'll never know what she saw. Right?"

"Wrong," I said. "I'll know when I talk to her."

"How will you do that? You said you don't have her address or her phone number."

"I don't. But I have a well-connected, computer-whiz girlfriend who could find those things out for me."

"Is that so." D.J. leaned back with a sly smile. "Who exactly is this woman?"

"The witness?"

"The girlfriend."

#

Back at the Den of Iniquity, which was what I called the offices of her destroyer-lawyer employers, my wisecracking fiancée was indeed able to locate the phone number and home address of our eyewitness, a Ms. Frances Elkins. She didn't tell me how she managed to get hold of the records of retired DMV workers, and I didn't ask. What I did do was call Ms. Elkins and make a four-o'clock appointment to come talk with her about the George Willard tragedy.

I arrived at her suburban home at four on the dot and was politely invited into a small and neat sitting room. She lived alone, she said, except for two cats that then received introductions as if they were family members. I introduced myself (to her, not to the cats) as Detective Tom Langford, which was true, I suppose, depending on how broadminded you happen to be, and told her I had personally known the late George Willard and wanted to confirm some of the things she'd discussed with my two colleagues (fingers were crossed behind my back when I said that) who had questioned her earlier today. She readily agreed, told me to call her Fran, which I had no intention of doing, and turned out to be the perfect subject for an interview: calm but not bored, helpful but not overeager, intelligent but not uppity.

"About this time yesterday," she began, "my sister Joanie and I went fishing—we do that a lot since both of us are retired. We left my car at a camping area at a scenic park on Union Road not far from town, and hiked a quarter mile to our favorite fishing spot, on Silver Creek. We stayed a couple hours, until just before sundown. After we came back to the car with our catch, I remembered I'd left my Igloo cooler on the creek bank and walked back, alone, to fetch it. On the way I happened to notice a tent pitched between the woods and the cliff they call the Overlook, and I also saw an older man, sixty or so, standing at the edge of the drop-off and staring out at the view. None of this was particularly interesting, I guess, except that I then saw a woman behind him, walking slowly up to him with her knees bent and her hands raised in front of her and her palms out, as if . . ." She stopped, and frowned.

"As if?" I said.

"As if she was going to push him." She shook her head. "I can't be sure of it, but that was my first thought. There's a big gully down below, probably fifty feet deep."

"Go on," I said.

"Well . . . I just stood there a moment in the shadows of the trees, frozen, not wanting to believe what I was seeing. And then suddenly, as I watched, the man turned around, looking pleased about something, and the woman approaching him quick dropped her hands and stood up straight. He said something to her, but I was upwind and a ways off, so I couldn't hear what was said. Then the woman turned, too, as casual as could be, and walked to the tent about thirty feet away. She stayed in there a long time, then came back outside, walked to the man, and handed him something that looked like a little plastic pill bottle, the ones you get from the drugstore."

"Are you sure about that?" I asked. "How far away *were* you?"

"Maybe forty or fifty feet. And yes, I'm sure. I might be old but there was still plenty of light and my eyesight's good."

"Of course. Please, continue."

She swallowed and said, "Well . . . he opened the little bottle, grinned like he was proud of himself, and poured something out of it, over the cliff. Then the two of them hugged and walked together back to their campsite."

"Did they see you?"

"I don't know. I don't think the woman ever looked in my direction."

"And that was it?" I said.

Ms. Elkins nodded. "That was it. I let out a breath I'd been holding and went on down to the creek to get my cooler and walked back to the car—it was darker then, and I noticed there was a light inside their tent—and I drove Joanie to her house and went home myself to eat supper. But later that night . . . what I'd seen really bothered me. I had the feeling that man had barely missed getting himself murdered. As for the deal with the medicine bottle, I couldn't figure that part out. Still can't."

Both of us stayed silent a moment. Finally I said, "Did you tell all this to the two detectives who visited you this morning?"

"Yes." Then she added, "The thing is . . . I did nothing about it last night, Mr. Langford. They told me what happened to that poor man. If I had called the police then to report what I saw, instead of waiting until this morning, maybe—"

"I doubt the police would've done anything at that point, Ms. Elkins. What could they do? And even if your call somehow kept the guy from dying—well, if the wife really did have deadly intentions, I suspect she would've eventually found a way to do him in. And nobody saw what happened overnight. It might've truly been an accident. Or a suicide."

"But—you agree there's a possibility she did it? That she killed her husband?"

I sighed. "Well . . . somehow I can't picture them walking back to the cliff in the dark, or him walking back and her sneaking up again behind him, or her knocking him unconscious and dragging him out and rolling him over the edge. Can you?"

"No. I can't." Something like relief crossed her face. "Maybe there's a perfectly innocent answer to all this."

Somehow I knew there wasn't, and I think she knew it too. I now had more doubts than ever. I let a few seconds pass, then I stood up and said, "Either way, I appreciate your time."

Frances Elkins walked me to the door. As I turned to leave, she said, "You're not with the police at all, are you."

I looked at her, and she was smiling a little. I decided I really liked this lady.

"I used to be," I said. "Now I'm just a concerned citizen. Like you."

"So you're working on this for free."

"'Fraid so."

She seemed to give that some thought. "And you're not going to let it go. Right?"

I didn't reply. Both our faces had turned solemn now.

"Don't let it go," she said.

#

Supper was at D.J.'s apartment, and although she asked me about the case as soon as I arrived, we didn't discuss it until afterward in the living room, cuddled up on the couch and waiting for a TV movie to start. (Actually a real movie, *Casablanca*, that was being broadcast for probably the thousandth time. But neither of us ever tired of watching Bogie and Bergman, or listening to the music.)

Ten minutes later, when I'd finished briefing her on the new info from Frances Elkins and she'd thought about it awhile, D.J. said, "Two things jump out at me, from all this. First, I think we now know the reason Alice Willard told the two cops all that stuff about the medicine bottle. She must've spotted Ms. Elkins watching her from the trees."

"I had the same thought. Alice might've figured that, just in case this stranger happened to see her sneaking up on George earlier, she'd look more credible if she told the cops the medicine-bottle part of the story as well, and gave it a positive slant." After a few seconds I said, "Not that it sounded all that negative—but it did sound strange."

"And the second thing is, Alice told the cops her *husband* had gone to the tent to get his bottle of pills. Ms. Elkins told you she saw *Alice* go to the tent—not George—and that Alice stayed awhile in there before bringing it out."

"That's right," I said. "Direct contradiction."

D.J. stayed silent a minute, then said, "One thing we haven't talked about's the fact that George suspected his wife of an affair awhile back, so much so that he hired you to investigate her. Does that tie into all this?"

"I'm not sure. All I know is, the only traveling Alice did when I was tailing her was local, and I was satisfied there were no trysts or secret liaisons going on. Maybe George was just beginning to sense something was amiss, and was looking at the wrong reasons for it."

"And maybe she was dissatisfied with him or with marriage or whatever. Maybe she was starting to think of getting rid of him, even back then." Neither of us spoke for a time, and I felt her snuggle deeper into my shoulder. Finally she said, "I think you were dead right to be suspicious, Tommy. I believe this woman killed her husband last night."

"I do too. But if that's true . . . how'd she do it?"

We both fell silent then. On the TV, the movie was in progress, and the customers in Rick's Place were quiet too, even though their lips were moving. D.J. had muted the sound.

"This medical thing," I said, "bothers me. This business about overcoming the phobia and celebrating by pouring out the pills that treat it—it's odd, yes, but it's believable, mainly because Frances Elkins saw it also. But there must be more to it. Something we've overlooked."

"Or didn't know about to begin with," she said. "Did it occur to you that all this, every bit of it, is secondhand information?"

"Not all of it. I have one advantage: I did know the victim. I even visited his house the day he hired me. And he was talkative, too—told me things about himself that I didn't need or want to know, things that might be meaningful now, if I could just recall it all."

"What kind of things? Try to remember."

Actually I'd already tried, but the truth is, some of what Willard told me months ago had gone in one ear and out the other. At the time I was more interested in what he said about his wife, and what I would need to know to get the job done.

"I do remember he boasted about his health," I said. "He told me he had only two medical conditions—the agoraphobia was one—and that neither was serious, which at his age was an unusual thing."

"Two conditions? What was the other?"

"He didn't say. Just that he was lucky to be as fit as he was, for sixty-one." As it occurred to me, I said, "Robbie told me Mrs. Willard mentioned something related to that also—you and I talked about it, remember? She said her husband took 'his other medicine' before going to bed. What other medicine?"

"Something to treat that other condition, I guess." D.J. frowned and said, "I think that could be important. What else did George Willard tell you, that day you took the contract?"

"Well . . . he mentioned that he rarely ever left the house, because of the fear-of-open-spaces deal. Said his wife was often away on trips, and because of that they had hired—"

I stopped in midsentence. This was something I *hadn't* thought about before. I felt a funny little tingle, in my spine.

"He said they had hired a lady to come in every day, to help out.

Rosa, I think, or Rosie. Technically she did housecleaning, he said, but when Alice was gone this woman also ran errands for him, to the dry cleaners, post office, pharmacy. . . ." I stopped again, and looked D.J. in the eye. "The pharmacy. To fill his prescriptions."

She sat up straight. "You have to get in touch with this housekeeper, Tommy. If you don't—and I know the HIPAA rules—you can't access medical records, even those of the deceased, without the signed consent of the patient or a relative."

"Get in touch how? I don't even know her name."

"But you know she worked at the Willard home. She probably still does—George has been dead less than a full day. If you could call there when Alice Willard's not around . . ." She brightened and said, "Wait, you know Alice's schedule, right? You shadowed her for almost two months—"

"I knew her normal schedule. But, like you said, her spouse just died. She could be anywhere at any time, from her house to her office to the funeral home to the police station."

"Try it anyway. Call the house tomorrow morning, with one of your burner phones."

"How do you know about burner phones?"

She snorted. "I watch TV, that's how. I mean, you're a PI, right? Are you going to try to tell me you don't have one or two throwaways stashed in your office?"

"I'm going to try to tell you to stop snooping around in my desk drawers when I'm not looking." But her idea about calling the maid was a good one. I sighed and turned to check the TV, where Peter Lorre had burst through a door and was having a frantic but silent gunfight with the police. "Turn the sound back on. Let's forget this for a while and watch the movie."

"Okay." She relaxed a bit, and cuddled close again. "But call her in the morning."

#

I did, around 9:45. I hated to wait that late, but I had a feeling Alice Willard was a late sleeper, dead husband or not, and I wanted to improve my chances of avoiding her. Finally I made the call, and—wonder of wonders—a young woman's accented voice answered.

"Hello—Willard residence."

"Is this Mrs. Willard?" I asked, knowing it wasn't.

"I am Rosita. Miss Alice not home, at the moment. May I take message?"

"Actually, you might be able to help me. This is Rick Blaine, at Mr. Willard's pharmacy. I just received word of the tragedy, and I've been asked to cancel his prescriptions. Could you verify for me which medications he was currently taking?" I shut my eyes, thinking this was the biggest load of bullshit I'd ever heard. No drugstore would contact someone after her spouse's death and say this. But what did I have to lose?

"I can do that," she said. "I am the one who picked up his medicine, every month."

Hallelujah. "What I need are medication names and dosages, Rosita. Could you give me those?" I grabbed a notepad.

"Sure—let me see . . . Two medicines, refilled once every month. First is Sertraline, one pill by mouth before sleep, for something called . . . ack . . . ack . . ."

"Agoraphobia?"

"That is it." She paused then, and I could hear a gulp and a sniffle. "Oh, that poor man." Then she took a shaky breath and said, "Other medicine is Estrazolam, also take one pill just before bedtime, they tell me it is for some nambulism. I do not know which one."

Nambulism? I was writing like mad. I checked the spellings of both medicines and thanked her sincerely. Why couldn't all my informants be this helpful?

I spent the next half-hour on Google, digging up all I could about these two kinds of pills. Sertraline, I found, had been proven effective in controlling and preventing panic attacks, which were apparently direct links to this fear of open/outdoor spaces. And Estrazolam was a sort of sedative that helped users fall asleep easier and stay asleep longer. I felt a bit of a letdown. Was this "other" medication no more than a sleeping pill? Was I barking up the wrong pine tree?

I went back over what I'd heard from Rosita and from Ms. Elkins, and I thought about Alice going back to the tent to fetch the bottle, and staying an unusually long time in there—

And it hit me. It happens that way sometimes, when you have a headful of all these little pieces of the puzzle but they won't fit together, and then suddenly the clouds part and the sun blazes through and you can see everything, the whole completed picture, as clear as crystal.

I knew what had happened to George Willard.

I picked up my phone, the real one this time, and called Robbie Robertson. "Lunchtime," I said.

"It's ten-thirty."

"Doesn't matter. O'Dette's, on East Main. Meet me there."

#

Twenty minutes later we were sitting in a back corner booth, staring at each other instead of our menus. "Okay," Robbie said. "What's so important?"

"First, tell me what's happening, on the Willard investigation."

"What's happening? Nothing. I sit in the cubicle next to Ratzen and hear almost everything he says, and I can tell you the case is practically closed. This morning he got the coroner's full report, and Willard's body had no knife wounds or gunshot wounds or any traces of poison in his system. And he was too big to have easily been a pushover, if you get my off-the-cliff humor. The man must've slipped and fallen, period. Both Ratzen and Andrews agree that the witness was wrong in her suspicions, and that the incident was—in the absence of a suicide note or evidence of depression, et cetera—a tragic but simple one-person accident."

"In which case, Mrs. Willard would collect on the life insurance."

"Yep." Robbie paused and said, "So what's your 'important' news?"

"She killed him," I said. "It wasn't an accident *or* suicide."

He sat back and gaped at me. "You're serious?"

"Yep. It was murder."

"Premeditated?"

"Not for long. Sweet Alice is a quick thinker. But yes, premeditated."

"Okay," he said, "let's hear it."

I first gave him all the backstory: my Frances Elkins interview, my and D.J.'s deliberations, my long-ago PI/client discussions with George Willard, my phone call to the housekeeper, my research into disorders and their treatment, etc. And with all that in mind . . .

"Here's what I think happened," I said. "Picture this. After a planned and barely missed opportunity for Alice Willard to shove her hubby into the next life, she listens impatiently to his announcement that he's now cured of his wide-open-spaces phobia and that he wants to jettison his pills to celebrate his victory, and—brainstorm!—she decides she might have another chance at murdering him. She—*not* George, as she told Ratzen and Andrews—goes back to the tent, supposedly to fetch the medicine George has told her he wants to throw away because he doesn't need it anymore.

But there isn't just one bottle of pills in the tent. There are two. Remember when Mrs. Willard mentioned 'his other medicine' to the interviewers, and I told you that he said he had a second medical condition? Well, when she goes into the tent and out of George's sight she *switches the medicines in the two bottles.* That's why she spends what Frances Elkins thought was a suspiciously long time in the tent. I think Alice pours the pills he asked for—the Sertraline, for the agoraphobia—out onto one of the sleeping bags or into her hand or someplace, and puts the other pills—the Estrazolam, which must've looked a lot like the Sertraline—into the Sertraline bottle. Then she puts the Sertraline pills into the Estrazolam bottle and leaves it there beside his sleeping bag or wherever it was. After that, she takes the bottle labeled Sertraline—the right bottle containing the wrong pills—back out to George. (It won't matter, now, if he happens to take a look at the label.) He empties the pills theatrically over the cliff, and later that night, just before they go to bed, either in the dark or in dim light, he as usual swallows a pill from the Estrazolam bottle, which now contains the Sertraline pills because Alice switched the contents."

Robbie stared at me awhile, then said, "Let me get this straight. His death didn't happen because of the medicine he took, at bedtime. . . ."

"Right. It happened because he didn't take the medicine he needed. Because he didn't have it anymore."

Another silence. "Then the big question is," Robbie said, "how did not taking what he needed . . . cause his death?"

"Because of the condition it was designed to treat. The housekeeper told me the Estrazolam was for some kind of 'nambulism.' "

"And . . ."

"She must've misunderstood the term. It wasn't 'some' nambulism. It was *somnambulism.* Also known as somnambulation."

"What?"

"Sleepwalking," I said. "The pills George no longer had, because he'd unknowingly emptied them out, prevented him from sleepwalking. His wife had made sure that before going to bed that night, he took one of the *other* pills. . . ."

"So he *did* sleepwalk," Robbie said.

"Right. In fact, right over the cliff. I wonder, now, if Alice might've even been the one to suggest they pitch the tent so close to the edge."

For a long time, neither of us spoke a word. At last Robbie said, "How can I prove this?"

"That, I don't know. But if you bring Alice Willard back in for questioning, along with Ms. Elkins, who witnessed what happened outside the tent, and you point out the holes in Alice's story and accuse her directly of doing exactly what I just told you she did . . . it'd be interesting to see her reaction. I think she'll crack, and spill everything. If she doesn't, threaten her with a polygraph, or whatever it takes—and while you're at it, find out how much life insurance her husband had. My investigation in April and May proved, as best I could, that Alice Willard wasn't cheating on her husband at the time, so I doubt that'd be a reason for murdering him—but a big insurance payout might be. Also, the fact that he hired me to watch her at least implies a less-than-ideal marriage." Another thought popped into my mind, and I said, "You might even want to search for any pills in the rocks and grass in the gully below the Overlook, where the body was found. If they're still intact and can be analyzed, the lab'll find that they're Estrazolam, not Sertraline. And the opposite will be true for the pills in the other bottle, if they're still there."

He nodded slowly, taking all this in. "Understood," he said. A waitress finally appeared, and both of us ordered. Robbie, a man after my own heart, chose a burger with onion rings, and I ordered fried chicken, extra greasy. When she'd left, he said, "You know, of course, that this is still Ratzen's case—you should've given this information to *him*. Why didn't you?"

"Well, first, I don't like him. Second, you're my buddy. And third, if all this can be proven, you might get promoted. I need big-shot friends on the force, not pipsqueaks like you."

"Ha. But you still haven't told me how you figured it all out. It was Debra Jo, right?"

"She does make a good Dr. Watson," I said.

"I think it's the other way around. Have I told you that I've decided you're marrying way above your station?"

"Many times. And since you're so smart, I think you should pay for lunch."

"What a buddy," he said.

#

A week later, Debra Jo and I were sitting in the noonday sun in an outdoor amphitheater near her office building, watching a ballet performance, of all things. To be honest, I wasn't doing a lot of watching. I was reading an article in today's paper, titled LOCAL REALTOR CHARGED IN DEATH OF HUSBAND, which described the surprising arrest and confession of real-estate professional Mary Alice Willard. At one point D.J. whispered, without taking her eyes off the leaping and tiptoeing dancers, "You having a good time?"

"Loving every minute," I said, looking up. "How much longer does this last?"

"You know, I've heard you don't just watch a D'aureville production. You *feel* it."

I shifted on the concrete bench. "I am feeling it."

The write-up went on to congratulate Officer Robert Robertson for discovering evidence that led to the swift resolution of the unusual and disturbing case. There was no mention of Detectives Allen Ratzen or Kevin Andrews, and I secretly hoped they'd been reassigned to security duty at the sewage treatment plant, or maybe teaching culture awareness classes to prison inmates.

Eventually D.J. leaned over, checked out what I was reading, and said, "Does it mention Sherlock Langford and Dr. Debra Jo Watson?"

"I think it's the other way around," I said.

She grinned. "You're sweet. And especially sweet to come with me to the ballet. Are you watching it?"

"I'm waiting for the nude scene," I said. Actually, I didn't say that. What I really said was, "It's fascinating."

When all the jumping around was finally done—thank God—and we were leaving, arm in arm, D.J. said, "Do you realize that if George Willard hadn't had your card in his wallet, you might never have known about his death, and if you hadn't, his wife probably would've gone free?"

"Maybe. Maybe not. If somebody smarter than Al Ratzen had been assigned to the case, they might've figured it out."

"Nope. She'd have gotten away with it. I think it was fate." She studied me for a moment. "Do you believe in fate?"

I looked back at her, and up at the autumn-tinted trees and the blue sky and the puffy white clouds, and suddenly I was very happy with this day and my job and my future wife. *The beginning of a beautiful friendship*, I thought, picturing Bogart and Claude Rains on the tarmac.

"I believe in old movies," I said.

THE THREE DOLPHINS

"I need a favor," a familiar voice said.

I looked up from my iPhone to see my fiancée, Debra Jo Wells, sitting across from my desk. I hadn't even heard her come in. That was a little annoying, because I'm a detective. The lettering on my office door says THOMAS LANGFORD, PRIVATE INVESTIGATOR.

"Playing chess with Ivan again?" she asked me.

I gave her a hurt look. "I was reading the weather report."

An electronic voice from my phone said, "Checkmate."

D.J. smiled and raised an eyebrow.

"Okay, I lied. And his name's Boris—you probably pissed him off." I put my phone down and leaned back in my chair. "I had him on the run, too."

"Of course you did," she said.

That was when I remembered her earlier statement. "What kind of favor?"

Her face turned solemn, which got my attention. I sat up straight. "Are you in some kind of trouble?"

"A friend of mine is," she said. "She needs your help, Tommy."

I leaned back again. "And . . ."

"And she can't afford to pay you."

"Which is where the favor part comes in."

"Right." She looked at her watch and said, "I have to get back to work. Can you take a long lunch?"

"Heaven forbid."

"Pasquale's, twelve o'clock." She rose from the chair, blew me a kiss, and left. A minute later I stood and watched her through my second-floor window as she hurried across the park toward her office. I wondered what I was about to get my lovesick self into.

"How about another game?" my phone said.

#

As it turned out, we didn't eat at Pasquale's that day. We just met there. As soon as I strolled up to the door at high noon D.J. appeared and waved me toward her parked car, and fifteen minutes later we pulled into the driveway of a huge Victorian home on an oak-shaded street on the other side of town. The lady who answered the door was in her late twenties, and somehow looked sad and scared at the same time. "Come in, come in," she said.

We followed her to a gigantic and elegant living room, where D.J. made the introductions. The young woman, Emily Burnside, began by telling me she and D.J. had met at a garden center a year earlier. I had already been informed of that, in the car, but that's all I'd been told.

"I've run into some hard times since then," Emily continued. "A bad divorce, a lot of therapy, et cetera. I'm fine now, but between jobs, so I'm housesitting to make ends meet."

"Well, if this is one of your clients," I said, looking around, "it must pay well."

"It does. Older couple, Andrew and Jenny Cullen. Used to know my father. They just moved here a couple weeks ago."

"What do they do for a living?"

"He's a retired filmmaker, she writes mysteries." Emily pointed to a corner of the room and said, "Everything's not unpacked yet, but stored in that open box over there are an Oscar for best documentary movie and an Edgar Award for best novel. Years ago, but still." She paused. "The Cullens are a strange combination: wealthy and talented and truly nice."

"Where are they now?"

"Mediterranean tour, this time. They've said they plan to take several trips a year, for weeks at a time. Which means . . ." She swallowed hard. "I can't afford to lose this job."

"You'll be okay, Em," D.J. said, and took her hand. "Tell him what happened, last night."

Her story didn't take long. In a nutshell, someone had broken into the house during the night and stolen a gold statuette from inside a display case in Andrew Cullen's home office. Emily said she heard nothing and saw nothing, and only this morning discovered it missing. She was about to call the police when she realized how bad it would look to her employers. She was, after all, solely responsible for the house in their absence, and there were no broken windows or splintered doors or any other signs of forced entry. That could mean she must've left something unlocked overnight, or—even worse—was in on the deal with the burglars and the theft.

"So I got scared," she said, "and called Debra Jo. She'd told me about you, and your . . ."

"Superior detection skills," D.J. said, eyes twinkling.

"Wait a second," I said to Emily, already shaking my head. "In order for your employers to claim the insurance on this . . . statuette? . . . there'll need to be a police report on file, of the burglary."

She and D.J. exchanged a look. Apparently this had already been discussed.

"Not if you can find it yourself," Emily said.

Now both of them were staring at me, with laser intensity. As I realized I was in trouble, a couple of appropriate quotations popped into my head. The first was *Okay, bub, time to earn your pay*. But since I wasn't getting paid, I settled on the second one. I seemed to remember Han Solo saying it several times, in dire situations: *I got a bad feeling about this. . . .*

I let out a long breath. "I'll need you to ask you some questions," I said.

Which took most of the next two hours. There were a lot of questions to ask.

This was done, by the way, without any mention of lunch, and without the assistance of the person who'd gotten me into all this. Before leaving, my sweetie had informed us that she had to get back to the office—D.J. was a paralegal at a law firm (in my opinion, an angelfish swimming among sharks)—and further informed Emily that she was being left in good hands. Bottom line is, I reluctantly set out to discover what had happened here, and how.

Emily and I began with a tour of the house, which did little good because all the doors and windows were indeed locked and intact. The only missing item, so far as she could tell, was the statuette, which she described as an 18-inch-tall, solid-gold likeness of three leaping and interlinked dolphins. She assured me the piece was probably obscenely expensive, which I didn't doubt for a minute. Its glass-walled display case, which probably cost a fortune, sat empty on a bookshelf behind a walnut desk in Mr. Cullen's home office. After that, there wasn't much else to see. She told me again that she'd noticed nothing at all suspicious or unusual during the night.

Back at our seats in the living room, I asked if she'd had any visitors to the house in the six days she'd been here. Like the cop I'd once been, I took a notepad and pen from my pocket.

"Visitors?" she asked.

"Anyone at all."

She frowned, thinking hard, and said, "Five, I guess. Let's see, this is Thursday. . . . A lady from up the street stopped by Sunday afternoon to bring a welcome-to-the-neighborhood casserole for the new couple, and the mailman rang the doorbell and had me sign for a package yesterday. Neither of them even came inside. But there were three service calls."

"Service calls?"

At that moment a landline phone in a nearby room—the kitchen?—rang in the old-fashioned, nerve-jangling way. I looked at Emily, but she waved it off. "That's Mrs. Cullen. She calls every day at one o'clock sharp. She doesn't expect me to answer, she's just telling me where they are today and how to reach them. Sometimes their hotels don't have cell coverage. I always let it go to the answering machine so the call's saved in case I need the number."

Sure enough, after a few unanswered rings I heard a woman's clear voice, giving Emily the location and contact info. Then the call disconnected and the answering device switched off.

"Do you get many calls on that phone?"

"Almost none. I think Mrs. Cullen's the only one who's ever left a message."

I made a note and said, to get back on track, "You mentioned three service calls."

"Right. One was from a plumbing company I contacted when I found that the sink in one of the bathrooms was clogged. The second was a guy from TempExact Heating and Cooling, who said he was here for a scheduled appointment."

I looked up from my notepad. "I thought you said the Cullens had just moved in."

"They did. But they kept the same contract with the heating and A/C service that the previous owners had, which includes preventive maintenance every few months. Checking the inside and outside units, changing filters, and such."

"Okay." I wrote that down. "What was the third service visit?"

"An interior decorator. He said Mrs. Cullen hired him just before they left on their trip."

"Hmm. This is probably sexist, but aren't most interior decorators women?"

"Around seventy percent, I think. This one wasn't."

I looked around the room again. "Wonder why they need him. The place seems laid out pretty well already."

"But not professionally, according to this guy. He said he's a designer as well as a decorator—apparently there's a difference— and Mrs. Cullen specifically wanted him to plan a reworking of the living room and Andrew's office."

"The office, huh?"

"Yes. For, among other things, a possible area rug and more bookshelves."

I gave all that some thought. "What dates and times were these three people here?"

"Well . . . the A/C man came at half past noon on Monday, stayed an hour or so."

"How about the plumber?"

"He was here Tuesday afternoon, from maybe two till four."

"Were both of them wearing uniforms? And driving company vehicles?"

"Yes and yes. A truck and a van. Both had logos and lettering on the sides."

"And this so-called decorator/designer?"

"So-called?"

"Did you see any ID, anything that would prove he was who he said he was?"

"No—and he came in an unmarked car. But he gave me a business card. It's here somewhere."

"I'll get it later. What day and time was he here?"

Emily frowned a moment. "Early Monday morning, from eight until nine or so. He looked at all the rooms, not just the ones he first mentioned."

"And these were the only times these people came, right?"

"Yes—to this house at least. I haven't seen the decorator again, but both the plumbing and heating/cooling companies must be popular around here. I saw the plumber's truck parked down the street several times in the past week, and on Monday and Tuesday nights the A/C van was parked in front of the neighbor's on the street behind me from ten to ten-fifteen."

"The street behind this house? How'd you happen to notice it back there, late at night?"

"Because I was outside. I water the little vegetable garden the previous owners planted out back, for fifteen minutes every night beginning at ten. In this heat it's best to water after dark, didn't you know that?"

"D.J.'s the gardener," I said. "I can't tell tomato vines from poison ivy."

"Well, take my word for it."

I made a few notes, but not about horticulture. "I'd like to see this garden," I said, "and also get a look at where you saw the A/C van."

Which took about ten sweltering minutes. Their backyard was the size of a football field, and almost as free of trees. Someone with binoculars on the street behind it would have a perfect view.

Back inside again, I said, "So when exactly do you go to bed?"

"Right after my plant watering. Around ten-twenty."

I paused, thinking. The house was so quiet I could hear the happy chirping of birds in the trees out front. I figured they must've gotten *their* lunch.

"Back to the plumber," I said. "Which bathroom needed fixing?"

"The half-bath adjoining Mr. Cullen's office."

"So he probably got a good look at the dolphins, on his way there."

"The plumber? I'm sure he did. So did the decorator, of course, and the air-conditioning guy too—the inside A/C unit's in the hallway, and the office door's always open. After discovering the statue was gone this morning I switched the light off in the empty display case, but it's usually lit up like a museum exhibit."

"And I assume you're certain the statue was still here after all three of these men left."

"Yes. I told you, it was taken sometime last night."

I gave that some thought. "You also told me you were worried the Cullens might think you'd left an outside door or window unlocked. Correct?"

"Yes. I mean, whoever it was had to get in somehow. And security's my responsibility." She sighed. "Everything's my responsibility, for these three weeks. That's why I get paid well."

"Did you?" I asked.

"Did I what? Get paid?"

"Leave something unlocked."

"No," she said. "Annabelle takes care of that, thank God. But I wish now I'd gone around afterward and checked every single door."

"Annabelle?"

Before Emily could reply, a small box-shaped device on one of the living-room end tables came alive, lighting up in dancing colors. "You rang?" it said.

Emily looked at it and said, "Annabelle, stop. You're not needed."

"Very well," it replied. The colored lights winked out.

"One of Alexa's cousins?" I asked, studying the device.

"Yeah. A voice-controlled assistant. She'll answer questions and play music, but mostly she's part of a system that handles the lights, thermostat, etc. One of her duties is making sure the outside doors and windows are locked, all day and all night."

"How about other security matters? Does she activate the alarm system?"

"There is no alarm system. In this part of town, the owners didn't think one was needed."

"No cameras either?" I said.

"Not a one."

"I wonder if they'll rethink that."

"Not if you can do what I hope you can," she said. All of a sudden her pretty face looked much older. "I'd prefer they never find out any of this happened."

I made no comment on that. In fact I was feeling less like Sherlock Holmes with every passing second. Even if I figured this out, retrieving the stolen merchandise would be another story. For the tenth time, I wished my adoring girlfriend had kept my noble profession to herself.

Neither of us spoke for several minutes. I studied my notebook while Emily studied me. The grandfather clock I'd seen in the entranceway struck two o'clock.

"What else do you need to know?" she asked.

I let out a lungful of air. This was like searching for an honest politician. I wondered if Annabelle had any advice.

As that thought occurred to me I said, "How often do you use Annabelle?"

At the sound of its name, the box woke up and started blinking. "You rang?" it said.

"Annabelle, stop," Emily commanded. It fell silent. To me she said, "A lot. If I want to hear a certain song, or check on how to spell something, or wonder what the weather'll be like tomorrow, I ask her. Just like Alexa or Siri. As for her regular duties, I can override those by telling her to raise the temperature or unlock a window or something—in fact, I remember doing that the other day, while the heating/cooling dude was here—I asked her to brighten the lights in the hallway where the indoor A/C unit is, so the guy could see well enough to check the filter. But like I said, most of what Annabelle does is scheduled and automatic."

"Did you interact with her at all while the plumber and interior decorator were here?"

"Probably. Does that matter?"

"I doubt it. Just asking." Another thought hit me, and I pointed and said, "How about the window shades and curtains? Those are manual, right?"

"Right. And since I'm here alone, I keep the shades down and curtains closed except in these front rooms. I like to be able to see the road and the driveway."

I wrote this down, after which we both stayed quiet awhile. As I studied my notepad I could again feel her watching me, probably hoping to see one of those cartoon light bulbs come on above my head. I hated to tell her I was as lost as Columbus on his way west. What I needed now was to take the information I had and go someplace and think.

I gave Emily my cell number, got her to find and give me the card the decorator had left, asked her to call me if she remembered anything else, and walked two blocks to a city park. It was there, as I sat sweating on a wooden bench in the shade of an elm tree an hour later, thinking about service calls and electronic devices and golden statues and locked-house mysteries, that understanding dawned. And the more I thought about it the more likely it sounded.

On impulse, I took out my phone and called Emily. At first I was afraid she might let my call go to the answering machine as she did with the homeowner, but she picked up right away.

"I need you to do something unusual," I said to her, and checked my watch. It was 3:28. "At exactly three forty-five, I'd like you to go into the back bathroom, the one next to Mr. Cullen's office, shut the door, turn the water on full blast in the sink, and wait there for fifteen minutes. Then—"

"What in the world for?" she asked.

"Humor me, okay? After fifteen minutes, at four o'clock exactly, turn off the water, leave the bathroom, and go about your business."

"But, Mr. Langford—"

"Tom," I said.

"—this is crazy. Can't you tell me why I'm doing this?"

"I'm trying something out. If I'm right, I'll tell you first thing tomorrow. Good enough?"

I imagined her rolling her eyes. "Okay." After a pause she said, "Three forty-five?"

"That's right. Don't forget to turn the water up as fast as it'll go." I disconnected, hurried back down the street toward the house, and looked again at my watch.

At exactly 3:47, I made another phone call.

#

What I'd suspected worked like a charm. Half an hour later I called for a taxicab back across town, climbed the stairs to my office, and fired up my computer. A little googling gave me exactly what I needed. Still looking at the notes I'd taken from my meeting with Emily, I called the business phone number I'd just found online and asked to speak with the manager.

"Bob Price. How can I help you?"

"Mr. Price," I said, "one of your employees called on the home of Mr. Andrew Cullen this past week. Nineteen Wisteria Lane. Andrew's a friend of mine, and he and his wife say they were extremely impressed with your representative but couldn't recall his name. Could you check and give it to me?"

"Sure. Hold on a minute." After a short silence, he came back on and said, "That would've been James Allgood. Jimmy."

"I think I might know him. Lives out on Cooper Road, right?"

"No, Jimmy's in town. Blackwell Street, I think."

I wrote that down. "My mistake. Well, thanks, Mr. Price. I'm thinking about using you folks, and apparently you got a good man, there."

"I agree," Price said, before I disconnected.

My next call was to my old friend Robbie Robertson on the local PD, and after running James Allgood's name through the system and making a call of his own, Robbie gave me a fact that might've proven Mr. Price wrong in his opinion of his employee. Allgood had a rap sheet as long as a telemarketer's nose. I doubted he'd mentioned that on his job application form.

What Robbie didn't have was a current address, but the name and the street name were all I needed to get that from the People-Locator system I used online. Within five minutes I had it, and at six o'clock, after a much-needed supper at the burger joint down the street, I was knocking on James Allgood's front door at 7320 Blackwell.

For some reason Jimmy didn't seem thrilled to have an after-hours visitor on his doorstep, and his mood didn't improve when I told him why I was there.

The rest of my visit was even more interesting.

#

D.J. arranged to come in late to the office the following morning. I picked her up at her place shortly after eight in my ancient

Camaro, which when sitting at the curb in front of her apartment looked like a frog on a plate of fine china. I was of course aware of my vehicle's uniqueness but didn't mind, and if she was aware of it she never said so. One of the signs of undiluted love, I'd decided, is when your girlfriend's willing to be chauffeured around in a car more than twenty years old. Mine was pushing thirty.

"You still keeping it secret?" she asked. All I'd told her on the phone last night was that there'd been a break in our case.

"I don't want to spoil the surprise."

She gave me a doubtful look, but I was used to that. "Tell me *something*, at least."

"Okay." My car started on the third try. I smiled at her and said, "Buckle your lap strap."

We arrived at the Cullens' home twenty minutes later, and when the grandfather clock struck the half-hour D.J. and I were again sitting in the living room with Emily Burnside. She still looked sad, and scared, too, but she now looked cautiously hopeful as well.

"Tell me," she said, staring.

I took a breath and said, "Your burglar was a guy named James Newton Allgood. The A/C serviceman."

Her eyes widened. "How do you know?"

I took a small black-and-white figurine from my sports coat pocket. "Because of this."

She gasped. "Mrs. Cullen's Edgar Award." She looked at the open cardboard box in the corner, then back at me. "How on earth did you get that?"

"Easily," I said. "After you went into the bathroom yesterday afternoon like I asked you to, I called the landline here at the house from out front—I wanted the water running to cover the sound of the phone ringing—and when my call went to the answering machine, I told Annabelle to unlock the front door. She heard my message and did as I asked, and I walked in through the door a second later. I took Mrs. Cullen's award you'd told us about from the box and left again, re-locking the door behind me. You never knew I was here." I paused and added, "I had to prove to myself, and to you, that such a thing could be done."

Emily thought about that a moment. "You're saying . . . my God, you're saying that's what this Allgood man did. He called and told Annabelle to unlock the door."

"Yep. Night before last. Two days after his visit here."

"But—if he did, and left a message on the answering machine like you . . . why didn't I hear the phone ringing?"

"Because you were outside, watering the garden. He didn't call in the middle of the night, Emily—he called between ten and ten-fifteen, while you were too far away to hear the phone."

More thinking. Then: "The house phone's a landline, but a lot of those use portable handsets. How'd he know I wouldn't have one of those in my pocket when I was out back?"

"Because he'd been here last Monday, and checked it out. No wireless handsets in use here. He probably checked *every*thing out."

"So . . . those two nights when I saw the A/C company's van out back—"

"The resourceful Mr. Allgood was watching you, learning your nightly routine. You are, I'm afraid, a creature of habit."

"But—wait a minute—the night he stole the statue, why didn't I see a 'new message' light on the machine when I came inside from watering? Or the next morning, at the latest?"

"Because he erased his phone message before leaving the house," I said. "Just like I erased mine, yesterday afternoon. And made sure the door was locked behind him when he left."

A silence passed, as Emily absorbed all that. At last she said, "How do you know it was the A/C man? It could've been the plumber, or the decorator. I told you I saw the plumbing company's truck in the neighborhood after-hours, too, and like you said, the decorator could've been anyone with a fake business card. Besides, both had seen the statuette, and I talked with Annabelle while both of them were here, not just Allgood."

"But Allgood was here at the right time of day," I said. "You said the plumber stayed from two to four, the decorator from eight to nine, Allgood was here from twelve-thirty to one-thirty. So he was the only one who could've heard Mrs. Cullen call you at one o'clock, and heard the answering machine pick up and repeat her message. I'm pretty sure that's where he got the idea for the burglary."

Another silence. I looked at D.J. She was nodding slowly, as all this sank in.

"But there's one difference," Emily said, "between your demonstration yesterday afternoon and the theft of the Three Dolphins statue the other night. The item you took wasn't readily visible. It was in a box—I wouldn't, and didn't, notice it was gone. The gold statue was out in the open. If I'd gone into Mr. Cullen's office that night before I went to bed, just after this man must've taken it, I'd have seen that it was missing."

"You're right, that was risky. But he would've noticed, in his surveillance, that your bedroom light usually goes off very soon after you go inside at ten-fifteen. Also, why would you go to Cullen's office anyway, before turning in? Your room's all the way on the other side of the house."

D.J., who hadn't said a word during all this, finally spoke. "Let me get this straight," she said. "We now think we know it was the heating/cooling man who stole the dolphin statue, and we know how he did it. What happens next? Do we tell the police?"

Again Emily's eyes widened. "No! If we do, my bosses'll find out about what hap—"

"The police won't need to know," I said. "I did ask a cop about Allgood's record, but he's a good friend, and I didn't give him any details anyway. He doesn't know why I asked. Your secret's safe."

"It won't be safe for long," she said. Her face, so optimistic moments ago, had gone pale as a bed sheet. Her bottom lip quivered. "Think about it: the statuette's still gone. And I bet it cost a hundred thousand dollars."

"It's not gone," I said. I took a heavy object from inside my jacket then, and handed it to her. The morning sun through the front windows glinted off the golden backs of the three frolicking dolphins.

For a moment she was speechless. Finally she said just one word: "How . . . ?"

"Mr. Allgood and I came to an agreement last night. I got the statuette; he got a chance to resume a career a little less rewarding but a lot safer than stealing from his customers." I paused, remembering. "I think he was actually relieved, in a way. In spite of his record, he's still an amateur. He had no idea where or how he could sell what he'd stolen."

Emily couldn't seem to take her eyes off the statue. "So—are you saying you're—"

"Yeah, I'm sure. Long as we three and Jimmy Allgood keep our mouths shut, his boss and your bosses and the Men in Blue will remain blissfully ignorant of any wrongdoing."

"In other words," D.J. said, smiling, "mystery solved. And case closed."

"One more thing," I said. I seemed to remember that the famous Mr. Holmes—like Sergeant Friday in *Dragnet*—always had the final word. "Suggest to your homeowners that they get a dog. A big one, German Shepherd maybe." I shrugged. "You could even add pet-sitting to your housesitting fee."

Emily Burnside smiled a bit, and this time I saw tears in her eyes. She rose from her chair and squeezed me until I saw stars.

"How can I ever thank you?" she whispered.

"Install security cameras," I said. "And give the bill to Andrew."

She was still smiling when we left.

Outside in my Camaro, D.J. scooted across the passenger seat and cuddled close, as if we were teenagers on a date. A vintage date, considering our ride.

"My hero," she said, her voice muffled by my neck.

"Unpaid though he is," I pointed out.

I felt her face move in a grin. "Maybe we can do something about that."

Which made me grin also. This time my car started on the first try.

"Buckle your lap strap," I said.

R.I.P., VAN WINKLER

Nurse Susan Harlow marched into the patient's room at Rosewood Pines Rest Home, chart in hand, and said, "Good morning, Mr. Winkler. How're you feeling today?"

She didn't bother to look at the room's only occupant or expect a response to her usual question. She was fairly sure Evan Winkler wasn't feeling anything at all. He'd been in a coma for almost five years.

She checked the feeding tube and bags and monitors with movements as automatic as her greeting had been, and she was about to leave when something made her pause and look at the face of the motionless body in the bed. And when she did, she saw Winkler staring straight back at her.

"Is this Heaven?" he asked.

Nurse Harlow gasped and dropped her chart.

#

Evan "Van" Winkler's sudden recovery produced a similar reaction in almost everyone who heard about it. The facility director swallowed her chewing gum, a doctor in the lounge dumped his coffee in his lap, and when Winkler's wife was called at home, she dropped her phone in her bowl of breakfast cereal. All this happened on a Friday morning. By that night, the news media was calling it everything from an unexpected development to a medical miracle. And the Miracle Man himself seemed to be doing well in both body and mind. According to sources at Rosewood Pines, Winkler thought Trump was still in his firm term as president and had never heard of COVID-19 or *Yellowstone*, but that was understandable. To him, today was five years ago.

As for me, I'd never heard of Van Winkler. I'm located sixty miles from where all this happened, and I seldom watch the news unless it involves one of my cases. But my fiancée, a paralegal named Debra Jo "D.J." Wells, does. In fact, she said to me, at our regular lunch spot the following Wednesday, that she and Winkler's wife had lived in the same dorm in college, and further told me she remembered the events that had put him into the coma in the first place.

"What events?" I asked.

"Well, his injuries came from a car wreck, but Alicia—the wife—has always insisted the crash was the result of some kind of feud between him and a neighboring farmer."

"A feud?" I couldn't help smiling. "Like the Garfields and McCoys?"

"Hatfields," D.J. said. "In this case, a fight over peach trees, of all things."

"Peach trees?"

She took a bite of her po'boy and nodded, chewing. "I think so. Some kind of crop issue that turned violent. The thing is, this neighbor—Morton's his name—was also the driver who hit Winkler's car."

"Big coincidence," I said.

"Especially since Winkler's ride was a Honda Civic and Morton's was a three-ton pickup. According to the wife, it was a planned and intentional murder-by-vehicle. Well, attempted murder. Investigations followed, but no blame was ever assigned, and nothing came of it. And now this, with Lazarus coming back from the dead. Anyhow, when I saw the news report, I found Alicia's number and gave her a call, and . . ."

Somewhere around this point in her story, I saw a stain on my shirt—mustard?—and started scrubbing it with my napkin. "So," I said, when I noticed she'd abruptly stopped talking, "this wife was your college roommate?"

I looked up to see my usually sweet fiancée staring at me the way her grumpy father had done, on the few occasions when I've been in the presence of my future in-laws. "I've never had a roommate, Tommy," D.J. said, "and I don't plan to unless you stop that and listen to me."

I stopped scrubbing and listened.

"We were in the same dorm," she said patiently. "My point is, since Alicia Winkler and I once knew each other, I called to tell her how pleased I was about her husband's resurrection."

"I heard that part."

"Well, then Alicia called *me*, this morning, with more news, which led me to tell her about you and your services."

"What 'more news'?" I said, interested now. "And why would she need *me*?" My name, by the way, is Tom Langford, and my services are private investigations.

"I'll let her tell you that," D.J. said. "She's driving here to see you this afternoon."

#

Which she did. As for why she needed me—

"I want you to find my husband," Alicia Winkler said. "He's disappeared."

The two of us were sitting in my small and currently un-air-conditioned office at three o'clock on an August afternoon, and I wondered if the heat had affected my hearing. "Disappeared?" I asked. "I thought he'd just reappeared."

"He did. Five days ago. They kept him at Rosewood Pines until yesterday, checking him over, then released him and sent him home with instructions to rest, do certain exercises, no visitors, et cetera. And then, this morning—"

She stopped and cleared her throat. I saw her eyes well up with tears.

"I woke up and he was gone."

"Gone how?" I said. "In a car?" A brief image of a long-expired driver's license flashed through my head.

"On foot." She wiped her eyes and took a breath. "I found his work boots gone, and a pair of coveralls. And his deer rifle."

It took a moment for that to sink in. "What kind?"

"Of rifle? Remington bolt-action. A seven-ten, I think."

If I hadn't already known she was a country girl, that answer would've told me. I said nothing while she stared blankly out the window. Not that there was much out there to see, except a hot day.

When she faced me again, I took a mini-recorder from a drawer, set it on the desktop, and said, "I think it's time for some background." I didn't tell her I'd already heard part of the story, from D.J.

Alicia Winkler's version took fifteen minutes. She was indeed the owner—actually co-owner, with her revived husband—of a sixty-acre farm in Hilton County, twenty acres of which were a peach orchard that served as its primary source of income. She'd grown up near there, she said, and so had Van (apparently no one called him Evan). They'd known each other in school but never dated until he'd finished a two-year stint in the Army and both had settled into jobs there in Rosewood. They soon tied the knot, and after several years of a sometimes-shaky marriage they quit their jobs to run Alicia's family farm when her father died.

The rural life, she said, suited them both. The only real speed bumps were their growing disputes with a man named Ben Morton, a transplanted Yankee who'd bought another peach-farming operation nearby. Morton was a natural bully, and Van hated him at first sight. Their relationship grew steadily worse, and soon resembled that of spoiled children on the playground: threats, accusations, even fistfights. Fires were set in orchards, fences cut, farm vehicles sabotaged. Both men were hunters, and on several occasions, shots were reportedly fired at workers from a distance. The law always responded but did nothing, which didn't surprise me—Hilton County's sheriff was known for both laziness and corruption. Both businesses continued, Alicia said, but each suffered from the other's presence.

And then, five years ago next month, Van Winkler was driving home from a trip to town in his wife's Civic when Ben Morton's F-350 truck plowed into him on a dangerous curve. No charges were filed, which I already knew, and a comatose Winkler took up residence in the local hospital and then in a long-term care facility. Morton said not one word to Alicia following the tragedy, and still hadn't. In her view, Morton had murdered her husband and gotten away with it.

"I'll never forgive him," she said, wiping tears. "Never."

Something in her voice said that was the end of the story. I switched off the recorder and we sat in silence. Outside and below my window, afternoon traffic honked and rumbled.

"One of the worst things about Van disappearing like he did today," she said dully, "is that he would probably be able to tell us the truth about the car wreck that night. He could tell us Morton hit him on purpose. Then the world would know what I already know."

After a moment I asked, "Did you and Van talk about any of that, yesterday? When he got home from the—facility?"

"No," Alicia said. "His doctor had given strict orders that no one should mention the coma—or the accident, or Ben Morton—to Van, and suggested I not mention it either, at least for a few more days. Van didn't seem to want to talk about much of anything anyway."

I let a few seconds go by. "So—that's it?"

"Pretty much," she said.

More silence. Finally I looked her in the eye. "What aren't you telling me?"

She blinked. "Excuse me?"

"I get it, about the feud, the resentment, the competition. I do. But for this Morton guy to try to kill your husband in a crash, risking his own life in the process—and for Van to wake up from a coma and grab a gun and run off without a word? I've been doing this a while, Ms. Winkler, and something sounds wrong." I kept my gaze steady. "What else is going on, here?"

For a long time, she said nothing. At last she lowered her eyes. "Ben Morton and I had an affair."

I waited, watching her. This time I left the recorder off.

"I told you there were rocky times in my marriage. The thing with Morton was a mistake, a bad one, six years ago. It didn't last long, and when I ended it and went back to Van it left the two of them despising each other even more." She swallowed. "That's what the car wreck was about. Morton tried to kill him because of me. Well, the farm, too, but also me. I'm sure of it."

Another silence passed.

"And now that Van's come out of the coma," I said, "you figure Morton'll try again."

"Yes. I think Van figures that, too."

"You think that's why he left the house?"

She nodded. "Yes. Van's scared, and not just for himself. He left here to try to protect me also." She hugged her elbows and said, "I know what you're thinking. Does Morton hate me, too, for breaking up with him, years ago? Or does he want me back?"

I studied her face. "You tell me."

She turned to the window again, frowning. "What he wants most is my farm. He's tried twice in the past few years to buy it, and I've refused. He'll probably run me out of business anyway, eventually, but he's not a patient man. If Van was out of the picture—for good, this time—and if I was dead, too, that'd solve all Morton's problems. So it doesn't matter if he hates me or not." She focused on me then and leaned forward. "What matters is, you have to find my husband, Mr. Langford. You see that, don't you? You have to find him before Morton does."

I thought about that. She was probably right. *Could this plot get any thicker?* "And you have no ideas, none, about where he might've gone?"

"None," she said.

For the next few moments, neither of us spoke. I didn't bother suggesting she contact the police because I suspected it wouldn't help. Even if they believed her, they stood little chance of finding her husband—and if they did, they'd bring him right back to her house, to the place where his life would be most at risk. Strangely enough, Van Winkler was probably as safe right now as he could be anywhere; he'd grown up on this land and was a hunter with military training. He knew the woods, and how to survive. I had a feeling that Alicia did, too.

"I better go see this Mr. Morton," I said. "Get a feel for what he's thinking. Maybe he's not thinking—or planning—anything."

Alicia shook her head. "He won't tell you, either way."

"Doesn't matter. I want him to know I'm working for you. That's the first step." I checked my watch. It was past four, and Rosewood was an hour away.

"Wait till morning," she said, reading my mind. "Morton has a bunch of workers who live on his place. They're all there at night, in close quarters. During the day they're spread out all over the farm."

That made sense. All things considered, who knew what might greet me at Morton's place? And Winkler might even return home tonight. I agreed, and she and I worked out the details of what I figured would be a short-term contract. When she'd signed it, she gave me some more information about the two farms and Morton and where I could find his place.

As I stared at my closed door after she left, I couldn't help wondering how it would feel to go to sleep and wake up five years later, and to remember that someone I knew had tried to kill me. And that he might try again.

I let out a sigh. Every time I thought I'd seen it all, something like this came along.

I locked the office, went down the stairs and out to my car, and headed south.

#

It was almost seven by the time I found a motel in Rosewood, gobbled down a burger at the Wendy's across the street, and dropped into a chair in my room. I caught the end of *Wheel of Fortune*—would Vanna White ever age?—before my phone buzzed in my pocket. It was D.J. She was home from work and calling from her apartment. I could hear a TV in the background. After reminding her that it was her fault I was out of town, I filled her in on the new case.

"So," she said, "Alicia thinks her husband left because this man who probably tried to kill him, still hates them both enough to try again?"

"It's possible."

"And he might even try to kill *her*?"

"We don't know. I think a lot depends on whether Ben Morton's really a murderer, and whether he suspects her husband might've told her, yesterday, that the crash five years ago was intentional. I mean, there could suddenly be a live victim who can testify to what happened."

"But Alicia told you she and her husband didn't discuss the accident."

"True," I said. "But Morton doesn't know that."

Silence. I could hear her dog yapping. Probably wanted his supper.

"D.J.?"

She sighed into the phone. "I'm beginning to wish I hadn't gotten you into this."

"I'll be fine," I said. At least I hoped so.

After another pause, she said, "Did you stop by your place, on your way out of town?"

"No need. I keep a travel bag in the trunk, toothbrush and all. You know that."

"So, you have your gun?"

"The revolver. It's in my bag."

"And what about Alicia? If she's in danger, too—"

"She told me she carries one in her purse. Short-barrel thirty-eight. Said she's a good shot, too, handgun *or* rifle."

I heard her breathing into the phone. "What a crazy situation this has turned out to be."

Neither of us spoke for a while. After a minute or so she said, "What all did Alicia tell you about—*ow!*"

I sat up straight. "D.J.? You okay?"

"No. Before you called, I tried to feed Rambo a dog biscuit—he hates 'em—and he bit the hell out of me. My whole hand's bandaged up." Rambo was her toy poodle, maybe six inches tall. She adored him, but he could be a pain. "I might take him out back and shoot him."

"He'd be too small a target. I've seen you shoot."

"Hold on a second," she said, ignoring that. "Let me cut this TV off."

After a moment and a few cusswords, she said, "Where was I?"

"You wanted to know what Alicia told me about—"

"Yes. Ben Morton. Who is he, exactly?"

I spent some time updating her. Single, fifty or so, raised someplace up North, moved to Rosewood twelve years ago. Handsome in a dark sort of way. Apparently he once survived a tornado that destroyed his barn while he was inside it, and, incredible as it sounded, he lost his left arm hunting alligators three years ago—

Alicia said she remembered it because it was the first summer of the pandemic—and almost died before the others in his boat got him to a hospital. I couldn't help thinking of Captain Hook. The point was, Morton was tough.

When I was done, she said, "Let me see if I understand this. Ben Morton, the man who most likely tried to murder Winkler, and who could now conceivably try to murder him a second time, and who hunts gators and lives with a dozen henchmen on his property—"

"Farm workers," I said.

"—is the one you plan to have a chat with, tomorrow?"

"Well, when you put it that way—"

"I'll put it this way," she said. "You be careful, Tommy. Understand?"

"Look who's talking. No dogs bit *me* today."

When we'd swapped I-love-you's and disconnected, I called Alicia Winkler to tell her where I was, took a shower, and watched old movies on TV until eleven or so. Long day or not, I wasn't sleepy. Finally I fetched my overnight bag, sat down at the room's little desk, and decided to do something I'd done regularly while in the Army but had neglected in recent years. And, just like in the old days, it made me feel better about whatever tomorrow might bring.

I cleaned my gun.

#

Thursday morning was overcast and smelled like rain. I was out the door by eight o'clock. I already had directions to Ben Morton's farm and figured now was as good a time as any. I was climbing into my car when my cell phone rang.

"Have you heard the news?" Alicia asked.

"What news?" It didn't take a detective to note the edge in her voice.

"Didn't you have breakfast at the motel? I'm sure they're talking about it."

"I skipped breakfast."

"Well, you can skip the trip to Morton's, too," she said. I heard her pause, and swallow hard. "Remember the directions I gave you, to my place?"

"I remember."

"Come quick," she said. "I'll probably be having other visitors soon."

#

I found her in a rocker on the front porch of a white farm-house, wringing her hands. In the distance was a long building that she'd already told me was filled with customers every spring, when the peach crop came in. It looked empty now. I studied her face as I approached the house. She looked old enough to be the mother of the woman who'd visited me in my office.

"Ben Morton," she said, "was shot dead in his barnyard last night."

I stopped halfway up the porch steps.

"He was standing there with half a dozen of his hands, just talking, and all of a sudden he dropped like a sack of potatoes. All six workers said they heard a rifle shot, from somewhere in the hills to the south." She patted her heart and said, "Bullet hole, right here."

I sagged into a chair facing her. "Who told you all this?"

"Sheriff's deputy, an hour ago. An old friend. He said they were called to Morton's at ten last night." Alicia looked at me with a face as pale as a gravestone. "It had to be Van. Right?"

Surely it was. Coma or not, a frightened man possibly bent on revenge vanishes with a rifle and shortly afterwards, his enemy dies from a rifle shot? But—

"I don't know," I said. "Did your husband's gun have a scope?"

"No. Why does that matter?"

"It matters because it was apparently a faraway shot, at night, at one man in a group of seven. How could Van have known for sure, at that distance, which one was Morton?"

She frowned, thinking. I could see a glimmer of hope in her eyes. But then it winked out.

"Because Morton was handicapped," she said. "I told you, remember? And he doesn't wear a prosthetic. You wouldn't need a scope to identify the only one-armed man in the group."

That made sense. And I had no other argument. "You're right. It must've been Van."

I was still stunned. There were always surprises in an investigation. But this? This was no longer a PI case—it was now murder, which was a police matter. I found myself wishing, for several reasons, that she—we?—had notified them sooner about Van's disappearance.

Well, they would know about it soon. They would come here with questions, and then there'd be a full-scale manhunt. The sheriff, and everyone else, was aware of the bad blood between Morton and the Winklers. "You'll need to tell them everything," I said, in case she hadn't realized that. "It'd be even better if you could help find him."

"How would I do that?" Alicia asked. "That's why I hired *you*." She drew a shaky breath. "I don't know any more now than—" She stopped suddenly and looked at me.

"What?" I said. Her eyes had gone wide.

"Unless he doesn't plan on coming back." Her voice was lower now, almost a whisper. "Maybe he never did plan to."

I knew what she meant. I hadn't even considered it—but now that Morton was dead . . .

She was sitting frozen in her chair. All the color had drained from her cheeks.

"We don't have many suicides here," she said, still whispering. "But when we do—there's a cliff, about two miles north—"

At that point, I think we both knew.

"Show me," I said.

#

She did, and sure enough, Evan Winkler was there. His body lay crumpled on the rocky ground at the bottom of the fifty-foot cliff. Ten feet away, and somehow undamaged because of a patch of soft grass, lay the old Remington. That would be the proof, when ballistics matched it to the bullet that killed Ben Morton— and I had no doubt it would. For the moment I'd forgotten Alicia, and when I looked at her she seemed about to faint. I helped her stumble to a flat rock near the body and eased her onto it, then phoned the sheriff's office and sat quietly beside her to wait. It was a sad day, and a terrible ending to a situation that had begun so happily last week. "I wonder what's worse," Alicia murmured at one point, as we sat there beside her dead husband. "To lose a loved one, or to be given hope and then lose him all over again." Once more I noticed how much she seemed to have aged.

At last the cavalry arrived. Hundreds of questions followed, some of them difficult. Bottom line was, Van Winkler had probably been released from professional care too soon, but that was water under the bridge. What everyone seemed to agree on was that the wife appeared to have not been involved in the resulting murder. She hadn't filed a missing-person report, but that required a twenty-four-hour wait, and Van hadn't been gone that long. Besides, there was the fact that she had hired me to find him.

During a break in the questioning, when we were alone, she

brought up the matter of my fee. I told her there *was* no fee. I hadn't located Van Winkler, *she* had—and I don't charge clients for work I didn't do. Much later, after constant grilling and head-shaking and hand-waving by just about everyone in Hilton County law enforcement, we were at last dismissed and allowed to return to her house, where I'd left my car.

When we arrived, Alicia and I trudged up the porch steps and dropped into the two rocking chairs we'd left earlier. She hung her purse strap over the arm of hers and I maneuvered my chair so I was beside her. We said nothing for a long time, just sat there looking out over the big front yard. Birds sang in the treetops; squirrels played in the lower branches. Somewhere to the west, behind the house, thunder growled. On the green hillside past the end of the driveway, three brown deer stood looking at us as if from a painting.

"It just occurred to me," Alicia said finally, "that both the person I loved most and the one I hated most are gone." She gave me a sad look. "Ain't that a note."

"But you're here now," I said. "That counts for something."

"Yeah, well." She took a long breath and said, "I'm also now the wife of a murderer."

There wasn't much I could say, to that. In fact, there wasn't much left to say at all. After a while longer I stood and held out my hand. She squeezed it and half smiled, and I left.

When I turned out of her driveway onto the paved road, the deer I'd seen were gone.

#

"So, how'd it go?" D.J. asked.

I was on my cell phone at the motel after a late lunch at Wendy's, packing what little I had into my travel bag. I'd started to call her earlier, on the way back from Alicia's, but didn't. I'd tuned in a country station instead, on the car radio. Sturgill Simpson and I seemed to agree that life ain't fair and the world is mean.

"How's your hand?" I said.

"Hurts like hell. I've been a lefty all day today—good thing I don't drive a stick shift."

Good thing for all the other motorists, too, I thought. "You still at work?"

"Yes," she said. "Stop stalling—and don't tell me I'll see it all on tonight's news."

I'd been ready to suggest exactly that. But I didn't blame her for wanting to know. I pushed my bag aside, sat on the bed, and gave her whole story. Outside, rain was falling.

When I'd finished, dead silence. After maybe ten seconds she said, "Unbelievable."

"I agree. But true."

"So—what happens now?"

"Nothing. One, an unlikely murderer is dead, by his own hand; two, a likely attempted-murderer is dead also, so no one'll ever know for sure what happened five years ago; and three, the only survivor of all this is in shock. So it's an ending, but not a good one."

"And I got you involved for nothing," D.J. said.

"Not for nothing. If I hadn't come here last night I'd have probably been at your place, trying to defend myself against Rambo the Devil Dog."

"Well, you can pay me back with dinner out tonight. I can't cook with only one arm."

"Deal," I said. "In fact, how about Jolene's on Lakewood? We haven't been there in—"

I stopped in midsentence.

"Tommy?" she said.

I sat rock-still, thinking about something she'd said.

With only one arm?

"Tommy? Are you there?"

I drew a deep breath and let it out. "Sorry, Deej. I'll have to call you back."

"What? Wait a minute. What's going—"

I disconnected, switched my phone to SILENT, and left the room. Afterward, I could hardly remember walking through the now-blowing rain to the car, climbing in, starting the engine. The pieces were fitting together fast now, one after the other. My overriding thought, as I pulled out of the motel lot and onto the wet highway, was *How could I have missed it?*

#

Twenty minutes later I was sitting again on the front porch of Alicia's farmhouse. This time I was alone. When I'd parked and walked through the downpour to the house ten minutes ago, I noticed her car was here and her purse was still hanging from the arm of her rocker, but there was no sign of her. I had taken a seat in the chair beside hers, and waited. Yellow lightning forked the sky. Thunder rolled. Eventually Alicia stuck her head out the door and looked at me.

"I thought I heard a car drive up," she said. "You all right?"

"Fine. Just thought of some questions, before I head back. Is this a bad time?"

"I was about to get started on the arrangements." She came out, rubbing her red-rimmed eyes, and slumped into her chair. "Ask away."

I hesitated, then said, "Tell me about the peach business."

She gave me a weak smile. "You thinking of investing?"

I chuckled. "No. I was just wondering how profitable it is, that kind of thing."

"Well, let's see—I got maybe three thousand trees, and they produce thirteen, fourteen thousand bushels of peaches a year. I also grow blackberries, plums, and pecans, and sell most of 'em on site. There's a ton of overhead—workers, pickers, equipment, and such—but on a good year, it can be a good living."

"*Can* be?"

"Not all years are good," she said.

I nodded, then asked, "How about Ben Morton's farm?"

"Size-wise, about the same. Production, too, I expect."

"But in the past, the two of you wound up splitting—or sharing, I guess—the market."

"We did," she said. Then, frowning a bit: "Why do you ask?"

"Well—it just occurred to me that you're now the sole owner of this place—I assume you were half owner, during the coma years— and that your only competitor is now gone."

She nodded also. "Guess that's true. I doubt Morton's kinfolks'll keep things going."

"Which could make you an extremely wealthy woman."

Alicia stopped rocking and gave me a look. "What's your point, exactly?"

I stayed quiet a while, holding her gaze. Around us—on all three sides of the porch—was a shining curtain of rainwater. Thunder crashed and boomed.

"We agreed your husband shot Ben Morton last night, out of that group of field hands, because he picked the one person who was missing a limb. The thing is, Ms. Winkler, he couldn't have known that. If the gator accident that took Morton's arm happened three years ago, Van was already in his coma."

It took a second for that to register. "Well—he must've been told—"

"He wasn't. You said so. Nothing about Morton or the coma circumstances was mentioned to him, by you or anyone else."

She didn't reply. Her face had shut down, her eyes hard as flint.

"Van never disappeared from here at all," I said. "It was you who shot Morton, using your husband's rifle. Problems solved, archenemy gone, all with one bullet. You said, yourself, you're a good shot. After that, you came back here to the house, knocked Van out with pills, or maybe a hammer, dressed him in his coveralls and work boots, drove him to the cliff, and pushed him over the edge. But not his rifle. You wiped his rifle clean of prints, went down afterward, and put it on that patch of grass beside him so it'd be in good shape for the ballistics test. Then, the next morning—this morning—you called me and told me about Morton's death. From that point on, it was all a performance." I paused. "That sound about right?"

Her mouth was a thin line, her face pale and drawn. Without a word she turned to look at the falling rain. So did I. Thunder rumbled but a bit softer now.

"You knew that hiring me would make you look even more innocent," I said. "A murderer doesn't pay a private investigator to try to find her victim."

I turned again to face her—and froze. Her purse was open now, and she was holding a revolver in her hand. It was cocked and pointed at my chest.

"Hiring you was a mistake, Mr. Langford. But not as big as the one you just made."

The two of us sat looking into each other's eyes. Hers had turned ice-cold.

"I told you yesterday that I carry a gun in my purse," she said. "A good detective would've remembered that."

She smiled and pulled the trigger.

The hollow *click* was loud, even with the noise of the storm. Her shocked gaze moved from me to the gun, and as she looked at it, I took the six .38 cartridges from my shirt pocket and showed them to her. "You're right," I said. "And waiting out here alone gave me time to think."

For another moment we stared at each other. I was tensed and ready for anything, but there was no need. Her shoulders and face sagged at the same time. Gently I took the empty weapon from her hand.

As if at a signal, the rain eased up and then stopped, and the only sound was the drip, drip, drip of water from the edges of the roof.

#

For the second time that day, I spent hours answering questions. This time I did it alone; Alicia Winkler had been transported to the jail in Rosewood. It was almost dark when I called D.J.'s cell phone, on my way back to the motel, to tell her I'd need to stay another night. It went straight to voicemail, which wasn't surprising—she was always careless about charging her phone. So, I called her landline, which turned out to be a mistake.

"Langford?" a man's voice growled, from her apartment. "Where are you?"

"Mr. Wells," I said, cursing my luck. I was too tired for this. "Is Debra Jo there?"

"She's gone to the store to bring her mother and me something to eat." I could hear Rambo barking in the background. "She said you were supposed to take us to dinner."

I was supposed to take HER to dinner. "Sorry, Mr. Wells. I'm still working." Thank God.

"Well, that's pretty inconsiderate if you ask me. We don't visit often." Then: "What's the matter with this damn dog?"

"He's probably hungry," I said. "But whatever you do, don't feed him a dog biscuit."

I heard him snort. "I'll feed him whatever the hell I want. Janice?" he called. "Hand me one a them dog biscuits." Then, he hung up.

I hung up, too. And felt better than I had all day.

Part 3 – Other Stories

GUN WORK

Will Parker sat alone on the wooden platform beside the pulpit in the empty church. He was watching, through one of the side windows, the bay horse he'd tied to the hitching rail half an hour ago and the rippling rust-colored leaves of the trees in the distance. It was a sunny October morning, bright enough to light up every corner of the little sanctuary, and the breeze through the open windows was cool but not cold.

Parker crossed his legs, took off his hat, and balanced it on one knee. The pews facing him were as empty as the church, but he had chosen this seat—which wasn't really a seat—because it offered a clear view of the front door. Whenever possible, he sat this way, facing a room with his back to a wall. He remembered what had happened to Bill Hickok.

For the tenth time, Parker checked his pocket watch. He'd been intentionally early, but it was now twenty minutes past the time his client had set, for this meeting.

His client. That still sounded strange to him, even after several years as a private investigator. But Parker liked the job, and the agency he and his brother had founded in San Francisco had been surprisingly successful. Granted, most of his recent work was dull—checking backgrounds, locating beneficiaries of a will, uncovering shady deals and/or relationships, etc. (unlike the tough assignments he'd had during his short time with the Pinkerton Agency years ago)—but occasionally he was given something interesting and challenging. He had a feeling this case might be both. After all, he wasn't often instructed to meet a client at a church in the middle of the week, in the middle of nowhere.

"Mr. Parker?" a voice said.

He looked up to see a tall man in a brown hat and vest standing in the front doorway. Parker had heard no hoofbeats, no footsteps. A quick glance confirmed that his own horse, rented from the livery stable in Dodge early this morning, was still alone at the hitching rail. So much for being watchful.

"Who else would I be?" he said. "We're probably the only two people within miles."

"Sorry I'm late," the tall man said.

Parker stayed seated, watching him. "How'd you get here?"

"Quietly. My horse is tied up some distance away." A smile

touched the man's lips, but only for a moment, there and gone. "The cautious, I have found, live longer."

"Cautious of what?"

"Of everything."

With that, the man strode casually down the aisle and extended his hand. "Cole Bennett."

They shook hands and Bennett took a seat in the front pew, facing Parker from a distance of eight feet or so. Cole Bennett appeared to be in his late fifties, maybe ten years older than Parker. But he looked strong and fit, and had what Parker's wife, Bitsy, would call a world-weary face. Bennett took off his hat and set it down beside him. "Thanks for coming," he said.

"You paid for my transportation," Parker reminded him. "I arrived on last night's stage."

"But not from San Francisco. Your brother wired me that you were already fairly close to here, at the moment. Redemption, he said?"

"Yes—my wife lived there when I met her. We're visiting her parents."

"That was convenient for me."

"Convenient for *me*, actually. Less expensive for you." Parker hooked his thumbs in his gun belt. "How can I help you, Mr. Bennett?"

Bennett blew out a long sigh. "First I need to tell you a story."

"I'm listening."

"Do you remember the Ford brothers? Jesse and Dalton?"

"Barely."

Again Bennett hesitated, obviously choosing his words. "Some time ago," he began, "a U.S. marshal, Sam Ewing, shot Dalton Ford during what was said to be the robbery of a bank up in Hays City. The marshal lived here in Dodge but was in Hays the day this happened. Anyhow, Marshal Ewing shot Ford and killed him. Afterward one of the witnesses said Ford was in the bank, sure enough, but wasn't robbing it—he said Ford was chatting with one of the tellers. Whichever way it happened, the marshal got word he was there, entered the bank, and Dalton Ford—a man wanted for multiple crimes—wound up dead as a pine knot. Dalton's brother Jesse, who was in prison at the time, heard about the killing, and when he was released a year later he showed up at Ewing's house just outside Dodge with two of his buddies."

"Looking for revenge."

"Yes," Bennett said. He paused and studied his folded hands. Will Parker waited, saying nothing.

"According to the official report," Bennett continued, "Jesse Ford—I'll just call him Jesse from now on—and his friends arrived one day in July to find Ewing and his twelve-year-old son, Andrew, home in their farmhouse north of town. Not far from here, actually. Mrs. Ewing had died three months earlier, some kind of fever, and Ewing had retired as marshal and took to raising crops and some cattle. Apparently Jesse and his men surprised them. They struck Ewing in the head in the kitchen, held him and the boy at gunpoint, and Jesse ordered his two men to go outside and wait. Five minutes later, Ewing got the jump on Jesse and shot him dead, then went out and killed one of Jesse's friends as well. The other one got away."

Parker thought that over. "The official report, you said?"

"Yes. It's what Ewing told the sheriff, afterward."

"Go on."

"No more to tell. That's the background," Bennett said. "The current situation is, I received word recently that things didn't happen the way everyone thought they did, that day at Ewing's house. I've been told that Jesse Ford was shot in the back. One of his two companions was killed with an entry wound in the chest, just like Ewing reported, but—again—Jesse's wound showed that he was shot from behind."

"And how did you find all this out?"

"From an old friend of mine. He'd been a sheriff's deputy in Dodge, back when the incident took place, and saw the two bodies the sheriff brought in. He told me this a few weeks ago, on his deathbed. A week or so after that, I noticed an ad in the newspaper about your agency, and sent the wire requesting your services."

Parker waited for more. When it didn't come, he asked, "So what is it that you need?"

Bennett turned to look out the window at the small stand of oaks Parker had been watching earlier. The wind had died; the leaves were still. Like Bennett's expression.

"I need to know what happened that day," Bennett said. "What really happened."

"Why don't you just ask the sheriff?"

"Because the sheriff is dead. So is former marshal Sam Ewing, and even his son Andrew. The son died young, from an accident on a cattle drive, south of here. They're all gone now."

Parker studied Cole Bennett for a moment. "What haven't you told me, Mr. Bennett?"

"I haven't told you *when* all this happened."

"When did it happen?"

Bennett let out a lungful of air. "Sam Ewing shot Jesse Ford twenty-two years ago."

"What?"

"My friend—the deputy—said he kept the secret all those years because the sheriff asked him to. Said everybody in town loved Sam Ewing, all the Ewings. Said the sheriff figured what good would it do to tell the whole story? Jesse Ford was dead, along with one of his cutthroat friends, and the world was better off for it. Why complicate things? The deputy said he and the sheriff, and of course Ewing and his son, were the only people who knew Jesse was back-shot. And that only the two Ewings knew *how* it happened."

Bennett went quiet then, staring down at his boots as if in deep thought.

Parker let the silence drag out, then said, "I think we have a problem here, Mr. Bennett. If this took place more than twenty years ago and everyone involved is deceased, why do you think I could find out any more than what you just told me?"

Bennett raised his head. "Because I don't think they're all deceased."

"You just said—"

"I said the deputy told me Sam Ewing and his son were the only people who saw exactly what happened. But I think there's someone else." He leaned forward in his seat, his eyes locked on Parker's. "I heard Sam Ewing's son, Andrew, had a childhood friend his own age, and I heard that in the summers they were inseparable, those two boys, especially in the months after Sam's wife passed. Way I heard it, this kid was at little Andrew Ewing's house most every day." Bennett paused, drew a breath, and said, "I'd be willing to bet—in fact, I guess I am betting, by hiring you—that whoever this boy was, he was probably there with Andrew the day Jesse Ford and his men came to call. I'm betting he never got mentioned because everyone involved was trying to protect him. Again, why make a simple matter complicated?"

Parker gave this some thought. "Do you have a name?"

"No. But I have confidence you'll come up with one. And when you do . . ." Bennett paused again, his face solemn. "When you find him, maybe he has what I need to know."

Another question was nagging at Parker. An important question.

"Why *do* you need to know?"

Cole Bennett settled back into the pew. "My wife," he said, "was a Ford. Jesse and Dalton, as worthless as they were, were her nephews. Her brother's sons. I told her what my deputy friend, before he died, told me about Jesse's death, and it's driving her crazy. She says she has to know what really happened in that kitchen that day."

Parker mulled that over. "All due respect," he said, "why do you need *me*? Why couldn't *you* ask the same kinds of questions you want me to ask?"

"Because you're the expert. I checked out the references your brother gave me." Bennett picked up his hat and stood. "I'm trusting you to solve this for me, Mr. Parker."

Parker, who had spent a lot of time doing this kind of work, knew a lie when he heard it. He knew Cole Bennett didn't want to ask around about this matter for the same reason Bennett had picked a remote spot for their meeting today: he couldn't afford to be connected to all this. *What are you hiding, Mr. Bennett?*

Parker rose to his feet also, and the two men stood facing each other.

"Your brother told me your name's Will," Bennett said.

"That's right."

"It occurred to me that you bear some resemblance to another Parker, well known in this part of the country years ago. By reputation, at least."

"What kind of reputation?"

"He was a gunman. A killer, I'm told."

"Is that so."

Bennett tilted his head, narrowed his eyes. "This man's name was Charlie Parker."

Parker felt himself shrug. "Sorry. No relation."

Bennett studied him a moment more, nodded, and left. Parker remained standing where he was. This time he did hear hoofbeats, moments later, receding into the distance.

Parker sighed. Everybody has secrets, he thought.

After another minute or so, Charles William Parker walked outside to the hitching rail, mounted the bay, and headed back to town.

#

It took Parker less than six hours to narrow things down a bit. Unlike the procedures he'd followed to gather information the last time he'd visited these parts—a missing-person case in the small town of Redemption—he didn't bother with the saloons and the stables and the blacksmith and the stockyards. This time he concentrated on places where he could find and talk with the womenfolk. After several hours of visiting the general store, a dress shop, the schoolhouse, and a church—this one with more pews and more windows than the one this morning—he'd discovered that young Andrew Ewing was well remembered by some of the older teachers and ladies. One, a widow with the unfortunate name of Ophelia Reardon, recalled that Andrew had indeed made one especially close friend during his long-ago school years.

"Truitt," Mrs. Reardon said, smiling at the memory. "Can't recall his first name, but little Andrew Ewing played a lot with Daisy Truitt's boy. Never saw one of them without the other."

"When exactly was that?" Parker asked. "When they were teenagers?"

"Earlier. When they were eleven or twelve, probably." A thought seemed to come to her, and Mrs. Reardon's smile faded a bit. "Around the time Andrew's mama died, and that outlaw Ford came and tried to kill Marshal Ewing," she said.

Which was exactly what Parker wanted to hear.

"Is Mrs. Truitt still here in Dodge?" he asked, holding his breath.

"Sure is. Husband died five years ago. She and her son live on the other end of town." Ophelia Reardon pointed toward the reddening sunset. "You turn left there at the stage office, their place is about a mile south, on the right side of the road. White house with a tall barn."

Parker thanked her and set out in that direction. Five minutes later he climbed the front steps of a white-painted home and rapped on the front door. The small woman who answered the knock looked about as old as Cole Bennett was, which made sense. Twenty-two years ago she would've been about the right age to have a twelve-year-old child. She was holding what looked like a damp washcloth.

Mentally crossing his fingers, Parker identified himself and, without giving a reason, asked if he might meet her son and ask him a few questions.

She stared at Parker a long time before answering. "You can certainly meet him," she said at last. "But I'm afraid questions won't do any good."

"Excuse me?"

She sighed and motioned him inside. The house was old but neatly kept. Parker followed her down a dark hallway and through a door to a room containing nothing but a bed and two small tables on each side. Propped up on pillows in the bed was a pale, thin-faced man in his thirties, with sandy hair. His eyes were closed, his breathing slow and peaceful. His forehead and cheeks looked wet. Parker now understood the washcloth.

When Parker turned to look at her, Daisy Truitt gave him a sad smile. "My poor boy, Wilson. He's been that way six months now," she said. "Got kicked by a mare while he was trying to shoe her. Doc says it caught him square in the left temple, at just the wrong place. When his brother got here he went out and shot the horse dead, not that that did anybody any good." She studied her visitor again and added, "He can't speak, Mr. Parker—he can't even hear us. Could I be of some help instead, with your questions?"

Parker, stunned, shook his head. "I doubt it, ma'am. Unless he might possibly have told you something—anything—about the day Jesse Ford was killed, up at the Ewing place."

She looked shocked. "Wilson? No, I'm afraid not. I doubt he knew anything about that."

"Well, then, I'm sorry to have bothered you."

"No bother at all."

They retraced their steps to the front door, but Parker was barely aware of it. His legs felt heavy, like chunks of firewood. What a disappointing way to end his search. And his assignment.

Parker thanked Mrs. Truitt again at the door and was turning to leave when it hit him. He stopped and looked at her in the gathering twilight. "You said his *brother* shot the horse?"

"That's right. My second son."

"You have another son?"

"Two years younger," she said. "His name's Tommy."

Parker swallowed. "Could he have known Andrew Ewing? The marshal's boy?"

"Oh my, yes. Those two were best friends."

#

Tommy Truitt, it turned out, lived in the town of Hopeful, about half a day's ride from Dodge. Will Parker, hopeful now also, sent a wire that night to his wife and another to his brother, Robert, at the agency's home office. He assured Bitsy he'd try to be back by the end of the week and informed his brother that he had met with Cole Bennett and was making progress. He rewarded him-self with a thick steak at a café called Delmonico's and a beer at the Long Branch, and after that retired to his hotel to sleep the sleep of the weary and guiltless.

Or at least the weary.

It was hard, Parker had decided, to escape the past. Years ago, young and reckless, he had chosen all the wrong friends and all the wrong endeavors, and his steely nerves and uncanny skill with firearms soon found him steady employment and built him a reputation from Fort Smith to Deadwood. Inevitably, many who heard about Charlie Parker wanted to challenge him, and those who did, died. When maturity and self-preservation finally convinced him to give up gun work, he went East, started using his middle name instead, and landed a job with the Pinkertons in Washington, one that required brains over bravado. Since then he'd done some security work, even a stint as a deputy, before joining his brother at Parker Investigations in San Francisco.

Even now, though, after all this time, a lot of people remembered the name Charlie Parker. When that happened he usually pled ignorance, which occasionally worked. He doubted that it had worked with Cole Bennett.

What a career change, Parker thought. He'd gone from being a hired gun to being a liar.

He fell asleep wondering which was worse.

#

Will Parker got up early, had a leisurely breakfast, and rode into Hopeful just past noon. The town was appropriately named, he decided; there seemed to be nowhere for it to go but up. He counted a dozen dreary houses and half a dozen dreary stores, all clustered around the intersection of a sluggish creek and a muddy road. He hoped Tommy Truitt lived on this side of the creek. The wooden bridge looked too rickety to support a man, much less a man on a horse.

At one of the buildings—a sort of combination saloon and dry-goods store—he was told that Truitt owned a small ranch west of town. There was no real road out that way, but the directions Parker received seemed simple enough. An hour later he found the spread.

He also found Tommy Truitt, on his knees in the doorway of a barn, shoeing a gray horse. Given the family history, Parker figured it to be a scary task. The horseshoer looked up as Parker rode in, and eased the gray's foreleg to the ground. Something about the man's eyes verified that he was the son of the woman Parker had spoken to the night before.

Parker stopped ten feet away and propped both arms on his saddle horn. "I've come a ways to find you, Mr. Truitt. Can I interrupt your work for a while?"

Truitt put down his tools, stood, and sleeved sweat from his brow. "Don't know. I'm having an awful good time, here."

Both of them smiled.

"Help yourself to water for you and your horse," Truitt said, pointing to a well and bucket. "I'll be right with you."

Fifteen minutes later introductions were made and Parker's task was explained. The two of them sat in rockers on the front porch of the house. Truitt's wife and daughter, he said, were visiting his wife's mother, in town. Chickens pecked and strutted in the dusty yard, and small white clouds cast moving pools of shade across the flatlands. The wind was chilly.

Tommy Truitt exhaled a deep sigh. "Yes, I was there that day," he answered. "And no, I've never spoken of it to anybody, not even my ma and pa."

"You didn't tell your brother?"

"So you know about Wilson? A sad thing, that horse kicking him. I go over as often as I can, help Ma with chores. . . ." Truitt paused, adrift in his thoughts. Then he blinked and said, "No, I never told him. Wilson was a bit older, and for some reason we never got along. Guess that's why I played so much with Andrew."

Parker, wondering how to proceed, decided to be direct. "Do you remember what happened, that day?"

"I'll never forget it," Tommy Truitt murmured.

A silence fell, during which Parker had the good sense to keep quiet. After a full minute or more, Truitt took a long breath and said, "We'd been playing in a patch of woods behind his house, with a bow and arrow we'd made out of sticks and a springy branch. We were trying to shoot a rabbit, and Andrew kept saying we needed that old eight-gauge shotgun his pa had, not a homemade bow and a little stick with an arrowhead tied to the end. He said his pa had put away all his weapons when he retired, but Andrew knew where the shotgun was stored. He said we ought to sneak it out and shoot that rabbit. Said there wouldn't be nothing left but a cotton tail."

He stopped for a beat, and Parker saw him smiling a little, at the memory. The smile didn't last long.

"That was when we heard hoofbeats, coming down the road from town," Truitt said. "By the time we got back to the house—"

#

—three horses were tied to the porch rail. Tommy Truitt didn't recognize any of them.

He and Andrew climbed the steps, crept inside, and found three men in the kitchen with guns drawn, and Andrew's father sprawled on the floor with blood on his forehead. Greenish-white peas were scattered on the floor, some still in their hulls, along with a broken bowl and an overturned chair. Tommy figured the intruders must've caught the marshal shelling peas and hit him with a gun barrel. "Pa?" Andrew cried.

When Marshal Ewing saw them—Andrew's pa would always be Marshal Ewing, to Tommy—he propped himself up on one elbow and groaned, "Run, boys. Get outa here."

One of the three men told him, in a bored voice, to shut up. This was the ringleader, Tommy could see that. He was the oldest and the meanest-looking, too. He had dragged one of the kitchen chairs over to the wall beside the spot where Andrew's father was lying and was sitting in it, leaning back against the wall. The glare he gave the two boys sent chills up Tommy's spine. The man said, to one of his friends, "Get rid of 'em, Dixon."

For just a second Tommy wondered what he meant, and then understood. The man the leader had spoken to seemed to under-stand, too. "No," he said.

The leader turned to face Dixon. "What did you say?"

"I said no. I'm not shootin' any kids, Jesse."

It was then that Tommy knew who the leader was. Jesse Ford. He'd heard the name mentioned, in town. Tommy had thought Ford was in jail.

But he wasn't. He was here, in Andrew's house, sitting in a chair against the wall and pointing a gun at Andrew's pa, lying at his feet. It felt like a dream, a scary one. But it was real.

"Then I guess *I'll* have to," Jesse Ford said.

"No." Dixon shook his head. "Nobody's shootin' a kid."

The two men stared at each other for what seemed a long time. Sam Ewing was still propped on one elbow, opening and closing his eyes and breathing hard. Finally Ford said, "What do you suggest, then? We can't let 'em go—they done seen us, and can tell the Law."

"So can that woman we saw in the field, a few miles back. She got a good look at us."

"We shoulda killed her, too," Ford muttered.

"Jesse's right, Dixon," the other man said, a short guy with a face like a weasel. "I'll do it if you won't."

Ignoring him, Dixon said, "We don't have to kill 'em. We could tie 'em up. Or lock 'em up someplace. All we need is time to get this done and get far enough away."

"You could lock us in the pantry," young Andrew said, speaking for the first time. Tommy turned in surprise to look at him, and so did everyone else. Even Marshal Ewing's eyes were open now, and watching.

"It's right there," Andrew added, his voice shaky, and pointed to the wall against which Jesse Ford's chair was leaning. "The only door's just around the corner, and it locks."

"Who in the hell would put a lock on a pantry?" Ford growled.

"My ma, years ago. She kept stuff in there, kerosene and poison and such, that I wasn't supposed to get into."

Dixon walked to the corner, then came back. "It has a latch, with an open padlock on it."

Jesse Ford sighed and nodded. "Get 'em in there, then."

Within seconds the two boys found themselves inside the long, dim pantry. Dixon had steered them through the door, and afterward Tommy heard the lock snap shut. Narrow bars of light seeped in under the door and through the spaces between the wallboards.

The first thing Tommy heard, from the other side of the shared wall, was Jesse Ford's voice: "You men go outside, you and Dixon both. Bring the horses round to the back door here and wait for me. I won't be long."

"You gonna kill him?" Weasel Face said.

"That's what I came here for. Now get out, both of you."

Tommy, who had been listening and peering into the kitchen through the tiny slits between the boards, heard Andrew moving around in the back of the pantry. "What are you doing?" he whispered. Andrew didn't answer.

On the other side of the wall—Tommy could see the dark outline of Jesse Ford's back as he sat in the chair only inches away—Ford said, "Well, well, Marshal. Here we are, just you and me. You beginning to be sorry you killed my brother?"

Weakly, Sam Ewing said, "Wish I'd had a chance to kill you, too."

Ford cackled a laugh. "I got news for you, Marshal. Them two boys of yours are gonna die too, soon as I finish with you. I'll just shoot the lock off the door and take care of 'em both. Might have to shoot Dixon, too, afterwards. Looks like he ain't got the grit I thought he had."

All of a sudden Tommy felt Andrew pushing him aside. Andrew had something in his hands, but Tommy couldn't make it out. He was about to whisper a question when Andrew placed one end of whatever he was holding—a long stick?—against the wall Ford was leaning back on and squatted down behind it.

"Ain't no use wastin' time," Ford's voice said. Tommy heard the click of a pistol being cocked. "This is for Dalt—"

Jesse Ford never finished the sentence. Tommy heard an explosion—it sounded like a blast of dynamite only inches from his right ear—and suddenly there was a fist-sized hole in the pantry wall. Light poured in from the kitchen, smoky gray light, and then he saw Andrew standing beside him. Andrew was saying something to him, shouting it, his lips moving, but Tommy could hear nothing. Finally he saw Andrew motion to him to get down. Tommy ducked and heard yet another explosion, above his head. He looked up to see that the pantry door was open, the wood splintered in a huge circle around the spot where the lock had been. Andrew stormed past him and out the door, holding his pa's double-barreled eight-gauge, and Tommy stumbled after him, ears ringing. Andrew was reloading as he ran, stuffing in fresh shells.

There was no need. They rounded the corner to find the kitchen empty. Jesse Ford's body was lying in the middle of the floor, lying where Andrew had blown him out of the chair and forward six or seven feet. Marshal Ewing was nowhere to be seen. Blood was everywhere.

Before Tommy could get his mind around all this, he heard—through his left ear—a pistol shot, and followed Andrew out the back door. Standing there in the yard were two men: Dixon and Marshal Ewing. Dixon had his hands raised, and Ewing was leaning against a tree, his smoking gun pointed and rock-steady. At first Tommy wondered where Ewing had found a pistol, then realized it must've been Jesse Ford's, picked up off the kitchen floor after Andrew had shot him. A short distance away, lying at the feet of one of the three horses, was the motionless body of Weasel Face. His shirt was bloody and a gun lay in the dust beside him.

For a long moment no one said a word. The boys gawked at

the two men and the two men stared at each other. Somewhere nearby, a crow cawed.

With the back of his hand Andrew's father wiped blood from his eyes. He was covered with it, from head to toe, and Tommy realized most of it was Jesse Ford's.

"Give me a reason I shouldn't kill you," Marshal Ewing said.

Dixon shook his head. He looked sad, and strangely unafraid. "I can't."

Ewing cast a quick glance at his son and Tommy, then said to Dixon, "You don't seem the same kind of man as those other two were. What are you doing in this bunch?"

"I'm more like them than not," Dixon said. "But there's some things I won't do."

"Like murder a child."

"Yes."

Another long silence passed.

"Get out of here, Mr. Dixon. And don't come back."

Without a word, Dixon lowered his hands, walked to his horse, mounted up, and rode away. Tommy and the two Ewings watched until he disappeared around the curve of the trail.

Then Andrew put the shotgun down and ran to his father. Tommy did too. Marshal Ewing scooped both of them into his arms, then stopped when his son cried out in pain. As it turned out, Andrew's right shoulder was badly sprained, from the kick of the eight-gauge. And he had even fired it a second time, Tommy remembered, to blow away the door lock.

All three of them, as if at a signal, turned to look at the shotgun, lying in the dirt.

"Guess I won't bother hiding it anymore," Ewing said.

#

"And that's what happened." Tommy Truitt looked at Parker and shrugged. "They're all gone now. Marshal Ewing, Andrew, everybody. Except me."

Parker nodded. He had started out taking notes, but had soon quit and just listened. "You all agreed, I guess, never to talk about it."

"That's right. To anybody. And the marshal insisted on hiding the fact that Andrew was the one who killed Jesse Ford, and that I was even there at all. If anyone else ever showed up looking for revenge, he said, simpler was better. Three men came, two died, one got away."

Parker wondered what it would feel like, to live through that and never tell anyone about it. Maybe telling it, at long last, had helped a little.

"Andrew was a tough kid," Truitt said. "And smart. He talked a bunch of killers into locking us in a room that had a gun hidden in it."

Parker nodded. "Smart *and* lucky. Lucky two of the three men were outside, lucky that Jesse Ford sat where he did, lucky that Sam Ewing was on the floor, underneath the line of fire."

Truitt didn't reply. He just sat, slowly rocking, looking out at the flat plains, and his memories. After awhile he blinked and studied Parker's face. "You said you came a long way, for this. Did you get what you needed?"

"I got what my client needed. You cleared up a lot of things."

"Now I plan to forget about it," Truitt said.

He rose to his feet, and Parker followed.

"You're welcome to stay for supper," Truitt said. "My family'll be home soon."

"Much obliged, but I need to go." Parker turned to leave, then paused. "One question. You said you'd heard the name Jesse Ford, before all this happened."

"That's right."

"Well, he wasn't the only one did gun work, back then. Ever hear of Pete Lawson, or Merrill Smith, or Charlie Parker?"

Truitt thought a moment, then shook his head. "Don't think so."

"Good," Parker said.

#

The temperature dropped like a stone that night, and the following afternoon was windy and cold and overcast. The orange, yellow, and red leaves of the trees outside the small country church seemed to be struggling to stay on the branches, and many of them failed. Parker arrived just before three o'clock. This time Bennett was early; Parker found him standing at the head of the center aisle. They shook hands and settled again into the same seats they'd taken earlier.

"Let's hear it," Bennett said.

Twenty minutes later the story had been told. Parker left nothing out. Using many of Tommy Truitt's own words, he told Bennett about the intrusion, the spoken threat to the two boys, Dixon's challenge to Jesse Ford's order, the locking of the boys in the pantry, the shotgun blast through the wall, the shootout in the backyard, the departure of the third attacker.

"I believe every word he said," Parker concluded. "That's the way it happened."

For a long time Bennett sat there in silence, fingering the buttons of his overcoat. At last he said, "It makes sense. I couldn't see Sam Ewing as a back-shooter. But I had to know." He stood up. "You've done good work, Mr. Parker. I'll be sending full payment to your office tomorrow morning." He turned and moved away toward the front of the church.

"Give my best wishes to Mrs. Dixon," Parker said.

Bennett stopped in his tracks. For several seconds he stood motionless, then turned again and locked eyes with Parker. Parker hadn't moved. He was still sitting there, on the platform beside the pulpit.

Very slowly Bennett walked back to the first pew. It was so quiet in the church Parker could hear the wood creak as Bennett sagged into the seat. His face was blank.

"Are you even married?" Parker asked him. "Or was that a lie, too?"

"I'm married. But my wife wasn't a Ford. And she has no nephews." Bennett paused for a beat, then said, "How did you know?"

"That you were the third man?" Parker sighed. "I'm not sure. Maybe it takes somebody with a guilty conscience to recognize it in someone else. Besides, you were so certain that Andrew had a playmate who would've been there at the time. Why were you so sure? And something else that bothered me from the start was that you felt you couldn't pursue this on your own. I finally realized that if you had, if you'd discovered the identity of Andrew's friend, and approached him yourself to ask him questions—"

"He might've recognized me. From that day."

"Right," Parker said. "And I assumed you had a reason why you'd rather not call attention to your past."

"My reason is, I'm an elected official now. A mayor. Back east a ways."

"I know. And I know where. My brother checked, and contacted me this morning."

Bennett stayed quiet a minute, gazing out the window.

"You think anyone'll find out?" he asked.

"About your former life? That you rode with Jesse Ford? No. Even if they do, so what? You're a changed man."

"What about Tommy Truitt?"

"The two of you live far apart. I doubt you'll ever meet."

Bennett rubbed his face wearily. "Maybe we should." He looked Parker in the eye and said, "I went there that day to help murder an innocent man. What I did got two people killed."

"What you did saved three people, too."

Bennett gave that some thought, and nodded. This time both of them stood. "Thank you, Mr. Parker."

"What should I call you?"

"My name's Morris Dixon."

They shook hands. "Have a safe journey home, Mr. Mayor."

"You, too."

Parker watched through the window as Dixon rode away, then he pulled up the collar of his coat and stomped outside to his own horse. He had already swung into the saddle when he saw a grizzled old man in a fur hat and a bearskin trudging up the road toward him. Parker loped over to the man and reined in.

The old-timer looked up and patted the shotgun he held in the crook of his arm. "Good day for squirrel huntin'," he said.

Parker burrowed deeper into his coat. "If you say so."

The old man chuckled, then frowned. He leaned forward and squinted. Parker knew what was coming.

"I know you, from someplace," the hunter said. "Ain't you Charlie Parker?"

Parker raised his head a moment, gazed up at the trees and the falling leaves and then at the woods and the straight, flat road that led to his wife and his brother and the rest of his life. He thought about past deeds and past decisions, and about Cole Bennett, also known as Morris Dixon. Then he looked back down at the old-timer.

"I used to be," Parker said.

MOONSHINE
AND ROSES

"Tell me the truth," Ruthie Ford said. "Why exactly did you come here?"

Joe McInnis didn't answer. The two of them were sitting hand-in-hand on the moonlit steps of her farmhouse outside Rayville, Kentucky. Fifty feet away, parked in an open shed, were a wooden mule wagon and a 1930 Chevrolet. The car, and house too, had belonged to Ruthie's late father, Parnell, until his death five months ago. Joe remembered him well, from when Joe and Ruthie were kids and their families were neighbors in Allen's Fork, a hundred miles west. He hadn't seen Parnell Ford or his wife—or Ruthie—since then, but he could easily imagine Parnell buying that car and grinning and lighting a cigarette and saying something like *It might be a Chevy, but it's a Ford now*. Ruthie's father had been interesting, to say the least.

"What's making you smile?" she asked.

"You," Joe said.

"Liar. I said I wanted the truth."

"The truth is, I was admiring your ride, there under the shed."

She followed his gaze, and smiled, too. "It'd work, if I had a mule to pull it."

"I meant the car."

"I know. The car won't run either." She leaned against him and squeezed his hand, like old times. "You gonna answer me, or not?"

"I was thinking about your family," Joe said, addressing one of her questions but not the other. "Back when we were teenagers in Allen's Fork." He didn't mention the fact that he and Ruthie had been madly in love at the time. Or thought they were.

A wave of sadness crossed her face. "Ancient history," she murmured.

It did seem that way, now. Ruthie and her parents had moved here to Rayville in the fall of 1924, almost ten years ago, right after she and Joe graduated from AF High. Joe's parents and sister had stayed put, but he soon moved also, took the train to Chicago to work a government job arranged by a distant cousin, and the next time Joe heard anything at all about the Fords was several years ago, when the agency he worked for found out Parnell was involved with a network of bootleggers in Burdette County, Kentucky. Then, not long before Joe's office at the former Bureau of Prohibition relocated to Cincinnati this past May, he heard that Parnell Ford and a man named Arliss Horton stole forty thousand dollars of liquor money from Jed and Isaac Sloane in the town of Rayville. Both Horton and Jed Sloane died in a bloody gunfight at the scene, but Parnell got away with the cash and led his pursuers on a chase that took them halfway across West Virginia. Everyone familiar with the situation knew who Parnell was running from, but nobody knew where he was running to, maybe not even Parnell. One thing for sure was that he failed to run far enough or fast enough, because he was caught and killed and the stolen forty grand was never found. Even so, the dark world of illegal liquor production and distribution continued throughout the hills and hollows of Ohio, Kentucky, and Tennessee, and the Sloane empire in eastern Kentucky remained powerful and ruthless. What also continued were the frequent and violent clashes between groups like Isaac Sloane's and their competitors, an activity that for years had been known to Prohibition agents as the moonshine wars.

When the officials in Frankfort tried to control the situation and failed, Joe McInnis's bosses at the newly formed Alcohol Tax Unit in Cincinnati decided to send an agent down to check things out. Joe was quick to volunteer. He had never forgotten Ruthie Ford and was convinced he never would, and saw this as a long-awaited chance at never-achieved happiness. He was dispatched the next morning to the mountain town of Rayville, and after a full day of halfheartedly searching for Isaac Sloane and fiercely searching for Ruthie, he located her. At five o'clock on the afternoon of July 31, 1934, Joe was standing on the doorstep of her home on Coaldigger Road in rural Burdette County, his hat in his hand and his heart in his throat, and when she answered the door she leaped into his arms. Some time later, when they'd calmed down and could think rationally, Joe drove her to supper at a café in Rayville, and they lingered there at a back corner table for three hours, during which time he learned all he could about Ruthie's life over the past ten years. There wasn't much to tell: two years of junior college in the adjacent county, a brief and failed marriage with no children, a job as a teller at the local bank. And ever since the unhappy and unexpected event that took away both Ruthie's pa and her job—the bank's president, though fond of bootlegged whiskey, decided he didn't want the daughter of a rum-running murderer handling its customers' money—she had been an unemployed caregiver to her ma, who had suffered a debilitating stroke two weeks before Parnell's death.

Afterward, Ruthie and her ma had stayed on, here at the house—where else could they go?—and lived on what Ruthie was able to raise in the garden and what she could earn through field work and household chores for the few neighbors who were friendly and charitable and the fewer who didn't know her history. But neither the friendship nor the charity lasted long, and those who didn't know her found out about her. The sins of the father and an ingrained mistrust of anyone not raised in or near Rayville finally left the two remaining Fords shunned by the townspeople and most of the country folk as well, and hated by Isaac Sloane and his crew. Since her ma's death three months ago Ruthie had truly been on her own.

As far as Joe McInnis could tell, she'd done a fair job of it. The farmhouse was neat as a pin, and the outbuildings were not yet in bad repair. A bone-dry but tidy lawn, an orchard of young plum trees, a green and lush vegetable garden, and, alongside the split-rail garden fence, a long line of rosebushes that—except for two plants near the end—blazed in every shade of red, white, and pink. Even now, here in the evening starlight in one of the poorest counties of one of the poorest states in the union, the setting looked like the front cover of *Successful Farming*.

As for the rest of the story, Joe also learned that Ruthie had found a note in the barn the morning after her pa's theft of the Sloanes' money, a note pinned against an inside wall by a shovel handle, where she'd be sure to see it when she came through to gather eggs from the henhouse. It said, in Parnell's rough printing, I'LL BE BACK FOR YOU AND YOUR MA. As things turned out, he hadn't made good on that promise.

All this catching-up made their otherwise happy reunion supper a somber event, but by the time they finished dessert Joe McInnis had already sworn to himself that they'd never again be apart, and he thought Ruthie felt the same. It was as they rose to leave the table and headed for the door that reality set in. The red-haired and oversized Isaac Sloane and his cousins stomped into the café, and when Sloane saw Ruthie he snarled an insult and grabbed her by the arm.

Ruthie, sitting beside Joe now on the front steps of her porch, adjusted the pretty white shawl that covered her shoulders—it was an unseasonably cool night, for late July—and stared off into the distance. "I wish you hadn't hit him," she said.

"Me, too—I wish I'd shot him."

"Were you carrying a gun?"

"No. It was in the car. But . . . the things he said to you . . . and then, when he grabbed your arm—"

"He got a surprise, didn't he." She paused, and smiled. "You hit him so hard I bet his dog farted."

Joe looked at her, and grinned also. "And then howled at the moon?" he said.

"And then ran under the house and hid."

They laughed aloud. It was a good sound, out here in the clear summer night. He said, "I'd forgot how much I missed you, Ruthie."

She turned solemn then. "Well, you'll soon be missing me again. You gotta leave here tonight. Or tomorrow morning at the latest."

"Why? Because of Isaac Sloane?"

"Him and his bunch."

Joe shook his head. "I'm not leaving you, Ruthie. I told you that. Ever again."

Her eyes teared up, sparkling in the moonlight. "You have to. You can't come to this town and do what you did tonight, to a Sloane. Not in public. And it's not just about you. Think about it—you were with *me*, and my pa stole money from him and killed his brother Jed." She swallowed hard. "Sloane'll come all right, and if he finds you here he'll kill us both."

"I don't think so," he said.

"Why not?"

"Because of that card I gave him."

Ruthie frowned, and Joe knew she was remembering what happened. Isaac Sloane had jerked Ruthie toward him and spat his obscenities and then Joe stepped up and punched him square in the face as hard as he could, and while Sloane was lying on his back on the floor with a flattened nose and out so cold that cartoon stars should be circling his head, one of Sloane's gang—Lester Coggins, Joe thought, from the photos he'd studied—looked at Joe and mumbled, "Who are you?" And Joe had taken a business card from his pocket and flipped it onto the unconscious man's chest. Then he and Ruthie walked out, never looking back.

Now, an hour later, Ruthie asked him, "You honestly think your name is gonna scare Isaac Sloane?"

"My name? He doesn't know my name."

"'Course he does. You left them your card."

"The card wasn't mine. It was my boss's. I happened to have one with me, and, well . . ."

Ruthie frowned. "I don't understand," she said. "Who exactly is your boss?"

"Eliot Ness."

Her eyes widened. All of a sudden it was dead quiet, there in front of the house.

"What did you say?"

"I'm sorry," Joe said. "That was one of the things I hadn't mentioned to you yet."

"You told me you work for the government, in Ohio—"

"Treasury Department." When he saw her blank look, he added, "Alcohol Tax Unit."

"You mean . . . Prohibition? That was repealed last year."

"That didn't stop the stills or the bootleggers. It's an illegal black-market issue, now."

She stayed quiet a minute or so. When all that sank in she said, in a hushed voice, "You once told me you were good with numbers, you wanted to be an accountant. So I figured—"

"I lied. I was never good with numbers."

"And—your boss is *Eliot Ness?* Does that mean . . . are you one of the—"

"Untouchables? No. He put that group together to get Capone, when we were in Chicago. I moved to Cincinnati when he did. I'm just a low-level agent."

"But they saw your face. Won't they know you're not Ness?"

"I doubt it. You ever seen a picture of him?"

"No . . ."

"Neither have most people. Besides, we look a little alike, and he's only thirty-one."

Ruthie was shaking her head. "Even if you did fool them, and that keeps 'em from coming after you—what good would it do?"

"It'd buy us time."

"Time for what? You told me you came here to do a job. You can't just leave."

"Sure I can," Joe said. "So can you."

"What?"

Joe turned and took both her hands in his. "I came on this trip for you, Ruthie. To find you. That's the answer to that question you asked, awhile ago. I was sent here to get information on Sloane's outfit, but *my* reason was to get *you*." Holding her gaze, he said, "I'll quit if I have to, take a different job. All I want is for you to leave here with me."

A silence passed. The only sound was the chirp of crickets in the woods beside the house.

"I can't leave, Joe. I got no money. In fact, I got a tall pile of debt. The bank says I'll soon lose the house."

He nodded, still looking her in the eye. He'd been wondering when to mention this to her, and maybe now was the time. "I been thinking about that," he said. "All through supper, and on the way here, after."

"Thinking about what?"

He didn't answer right away. He looked again at the garden fence and the row of bright flowers alongside it, and when he focused on her and was about to reply, he stopped. She was staring past him, her eyes wide. He turned also, to face the winding dirt road that led to town.

A cloud of smoke, chalk-white in the moonlight, hung in the distance. It seemed to be growing. Then Joe saw that it wasn't smoke at all. It was dust, and it was moving toward them.

With a jolt he realized Ruthie had been right. Not only had Sloane and his thugs known Joe wasn't Ness, they'd probably pegged him as a revenuer. Add that to the knockout punch at the café, and his fate was sealed. For Sloane, getting payback against Parnell Ford's daughter would just be icing on the cake.

In what he hoped was a steady voice Joe said, "You have any guns in the house?"

She nodded, still gazing at the approaching dust cloud. "Pa's pistol and a shotgun."

"Can you find 'em quick, in the dark?"

"Yes."

"Go," he said. "Meet me in the barn."

"The barn?"

"They'll think we're in the house. Go!"

She jumped up and dashed through the door while he sprinted to his car, a black '32 Buick. From the backseat Joe grabbed his holstered revolver and a lever-action Winchester rifle. Then he jogged downhill past the house to the barn he'd seen earlier, an ancient building with two small, shoulder-high windows flanking a wooden door. He didn't bother to look back at the road; he could now hear the motor of the approaching vehicle. It was maybe half a minute away. From the corner of his eye he saw Ruthie come out the back door of the house and head toward him. She had a weapon in each hand, her white shawl streaming behind her as she ran. He got to the barn first, opened the door, and when they were both inside pulled it shut again. For a moment they stood there, breathing hard and staring at each other in the sudden darkness.

It wasn't pitch black, but almost. The front of the barn faced north, toward the house, and was in shadow, so they could see out the two paneless windows but no one could see in from outside. The only lights in the rest of the building were narrow slats of moonlight through the gaps in the boards of the back side. He could make out several empty stalls and a ladder to a loft.

"Maybe it's not Sloane," she said, still out of breath.

"Who else would it be?"

She nodded her agreement. No visitors came here anymore, before dark or after.

Joe looked out the window, thinking hard. The car he'd seen and heard should be here by now—what was taking it so long? "Are those loaded?" he asked, pointing to her two guns.

"Yes. And I know how to use 'em."

She'd turned tough since he last saw her, Joe thought. He guessed she'd probably had to.

Moving carefully in the gloom, Joe leaned his rifle against the wall, shucked his suit coat, strapped on his shoulder holster with his revolver, and took Ruthie's pistol—a .45 automatic—and shoved it into his belt at the small of his back. Then he put his coat on again and said, "If things start happening, hide in one of the stalls and keep your shotgun ready." He ran his fingers along the dim outline of the long gun in her hands. "My God, is that an eight-gauge?"

"Yep. And you don't even want to know what Pa put inside these shells. I shoot somebody with this, their head's comin' right off."

"I'm hoping you won't have to." Joe had picked up his rifle and was peering through one of the windows, studying the scene. Then he caught the yellow glow of headlight beams against the trees beside the house, a second before they winked out. As he watched, his heart pounding, a dark-colored car eased to a stop beside his, and several doors popped open.

Ruthie was watching too, kneeling a few feet away. "Should we go up in the hayloft?"

"That only works in cowboy movies," he said. "I want us to be able to run if we have to." In fact he wished they'd gone straight to the woods, or at least thought to hide his car behind the barn. Too late now.

And then he saw them, three men, spreading out in the side yard. One disappeared around the front of the house, one crept toward the back door, and the third—Joe recognized Isaac Sloane from his size and from a white bandage on his nose—stayed put, waiting. All three were holding pistols. Not as bad as it could've been, Joe thought. At least no Thompson machine guns.

As long as they didn't search the barn . . .

The two who'd gone to the house spent a long time inside, and finally came out the back door together. All three held a conference, and after a look in all directions they seemed uncertain. One of them—Coggins?—motioned toward the car. Then Sloane stopped, marched to the middle of the backyard between the barn and the house, and picked something up off the ground. Something white. Joe hadn't even seen it lying there because the moon was so bright.

Beside him, he heard Ruthie suck in a breath. It was her shawl.

The three men turned, together, to stare at the barn.

Joe dropped below window level, quietly cocked the Winchester, and rose again to rest the gun barrel on the sill. He could see all of them, but knew they couldn't see him. Without looking away, he hissed to Ruthie, "Hide someplace, *now*."

Sloane and his men, weapons pointed, started walking downhill toward the barn.

When they were thirty feet away Joe called, in a level voice, "Stop right there."

All three froze.

"My name's McInnis, and I'm a federal agent. Drop the guns."

For a long moment no one moved. And then four things happened, in quick succession: (1) Isaac Sloane jumped behind Lester Coggins, (2) Coggins fired a shot at the barn window, (3) the third man fired also, and (4) Joe McInnis shot them both.

Sloane didn't hesitate. Since his human shield was gone—along with his courage—he turned and ran to Joe's left, heading for the parked car. Joe pushed the barn door open, walked into the yard, and shouted to him to stop. He did.

Slowly, Sloane turned again, pistol in hand. The two men faced each other in the moonlit yard. Joe stood with his rifle shouldered and ready, the barn to his left, the house to his right, the two dead gunmen lying nearby, and Sloane straight ahead.

"Put it down," Joe said.

And saw, in the brilliant moonlight, a smile spread across Sloane's face. Before Joe had time to process this, something punched him in the back—it felt like a sledgehammer—and he heard the flat *crack* of a gunshot. He pitched forward and landed facedown in the dirt, pain knifing through his body. He had dropped the Winchester. Moaning and gasping, he rolled over onto his back and looked up at the stars.

He lay there for what seemed a long time, and heard, more than saw, Isaac Sloane walk around him to stand just beyond his feet, staring down at him. With an effort Joe raised his head to look at Sloane, and when he did he saw a fourth man walking toward them in the distance, holding a rifle. It was this man, Joe knew, who'd shot him from behind, and he also understood, now, that this was the reason Sloane's car had taken a little too long to reach the house. It must've stopped on the way, while Joe and Ruthie were making preparations, and let one of its passengers out, probably to get a rifle out of the trunk and circle around on foot and come in from the other direction. And it had worked.

Joe squeezed his eyes shut, rigid with pain, opened them again, and saw Sloane—he was still smiling—cock his pistol. "You ain't Eliot Ness, kid," he said. "In more ways than one."

And then Joe heard another blast, this one earsplitting, from the open barn door ten feet away, and Isaac Sloane disappeared as if someone had snatched him aside. Joe, head still raised, heard Sloane hit the ground somewhere to the left, but didn't try to look; he now had an unobstructed view of the rifleman in the distance, and before the man could react Joe snatched the revolver from its holster, and—aiming between the V of his own shoes as he lay on his back—shot the man twice in the chest.

And passed out.

#

He woke up lying with his head in Ruthie's lap, both of them there on the ground outside the barn door. He looked up into her face.

What an ending, Joe thought. He remembered her saying there was no telephone in the house, and he doubted she'd be able to drag him to his car, get him into it, and drive him all the way to a doc in time. Oh well. He could think of worse places to die than in her arms.

She put a palm to his cheek and said, "You feeling better? We got things to do, here."

He shifted position and winced. "Be sure you tell the sheriff they shot first. Okay? And tell Ma I love her—"

"You can tell her yourself. Come on, try to stand up."

"Stand up?"

"You're not dying, Joe. You might feel like it but you're not." With her free hand she held something up so he could see it. At first he thought she'd retrieved one of the dead men's weapons, but what she held in her hand was bent and twisted—

He blinked. "Is that your pa's gun?"

"It saved your life," she said. "I rolled you over and pulled your coattail up to see the wound, and found this instead, stuck in your belt."

Joe couldn't speak. He could only stare at the dented pistol.

Still cradling his head, she said, "That last guy musta been a good shot. He hit you—and *this*—dead center."

With a deep grunt Joe sat up, reached behind him, and felt around. It hurt like hell, but she was right—he had no bullet holes in his back. Just one in his suit coat. Ruthie stood up and helped him to his feet. He still couldn't believe it.

Moving slowly, he followed her to each of the fallen moonshiners. All were indeed stone dead, and Isaac Sloane looked as if parts of him had been through a sausage grinder. An eight-gauge at close range would do that. "Looks like both those guns of your pa's saved me," Joe said.

She helped him limp to a bench underneath a big oak in the side yard. He slumped onto it and flexed his legs and back, groaning but counting his blessings. "Give me a minute," he said.

She sat beside him, a little gingerly, he thought. "Are *you* okay?" he asked her.

"Yeah. It's just my shoulder. That shotgun's got a kick." They leaned against each other a moment, both of them dog-tired and shivering and lost in thought. Finally she said to him, "What were you about to say, earlier, just before we saw 'em coming?"

"What?"

"I'd just finished telling you about my debts, and the house, and you said—"

He nodded, remembering. "I said I'd been thinking about that."

"Yes. And you got a strange look on your face and turned to stare at the garden. . . ." She looked in that direction also, then back at him. "What was it you were gonna tell me?"

He hesitated, gathering his thoughts. Somewhere in the woods, a night bird called. It was eerily silent underneath the tree.

"I was gonna say they never found that money your pa took from Jed and Isaac that night. Right?"

"Right. Everybody knows that."

"And that note your pa left you, in the barn. You told me it was up on the wall in a place that he knew you'd walk past, the next morning."

"That's right."

Joe studied her face. "I ain't the smartest guy in the world, Ruthie, but I been doing investigative work a long time. I'm observant, and I listen close."

She sat up straight, staring at him. Waiting.

Joe cleared his throat and said, "Were there any nails in that wall, any hooks, anything else your pa coulda used to hold the note up at eye-level, where you'd see it?"

She frowned. "Now that you mention it . . . yeah, I guess there were. Why?"

"And was the barn a place where he kept hand tools? Rakes, hoes, shovels, and such?"

"No. Those were in the toolshed. Still are."

"But that night, when he left you the note, you said he used a propped-up shovel handle to pin it against the wall."

She let out a breath. "What are you getting at, Joe? We got four bodies layin' here, people you and me shot dead. There are things we gotta do."

"One more question," he said. He shifted position a bit, felt another stab of pain. "You ain't had rain here in a while, have you? Road's dusty, grass is dry. Correct?"

"Yes . . ."

"But you been tendin' to your peas and beans, and flowers." He pointed, holding her gaze, toward the garden. It glowed almost as bright as day underneath the full moon. "You water 'em regular, from the well. You have to, for them roses to be so big."

"Yes, I do."

"Then why ain't those last two rosebushes as pretty as all the others? They're practically dead."

She blinked, and drew her brows together. "I don't know. I water 'em all the same way."

He said nothing, staring at her.

Ruthie shook her head. "What's all this about, Joe? What are you saying?"

"I'm saying you need to go fetch that shovel."

\#

It took twenty minutes for the two of them to dig up the last two rosebushes in the row beside the garden fence, Joe working while Ruthie held her shoulder and then swapping out with her until the pain eased in his bruised back. It took another five minutes to haul out the metal box they found underneath, and open it.

Only then did she fully understand. She clapped a hand over her mouth, took two steps backward, and sagged to a sitting position in the grass. The box was packed with cash, in bundles of everything from fives to hundreds. It would take a long time to be sure, but Joe did a quick count. When he was done he said to Ruthie, "Forty thousand looks about right."

Her eyes were wide as quarters. "I never woulda known. . . ."

"Maybe he didn't intend you to. He might've just wanted to hide it someplace he knew was safe, where nobody'd look."

"Except you."

He shrugged. "I just noticed something musta been keeping those bushes from growing."

Both of them stayed quiet a while. A light wind had picked up, but Joe barely felt it.

At last Ruthie said, "So, what now?"

"Now we drive to town and tell the sheriff to follow us back here and pick up the bodies. And find a phone so I can report to my office in Ohio."

"Your boss, you mean? This time of night?"

"Dern right. You and me just derailed the biggest bootlegging outfit in this state. Maybe the whole country. I know a lot about Isaac and his operation—without him, it's finished."

"And the revenge thing, about what Pa did to him and his brother?"

"That's done, too. Nobody'll bother you anymore."

She seemed to think that over. "So, what about . . ." Her gaze drifted to the metal box.

Joe looked at it also, and for the first time in an hour or so, felt a smile on his face. "That's your decision. It's your money."

"No," she said. "It's not."

"Then whose is it? This is cash from illegal hooch that's long since been delivered and drank up. It's not like it came from an honest business, or somebody's savings, or a bank vault."

"But . . . don't we need to turn it in, to your boss? He'd be happy, right? You'd probably get promoted."

"Oh, he'd be happy for sure. And yeah, I probably would. But think about what this money could mean to you, Ruthie." He waved a hand around him, at the land, the house, the useless car in the shed. "A fraction of it could pay off every debt you have."

She paused, tilted her head, and gave him a long, thoughtful look. "Actually," she said, "you might've miscounted."

"I what?"

She pointed to the box. "Now that I think about it, I bet it's really only twenty thousand, in there. I bet Pa divided it up and buried half here and half someplace else. In fact, I doubt anybody'll ever find the rest."

He stared at her, then at the box, then at her again.

"The only right thing to do," she added, "is give all this money we found—it's twenty thousand, remember—to your boss. And if he chooses to reward you somehow, well . . ."

He looked at her for a long time. Innocent little Ruthie Ford, whose life had taught her to be tough, so tough she could kill a man with a shotgun if she had to. Sweet Ruthie, who he once thought he'd forgotten but now realized he had loved all along—and who seemed to be trying, at this moment, not to smile.

He gave her a solemn nod. "Sounds good to me. And you know what?—a promotion might mean I could afford to get married. Maybe look for a nicer place to live."

"My thoughts exactly. You might even marry someone rich." She stood up. "Come on, let's fill up this hole and put the box in the house."

Joe didn't move, still staring into her eyes. "Just one thing. After all this digging, I might not be able to get down on one knee . . ."

She did grin then, the look on her face as bright as the moon. "I bet you can manage," she said. "And by the way, you shouldn't feel bad about miscounting, just now."

"I shouldn't?"

"No." She picked up the shovel, scooped the first bladeful of dirt into the hole, and looked at him. "You were never good with numbers."

WELCOME TO ARMADILLO

I was unlucky last night, for two reasons. First, I missed my ex-wife. Second, I ran out of bullets.

But I was lucky, too. The creak of a loose floorboard made me dive out of bed an instant before the knife stabbed the spot where my chest had been. I fumbled my old two-barrel derringer out of the night table drawer and got off a shot, but—as I said—it missed its mark. The other chamber was empty, and by the time I retrieved my real and fully loaded gun from under my pillow, Penny was out the door and gone. Insult to injury, the hunting knife sticking out of my bed was the one I'd let her use on our camping trips. Back before she wanted to kill me.

Just so you know, my name's Russell West, I'm a private investigator, and this wasn't the first attempt on my life. Or even the first attempt by the former Penny West. It's a long story, but what happened was, one of my cases last year involved following a husband suspected of having a torrid affair. Turned out I spotted him in a hot-sheet motel parking lot, but he spotted me, too, got spooked, and shot at me. He missed and I didn't, and as I stared down at his dead body on the pavement I couldn't help noticing that the woman standing in the motel-room doorway was my wife, Penny. Tears and hysteria followed, and she never forgave me. It didn't seem to occur to her that she might need some forgiving herself. (Penny grew up rich, and never got over it.) Anyhow, she moved out and I stayed, and now here we were, eight months later, with me having to look over my shoulder every day—and night, too, apparently. I watched from my bedroom window as she screeched away from the curb in the vintage yellow Mustang her daddy'd bought her.

I sleepily weighed my options. As I said, Penny had tried this before. Not long after our divorce, she'd taken a shot at me from the nearby woods one afternoon as I checked the mail. Obviously, it didn't work—all I suffered was a bullet hole through my mailbox and my water bill. But going to the cops didn't work either. I had no proof it was her, and one of her lying girlfriends supplied her with an alibi. Same thing would probably happen this time, if I reported it. Besides, there was someone else who wanted me dead also, probably more than Penny did: a sleazebag named Ollie

Bonatello. I had helped put him away a long time ago, and I'd heard he was out now and gunning for me. Just one more thing to worry about. As for Penny, on the one hand I wished I'd shot her tonight and on the other hand I was glad I hadn't. It's complicated.

In the end, I did nothing. Fortunately I had no more nocturnal visits, and the next thing worth telling happened two weeks later. June fifteenth, my mother's birthday. She lived alone in the small town of Catlow, two hundred miles across the desert, and I planned to drive over and spend the day with her, something I'd done every year since my dad's death in '09. This time, though, my car was in the shop so I took the bus. Penny and I had done that together several times in the past, since we'd both grown up there (on different sides of the tracks, so to speak) and her parents still lived there, too, and we thought riding the bus was fun, back then. I'd even done it alone last Christmas, after Penny and I had split up and the roads were icy, and I had slept the whole way. I was planning on another restful trip.

Little did I know.

#

At nine a.m. I walked downtown and caught the bus, armed with a birthday gift for my mother, a change of clothes, and hopes for a mini-vacation away from those who might wish me dead. I settled into an aisle seat near the back of the bus, pulled the bill of my baseball cap low over my face, and nodded off. We'd been on the road for maybe two hours when I woke up to see a twentysomething red-haired woman standing in the aisle beside my seat, chewing gum and looking at me. I rubbed my eyes and said, "Sorry. Did you say something?"

"I said, could I scoot by you to the window? It's been too crowded up front."

"Sure." I moved my knees so she could squeeze past. My backpack was in the middle seat, so I moved it to my lap to give her more room. She sat, studied the dreary landscape a bit, then turned to me and held out her hand.

I shook it, and we exchanged names—Nancy Reed, she said—and did the small-talk thing for a minute or two, in low voices. Her face seemed vaguely familiar, but I couldn't place it.

"I heard we'll make a lunch stop soon," she said.

I nodded. "Armadillo."

"I hope you're not saying that's on the menu."

"I'm saying that's where we'll stop. I've made this run before."

"Never heard of it."

I smiled. "No reason you would've. I think it has one stoplight."

"Where is it you're going?" she asked. "Final stop, I mean."

"My hometown—place called Catlow. Not much bigger."

The redheaded woman seemed to give that some thought. "Only Catlow I remember's an old Western movie. Main guy was that dude from *The Magnificent Seven*."

"Steve McQueen?"

"The other one," she said, chewing away at her gum. "You like movies?"

"I like detective shows." I wonder why.

"Me, too." She paused and took a long look around. "Okay—that should be enough."

"Enough what?"

She leaned toward me. "Conversation," she whispered. "I needed to make sure other passengers saw us talking."

"What do you mean?" I said.

She smiled and stood up. "Excuse me. I'll be right back."

I moved my legs again so she could ease past, then watched her march away toward the front. A moment later the bus slowed and pulled to the side of the road. When we'd stopped, Nancy Reed returned, followed by the bus driver, a huge man with a shaved head and tired eyes.

"That's him," she said, pointing to me. "He said he has a bomb in his backpack."

I felt my jaw drop. *What?*

"He told me he's going to blow us all up."

I tried to speak but couldn't seem to form words. My body had gone numb.

The bald driver was glaring at me. "Let's see your hands, buddy."

I showed him both palms while he took my pack from my lap. In a hopefully calm voice I said, "There's nothing in there but clothes and a book."

"A book?" He'd unzipped the pack and was looking inside.

"Birthday gift." Hands still raised, I added, "This woman is lying to you."

"He's the one who's lying," Nancy Reed said. "He told me he was going to kill us all."

By now the driver had finished his search. Everyone was staring at us. He looked around and asked, "Anybody else hear this, what he said?"

"I did," said a scowling, dark-haired woman in the next row. "He said he had a bomb."

I let out a breath, tried to tell myself this wasn't happening.

He tucked my pack under one giant arm. "Stand up."

I did, and he gave me a thorough pat-down. Meanwhile, I kept my eyes on the redhead. She stared back at me without a blink, still smacking her gum. *Why was she doing this?*

Apparently satisfied, the driver told her to have a seat and guided me by the elbow up the aisle and off the bus. Outside, he handed me my backpack and stood there looking at me.

"Want to tell me what's going on, here?"

I shook my head, still stunned. "I told you already. That woman in there's crazy. I never said anything about a bomb."

"How about the other lady?"

"She was lying, too." Realizing how lame that sounded, I pointed east and said, "Look, I figure we can't be more'n twenty miles from Armadillo. You want to call the cops, call 'em. I've done nothing wrong."

He studied me a moment. "It's eight miles. But there's no police there. No tellin' how long it'd take the cops to get here." He folded his arms across his barrel chest. "I dunno what your game is, mister, but we take this kind of thing serious. I got two passengers saying you made a bomb threat. The first one suggested I throw you off the bus. I think that's a good idea."

I couldn't believe my ears. I said, as he turned away, "You're leaving me here? What am I supposed to do?"

"Thumb a ride, or walk." He paused with one foot on the door-step. "Don't matter to me."

And that was that. The door closed, and moments later the bus roared to life and eased back onto the road. Faces stared at me through the rear window. I stood and watched until the bus was no more than a tiny dot miles away on the horizon, then it vanished from sight.

I sighed and studied my surroundings. Nothing but yellow-brown desert on all sides. Straight ahead and behind me was the two-lane highway, ahead and to the right was a scattering of rocks and boulders, and in the distance to the left was a line of purple mountains. A stiff wind from the west helped make the midday heat a little more bearable. I knew the desert: tonight would be cold.

I checked my cell phone, which without any service bars was as useless as a stick of wood, and studied the time-worn state road, which I already knew was rarely traveled.

Eight miles? I supposed it could be worse.

I strapped on my backpack, adjusted my cap, and started walking.

#

I'd gone maybe a mile when it hit me. I stopped in my tracks.

I knew where I'd seen my redheaded accuser before. The hair had thrown me off.

She'd been a blonde then, in the back row of the audience at Ollie Bonatello's trial. Probably along with the other lying woman on the bus. It took several seconds for the full impact of that to settle in. Here I was, alone and unarmed on the back side of nowhere, and the person who had put me here was connected to the man who had sworn to kill me.

I realized I might be in a lot more trouble than being stranded.

It was at that moment I saw another little dot in the distance ahead, three or four miles away. This one was moving toward me. Bonatello? I had no way of knowing. But I had to assume it could be.

I took another quick look around, this time searching instead of observing. Whoever was coming couldn't see me yet, but he would soon. I had only a minute or two.

I was now about even with the cluster of big rocks I'd seen earlier, off to my right. That seemed to offer the only cover. I headed for it, and on the way there I put together a flimsy plan. Veering farther right and stripping off my pack and shirt as I ran, I spotted a lone, squarish boulder about two feet by two feet, not far past the rock pile. I also picked up two smaller rocks on the way. One was the size of a baseball, which I stuffed into my pants pocket, the other a head-sized stone with a flat bottom. Still running, I fitted my baseball cap onto that one, tight enough that the wind wouldn't blow it off. When I reached the lone boulder I draped my shirt over it all the way to the ground, pulled the collar up high, and balanced the cap-covered stone on top, with the cap's bill facing away from the road. If my suspicions were right, "Nancy Reed" would've by now reported my location and what I was wearing, either by phone or in person, in Armadillo, and I hoped that from a distance my hastily dressed dummy would look like the back of a seated man with a red shirt and blue cap. It was the best I could do.

It occurred to me that she had also seen the driver search me, and would've reported that I was unarmed. Things just kept getting worse.

I sprinted back toward the tall cluster of boulders, keeping my head down and keeping the rocks between me and the approaching car. If the driver did get a glimpse of me, my white T-shirt and khaki pants would blend in a lot better than that red shirt would've. The car was still a long way off, and though I'd not yet had a real look at it, I could hear it. It didn't seem to be moving fast, which made sense, if it was Bonatello. He'd know roughly where I was, and he'd be watching for me.

I would soon know for sure.

I reached the rock cluster and found a hiding place between two of the boulders. Sure enough, wiggling in on stomach and elbows, I heard the squeal of brakes—he must've seen my decoy—and the crunch of gravel as he stopped on the road's shoulder. Then I heard a car door open and shut. One car door. At last, a bit of luck: if it was more than one person, I was dead.

Lying flat, my backpack under my left arm, I held my breath and listened. For a moment I heard nothing but the steady whisper of the wind. Then, footsteps. I risked a glance past the edge of one of the boulders.

It was him, all right. Ollie Bonatello. Older, but still skinny. He was creeping past my hidey-hole, eyes fixed on my fake self fifty yards away. He had a gun in his hand, a big revolver.

My mouth was dry, my heart pounding. I knew I couldn't chance throwing the rock I had in my pocket, and missing. I would do better trying to sneak up behind him and use it to crack his skull. The odds were slim, but it was my only hope. I reached down with my right hand for the rock—

And it was gone. My heart leapt in my chest. The rock must've squeezed out of my pocket when I knelt to adjust my shirt and cap.

I let out a long breath, closed my eyes. I was out of options, not to mention weapons. In the next minute or so Bonatello would discover my ruse, realize where I had to be hiding, and kill me as dead as my colorful decoy. I might as well stand up and surrender.

Then I heard the rattle. It was more of a low buzz, almost lost in the sound of the wind, and only a couple of feet to my left. I had no time to think; I just rolled to my right and thrust my backpack between me and the snake as it struck. Only then did I see it. It was huge, thicker than my wrist. Its fangs hit the pack hard, and as they released it I grabbed the snake with my right hand just behind its head. A moment later I found its tail with my left hand, and hung on. Lying now on my back with six feet of writhing, twisting snake between my hands, I craned my neck to look past my rock. Bonatello hadn't heard me. He was still moving toward the red-shirted diversion, even more slowly now, his revolver in a two-handed grip. And I had a new plan.

What happened next happened fast. Trembling from head to toe, I wiggled back out, struggled to my feet, and walked as quietly as I could toward Bonatello's back. I was fully exposed; if he turned the least bit, he would see me. The big snake bucked and jerked but I held on, one hand behind its head and one clutching its tail just above the now-silent rattles. I was surprised how heavy it was. Bonatello was now ten feet from the dummy. He raised the gun.

"Well, Mr. West," he said, aiming at the back of the red shirt. "Guess who's here."

By that time I was right behind him, and I never hesitated. I tossed the giant rattlesnake onto his neck, head over his right shoulder, tail over his left, and stepped back. Fast as lightning, the snake buried its fangs into his throat, released, and bit him again. His revolver fell to the ground and so did he, screaming and cursing. I darted forward and snatched up the gun. The snake was wrapped around him, striking his neck and head, again and again. It didn't take long. I think Bonatello probably saw me before he died, but there was so much thrashing and kicking and moaning I couldn't be sure.

When it was over, after the snake that saved my life had crawled away, I picked up my shirt and cap and put them on, searched the dead man's pockets, wiped his revolver clean of prints and tucked it back into his holster, and went back to the rocks to fetch my backpack. I remember standing there beside the boulders a moment, and then sagging down to sit in the dirt until the trembling passed.

Finally I trudged back to the road, and to the car. When I looked at it for the first time, another puzzle piece fell into place. After all, how could he have known I would leave town this morning? He didn't know my mother, or her birthday, or that I was always there for it. And how could he have known my car was in the shop, that I would take the bus? That *particular* bus?

He knew because someone had told him.

The car was Penny's, the fancy yellow Mustang she'd parked in front of my house two weeks ago last night, when she'd tried to murder me with my old hunting knife.

I could picture the two of them, probably at the bus station up ahead, him saying to her: *Wait here for me. I'll enjoy the job more if I borrow that fancy ride of yours.*

Maybe now was the time to return it.

I climbed in, started the car with the key I'd taken from Bonatello's pocket, did a U-turn, and headed east. The face I saw in the car's mirror looked older that it had this morning.

It had been a long day, and it wasn't even noon.

#

I stopped at a store across the road from a sign that said WELCOME TO ARMADILLO. Inside, I bought a cheap cowboy hat, a throwaway cell phone, and oversized sunglasses, then used their restroom to change into a purple Phoenix Suns T-shirt from my backpack. Not a big difference, but it would have to do. Back in the car, I passed two greasy-haired guys with gaudy jogging suits and neck chains and a red duffel bag walking on the side of the road and wondered which of the three of us looked the silliest.

A moment later, I turned off the main road a block before the little café that doubled as a bus station and approached it from one of the back streets. The lot behind the station was almost empty. I parked Penny's Stang there, in a spot that I was sure couldn't be seen from the café, put on my hat, walked into the station, and checked the bus schedule. Then I entered the café through a connecting door. From inside, I could see through a side window the bus I'd been evicted from, and its driver standing near its door. He was talking with an old lady, and examining some kind of suitcase. His bald head gleamed in the sun. I was glad he was outside and I was in.

And—sure enough—I also saw Penny, sitting alone at a table beside a front window and staring at the street. The café was crowded, and I recognized several passengers from the bus. They seemed to be getting ready to leave, and no one seemed to recognize *me*. Including Penny. That made sense. She was watching for a pale, skinny jailbird, not a tall, weary cowboy. Two faces I *didn't* see were those of my red-haired friend or the other witness, both of whom had probably been recruited by either Penny or Bonatello.

As I stood there I saw the two jogging-suited dudes enter through the front door. They seemed suddenly upset for some reason, and kept watching my old pal the bus driver through the window. Whispering to each other, they found a table near the back and sat down.

I could tell something was fishy with those two, but they weren't my concern. I sauntered to the darkest corner I could find, not far from them, and picked up a plastic menu while keeping (1) my head down, (2) my dumb hat and sunglasses on, (3) and my attention fixed on my ex-wife and her table. Who said I couldn't do undercover work?

The question was, why was I in disguise at all? Why didn't I just confront Penny right now, and accuse her? For that matter, why hadn't I called the police already, to report what I'd found, and all the things that had happened to me on the bus and in the desert today?

One answer was that I didn't trust the cops to carry through on all this. I knew and understood how rich and influential Penny's father was, and how far his tentacles reached into this state's businesses and politics and law enforcement. I had decided, at some point in the past hour, that—for better or worse—I would need to handle this alone.

But all I had was a big-picture plan, with few details. Short-range, I wasn't certain what to do next. Which was why I was here watching instead of doing, and dressed like Willie Nelson instead of Joe Mannix.

My thoughts were interrupted by a bored waitress, standing beside me and waiting.

"Want me to read the menu to you?"

I looked up at her. Her nametag said ROXIE. "Why would I want that?"

Before she could respond, one of the two guys in jogging suits pushed past her, holding the duffel bag. His partner followed. Together we watched them turn the corner to the restrooms.

"When you gotta go, you gotta go," she said, and faced me again. "What was you sayin'?"

"I was saying, why would you—"

"Oh, yeah. Read the menu out loud?" She smiled a little. "'Cause I doubt you can see anything in here with them sunshades on."

I chuckled. "I can see just fine. Except things that maybe happened before I got here."

She squinted. "'Scuse me?"

I tipped my hat toward Penny, who was still street-watching. "See that lady over there?"

"What about her?"

"Well—I'm told she might be meeting a couple of her girl-friends here today. Friends that aren't friends of mine."

"So?"

"One's sorta cute and redheaded, the other one's brunette, looks like she just bit into a lemon. I was wondering, you happen to see anybody like that?"

Roxie studied me a moment. "Yeah, they was here. Came in together, off the bus."

"You see her give 'em anything?"

"How'd you know she did that?"

"Just asking."

"Yeah," she said. "Envelopes. One each. They stuffed 'em in their purses and left."

I nodded. I had needed to be sure. "Okay. Thanks, Roxie. And by the way—don't count on much of a tip from the woman in question."

She gave Penny another look and snorted. "I figured that out half an hour ago." She pointed to my menu. "You gonna eat, or what?"

I ordered coffee and a sweet roll and made a quick call to my mother, telling her I'd been delayed. What I didn't tell her was, I hadn't yet decided whether to drive Penny's car there or leave it here and catch the next bus. According to the schedule I'd seen on the way in, it would depart at 2:20. Two hours from now.

I had finished my call and was looking through the window, where a line of irritated people had formed outside the door of the bus, when Roxie showed up with my food.

"One more thing," I said to her. I pointed to the crowd waiting to board the bus. The two goons in jogging suits had returned from the restroom and joined the line. They were sweating and fingering their gold neck-chains and glaring at everyone. "What's going on, out there?"

She turned to look. "Oh. The driver, the big baldheaded guy? I heard he run into trouble this mornin', bomb threat or some-thin', and now he's searchin' everybody when they board."

"He's what?"

"Searchin' the new passengers. Lookin' through their bags and such, 'fore they board. Crazy, huh?" She nodded toward to my coffee and pastry. "You gonna need anything else?"

I just shook my head. My mind was no longer on my order, or

Roxie, or even on Penny. I was watching the two nervous guys in the jogging suits, for one simple but interesting reason.

Neither of them was carrying the duffel bag.

When Roxie left, I rose and quietly made my way to the men's room. It was empty. Within a minute I had checked inside all the toilet tanks and wastebaskets, and wound up standing beside a tall metal storage cabinet beside the sinks. The door to the cabinet was locked. That left only one other place to look.

Quickly I stepped up onto one of the sinks, raised up to my full height, and checked the top of the cabinet—and there it was. I grabbed the duffel, climbed down, walked to one of the stalls, and shut the door. Inside the bag I found three brick-sized packages wrapped in duct tape. I used my fingernail to burrow underneath the tape on one of them and check the contents. Satisfied, I repacked the bag, zipped it, and put it back in its hiding place on top of the cabinet.

Lost in thought, I returned to my table. The bus and its passengers were gone. I sat and watched Penny, who was still in the same place, staring at both the window and the front door. Only her profile was visible, but her face looked hard, and hateful. And something else, too. I could've sworn she was smiling a little, as she waited. I think that was what made up my mind.

I wolfed down my sweet roll, gulped my coffee, and realized I had a plan after all. I left Roxie a twenty-dollar tip when I left.

#

"You got two little side-by-side holes in your T-shirt," my mother said, studying my shoulder.

I looked down at the purple fabric. She and I were standing in the kitchen of my childhood home, having finished the best supper I'd eaten in a long time. She was washing dishes and I was drying. I was stuffed to the gills.

"And you still got good eyes, Ma." I decided not to tell her there would also be two matching holes in the side of the backpack I'd left upstairs, or that the biggest rattlesnake I ever saw had put them there during a moment of some duress.

She'd stacked the last plate into the drainer when the phone rang in the living room. "Probably a telemarketer," she said, grabbing a dishtowel. "Be right back."

She wasn't. It took a while. When she returned I had finished drying everything and was sitting with my phone at the table, checking the stock-market numbers.

I looked up and saw the concern on her face. "What's wrong?"

She sat also, and seemed to be choosing her words. "That was Ethel Draper, worked with me for years at the library. She's a friend of Anna Gooden's. She said . . ." Ma paused, frowning.

Anna and Donald Gooden were Penny's parents. "Said what?" I asked.

"Ethel said Anna told her Penny was arrested this afternoon. Said the state police, acting on an anonymous phone tip, stopped her car and found three kilos of cocaine hidden under some stuff in her trunk. Almost two hundred thousand dollars' worth."

"Whoa," I said.

"Whoa is right. And that's not all. Penny's father's contacts said the police found texts on her cell phone between her and a gangster named Bonaparte, or Bonalisa, or something like that. That part was a little hard to follow."

It wouldn't be hard to follow once they found Bonatello's body, I thought, and the cell phone in his pocket. In fact they'd probably already done that, from my second tipoff call, both of them made from the burner phone I'd bought earlier. I'd made the calls from a gas station near the café while I passed the time until I caught my bus at 2:20. I also sent Penny an anonymous text from that phone to tell her where her car was parked and that the keys were under the floor mat. Last but not least, using my own phone this time, I texted one of my few cop friends, to tell him about the mix-up on the bus, in case the driver reported it, and the fact that I'd been left stranded, but in my version I hitched a ride with a long-haul trucker who dropped me off at the Armadillo station so I could catch the midafternoon bus to my mother's. I made no mention of Penny or her Mustang or Ollie Bonatello. Unless the police were blind they would soon see that Bonatello and Penny had worked together to try to kill me, and would also discover that Bonatello died by snakebite rather than foul play, so there'd be no reason to link me to his death. As for the coke in Penny's trunk, the D.A. would love that little twist. Any woman who would hire an ex-con to kill her husband could certainly be dealing drugs as well. Let's see Daddy try to get her out of all *that*. Oh, my, the evil in this world of ours.

My mother was staring at the tabletop, still clutching her dish-towel. "That poor girl. What in the world turned her this way?"

Well, she was raised by Anna and Donald Gooden, for one thing. But I didn't say that.

We sat there a while longer, thinking about this news. My thoughts, of course, were probably far different from my mother's. What a day this had been.

Finally I said, "Let's watch a movie, Ma. Like we used to."

"Good idea." She scraped her chair back from the table.

As we walked arm-in arm to the den, she said, "I actually signed up for Netflix last month. What's your preference?"

I smiled and said, "Detective shows."

She smiled back, and squeezed my hand. "I wonder why."

RHONDA AND CLYDE

The strangest two days of Helen Wilson's life began with a skiing trip to Appaloosa Resort one Sunday in January. The trip itself wasn't unusual: Appaloosa was a popular location, and only forty miles from her home in the town of Lodgepole, Wyoming. What was unusual was that Helen had gone there in the company of friends. Helen Wilson didn't have many friends.

Even as a child she'd been a loner, and her school years had given her little reason to change. She also had no desire, after graduating with an accounting degree from UW, to leave her hometown to pursue a career. Instead she hired on as a bank teller, a safe and unpretentious job on a safe and unpretentious street near the house her late parents had left her. Ten years later Helen was still there, a sensible woman of reasonable means but no ambition, one of those rare people who doesn't require much in order to be happy. Even so, she was pleasantly surprised when two total strangers engaged her in conversation one day at a neighborhood coffee shop, and even more surprised to find that she enjoyed their company.

Rhonda Felson and her husband, Clyde, were new to the area, Helen discovered—writers who had rented a cabin in the mountains nearby and who spent most of their time hiking and sightseeing and creating what Helen suspected would one day be masterpieces of literature. During the days after that first meeting, the three of them had gotten together twice for dinner in local restaurants, and the following weekend Rhonda had invited Helen to accompany them to Appaloosa. The trip ended badly. Helen, who had never before been near a pair of skis, suffered the fate of many first-timers: six hours later she found herself medicated and hobbling on crutches through the exit doors of the local ER. More painful to her than her injuries was the knowledge that she'd been so much trouble to her new friends—they'd driven her to the hospital and then home afterward—and she found herself apologizing nonstop for spoiling their outing.

"Nonsense," Rhonda said, for the tenth time. She used Helen's key to open the house door and stood aside as Clyde helped her maneuver down the hallway to her bedroom. "These things happen. I'm just sorry it happened to *you.*"

Helen sagged backward onto the bed, propped her bad leg up on pillows, and sighed. "Thanks, guys," she said. "I'll be okay now."

Rhonda was frowning. "Maybe I better stay. Clyde can come fetch me in the morning—"

"I'll be fine," Helen said again. "Oh, I just remembered—where'd we put my purse?"

"It's in the other room."

"Could you get it for me? My cell phone's inside it, and I need to call my boss."

"Now?" Clyde asked. "It's past ten."

"He stays up late. He knows a lot of the folks at the resort, and if he hears about my mishap I want him to know I'll still be coming in to the bank tomorrow."

Both Felsons blinked at the same time. "You're going in to work?" Rhonda said.

"This isn't exactly life-threatening. I just want to forewarn him. I don't want everybody mooning over me when I limp in with my cast and my new wooden legs." Helen closed her eyes for a second and added, "Whoa—I can't believe I'm so tired."

"Tell you what. I'll make the call for you. You need to rest. What's your boss's number?"

Helen gave it to Rhonda and watched sleepily as the two of them left the room. It occurred to her that from now on she would stick to tennis. . . .

#

Sheriff Marcie Ingalls had never fully adjusted to cold weather. Her parents had moved the family here from Alabama when she was nine, and she was sometimes convinced that she'd lived in balmy climes just long enough to thin her blood. But she'd married a local guy and her mother was still here, so Marcie made the best of it. She dressed in three or four layers, never complained, and even on subzero mornings usually got to the office before anyone else.

Today, though, she arrived to find the door unlocked and coffee brewing. Jerry Pearson, her only deputy, was at his desk in the back corner, feet propped up and a copy of *Guns & Ammo* in his hands. "You're early," Marcie said. What a detective she would've made.

"And full of news," Pearson replied, in a bored voice. "I put a ticket on a car parked in the alley off Fourth Street, a twenty-foot limb fell from an oak in front of the courthouse, and the bakery has jelly donuts on special today."

Sheriff Ingalls shrugged out of her heavy coat and took a seat at her desk. "Was it blocking traffic?" she asked.

"What, the limb?"

"The car."

"No, just blocking the alley." Pearson tossed the magazine onto his desktop. "Illegally parked. You saying I shouldn't have tick-eted it?"

"I'm just saying it's not even seven a.m., and nobody ever drives through there anyhow."

He snorted. "Where I come from, they'd tow it away."

"You're not where you came from, Jerry. We do things a little different, here."

"You can say that again." He nodded toward the window. "Hear that sound?"

Marcie frowned, listening. Sure enough, someone was pounding on something, in the distance—*bam...bam...bam...*, sharp and clear in the brittle morning air. She was about to reply, then stopped as Wanda Stalworth, the dispatcher, pushed through the door in a bright red parka. They exchanged greetings, Wanda headed for her desk in the other room, and Marcie looked again at Jerry Pearson. "I hear it," she said. "What is it? Hammering?"

"Yeah. Roscoe Three Bears. He's fixing Maude Jessup's front steps."

"Good. She's almost ninety, and that's a high porch—it'd be too bad if she fell."

"What I can't figure is why he does it. Splits her firewood for her, too. Roscoe's banned from the rez and dirt poor, and I hear she never pays him. Probably never even thanks him."

Marcie took a pair of reading glasses from her pocket and started riffling through her in-basket. "He does it because Maude's old and there's no one else to help her, Jerry."

He shook his head. "Maybe one of these days I'll understand that kind of thinking."

"I doubt it," she said.

From the dispatch desk Wanda called, "Are you two arguing again?"

"Not me," Pearson said. He rose to his feet and picked up his coat. "I'm going to do something to make me feel good, for a change."

"You quitting?" Marcie asked.

"Not that good."

"Where you going, then?"

"To buy some jelly donuts."

#

Two hours later and two blocks away, in the bank on the corner of Western and Fourth, branch manager Spencer E. Spencer looked up from the papers on his desk to see loan officer Ernest Polk standing in his office doorway. Both men were wearing thick winter jackets, and Polk even had on a fur hat with earflaps. He looked like a movie poster for *Fargo*.

"Any word on the heating situation?" Spencer asked him.

"They're sending a repair crew from Casper," Polk said. "It'll take a couple hours. Until then I guess we'll just have to stay bundled up."

Spencer sighed. He had come in this morning to find the bank lobby as cold as Siberia, although the lights and the computers all seemed to be working. When he'd phoned the bank's home office, they had instructed him to call the heating-system people and to—above all else—remain open for business. He glanced through the glass wall of his office at two of his tellers, who were huddled at their stations like ice fishermen. Both were wearing mittens and had the hoods of their coats pulled up over their heads. He found himself dreaming of Florida.

Spencer E. Spencer was still staring at the lobby when his third teller clomped through the door on a pair of crutches. Helen Wilson was encased in a brown parka from the top of her head to her knees, and what little of her could be seen wasn't good: one eye was squeezed shut, her nose was bandaged, and a long comma of black hair hung in her face. Looking at no one and saying not a word, she solemnly made her way to her teller cage and wrestled herself onto her stool. The other two women muttered sympathetic words to her, their breath making little white clouds in the air, but otherwise the room was dead silent.

The two men in the office couldn't help staring. "She's in worse shape than I expected," Ernest Polk whispered.

Spencer, who had already alerted the staff, said, "That friend of hers—the one who called me last night to tell me Helen was coming in?—said she skied into a tree."

"She must've knocked it down."

"Tough lady," Spencer said. He reached for his phone and punched a number. When he saw Helen Wilson pick up her receiver, he said, "Sure you feel all right, Helen?"

"I'b vine," her voice said. "Doesn'd hurd doo bad."

"Looks like it would, from here. And what's wrong with your voice?"

"My doze is all stobbed up, dad's all. Like I god a gold."

"Okay," he said. "You let me know if you need anything." He hung up and said to Polk, "Maybe she'll have an easy morning—we shouldn't get many customers anyhow, with no heat."

But as soon as he uttered those words, the front door opened again and a short redheaded man entered carrying two duffel bags. On the nearest bag were the printed words PARADISE VALLEY CASINO. He walked to Helen Wilson's station, set the bags on the counter, and grinned at her. The tired smile she gave him in return looked more like a grimace to Spencer, but the man didn't seem to mind. He also didn't seem bothered by the frigid temperature.

"Thank God for the casino," Spencer said. "They deposit more money in a week than most of our customers deposit in a year."

"I believe it," Polk said, as he turned to leave. "I'll keep a watch out for the repair folks."

Spencer nodded and went back to his paperwork, wishing he could do it with his gloves on. He also wished he didn't know the Paradise Valley Casino quite as well as he did. Sadly, some of those funds being deposited had probably once been his.

#

It took him twenty minutes to sign off on the earnings reports and finish a long phone call with the bank's IT crew about an upgrade to his ATM software. Finally Spencer leaned back in his swivel chair, burrowed lower into his coat, looked over at the tellers—and frowned. No one was sitting at Helen Wilson's station. Earlier, around the time the casino courier was here, Spencer had noticed Helen leaving her stool to make several trips to the vault. That made sense: the casino's deposits were always large, and her crutches would prevent her from carrying too big a load at once. But now she was gone. He picked up the phone to call the head teller, but before he could hit the intercom button, Ernest Polk stuck his head into the office.

"Know what we should do, Spence?"

"What."

"We should have a promotion and give away those big duffel bags like the casino does."

"What?" Spencer said again. His mind was on injured employees, not bank giveaways.

"You know—those bags like the ones the guy was carrying earlier, with the name printed on the side. That's great advertising, and—"

"Wait a minute," he said, still holding the receiver. "Are you saying the casino lets anybody have those, for free?"

"Well, not free," Polk said. "You have to spend at least fifty bucks at the slot machines. But that doesn't take long."

Spencer frowned. A vague uneasiness had crept into his bones. Shaking it off, he said, "Thanks, Ernie. I'll consider it." Then, without waiting for a response, he pressed the button for the head teller and, when she answered, said, "Libby? Is Helen taking her break?"

"She left for home ten minutes ago, Spence. Said she wasn't feeling well after all. I'm not surprised—she shouldn't have tried to come in."

"Thanks, Lib. I'll give her a call." Which he did, after allowing her five more minutes to get home. That should be plenty—Helen's house was barely a mile from the bank.

But her cell phone didn't answer. It rang four times, then went to voicemail. Rather than leave a message, he found her home number and tried her landline. After three rings, she picked up.

"Helen?" he said. "It's Spencer, at the bank. Just wanted to make sure you're all right."

Helen Wilson said, a little groggily, "I'm fine—thanks for checking on me."

"Well, you sound better, anyway. More like yourself."

"Excuse me?"

"Your clogged nose," Spencer said. "It must've cleared up, right?"

Hesitation. Then: "It's my leg, Spence, not my nose. I broke my ankle."

"But—when you were here, earlier . . ."

"There? I wasn't there. I've been here at home all morning."

Spencer felt a cold ripple move through his stomach. "What?"

"My friend Rhonda phoned you last night, right? At first she was going to call and tell you I'd be coming in anyway, but she later said she'd taken the liberty of telling you I'd be staying home sick today. She was right, I guess—I needed the rest. So I stayed home."

Silence. Spencer tried to respond, but his throat seemed to have closed up.

"Didn't she call you?" Helen asked him. "What's going on?"

He swallowed. "I don't know. I mean—the person who called said you'd be coming in, like always. She didn't say anything about taking a sick day."

"Oh my. She must've misunderstood. Or maybe I misunderstood *her*. . . ."

"Listen, Helen—this is important. Who's Rhonda?"

"I told you, a friend. I met her last week, she's the one who invited me to go skiing with her and her husband yesterday. The one who fell on my leg."

"Fell on it?"

"Well, it was an accident, but yeah, she fell and landed on my leg."

Spencer was sweating now, his heart thudding in his chest. "Hold on a second, okay?"

He rose and walked stiffly into the lobby and around to the teller area. Underneath the counter, in front of Helen's chair, he found it—a huge stack of bills. But they weren't bills at all—they were cash-sized bundles of blank paper. Helen's trips to the vault, he realized now, weren't to transport cash to it. They were to transport cash from it. If he'd been paying attention, he'd have noticed that the duffel bags the casino man had taken out of the bank were probably stuffed as full as they had been when he came in—but with real bills this time.

Quick as a flash, he pressed the alarm button under the counter, to alert the sheriff's department, then sprinted back to the phone in his office. "Helen?" he said. "What did they look like, your two friends?" But he was afraid he already knew.

"Look like? Well . . . the guy's short, reddish hair, glasses. His wife is—I don't know, about my height and weight, I guess. In fact it's a little spooky how much she does look like me, with the black hair and—"

"Names," Spencer blurted. "Do you have names?"

She gave them to him: Clyde and Rhonda Felson. He scribbled them onto a pad, looked up at the window, and saw Sheriff Ingalls's patrol car screech to a stop at the curb. As he leaped from his desk and hurried to meet the cops, Spencer realized he was trembling.

But not from the cold.

#

"I can't believe it," Helen murmured. She was still propped up in her bed, her leg cast resting on a pillow. Her face was noticeably free of bruises and bandages. "Rhonda told me she told you I wasn't coming in . . . when in fact she told you I *was*. She was setting the stage for"—Helen swallowed hard—"for impersonating me."

Gathered around her were Sheriff Marcie Ingalls, Deputy Jerry Pearson, and branch manager Spence Spencer.

"That seems to be what happened," Marcie agreed.

Spencer, who seemed to have aged ten years, said, "You didn't hear her make the call?" Helen shook her head. "No, she used my cell phone, from the other room. I was a little woozy anyhow, from the painkillers. But I remember her coming back in and waking me up and telling me you'd said that taking a day off was fine, and to get well soon."

"She must've been crazy, to stroll into the bank like that," Marcie said. "But it worked."

"Without that damn parka it wouldn't have worked," Spencer said. "Between it and the fake bandages, we couldn't see much of her face. Also, she disguised her voice."

"And her partner, husband, whatever—he walked out with . . . how much?"

Spencer shrugged. "We don't know yet. A lot." He ran a hand over his face. "With bags the casino gave him for free, for playing the slots. Insult to injury."

"You'll get me the security video, right?"

"Ernie Polk's holding it for you. And our main office has already offered a reward."

The sheriff nodded and looked at Helen. "Clyde Felson, you said? And Rhonda?"

"Yes." Helen repeated the descriptions she'd given to Spencer on the phone. "She really does look like me. She's prettier than I am, though." She sighed. "He called her Ronnie."

"Ronnie and Clyde?"

"Why not?" Deputy Pearson said.

Everyone turned to look at him.

Pearson shrugged. "They rob banks."

#

Marcie and Pearson continued questioning Helen for another half hour, trying to come up with some kind of lead. The only thing helpful at all was the fact that the robbers and fake friends (Helen had to admit that's what they were) drove a black Toyota Tundra. At least that's the vehicle they'd taken Helen to the resort in. As for today, nobody remembered seeing what the imposter had driven to the bank. Sheriff Ingalls said it had probably been Helen's Ford Focus, because of the possibility that someone *might* see it—and the fact that its keys were missing from her purse. In any case, the Ford was now parked in its rightful place behind Helen's house. The sheriff said they would check it over for prints, but that it would probably yield no clues; Rhonda Felson would almost certainly have kept her gloves on during the drive to and from the bank.

"Wait a second," Helen said. "I think they might've had *two* cars. One that I never saw."

"Why would you think that?" Marcie asked.

"We went to the resort in the Toyota, but Rhonda drove. Once, on Sunday, I saw Clyde take a set of keys from his pocket. It was only for a moment—he was looking for his ticket for the ski lift—but the biggest key on the chain wasn't for their Tundra."

"What kind of key was it?"

"A Honda."

"Are you sure?"

"Yes. It had that funny curved 'H,' that's bigger on top than on the bottom."

The sheriff and her deputy exchanged a look. Both were thinking the same thing: since the robbers knew Helen had seen the Toyota, they would probably ditch that vehicle someplace and use another for a getaway. They could always steal one, but if they already had a second car waiting in the wings . . .

"Okay, that helps. They're probably driving a Honda," Marcie said. "Anything else?"

"Not that I can think of." Helen heaved a sigh. "They even stole my crutches."

A silence passed. Marcie used it to look carefully around the room. When she noticed the old-fashioned telephone sitting on the floor between Helen's bed and the potty chair, she blinked.

"Helen, is that the phone you used earlier, to talk to the bank?"

"Yeah, Spence called me on it. I had to dig it out from under the bedside table. It's still connected, obviously, but I haven't used it much since I got my cell phone."

"Where's your cell phone now?"

"Same place as my crutches, probably. Rhonda used my cell to call Spence last night, and must've kept it." Helen looked up and added, "I bet they figured they were taking my only phone, so I wouldn't be able to call anyone at the bank today—or get a call *from* anyone—and screw up their plans. They wouldn't have seen my landline."

The room fell silent again. Then Marcie had a thought.

"If your cell phone's still turned on," she said to Helen, "we can track it."

"It's still on," Spencer E. Spencer said. "Or at least it *was*, after the robbery." Everyone turned to face him. Marcie had actually forgotten he was still there, and then realized he was probably reluctant to go back to an unheated bank and a heated interrogation by his bosses. As he'd mentioned, he hadn't even determined yet how much money was taken.

"How do you know her cell phone's on?" she asked him.

"Because I tried to call her on it, first, and it rang. No one picked up, but it rang several times and went to voicemail—it didn't give me a 'not in service' message or anything."

"Okay," Marcie said, deep in thought. "That's good. We'll see if we can get the cell towers to triangulate the signal, try to pin down the whereabouts of the phone."

All of a sudden Helen's eyes widened. "You won't have to," she said.

"What?"

For the first time today, Helen Wilson smiled. "It has a GPS chip."

"Excuse me?" Marcie asked.

"A GPS locator. My aunt bought me the phone, a few months ago, and said if I ever lost it, this feature'll find it. There's an app that'll point us straight to it."

"How exactly does that work?" Pearson said.

"We just need Aunt Lettie's phone. It's tied to mine—you click the app on her phone and it shows where my cell phone is, on a map. And where the Felsons are, if they still have it."

"Where does she live, your aunt?"

"Over past Battle Creek, near the edge of the reservation. About twenty miles—"

"I know her house," Marcie said. She pointed to the landline. "Will you call her?"

#

Within minutes Sheriff Ingalls and her deputy were in her cruiser and headed for Lettie Wilson's home. As usual, Jerry Pearson sat silent and brooding in the passenger seat. Marcie glanced at him from the corner of her eye. She liked him, but could never quite figure him out. He'd been a Seattle cop for years before moving here to be near his wife's folks, and had always seemed either unable or unwilling to adapt to local ways. Marcie sighed. Here she was, in a high-stress/low-pay job, freezing her butt off every year between September and May, with a deputy who was always in a bad mood. She couldn't imagine two better examples of ducks out of water.

She forced her mind back to the matter at hand. "Something's worrying me here, Jerry," she said. "Remember what the banker said, about the heat being off, in the building?"

"I remember. What about it?"

"He said if it hadn't been off, if the imposter hadn't stayed bundled up in winter gear, he and the staff would've probably recognized that she wasn't Helen."

"And?"

"Seems pretty convenient," she said, "that heating-system failure."

Pearson lapsed again into silence. Then: "Are you thinking they—"

"I don't know." Marcie chewed her lip a moment. "But the people coming to fix it should be there by now. Why don't you call Wanda, have her connect you to the bank. Ask to speak to the head fred on the crew." She turned, and they locked eyes. "Humor me," she said.

Two minutes later they had the repairman on speakerphone.

"You fellas see anything strange?" Pearson asked him.

"Dern right we did," the guy said. "The wires were cut to the heating system."

Pearson blinked. "Did you say 'cut'?"

"Yep. As in 'severed.' Somebody took a crowbar to the panel door and cut the wires. The *correct* wires—nothing else was affected. Whoever did it knew his way around a power board."

"Where is this panel? Somewhere in the bank?"

"Above the bank. On the roof."

Pearson thanked the man, disconnected, and turned to the sheriff. "Whoa," he said.

"Sounds like they decided to improve their odds a bit."

"Sure does," Pearson said. "They get two bags with the casino's logo, find a bank employee with the right looks, befriend her, cause her to have a disabling accident, create a situation that makes a disguise even easier . . . They know what they're doing, these two."

"So do we, now. We know one of them has teller experience and one's an electrician."

"Does that make us any closer to catching them?"

Marcie shrugged, her eyes on the road. "The more we know, the better off we are."

"We also know they're smart," he said.

"Let's hope they're not smart enough to turn off Helen's phone."

#

Helen's aunt Lettie took awhile to find her cell phone, but when she did, she loaned it to them with her blessing. Marcie and Pearson arrived back at Helen's apartment within an hour.

And found that they had company.

Two men in dark suits were standing in the bedroom. One of them, who looked like he'd just taken a bite out of a lemon , said, without a handshake, "Detective Murphy. State police." He pointed to his partner and added, "This is Detective Ellington. We'll take it from here."

Marcie glanced at Spencer, gave him a *Did you do this?* look. He shrugged and appeared clueless. She figured the big boys at the main bank had called the big boys in Cheyenne.

"I doubt you have the vast resources required for something like this," Murphy said.

Grinding her back teeth, Marcie said, "The crime happened in my county, Detective."

"But I suspect the criminals are no longer in your county, Sheriff." He looked down at the cell phone in Marcie's hand. "And it sounds like this will tell us for sure. Ms. Wilson, would you do the honors?"

Helen, still in bed, took her aunt's phone from Marcie, tapped some buttons, studied it a moment, and handed it back. Everyone crowded in to see.

On the screen was a map with a red dot in the middle. The location wasn't approximate; it was exact. According to the GPS, Helen's missing cell phone was now at an address on the northeast corner of Hill Street and Lancaster, in the small town of Florence. Sixty miles south.

They watched the screen for several minutes. The red dot didn't move.

Detective Ellington took out his own phone and googled the address shown on the GPS map. After a moment he looked up at his partner. "Two-twenty Lancaster Street," he said, "is a place called the Traildrive Motel."

Murphy nodded, his eyes on the screen. The red dot stayed put. "We got 'em," he said.

#

Rhonda Felson, although that wasn't her real name, kicked off her shoes, stretched out on the too-small bed, and blew out a sigh. Her husband Clyde, although that wasn't his real name, hefted both duffel bags onto the rickety table in one corner of the room and stared at them lovingly. "So far so good," he said.

"I'm glad you're pleased," she murmured, her eyes closed. "I'll be pleased when we're in Florence, Italy, and not Florence, Wyoming."

"All in good time, Ronnie my dear."

Outside, the traffic on Lancaster Street, which consisted mostly of pickup trucks, was sparse. That was to be expected, probably: it was eleven a.m. on a weekday. But Clyde had a feeling traffic here was always sparse.

"So this is part of your plan?" she said. "Check into a motel only an hour away from the scene of the crime, in broad daylight?"

"This is one of the final phases of my plan," he said. "We're almost done, here."

"We'll be done, all right, if they find us."

He smiled, still looking at the bags. "They won't find us."

#

Sheriff Marcie Ingalls pushed through the door of her office, tossed her hat onto the desk, and sagged into her chair. Deputy Pearson followed. Seconds later Wanda Stalworth stuck her head in, from Dispatch. "What are you guys doing back?" she said. "Did you catch 'em?"

"We're here because we were told to be," Marcie said. "It's not our case anymore."

"Then why are you frowning?"

Marcie rubbed her eyes. "Because something's bothering me." She looked all around, studying her surroundings if seeing them for the first time. "Something small, something I think we talked about, right here in this office. I just can't put my finger on it."

"You think the state cops are wrong, about heading down to Florence?" Pearson asked.

"I'm just saying we're missing something. As for Florence, those two detectives are in no hurry. I heard Murphy say he'll be taking several state troopers along with them, and making this a big deal. He wants all the glory, I promise you that."

Pearson snorted. "While we stay here and write parking tickets. Right?"

Marcie blinked, then scowled. Slowly, she turned and focused on her deputy.

"What's the matter?" he asked.

"That's it. That's what I was trying to remember. That car you said you ticketed this morning, in the alley."

"What about it?"

"That alley runs beside the bank, Jerry. Right beside it."

"So?"

"And I bet there's a ladder on the side of the building, to the roof."

They stared at each other for a long moment.

"The car," she said. "Was it a Honda?"

#

Seventy-eight minutes later, Clyde Felson was relaxing in the room's only chair, reading a travel brochure he'd found in the drawer of the nightstand, while Rhonda counted the money in the two bags. She'd been counting for half an hour now.

In spite of Rhonda's doubts, the motel was everything Clyde had wanted: small, cheap, quiet, and perfectly located. He didn't plan to be here long.

He turned to Rhonda, idly watching the glow of the lamplight on her jet-black hair. He had just opened his mouth to speak to her when he heard the screech of tires somewhere outside the open window. A lot of tires. Then the slamming of car doors.

Clyde was on his feet in an instant, dashing to the window and easing the curtains aside to peek out.

The Law had arrived.

#

Detective Michael Murphy was pleased with what he saw. As soon as he had assembled his team of patrolmen, they had hit the road and headed south. Now they were spread out evenly along the inside of the U-shaped row of twenty-four motel rooms. Ellington had already fetched the Hispanic owner—a man named Roberto Gonzales—from the motel office, and had learned from the register that only one couple was checked in, at the moment: a Mr. and Mrs. Curtis Allen, from Laramie, in Room 12. Murphy was now standing outside that door, his weapon drawn and his mouth dry. As planned, he caught Ellington's eye and nodded once.

Ellington took Aunt Lettie Wilson's cell phone from his pocket and punched in Helen's number . . . and everyone went dead quiet. Helen had told them her ringtone was loud and distinctive: the "Throne Room" theme from *Star Wars*. Every cop on the scene held his breath, waiting and listening. Five seconds passed.

And then Murphy heard it. It was ringing. The phone was here.

But not behind the door of Room 12. The ringtone was coming from somewhere off to Murphy's left. He turned, alert and searching, and saw others turn as well. Moments later they found the source of the music: a small blue mailbox on the outside wall of the motel office.

Frantically Murphy signaled one of the troopers, who fetched a tire iron from the trunk of a cruiser and pried open the lid of the mail drop. Inside were half a dozen stamped envelopes and a model 5 iPhone, which had finally stopped playing John Williams's music and was now calmly instructing the caller, in Helen Wilson's recorded voice, to please leave a message.

But that wasn't all. Rubber-banded around the phone was a scrap of paper with the printed words:

PLEASE RETURN THIS TO HELEN. THANKS, AND ADIOS.

Murphy stared at it silently for a minute or more, ignoring the looks of his fellow cops and a confused-looking elderly couple standing in the now-open doorway of Room 12.

Detective Ellington and Mr. Gonzales were both peering over Murphy's shoulder to study the message. Ellington looked at Murphy and asked, "*Adios?*"

"*Sí,*" Gonzales said.

#

A hundred yards away, on the other side of Lancaster Street, the Felsons stood at the back window of Room 7 at the tiny Hamilton Inn, watching the festivities across the road. The room's curtains had been pulled back and the lights switched off so no one could see in from outside. Rhonda had brought Clyde the binoculars he'd placed on the bedside table an hour ago, and he was smiling as he watched the policemen in the Traildrive Motel's parking lot mill around, disperse, and leave the scene. When all activity had died down he closed the curtains, switched the lights back on, and returned the field glasses to Rhonda's travel bag.

She stood there staring at him. "That was stupid. You know that, don't you? Stupid and risky. We should be miles away from here by now."

His gave her a smug look. "It was necessary. I wanted to know how safe we are."

"What do you mean?"

"I mean, they sent the big guns after us. State troopers, suits, everybody at once. That tells me that pinpointing her phone with that app you saw on her screen—that was all they had. They know nothing else about us."

Rhonda didn't respond, but she did seem to relax a little.

"They'll never catch us now," he added. "We're home free."

"It was still stupid," Rhonda murmured.

He sat on the bed, put his shoes on, and laced them up. "Come on, let's get out of here."

"Thank God. I was afraid you'd want to stay the night."

"I've seen what I needed to see." He looked up at her. "We'll double back and be in Canada by tomorrow. Then, the world."

"Why'd you write '*adios*,' on the note?"

"Misdirection never hurts," he said. "Whether they're after us or not."

Within two minutes they'd gathered their belongings. Rhonda handed Clyde her travel bag, then turned to leave the room key on the dresser. He looped the straps of the two casino bags over his shoulders, took his car keys from his pocket, and pulled open the door.

The gray Honda Accord was parked nose-out in the space directly in front of the room. Clyde pushed the button to pop the trunk even as he stepped out onto the sidewalk, his wife right behind him in the doorway. Head down and intent on his task, he loaded the two bags into the trunk, tucked Rhonda's bag in beside them, and closed the trunk lid.

And saw, for the first time, that he wasn't alone.

Two uniformed policemen, a man and a woman, were standing against the motel wall, ten feet from the door. The lady cop had a sheriff's badge, and her gun was drawn and pointed.

"Guess I don't have to ask if this is your car," she said.

#

For a long moment the two suspects stood there, staring. Their expressions weren't scared, or angry, or even disappointed. Mostly, they looked stunned.

Marcie Ingalls said, in a level voice, "Turn around, both of you. Slowly. Hands behind your backs." She kept her automatic aimed and ready while Pearson cuffed them. When they turned again to face her, the man—Clyde Felson, Marcie assumed—said, "How'd you know?"

She shook her head. "We didn't, at first. My deputy and I arrived at the other motel long before the cavalry did, and when we found that you weren't there we looked around to see where else you might be. In case you decided to hide and watch from a distance."

"Watch? What made you think we might do that?"

"Nothing. But it happens sometimes, and it was worth a try." Without turning, she asked Deputy Pearson—who had already taken the car keys from Clyde—to check the bags. He opened the trunk and unzipped the two duffels.

"The money's here," he said.

"Main thing is," Marcie continued, "we knew you weren't at the other motel because your car wasn't in the lot. All we did then was check possible vantage points until we found it." She nodded toward the still-open doorway to Room 7. "The lady in the office confirmed that this was the room that went with the car."

"But—you had no way to know about our car."

Marcie smiled, took the parking ticket from her pocket, and held it up. "Yes, we did—not only the make and model, but the license plate number. Thanks to my deputy here, who wrote a citation for your Honda earlier today, in an alley beside the bank building. An alley with the only outside access to the roof." She smiled, watching their faces. "That was smart, disabling the heating system. Everything you did was smart, except for parking in the wrong place this morning and hanging around here too long now. Which, by the way, was downright foolish."

"I told you," the woman growled.

Clyde's jaw tightened. "Shut up, Ronnie."

Marcie took out her cell and called Dispatch while Pearson finished checking the cab of the getaway vehicle. "Wanda? It's me," she said, into the phone. "Do me a favor. Track down Detective Murphy, and tell him he might want to turn himself and his vast resources around and head back here to Florence. We have the two suspects in custody, along with the stolen cash. Yep, that's right. Tell him we're across the street from the red dot. He'll know what I mean."

She disconnected and turned to Pearson. "Find anything interesting?"

"A couple things." To the Felsons he said, "What kind of people steal a woman's crutches?"

Rhonda snorted. "Good old Helen. Guess she was at the wrong place at the wrong time."

"I agree," Pearson said. "And she was wrong about something else, too."

"What's that?"

"She told us you were prettier than she is."

Rhonda glared at him.

"Okay," Marcie said. "Let's go." Pearson gripped Clyde's elbow and steered him and his wife toward the cruiser.

"Ronnie and Clyde," Marcie added, walking behind them. "What are your real names?"

The man turned and gave her an even darker look. "Thelma and Louise."

Marcie smiled.

"They didn't end well, either," she said.

#

Two days later things were back to normal. Around nine a.m. Sheriff Ingalls was sitting at her desk, sending an email to the mayor regarding his highly publicized but understaffed Pot-hole Prevention Program. For some reason, complaints about the poor condition of town streets were finding their way to the county sheriff instead of the city Public Works Department, and Marcie considered it her duty to place that particular monkey on the correct back.

Aside from the usual administrative headaches, though, all was going well. The quick arrest of the bank-heist suspects and the recovery of the stolen loot had put smiles on the faces of everyone except the two robbers and egg on the face of one Detective Michael Murphy. An additional but unexpected result of the incident was that the injured but wiser Helen Wilson now had an upcoming dinner date with Detective Scott Ellington. Proof positive, in Marcie's view, that clouds do have silver linings.

She had sent the mayor's email and was scrolling through the others when Wanda Stalworth ambled in from the other room. Marcie looked up, then turned back to her computer and said, "For what reason has the Wanda Woman abandoned her post?"

"Business is slow. Where's Pearson?"

"Out front, trying to fix our flagpole," Marcie said, eyes on her screen. A windstorm last night had snapped it off, along with three trees and the steeple of a nearby church.

Wanda, never one to be distracted from the important things in life, said, "Is that a box of donuts, on his desk?"

"Half chocolate, half cream-filled. Help yourself."

"You want one, too?"

Marcie shook her head. "One of my rules: I only eat sugar when I hear good news."

"Why's that?"

"You got any good news?"

"I guess not."

Marcie nodded. "Well, there you go. It helps me stay skinny."

Wanda picked out a donut and took a bite. Chewing, she said, "I do have some gossip. I heard you told the bank folks that Jerry Pearson caught the robbers the other day."

"That's not gossip. It's a fact."

Wanda stared at her. "But he didn't, Sheriff. *You* solved the case—I was standing right here when you linked the criminals to the car that was parked beside the bank that morning."

"I didn't say Pearson *solved* it," Marcie corrected. "I said his actions led directly to their capture. If he hadn't ticketed that parked Honda, there would've been no record of the license plate, and we couldn't have found them." She leaned back in her chair, holding Wanda's gaze. "If law officers were eligible for such things, I'd have made sure Pearson got that reward the bank offered. And I'll tell you something else: If it'd been me, I wouldn't even have written that ticket. Pearson did what he felt was right, and it turned out to be the only thing that pointed us to the guilty party."

Wanda finished her donut and wiped her mouth with a napkin. When her hand came away, Marcie saw that she was smiling.

"What's so funny?"

"I seem to remember you hinting, that morning, that Pearson should change his way of thinking."

"Well, I take it back," Marcie said. "I'm not sure I *want* him to change."

Wanda seemed to consider that, then said, "You might be a little late."

"Why?"

"Because of the reward." Wanda tossed the wadded-up napkin into a trashcan and sat down on the edge of Pearson's desk. "Do you recall telling us, yesterday, that the bank had withdrawn the reward offer because no one had come forward with information leading to the arrest and capture, blah blah blah?"

"Yes," Marcie said. "What about it?"

"Libby Anders, the head teller at the bank, called me this morning. She said Deputy Pearson told the bank manager last night that the reward would have to be paid. Said that he—Jerry Pearson—was informed by two alert citizens early Monday morning that a strange car was parked in the alley beside the bank. Said he wouldn't have noticed it otherwise. Since information from that ticket, as you said, later led to the apprehension of the two suspects, Pearson insisted that those two people should be given the full reward. Thirty grand, divided between them."

"Who were these two observant citizens?"

"Roscoe Three Bears and Maude Jessup."

Marcie blinked. "You're kidding."

"Nope. Pearson said they mentioned the illegally parked car to him on his way to the office that day. Then he walked over and wrote the ticket."

"But . . . " Marcie stared into the distance, thinking. "Roscoe was working on Maude's house at the time. Repairing her porch steps. To even talk to them, on his route to work, Pearson would've had to climb three fences and cross two yards."

Wanda narrowed her eyes. "Are you wondering if that's what really happened?"

"Well . . . I'm wondering what Roscoe and Maude would say, if asked about it."

"Pearson said they shouldn't have to be contacted."

"What?"

"He said Roscoe doesn't speak much English, and Ms. Jessup forgets things sometimes."

Marcie thought that over, and felt a smile spread across her face. Slowly she rose from her chair and crossed the room to the front window. On the snow-covered lawn between the office and the street, a man in a furry brown coat stood surrounded by tools, his fists on his hips and his eyes on a new brace that had been bolted to the pole supporting the Stars and Stripes.

Marcie stared out the window at her deputy for a long moment. *Flagpoles aren't the only things you can fix, are they, Jerry?* She was surprised at the sudden warmth she felt in her heart.

"That sounds reasonable to me," she murmured.

"What?" Wanda said.

Before Marcie could reply, she caught a glimpse of Helen Wilson's maroon Ford. She saw it putter its way up the snow-cleared street and pull into a parking spot, saw Helen climb out and limp on her recovered crutches to the front door of the bank. Spence Spencer appeared then, as if he'd been waiting for her to arrive. Marcie watched as he held the door open for Helen, bowed theatrically, and followed her inside. First, though, Spencer turned and stared directly down the street, at the sheriff's office. Directly at *her.* Marcie knew he couldn't see her from that distance, but he raised a hand anyway, and so did she. She thought she saw a grin on his face.

"What was it you just said?" Wanda asked again.

Marcie blinked and turned from the window. "I said I think I'll have a donut after all."

"Chocolate or cream-filled?"

Once more, Marcie felt herself smile. "One of each."

RIVER ROAD

Daniel Becker was sitting on the pond bank behind his building in a short-sleeved shirt and cuffed blue jeans when he heard someone behind him.

"Is this your outer office?"

Becker turned and squinted up into the sun. "Have we met?" he asked.

The man who'd spoken stepped to the edge of the water. Fifty-ish, bushy gray mustache, barrel chest, dark suit and hat. His tie was loosened in the noonday heat. "My name's Wolf McDade, Mr. Becker. I have a farm, west of here. I'd like to hire your services."

"Wolf?"

"Wolverton, actually."

Becker stood up and brushed the dirt off the seat of his pants. "'Fraid you're a little late, Mr. McDade. My office is closed."

"So I noticed. For lunch?"

"For good. Soon's my car's fixed, next door, I'm leaving for the Coast."

This time McDade was doing the squinting. "I was told you were a private investigator."

"I was, till yesterday," Becker said. "Hard to make a living at that, in a small town."

"Move north, to Jackson. Or down to New Orleans."

He shook his head. "Too big, for me. I hear the beach hotels are hiring security people."

McDade's frown seemed to indicate what he thought of the Gulf Coast. For a moment the two men studied each other. Wolf McDade looked as fierce and odd as his name, and the vest buttons across his chest seemed ready to pop. Becker was suddenly reminded of the old joke about the forgetful professor who unbuttoned his vest, took out his tie, and pissed in his pants.

"Why are you smiling?"

"Mental pictures," Becker said. "You know, you don't much look like a farmer."

"I left my straw hat at home. By the way, you don't look like a private detective."

"So I'm told. I try to blend in."

After a pause McDade raised his chin, put on an "enough of this" look, and said, "Tell you what, Mr. Becker. If you'd consider one last job, I'll make it worth your while."

"How much would my while be worth?"

"How about two thousand dollars?"

Becker stared. Maybe the newspapers were right, he thought, and the Great Depression *was* over. "You must want somebody killed," he said.

"I want somebody found." McDade let out a sigh and took off his hat. His gray hair was a shade lighter than his mustache. "My wife is missing."

Before Becker could reply, the older man spelled it out: Elizabeth McDade disappeared a week ago. She was always walking around on their land—the woods, pastures, everywhere, she loved to walk more'n anybody he ever knew, McDade said—and at first he figured she'd gotten lost, or hurt. But his people had searched every inch of his property. Lizzie was gone, period. McDade added a description, and handed Becker a photo he said was taken a year ago.

"Is your car missing, too?"

"No. And she didn't ride away with anyone, either, unless they forced her."

"What do you mean?"

"I mean she can't travel by automobile. Train, either." McDade ran a hand through his sweaty hair. "Lizzie suffers from motion sickness, always has. Anything faster than walking, or maybe riding a horse, makes her deathly ill, throwing up everything but her shoelaces. It's why she never learned to drive, not that a woman needs to."

"You're saying she stays home all the time?"

"That's right, or close by."

"How far you think she could walk?"

"Who knows? Miles and miles. She's a tough woman."

A silence passed. Becker was trying to picture such a thing. Somewhere on the far side of the pond, a fish jumped and splashed. Probably bass, or perch.

"If I find her," he said, "and she can't travel, how am I supposed to bring her to you?"

"That's up to you. Knock her out with laughing gas, or tie her to the car seat with a bucket to barf in. Point is, my wife's gone, either kidnapped or on her own, and I want her back."

Becker thought that over, especially the "on her own" part. "What if I find her and she doesn't want to come back, and I just let her go on her way?"

"Then you wouldn't get paid."

"So it's all or nothing, this deal."

"All or nothing." McDade put his hat back on and said, "How about it?"

#

Becker stood there in the sun for ten minutes after his new client left. In his hand was the photograph—a grainy shot of an unsmiling but attractive woman with jet-black hair—and in his mind was a blizzard of growing doubts. When he'd pressed McDade on the possibility of a kidnapping, which would make this a police matter, he'd been assured those odds were small. It seemed Lizzie McDade had pulled stunts like this before, and each time she'd come home relieved and apologetic. Her husband insisted she was just an impulsive and free-spirited young lady. Becker wasn't sure he agreed. In his view, thirty wasn't all that young, and rural southern wives rarely ran off.

But what could he do? Two thousand bucks would open his office again, either here or elsewhere, and give him a second chance at doing what he loved. He really had no choice. If Wolverton McDade was willing to pay him a fortune to fetch a wandering wife, so be it. She could always leave again later.

Finally Becker left the pond and headed for Carl's Auto Repair, in the cluster of shops fifty yards away. His old Ford wasn't yet ready so he gobbled a sandwich at a café across the street, bought a folded state map at the counter, and went back to Carl's smoky waiting-room. With the photo tucked in a pocket Becker studied the map until he figured out which direction Lizzie McDade had probably gone. Assuming she was afoot, west was the Mississippi River, an eventual dead end. East would take her back through town, where she might be recognized, and he doubted she'd want to waste time skirting around it. South, toward New Orleans, was also out: if she went far enough, that path led to the impassable swamps of south Louisiana.

Becker's guess was, she'd headed north.

He wondered what she'd taken with her. A bag of food and clothing and money, most likely, along with a gun in case of bandits. He decided she would probably also change her appearance—maybe already had—and would use a different name. Everything depended on how serious she was, about this.

He knew he was serious about finding her. On the one hand, it was a needle in a haystack. On the other, he had a picture and a probable direction and plenty of time. She would have to stop at towns occasionally; no one could walk forever in the woods. She would be seen, and noticed, and remembered. He just had to ask the right questions.

Sooner or later, he would track her down. And bring her home.

#

Utica, Mississippi
Monday, August 7

It was an almost-typical summer night at Susie Q's Diner. Music from the jukebox, clatter from the kitchen, the smell of grease and onions, the rush of heat (even at 7:30) whenever the street door opened. The only thing missing was customers. At the moment there were only six: an old baldheaded man at a booth next to the door with a heavy black walking-cane propped against his table, a teenager and his date eating ice cream, a red-cheeked fat man in a cowboy hat, and a pair of hard-faced workmen with wide shoulders and overalls. The sparse crowd was a welcome sight, to Elizabeth McDade. She deserved an easy night, she thought as she pushed through the door from the kitchen with a tray of coffee and hamburgers.

She knew she'd been lucky to find this job—any job—and a cheap hotel room across the street. The diner's owner, Susan Quinton, was a friendly soul, giving her a fair wage and a uniform and plenty of motherly advice. And even though Lizzie wouldn't call herself thrilled, she was a lot happier than she'd been with Wolf. His huge farm near Brookhaven had never been home, not to her, during their two miserable years of marriage.

When Lizzie made her decision to escape, she'd considered taking the buggy and one of the horses, but decided that traveling on foot would make her harder to track. Apparently she was right. There'd been no sign of her husband so far, and she was currently just earning cash to keep going north, maybe to Memphis. Someplace where Wolf would never find her.

She knew she couldn't stay here long. Susie Q's was too public, too risky—and she'd heard trouble might be coming. One of the cooks here at the diner, her only confidant, told her his cousin at the filling station out on the highway had heard a private eye was asking around about a dark-haired lady on the run. Lizzie wasn't overly worried—she was a blonde now, thanks to a drugstore south of here, and wore the ugliest pair of eyeglasses she'd ever seen outside the circus. She'd bought them at the dime store up the street.

It was then, as Lizzie stooped to serve the burgers and coffee to the two laborers, that it happened. The bigger of the two winked at her and pinched her bottom. Even as she yelped and felt her face heat up—which seemed to make the doofus grin even wider—his tablemate laughed about it. Afterward, she decided it had been their leering grins that set her off.

With teeth clenched Lizzie picked up a coffee cup and threw its blazing-hot contents into the pincher's lap. He screamed and leaped from his seat, the crotch of his overalls steaming, and grabbed her by the throat. She didn't cry out—she could barely breathe—and her struggling did no good. Her vision blurred; her knees weakened. Her glasses fell to the floor and broke. From what seemed like far away she could hear him cursing, could hear his companion cackling, could hear Kate Smith on the jukebox, telling the river to stay away from her door. Lizzie also heard the diner's front door open and close, and footsteps approaching.

The next thing she knew, she was leaning back against a wall, head ringing and throat aching. The man who'd attacked her lay motionless on the table with his face in his french fries and a dent in his head, and his friend was sprawled beside him. Both were out cold. Dully she turned and saw a tall stranger about her own age, staring down at the two men. She saw the look on his face, and the black wooden walking-cane gripped in both his hands. And understood this was the person she'd heard come in the front door while she was being choked.

She also realized everyone was gawking at her. Kate Smith had finished singing now, the room dead quiet. During the silence the overweight customer with the rosy cheeks and cowboy hat walked up to her and said, "How would you like a job, missy?"

Lizzie swallowed and winced at the pain in her throat. "I got a job."

"Well then, how'd you like to double your pay," he said, nodding toward the two men on the table, "and not have to play nursemaid to people like them all day?"

When she didn't answer, he added, "I'm Earl Duffy, case you don't know, and I got a place south a here. Since this pair a turds won't be working for me no more, I got two openings." He looked at the man with the walking stick and said, "That goes for you too, mister."

The stranger studied him a moment. "Much obliged, but I'm happy at the sawmill."

"Let me know if you change your mind," Duffy said, handing them cards with a phone number. "Both a you."

Dazedly Lizzie watched him waddle to his table and resume his meal. When she turned back to the table covered with uneaten food and unconscious bastards, the stranger was gone. She then looked at the door, which was swinging shut, and saw only the old bald man watching her from his booth, his black cane propped once more against his table.

#

Southwest Hinds County
Wednesday, August 9

Lizzie looked up from packing a wooden case with mason jars to see a familiar face gazing back at her. She'd noticed him earlier, on a wagon rumbling through the front gate, but thought it was someone else.

"How's your throat?" he asked.

She grinned then, and realized it was probably her first smile since she fled from Wolf and her former life. Certainly the first since leaving her waitress job the other night.

She'd found that working conditions weren't the best here, but the money was good, especially in these times. Earl Duffy's "place" turned out to be a dozen tin-roofed buildings in the wooded hills three miles from town. Not a long hike, for a walker like Lizzie, and she only had to make the trip once: the job included room and board, her lodging being a one-room shed that she shared with a sweet Negro woman named Loretta. The product of this enterprise had quickly become clear: Earl Duffy made moonshine, and a lot of it.

Apparently, he had dozens of locals on the payroll, and since production never shut down, he allowed them the option of working all seven days of the week. Many of them did. There were people to haul in the cornmeal, yeast, sugar, and water; ferment the barrels of mash; heat and monitor the still; ice and add the cold water; collect, load, and transport the liquor; maintain the condenser and tubing; keep records; serve as lookouts for Feds; and plenty of other tasks Lizzie knew nothing about. She'd heard about places like this, mostly across the river in Louisiana, but had never seen one. Here she saw cars with back seats removed to make room for cases of 'shine, switches to cut off taillights during a pursuit, false gas tanks to hold liquor, real tanks concealed under floorboards, etc. What would her dear departed mother have thought?

Lizzie's duties involved packing the jars into cases of twelve each, and this was what she was doing when her rescuer from the diner reappeared in her life and asked her a question.

"Throat's okay," she answered, opening the neck of her baggy dress to show him the bruises. "Could've been a lot worse."

He made no reply to that, just gave her an appropriately solemn look, and she knew they both would always remember what happened that night. Secretly Lizzie wished her two assailants had gotten more than just a beating with an old man's cherrywood walking-cane. If she'd had her gun in her uniform pocket at the time—a tiny 1903 Colt .32 automatic she usually carried everywhere—things might've been different.

"I never asked your name," she said to him.

"Parrish."

"First name?"

"Allen," he said. "But nobody calls me that."

"Allen Parrish. Nice to meet you. I'm Lucy Nelson." She shook his hand with a right arm still stiff from an old injury. After an awkward pause she pointed into the distance and said, "Is that your wagon? I saw you driving it in, this morning."

"Yep. My mule, too. I used 'em to haul lumber for the sawmill, till today. Ain't had time to sell 'em yet."

"So you took Earl up on his offer? I thought you said you were satisfied, jobwise."

"Well, the lady who runs the diner—"

"Susie Quinton."

"Yeah. She told me yesterday you'd decided to come here, and well . . ."

Lizzie felt pleased and embarrassed at the same time. She couldn't help grinning.

Red-faced, Parrish looked around and asked, "What do you think of this place so far?"

"My lunch break's in twenty minutes," she said. "I'll fill you in."

#

They wound up together on every work break for the next two days, and at meals, too, which for the "live-in" employees consisted of either sandwiches or country-style vittles fried by an old cook suitably nicknamed Grumpy. By Sunday, Lizzie and Parrish were spending every spare minute together, especially the free hours between supper and the crew's early bedtime. Married or not, runaway or not, Elizabeth McDade was smitten, and she felt pretty sure Allen Parrish was, too.

On Monday morning Parrish hurried to her packing station, grabbed her by the elbow, and steered her to a dark corner of the shed. "Are you wanted for anything?" he asked.

"What?"

"By the police."

"No," she said. "Why?"

He glanced around, but everyone else seemed busy. "According to Earl, somebody's been asking questions about a woman who might be new to town, or passing through. Thirty, good-looking, brunette, blue eyes. Won't say why, but this guy's for sure looking for her."

"Why are you telling *me* this?"

He calmed down, kissed her forehead, and said, "You're a smart girl, Lucy, but come on—blond hair and black eyebrows? And if I can figure it out, other folks can, too."

Her shoulders sagged. "I should've told you."

"Tell me now," he said.

So she did. Not the whole story, but most of it. The important thing was, her deceitful actions didn't seem to bother him. It was then that she made up her mind, about Allen Parrish.

Still, she held off on committing herself. Even with this talk of someone on her trail, she needed time to think. She had grown used to this newfound freedom, had decided she'd had her fill of wedlock, and romance in general. But Parrish had changed all that.

Finally, the following Wednesday, during their lunch hour on the one-week anniversary of Parrish's employment here, Lizzie looked at him through her taped-up glasses, took his hands in hers, and voiced what she'd been rehearsing in her mind. "Let's run off together," she said. They were sitting at a picnic table under an oak beside one of the sheds. She had an untouched ham sandwich on a napkin in front of her and he had a half-finished hotdog in his hand.

He stopped chewing. "That's the best thing I've heard in a long time," he said.

"I'm serious. Believe me, I know a little about running off." Which of course he knew by now. Except that her confession about her unannounced exit from Wolf McDade's life hadn't included the fact that Wolf was her husband. The version she'd told him had cast Wolf as her evil uncle on her mother's side. Why should a girl tell her beau every little thing?

Parrish put down his hotdog and said, "What if we do? What comes next?"

"Does it matter, long as we're together?" She squeezed his hand. "First things first. Will you go with me?"

He smiled then, a grin that lit up his face. "Sure I will. But . . . we'll need a car. And I don't do grand theft."

"We won't need a car." Her traveling phobia was another thing he didn't yet know about, but she'd told herself it didn't matter. She leaned forward and said, "I'm good in the woods, Parrish. I can make fires and fishing poles and trap rabbits and shoot squirrels, I know which berries are good to eat, and I got almost a hundred bucks saved, plus what I already had. All we'll have to do is stop by a country store now and then for food, and when we run outa money we'll find jobs. And if you feel bad about running out on Earl, we can leave him your mule and wagon." She paused. "I realize Uncle Wolf's looking for me, but they'll never find us on foot."

Parrish stayed quiet a moment. "I dunno about walking, Lucy. But I got another idea." He pointed past the shed. "Come bedtime, I can load a couple dozen cases of liquor in my wagon, pad 'em tight with straw so the jars won't break, cover it all with blankets, and we can be gone five hours before sunup. By the time Earl misses us and finds out some cases are gone and puts it all together, we'll be long outa here. As for whoever's hunting *you*, they'll be looking for a lady on her own, not two people traveling together in a mule wagon."

She thought that over. "But even if it worked—where would we sell the 'shine?"

"That's the best part," he said. "I know a fella in Natchez who works at the boat landing at the bottom of Silver Street. You ever heard of Natchez Under-the-Hill?"

She saw where this was going. "I'm not riding on a boat, Parrish."

"I didn't say we would. My friend told me moonshine gets bought and sold there all the time, to be loaded onto the steamboats headed to New Orleans. No telling what we could get paid, for a wagonload."

Again she fell silent. "I thought you said you didn't hold with stealing."

"I don't. What we'd be taking with us is bootlegged liquor. You can't steal something that's already illegal."

That didn't seem to Lizzie like sound reasoning, but she liked the wagon idea. A wooden buckboard wouldn't go fast enough to make her sick. Unless . . .

"Natchez must be more'n fifty miles from here," she said. "We can't go bumping down a public highway in a mule-drawn wagon. Earl's men would catch us for sure."

"We won't. I know this part of the country—I was born in Louisiana, but grew up south of Vicksburg. We could take back roads the whole way. Some of the trails I been on, even Earl wouldn't know about." He paused, thinking. "Best way from here'd be west, almost to the river, then south on a cow-track called River Road, past Port Gibson. We could be in Natchez in three days, depending on the weather." He focused on her and said, "It'd work."

Maybe it would, she thought. If it did, she'd have the man she loved, she'd be free and clear of the man she didn't, and she'd have money of her own for the first time in her life. She found herself nodding, and the more she nodded the more she smiled.

"When would we leave?" she asked.

"How about tonight?"

The smile widened. She took a bite of sandwich and said, "River City, here we come."

\#

West Claiborne County
Friday, August 18

The trip was taking a long time. The roads were even worse than expected, and twice they'd had to backtrack to avoid washouts or downed trees. Also, they'd traveled mostly at night, forcing Parrish to slow up every time the moon went behind a cloud. During some of those delays they'd stopped for what Lizzie thought of as "romantic interludes." Which was fine with her, but afterward Parrish seemed to turn moody. At one point she said, "What's wrong?"

"Nothing."

After a mile or two she asked, "Are you having doubts?"

"People who don't know what they're doing always have doubts."

"But not about me?"

He looked at her and smiled. "No, not about you."

Just before sundown, when he finally reined in and stopped, it was on a weed-choked dirt road. On both sides were tall stands of oak and sweetgum and kudzu, with what looked like a grassy clearing ahead. When she asked where they were, he said nine or ten miles west of Port Gibson. About halfway to their destination. "Let's make camp and sleep proper tonight, instead of riding," he added. "We're plenty far away from Earl and his still."

Lizzie climbed down from the wagon and stretched her legs. A soft breeze was blowing, and birds sang and played in the trees overhead. As Parrish unhitched and hobbled the mule, she gathered some of the food and wandered toward the clearing to spread a blanket—

And stopped in her tracks.

After a moment of stunned silence she turned to look at Parrish. He was watching her, one hand on the mule's neck and a tiny grin on his face.

"What is this place?" she whispered.

He walked over to stand beside her and followed her gaze.

Ahead of them in a huge open space stood more than twenty Corinthian columns, each almost four feet thick and soaring forty-five feet in the air. A fancy iron railing connected some of them about halfway up, and a grand staircase leading to nowhere rose from the grass.

"The Windsor mansion," Parrish said to her. "Biggest in the state. It burned down more'n forty years ago, but what's left is still impressive." He pointed west. "The river's only two or three miles away. I've heard that guests on the third floor could watch boats passing by."

"Unbelievable," Lizzie murmured. A ruined castle, in the middle of nowhere.

It was almost dark now, the western sky streaked with pink and orange. When they finished exploring, and trying to picture what used to be here, they sat and cuddled, leaning back against one of the square-based columns. The woods around them buzzed with crickets.

After several minutes she looked at him and said, "I haven't been honest with you."

He frowned, his eyes sleepy. "What do you mean?"

"I told you Wolf was my uncle. He's not. He's my husband."

A heavy silence passed. "You're . . . married?"

"He was mean to me, Parrish. Brutal. It's the reason my arm won't work right. I wasn't a wife to him, I was a slave." She paused, holding her breath. "You have to believe me."

Slowly, he nodded. "I do."

More silence. He lowered his head, then faced her again. "I haven't been honest either."

"What do you mean?"

Ten seconds dragged past. Somewhere to the south, a bird called. A warm wind rustled the leaves overhead and bent the long johnsongrass around them. Then Parrish blinked and looked past her into the woods. Muscles were twitching in his jaw. "Get in the wagon," he said.

"What?"

He jumped to his feet, snatching up the food. "Grab the blanket. Let's go."

"But . . ."

"Do what I tell you, *quick*! Get in the—"

"What's your hurry?" a deep voice said.

Both of them froze. Parrish just stood there, focused on something in the gloom. Lizzie had half risen, the blanket clutched to her chest. Her heart was pounding in her ears.

She knew that voice.

Twenty feet away, Wolf McDade stepped from the shelter of the forest. Beyond him, deep in the trees, was the dim rectangle of a license plate. He must've parked there and waited.

But how could he be *here*?

She turned to Parrish. He was staring back at her, his eyes wide and pleading. Finally, she understood.

"You're the one who was looking for me," she whispered.

"And took his time about it, too," McDade said. He looked amused and hateful and triumphant, all at the same time.

Lizzie kept her eyes on Parrish. She felt herself sag against the column. "How . . ."

"I called him," he said, in the saddest voice she'd every heard. "God help me, I called him just before we left, using Earl's phone."

"But why? How could you *do* that?"

"Because I hired him to bring you back," McDade said. "Right, Becker?" He stepped closer, a grin on his face. "Get over here, Lizzie. You're coming with me."

"No. She's not."

McDade stopped. The two men glared at each other in the fading light. "What did you say?"

"I said she's not going anywhere, with you."

McDade's voice hardened. "Look, if you want to get paid—"

"Keep your money." The younger man turned to Lizzie, his face contorted. "I didn't know then," he said to her. "I didn't know how I really felt about you. I don't think I knew for sure until just now."

She looked back at him, her mind spinning. She'd never been more confused in her life.

When she turned to her husband, she saw the gun in his hand. A big revolver.

"I told you to get over here, Lizzie. Now."

"No," she said, her voice trembling. "You'll have to kill me."

McDade grinned. "You might wish I had, later. I been here awhile, watching you two and listening. So right now it's not you I plan to kill."

"Wait!" Lizzie said. "That wagon's loaded with moonshine, Wolf. It's yours if you'll let us go. Mule, wagon, everything. For the love of God, let us go. Let us walk away."

"Why should I?" The grin became a sneer. "I can take it all anyway."

The two men locked eyes again.

"Too bad, Becker," McDade said. "Maybe you *should've* gone to the Coast."

And cocked the revolver.

"*No!*" Lizzie shrieked. . . .

#

Danny Becker saw the gun swivel toward him, heard the hammer click back, heard Lizzie scream—

And thought, *It's my own fault.* He'd somehow found the woman he was paid to find, realized she wouldn't go back voluntarily, tricked her so he could finish the job—and then fell in love with her. And, on top of all that, he left his gun under the wagon seat.

He closed his eyes knowing anyone that stupid deserved to die.

When the shot came, he stiffened but felt no pain. Not until he heard Lizzie sobbing beside him did he realize he was still alive.

Wolf McDade was not. He lay face-up on the ground, eyes and mouth wide open, probably the most surprised corpse Becker'd ever seen. When his muscles unlocked Becker stumbled to the body, prodded it to make sure, and put the fallen revolver in his pocket. Then he trudged back to Lizzie and gently pried the smoking automatic from her hand. She was trembling like a leaf in the wind. It was full dark now—he couldn't see her face—but he pulled her to his chest and hugged her tight. His left ear was still ringing from the gunshot.

Much later, as they sat together in the starlight, she said, "Tell me everything."

#

It was a long story, one that hurt him to remember because he knew he had hurt *her*, but he told it slowly and honestly. "One of my contacts pointed to Susie Quinton's diner but I wasn't dead certain the waitress was you," he began.

He'd been watching from across the street that night when he saw through the windows Lizzie's struggle with the customer, and came to her aid. Afterward, there was no way to talk to her there so he left. The following morning he poked around some more and wound up questioning Susie's cook, who said Lizzie was a friend, and because of Becker's role in the previous night's events, the cook told him all he knew, which was that Lizzie'd said she would never return home. Then, later that day, Becker found that Lizzie had hired on with Earl Duffy.

Earl's job offer made the rest of it easy. Acting on the lie he'd made up about the sawmill, Becker found a local farmer willing to loan him a wagon and mule to make him seem more convincing, in exchange for the use of Becker's car for a week or two. Then he took the rig out to Earl's the next day and signed on as a moonshiner. The plan, at that point, was to somehow persuade Lizzie to escape with him and make her think it was her idea. A week later, that happened. What Becker hadn't expected was to fall in love.

"Which I did," he said to her. "Mostly during our wagon ride.

That might be the only thing I've told you, before now, that was the truth."

Both of them thought about that awhile. Finally Lizzie said, "Allen Parrish?"

"It's where I was born," Becker said. "Town called Oakdale, in Allen Parish, Louisiana."

Lizzie had to smile a little, at that. "My alias didn't require that much imagination. I've always wished I was a Lucy, and I just used my maiden name."

"You'd never make it as a criminal."

When both their smiles had faded she said, "What do we do now?"

"We hide the body. Throw it into a kudzu-filled gully."

"Which would make both of us criminals."

"No, it wouldn't. You shot Wolf McDade to keep him from murdering someone else. If I'd had my gun I woulda done it instead." He gave her a long look. "You saved my life."

"So . . . what happens after that?"

"We get rid of the car, too. Roll it into a different gulch. Nobody'll find it for years."

She fell silent again. It was a warm night, the moon high now above the trees to the east.

"And then?" she said.

"We take the wagon back to my farmer friend in Utica, get rid of your gun somewhere along the way, and pick up my car."

"We can't do that—Earl's people are looking for us, up there. We stole his booze."

"No, we didn't. There's nothing in the wagon but blankets and straw and a few rocks underneath. I never planned on going to Natchez, remember?" Becker sighed. "I told you awhile ago, when Wolf had us at gunpoint, that I'd called him from Earl's office. That was the truth. I told him to meet us at the Windsor ruins sometime today. We just got here a little late."

"You really were a son of a bitch, to fool me that way."

"I was. But I swear I didn't know, then, how much you meant to me, or that he'd treated you the way he had. Wolf told me you had run off before, and came back gladly."

"Well then, you and I aren't the only ones been telling lies."

Becker sighed. "I should've figured all that out. I'm a detective." After some thought he added, "Unemployed detective. Guess I should've stolen that 'shine after all."

"Well, we're not flat broke. You got your car." She snuggled closer. "And me."

"And whatever's in your husband's wallet, right? He sure won't be needing it anymo—"

Lizzie sat up straight.

He frowned. "What's wrong?"

"That's it," she said. "If we take the money it'll look like somebody robbed him. Then we wipe your prints off his gun, put it and him back in his car, and tell the police we found the car and his body when you came here to meet him after locating me."

"What?"

"Don't you see? It's not enough that Wolf goes missing. His body needs to be found."

"Why?"

"So I can collect the life insurance and claim his worldly assets." Lizzie stared at him in the moonlight. "I'm his wife, Becker. His only heir. I know because I actually thought of killing him myself last year, and called his lawyer to make sure about the will."

Becker felt himself smile. He'd always admired people smarter than he was.

It took them less than an hour to properly set the scene. The following morning, when they'd gotten some sleep and climbed onto the wagon seat for the trip to retrieve his car, the tall, bare columns rose like ghosts above the ground mist. Gazing up at them, Becker said to her, "Tell me—do you know the first thing about farming?"

"No. Neither did Wolf. But the people who worked for him do. And they'll be working for me now."

"Make 'em wear straw hats and overalls," Becker said. "Farmers should look the part."

He could feel her smiling at him as he clucked to the mule and they got underway. "You know," she said, "you don't look much like a detective."

He grinned. For the first time in a while, he felt calm and happy and content. And loved; who would've thought it? He drew in a long breath of summer air, full of woods and fields and flowers.

"So I've been told," he said.

Sources

Part 1 – Sheriff Ray Douglas Mysteries

"Trail's End" – *Alfred Hitchcock's Mystery Magazine* (July/Aug 2017)

"Scavenger Hunt" – *Alfred Hitchcock's Mystery Magazine* (January/February 2018)

"Friends and Neighbors" – *Alfred Hitchcock's Mystery Magazine* (March/April 2021)

"The Dollhouse" – *Alfred Hitchcock's Mystery Magazine* (May/June 2022)

"Going the Distance" – *Alfred Hitchcock's Mystery Magazine* (Jan/Feb 2023)

"The POD Squad" – *Alfred Hitchcock's Mystery Magazine* (Sep/Oct 2023)

Part 2 – PI Tom Langford Mysteries

"Mustang Sally" – *Black Cat Mystery Magazine* (Issue #7, Oct 2020), winner of the 2021 Shamus Award

"Sentry" – *Strand Magazine* (Issue #68, Dec 2022)

"A Trivial Pursuit" – new story

"Overlooked" – new story

"The Three Dolphins" – new story

"R.I.P., Van Winkler" – *Black Cat Weekly* (Issue #119, Dec 2023)

Part 3 – Other Stories

"Gun Work" – *Coast to Coast: Private Eyes* (Jan 2017), selected for *Best American Mystery Stories 2018*

"Moonshine and Roses" – *Alfred Hitchcock's Mystery Magazine* (July/Aug 2024)

"Welcome to Armadillo" – *Strand Magazine* (Issue #73, Dec 2024)

"Rhonda and Clyde" – *Black Cat Mystery Magazine* (Issue #5, Nov 2019), selected for *Best American Mystery Stories 2020*

"River Road" – *Prohibition Peepers: Private Eyes During the Noble Experiment* (Sep 2023)

RIVER ROAD AND Other Mystery Stories is printed on 60-pound paper, and is designed by Jeffrey Marks using InDesign. The type is Baskerville Display. The cover is by Gail Cross. The first edition was published in a perfect-bound softcover edition and a clothbound edition accompanied by a separate pamphlet of "Quarterback Sneak." The books were printed and bound by Impress Printers. The book was published in November 2025 by Crippen & Landru Publishers.

Crippen & Landru, Publishers
P. O. Box 532057
Cincinnati, OH 45253
Web: www.Crippenlandru.com
E-mail: orders@crippenlandru.com

SINCE 1994, CRIPPEN & Landru has published more than
100 first editions of short-story collections by important
detective and mystery writers.

*This is the best edited, most attractively packaged line of
mystery books introduced in this decade. The books are equally
valuable to collectors and readers.* [Mystery Scene Magazine]

*The specialty publisher with the most star-studded list is
Crippen & Landru, which has produced short story collections
by some of the biggest names in contemporary crime fiction.*
[Ellery Queen's Mystery Magazine]

God bless Crippen & Landru. [The Strand Magazine]

*A monument in the making is appearing year by year from
Crippen & Landru, a small press devoted exclusively to publishing the criminous short story.* [Alfred Hitchcock's Mystery
Magazine]

Previous
Crippen & Landru

Nothing Is Impossible: Further Problems of Dr. Sam Hawthorne by Edward D. Hoch. Full cloth in dust jacket, signed and numbered by the publisher, $45.00. Trade softcover, $19.00.

Swords, Sandals And Sirens by Marilyn Todd. Full cloth in dust jacket, signed and numbered by the author, $45.00. Trade softcover, $19.00.

All But Impossible: The Impossible Files of Dr. Sam Hawthorne by Edward D. Hoch. Full cloth in dust jacket, signed and numbered by the publisher, $45.00. Trade softcover, $19.00.

Sequel to Murder by Anthony Gilbert, edited by John Cooper. Full cloth in dust jacket, $29.00. Trade softcover, $19.00.

Hildegarde Withers: Final Riddles? by Stuart Palmer with an introduction by Steven Saylor. Full cloth in dust jacket, $29.00. Trade softcover, $19.00

Shooting Script by William Link and Richard Levinson, edited by Joseph Goodrich. Full cloth in dust jacket, signed and numbered by the families, $47.00. Trade softcover, $22.00.

The Man Who Solved Mysteries by William Brittain with an introduction by Josh Pachter. Full cloth in dust jacket, $29.00. Trade softcover, $19.00

Constant Hearses and Other Revolutionary Mysteries by Edward D. Hoch. Full cloth in dust jacket, signed and numbered by Brian Skupin, $45.00. Trade softcover, $19.00.

THE ADVENTURES OF THE PUZZLE CLUB AND OTHER STORIES by Ellery Queen and Josh Pachter Full cloth in dust jacket, signed and numbered, $47.00. Trade softcover, $22.00.

THE ADVENTURE OF THE CASTLE THIEF AND OTHER EXPEDITIONS AND INDIS-CRETIONS BY Art Taylor Full cloth in dust jacket, signed and numbered, $47.00. Trade softcover, $22.00.

A QUESTIONABLE DEATH AND OTHER HISTORICAL QUAKER MIDWIFE MYSTERIES by Edith Maxwell. Full cloth in dust jacket, signed and numbered, $47.00. Trade softcover, $22.00.

THE KILLER EVERYONE KNEW AND OTHER CAPTAIN LEOPOLD STORIES By Edward D. Hoch with Introduction by Roland Lacourbe. Full cloth in dust jacket, signed and numbered, $47.00. Trade softcover, $22.00.

SCHOOL OF HARD KNOX Edited By Donna Andrews and Greg Herren and Art Taylor Full cloth in dust jacket, signed and numbered, $47.00. Trade softcover, $22.00.

THE SKELETON RIDES A HORSE AND OTHER STORIES By Toni LP Kelner Full cloth in dust jacket, signed and numbered, $47.00. Trade softcover, $22.00.

THE WILL O' THE WISP MYSTERY By Edward D. Hoch Introduced by Tom Mead Full cloth in dust jacket, signed and numbered, $47.00. Trade softcover, $22.00.

THE INDIAN ROPE TRICK by Tom Mead. Full cloth in dust jacket, signed and numbered, $47.00. Trade softcover, $22.00.

WITH LOVE, MAJORIE ANN by Marcia Talley. Full cloth in dust jacket, signed and numbered, $47.00. Trade softcover, $22.00.

Subscriptions

www.ingramcontent.com/pod-product-compliance
Lightning Source LLC
Chambersburg PA
CBHW030022200726
48283CB00012B/767